INTO the FIRE

Into the Storm Trilogy
Book Two

Serene Conneeley

Blessed Bee Books

INTO THE FIRE: Into the Storm Trilogy Book Two

First edition copyright © Serene Conneeley 2018

Conneeley, Serene
Into the Fire by Serene Conneeley
ISBN: 978-0-6484016-0-5

Website: www.SereneConneeley.com
Email: serene@sereneconneeley.com

Published by Blessed Bee Books
PO Box 449, Newtown, NSW 2042
Australia

Cover artwork: *Lady of Fire* by Selina Fenech
www.SelinaFenech.com
Illustrations: Daniella Spinetti and Justin Sayers

Fate whispers to the warrior:
"You'll burn up in the fire."
The warrior roars back:
"I *am* the fire!"

Contents

"Set your life on fire.
Seek those who fan your flames."
Rumi, Persian poet

Chapter 1

Night of the Dead

Snow was starting to fall, and Beth rushed up the steps of her cosy cottage in an attempt to escape it. Then stopped abruptly. She didn't have her key. She didn't have anything. Shivering, she knocked on the door, but her knuckles didn't make a sound. Puzzled, she peered in the window. Candles were flickering, and she could see the shadow of her husband moving in the kitchen out the back.

As she wondered how to get his attention, she heard the crunch of footsteps behind her, and turned to see Rose walking up the path towards her, hand in hand with a young girl she'd never seen before – although she looked so much like her old friend Violet, Rose's daughter, that it spooked her. But that wasn't possible. This girl was around her daughter's age, not her own. Which was... what? How old was she? Fear spread icy fingers through her gut. *What was wrong with her? Why couldn't she remember something so basic?*

"Rose, hello," she said quickly, shrugging off the mystery in her relief that she'd be able to get inside. It was freezing out here. But the priestess she'd known for more than twenty years ignored her. Didn't glance in her direction, or even acknowledge that she was there. Before Beth could process the snub, the young girl walked towards her – and passed right through her.

Oh goddess, was Rose dead? Was she seeing the ghosts of the priestess and her long-lost daughter Violet, reunited at last?

That would explain how the girl had walked through her. Yet when the dark-haired teenager knocked on the door, Beth heard it. And squinting through the window again, she saw her daughter Rhiannon run down the stairs in response and fling open the door.

"Carlie, Mrs Tyler, come in!" she said, her face wreathed in smiles. "I'm so glad you could come tonight, it means so much to us."

Horror clutched at Beth's heart. What was going on? Why was her daughter ignoring her? She tried to hug her and draw her close, but Rhiannon kept walking, leading her guests into the dining room. Trailing behind them, scared and confused, Beth tried desperately to figure it out. Her panic finally receded when her husband came in with some drinks. It would all be explained now.

"Sweetheart," she said with a smile, throwing her arms around him. It felt like ages since she'd held him, which didn't make sense. They never left the house without hugging and saying "I love you," and she missed his warmth. But her arms slipped right through him. Terror washed over her, and she felt her grip on reality start to shatter.

Taking a deep breath, she forced herself to calm down, and finally managed to laugh. It was just a nightmare. The first icy touch of winter signalled Samhain, when the veils between the worlds thinned and the spirits of those they'd lost came closer. Preparing for the ritual with her coven must have triggered these thoughts of ghosts and death. Relaxing now that she understood what was happening, she tried to enjoy the knowledge of her dream awareness. As soon as she woke up, everything would be fine again. Relief flooded through her, so when her son Brodie came into the dining room and ignored her too, she didn't totally fall apart.

Not until she saw the three empty seats at the end of the table...

Comprehension of their meaning dawned slowly, beginning in the mind of the stranger girl, whose thoughts she could somehow pick up. She seemed to be a friend of Rhiannon's, yet connected to Rose, which was puzzling. Putting aside her disquiet at her daughter having a friend she'd never met, she focused on the girl. For some reason she could sense how overwhelmed she was, and how uncomfortable she felt, but she didn't know who she was, or why she was radiating such thick, heavy waves of guilt and sadness.

Following the girl's gaze, Beth marvelled at the prettiness of the room as the stranger did. The long table they only used for special gatherings was beautifully set, with white candles glowing in the centre and pretty name tags at each place setting. Orange and black candles burned in an elaborate silver candelabrum on the side dresser, and the rich scent of cinnamon and nutmeg rose from a wrought iron incense holder.

It was the Samhain ritual, she realised, heart in mouth and fear slamming back into her. The stranger girl – Carlie, she remembered, from her daughter's greeting earlier – shivered as she looked at the end of the table. Summoning all her courage, Beth made her way over and glanced down at the name tags.

Her mouth opened in a silent scream. Her name was on one of them, along with Violet's, and a man called Oliver. A place had been set for each of them, with crockery and cutlery and a silver chalice, but these were ghost settings, left out for the dearly departed.

She was dead.

A swirling blackness opened up around her, and she felt herself losing consciousness as she fell back into the dark of oblivion.

Some time later, Beth felt herself pulled back into the room. Although she fought the sensation, it seemed that Carlie was holding her there, her grief and confusion pushing outwards in a whirling storm that Beth had somehow been caught up in.

Staring around wildly, she tried to focus on what was going on, and what was being said. As she watched, Rose turned to Carlie with a sad smile and shook her head, yet Beth hadn't heard the girl ask a question. Then again, Rose was priestess trained, and she'd always wondered if she could read people's hearts and minds. It was no great shock to discover that this was true.

"No Sweetheart, not strange," the older woman was saying. "There were sad moments, of course, but I am so grateful to Mike, and to Beth, for letting me share a little part of their family with them over the years – inviting me to Christmas celebrations, birthday parties and school performances, sharing their good news and good fortune, and letting me offer a little back in the harder times.

I've always loved Rhiannon and Brodie so much, and it fills my heart with joy that you two are such close friends."

In response, Beth's husband offered gratitude to Rose for all she'd done for their family over the years, hugged Carlie, then led Brodie out to the kitchen, leaving Rhiannon alone with their guests. Beth floated closer – *dear god, she was floating* – and settled in the place they'd set for her. It seemed rude not to. She felt a moment of hope when Rose stared right at her – but then the priestess shrugged and turned back to the girls, and Beth wanted to dissolve into tears. Instead she listened impatiently as Rose explained the seasonal festival they were celebrating to Carlie.

"Samhain is when the spirits of those who have passed are closest to us, so I always feel so close – yet so far – from Violet and Louis at this time. But I worry about Mike. He's still mourning his beloved wife, yet also feeling the loss of Violet all over again..." The rest of her words faded into the background as Beth focused on the ones just spoken.

Mike was mourning her. She really was dead.

And what the hell? Violet was being mentioned again? Must she overshadow everything in her life? *In her death?*

Beth wished she could fade away right then and there, and drift back to wherever she'd existed until this night, until this *girl*, had drawn her back to awareness. But the sharp scent and vivid colour of the jug Mike and Brodie returned with grounded her there in the room, the beauty of the deep purple grape juice spiced with cinnamon, cloves and ginger so intense her mouth watered. Brodie filled everyone's glasses, including the three at the end of the table, and seeing his lip tremble as he poured the punch into the silver chalice in front of her was a fresh dagger to her heart. Tears welled in her eyes – although was that even possible now she was dead? – and she noticed that Rose's eyes were wet too.

Yet the priestess was as professional as always. "Tonight we honour the ancestors who have gone before us, who watch over us and guide our feet," she said, her rich voice sadly compelling. "And especially we have joined together to pay tribute to and share our love for three special people. Beth was a beautiful soul, a devoted mother, a loving wife, and a close friend to so many of us. But she lives on in the two children she adored, and I can see her in both of you – her strength and independence in you Rhiannon, and her cheekiness and sense of humour in you Brodie."

The sorrow that the five living, breathing people shared was so thick Beth thought it would choke her, and the sad, stoic look in her daughter's eyes filled her with pride as well as despair.

"To Mum," Rhiannon whispered.

"The best mum ever," Brodie said in his sweet young voice.

Mike lifted his glass too. "To Beth – my wonderful wife, your beautiful mother. So deeply missed, and yet here with us always."

Beth tried to move, tried to reach out to her beloved husband at the other end of the table, desperate to comfort her grieving family. Desperate for someone to comfort her. But she was frozen, stuck in her chair. It wasn't fair. For a moment she forgot how curious she'd been about the other two empty place settings, and let herself drown in sadness, until Rose's poignant words dragged her back.

"And to Violet and Oliver. My beautiful daughter, who I have missed every day since she left us more than twenty years ago, and her husband Oliver, who I so regret never having the chance to meet. I honour you both for the gift you have given us all, in Carlie, and I welcome you both – you have a special place in my heart, and on my altar, and you of course live on in your daughter, who has brought me so much joy in my old age."

Beth recoiled in shock. So Violet hadn't died, not back then, but she was dead now. And she'd had a daughter, yet the girl had only just found her way to Rose. Now Carlie's caution made sense – her discomfort and unfamiliarity with the sabbat, with any kind of magic, and even with Rose. There was something rocky between them, something painful, and their relationship was still very new.

Her head spun back to her own family when she heard Mike laugh. "You will never be old Rose," he grinned, then he lifted his glass and looked serious again.

"To Violet, my dear friend. I regret that I never had the chance to see you grow up and achieve your dreams, and that you didn't get to meet my beautiful family. And to Oliver, a man I wish I could have known and called friend. I honour your memory, and I hope that somewhere, wherever it is you all are, you have met my wife and you can all feel happiness and pride at the wonderful ways you have all touched our lives."

Beth's heart was breaking, but when Brodie, her baby, spoke, it destroyed her completely. "I'm so sorry you lost your mum and your dad Carlie," he said, and she was shocked at the wisdom and sadness conveyed in his voice. "I couldn't imagine losing both my parents – it was hard enough losing my mum." As the sorrow crushed her, Mike reached over and grabbed their son in a hug. It was almost painful to watch their closeness, but it was touching too.

Sobs wrenched free from Beth, but no one could see her, or hear her, no one even sensed her, and that shattered her heart all over again. But what about the other two ghosts, if that's what she was? Nervously she gazed around the room, then squinted at the empty seats next to her. She couldn't sense the presence of anyone else though. Were Violet and her husband stuck in some other dimension? Or some other location? Could ghosts travel, or were Carlie's parents tied to wherever it was that they'd died? *Was she?*

Panic rushed through her veins – or whatever the ghostly equivalent of that was – as she realised she had no idea what was happening to her, and more importantly, no idea if it would ever happen again. Now that she had become aware, would she remain that way? Or was this just a once-a-year occurrence? Was the thinning of the veils at Samhain the only reason she was here, and would she plunge back into the abyss once the sun rose tomorrow? If that was how it worked, she had to absorb every single moment she could.

Focusing again on the conversations and events swirling around her, Beth smiled with pride as she watched her growing-up-so-fast son serve out the dinner, then sweetly ask Carlie to tell them about her parents. Impatience swamped her – she didn't want to waste precious time hearing about strangers! But she was moved despite herself when she realised that the girl had only recently lost both her parents, and her heart was soothed as she listened to Carlie describe her mum and dad and their relationship. Somehow Violet had escaped from Andrew, the abusive guy they'd both dated, and found real love. Relief flooded her. That was one less burden she had to bear, one less making of amends.

Mike was smiling as the girl spoke, and for an instant Beth wondered how deeply his feelings for his first love still ran. But then she put her pettiness aside – *what was the point of one ghost being jealous of another ghost anyway?* – and forced her attention back to the five flesh-and-blood people before her. She could feel the grief radiating from everyone, and the longer she sat at the table with them, as they swallowed the sabbat feast along with their pain, the more she started picking up the subtleties of emotion.

It was clear Brodie was hurting. His face wore a pained expression too heavy for someone so young, and there was a crease of bewilderment on his forehead. She wanted to scoop him up in her arms and comfort him, kiss his forehead and promise it would all be fine, like she had when he fell over and scraped his knees. But she couldn't. She could only sit here, mute and motionless, and watch helplessly as her family revealed how lost they were without her.

Peering at Rhiannon, she noticed how distressed she looked, worn down with the responsibility of looking after the family. But she had a quiet strength too, a maturity, and when she spoke to Carlie, something lightened within her, so she exuded joy. She was protective of her, recognising someone in even more pain than she was. Beth was intrigued when a flash of vision revealed that Carlie's many losses were making Rhiannon more grateful for what she still had, and bringing out all her nurturing instincts.

Curiously she turned her attention back to the stranger. Her grief was raw, like a gaping wound that had never been stitched up. And her connection to Rose was recent. There was wariness on her part, and even a little fear. But if Carlie's grief was so new, how old was Rhiannon's? How long had *she* been dead? Staring at her children, she tried to work out how much older they looked now, but memories of them at every age swam through her mind and thwarted her. Her husband wasn't much help either – although his hair had greyed and his face was worn and lined, she knew grief could have wrought those changes in a heartbeat. Frantically she floated around the room, examining books and swooping around trinkets.

It was a picture in a frame that floored her. Brodie was smiling next to a huge cake in the shape of a lion, with six candles on it. *Six?*

Desperately she tried to remember something, anything. She recalled baking Brodie's fifth birthday cake, a star-shaped riot of colour, for his party at the end of July, then they'd spent the August summer holidays away together, on a family adventure to Scotland. Racking her brain, she finally dredged up a memory of the kids returning to school at the beginning of September – then a shiver ran through her as she pictured the moment her cancer had returned, and all her hope had crumbled.

Now she couldn't turn it off. The image of Rose coming to visit her because she'd been too sick to attend the Mabon ritual. Having to tell the principal that she couldn't go back to work. Mike's worried face, Brodie's confusion. Then the premonition she'd had a few nights later, of Rhiannon standing naked in the woods with a strange man, and her own desperate race against time, stumbling in the dark, to rescue her. Her daughter had been shell-shocked, shaking and pale when she finally found her, trembling with fear and shame, angry that the healing ritual she was attempting for her mum hadn't been completed, devastated that the man had betrayed her trust, and terrified of her dad finding out what she'd done. Beth had held Rhiannon while she cried, kept her secret from Mike – and had planned to find out how to help her the next day.

But in the morning she'd been rushed back to hospital, her daughter taking charge when her husband fell apart, and she guessed that must have been when she died. And it was Samhain now, which meant she'd been dead for more than a year. Her family had been grieving for more than a year. *Dear goddess, where had she been for more than a year?*

Choked up with emotion and regret, she turned her attention to her husband. He was putting on a good act for their children, but she could see through to his core, and it was more than she could bear that he was still so broken inside. He'd accepted that the kids needed him to be strong, but the effort it took him just to get up in the morning, just to speak to people, let alone entertain, was beyond what he could handle. She wondered why he was hosting this dinner party – surely Rose would have done it? But then it dawned on her that her clever beloved had sensed how much Rhiannon needed this ritual, this marker of time and progress. An honouring of her mother, and the ability to be sad, but also to celebrate the memories of all the precious times they'd had as a family.

With a stab of pain she realised that Mike needed it too, because the knowledge of Violet's recent death had upset him deeply. She'd felt the knife in her heart again when she heard his voice tremble as he spoke of her. Violet had been his first love, she'd always known that. But could she feel jealous now, in this place and state she was in? *Was* she jealous? And was there any point being jealous of a dead woman? She'd always known he loved Violet, and that if she hadn't disappeared he may well have married her, had a family with her, given Rose grandchildren.

Or maybe not. Perhaps their teen love, as intense as it was at the time, would have fizzled out in the harsh reality and day-to-day life of adulthood. Sometimes she wished that *had* happened, that the mystery of Violet and the pedestal Mike had put her on hadn't always occupied a place in her husband's heart.

Yet she had to admit that the spectre of Violet had only ever been in her own mind. Her husband had never once made her feel second best. On the contrary, he'd spent every day of his life showing her that she was first in his heart. He was worried, of course, when Violet disappeared – she had been too – and he'd been so supportive of Rose in her grief, which had just made Beth love him even more. But he really had been the most amazing husband, the most loving partner, and the perfect father.

She had known every single day that he loved and adored her. Had never once had cause to question his love for her, or his loyalty. He had been kinder and more devoted to her than she deserved, which was making it even harder for him now. Their lives had been so entwined, each of them so beautifully dependent on each other, that she knew how hard he was struggling to cope. She missed him with a pain that cut deeper than anything she'd ever experienced

– and she didn't even have a physical body. How was he surviving? And what could she do? How could she help him?

Gazing over at Rose, she wondered how powerful the old priestess was. Could she sense her presence? Was there a way to communicate with her? She focused all her energy on her, willing her to see her, or feel her. But she and Mike were totally engrossed in whatever they were talking about. Sighing, Beth was just about to give up, when Rose turned and stared right at her. Instantly she felt paranoid, exposed. She wanted to hide, or fade away – which was stupid, since she'd been trying to get her attention, and pointless, because she was already as insubstantial as air, as mist. As ghost.

"Are you okay Gran?" Carlie asked in her strange accent, peering at the end of the table and trying to see what her grandmother was staring at. Smiling absent-mindedly, Rose nodded and focused back on Mike, continuing their conversation, but she seemed a little distracted now, as she tried to identify what she'd sensed.

"Rose!" Beth shouted, trying with all her might to get through to the priestess. "I need you to tell Mike that he has to start living again." Desperately she waved her arms as well, but that didn't work either. When Brodie asked Rose a question, Beth sighed, disappointed that she'd lost her attention. And yet...

"Sweet boy, of course. You'll always love your mum, and I know her love for you is eternal. But you also have to live your own life," she said, then glanced back at the empty end of the table before looking directly at Mike. Ostensibly she was still speaking to Brodie, yet this message was clearly for his dad. "Your mum is in a better place now, free of the pain that her poor body had to struggle with for so long while she was here. And she wants you to know that she's okay. She wants you to start living again."

Tears filled Mike's eyes, and Rose turned back to Brodie. "She'll always be a part of you, but she wants you to make the most of your lives, and to honour her memory by living the best way you can."

Shock crossed Mike's face, and he peered at the end of the table too. Was he imagining he could see his wife sitting there with them, laughing as she used to, being the life of the party? Beth almost laughed at the irony of that expression, but then her beloved stood abruptly and took some plates to the kitchen, and her heart swelled with pride as Rhiannon followed him out to comfort him.

T
ime stretched out interminably for Beth, but finally Mike put away the last container of food, washed the last dish and blew out the last candle, and she followed him up to his bedroom – their bedroom – and watched with the sensation of tears in her eyes as he brushed his teeth in the little ensuite, changed into a set of worn but warm pyjamas, then switched on the bedside lamp. The familiar actions were so ordinary, yet seeing him do them reminded her just how precious every second of their life had been. The romantic trips to France, the magical proposal and the exotic anniversary celebrations were wonderful, but it was these precious moments of normality that she missed the most. The very ordinariness of the life they'd created. Curled up reading together in bed, occasionally turning to the other one to share a meaningful story or choice of words. Making dinner together. Drinking cups of coffee as they chatted about their days. Walking through the countryside hand in hand. Sleeping in on weekends while Rhiannon looked after Brodie...

After switching off the main light, Mike sat down on the side of the bed – her side of the bed – and lifted something from the small chest of drawers. Curious, she drifted closer to him, and was overwhelmed with a bittersweet sensation of both sadness and joy as she saw that he was holding a photo of her.

It wasn't a glamorous picture. It hadn't been taken at some special place, or on some special occasion – it was just her, wearing jeans and a baggy t-shirt, with no make-up, and her unwashed hair swept back in a messy bun. But she remembered the exact moment he'd taken it, one morning when she'd been up to her elbows in soapsuds as she washed the dishes and he dried. She'd been laughing at something he'd said, and when the sun started pouring through the window and lighting up her face, he'd grabbed the camera, wanting to capture the joy they felt in each other's company. He'd always said it was his favourite photo of her, because it revealed her essence, her happiness at being alive, and their deep love for each other. She was glad it was the one he kept on his bedside table.

He held it close to his heart for a moment, then she heard him whispering. "I miss you so much darling," he sighed, running his hand delicately over her face in the frame. "I'm trying my hardest to be strong for Rhiannon and Brodie, but I still fall apart whenever I'm alone and I don't need to put on a brave face."

After he kissed the photo then carefully set it back down, he crawled under the thick quilt, still vivid in colour and meaning so many years after she and Rhiannon had made it together. It touched her deeply that her husband slept on her side of the bed, trying to stay as close to her as possible, but his obvious distress was agonising. Oh, she wanted to stroke his head, and kiss his check, and gently wipe the furrow of bereavement from his brow, but her hand passed right through him when she tried.

The place where Beth's heart had been trembled with pain, and she lay down next to him and breathed in time with him, attuning herself to the beating of his heart and the muffled sobs as he tossed and turned. Then as he finally drifted off to sleep, she focused her attention and her will on him, and slipped into his dream. She was startled to see him sitting on a long, deserted beach, the grey waves crashing onto the sand and the seagulls wheeling overhead the only movement for miles. It was nowhere they'd ever been together, and she wondered what the significance was.

"Alone," his voice croaked. "Like the only survivor of a shipwreck, trapped on a tiny island all on my own. Isolated, lonely, and my mind playing tricks on me." Beth inhaled sharply, his pain a physical sensation that rolled off him in waves, and into her. This was so much worse than she'd expected. By now he should be coping much better than this, surely. Sad yes, but not still paralysed by his grief. Not still crying himself to sleep every night.

She knew she had to do something to help him, to somehow let him know it was okay to move on. And she had to help Rhiannon too, make sure she had dealt with the after effects of that night in the woods, which must have been compounded a hundred fold  when she lost her mother the next day. Goddess, between Mike and her daughter, she certainly had a lot of unfinished business to sort out.

Curling up around her husband, she stroked his hair and whispered her love to him, hoping he could feel her presence on some level. When his tears finally stopped, she kissed him on the forehead then floated down the hallway to Brodie's room, a little more confident of her disembodied state now, and praying that her brave boy was coping better than the rest of the family. She shuddered to see that he had a lamp on – he'd been so proud when he'd stopped needing a night light, but her loss must have triggered his insecurities.

Suspended above him, she reached out tenderly to smooth his curls back from his forehead, but she had no strength, no physicality. It reminded her of the awful final weeks of her illness, when she'd been so weak, so helpless, so brutally fragile after a lifetime of good health and high energy. Instead she lay next to him, hovering her strangely transparent arm across his chest, and lingered there for what felt like hours, trying to impart all the comfort and confidence she could conjure, desperate to make sure he knew how much she would always love him. He stirred for a moment, and called out "Mum", and she prayed that some part of him knew she was there.

For a while she lost consciousness of her self, but she woke abruptly when she heard the back door open and someone tiptoe quietly up the stairs. *Rhiannon? Where had she been?*

Beth drifted through Brodie's door, which freaked her out so much that she exploded into a hundred pieces, and had to concentrate hard to draw herself back together again. Once she had, she darted along the hallway after her daughter and followed her into her room. Rhiannon's cheeks were flushed red with cold and excitement, and she radiated the scent and vibration of magic. She must have gone somewhere to do her own Samhain ritual, and for a moment Beth quaked in fear that it was that man again, until she picked up an image of Carlie, and sighed with relief.

Hungrily she watched her daughter's face as she changed into her pyjamas and slid into bed, then picked up a pretty purple journal. This time she saw a vision of Rose's face as she'd handed it to Rhiannon. Laughter rippled through her as she glimpsed the cover and realised it was a Book of Shadows. So, her little girl *had* grown into a witch. She was relieved when she sensed the energy and strength of the priestess, as well as her new friend Carlie, weaving into her magic and holding her safe. Her heart soared as she soaked up the scene before her – Rhiannon writing fast, determined to capture every nuance of her ritual before she forgot – but she also felt a pang of longing. She'd wanted to introduce Rhiannon to their circle. She'd wanted to be her daughter's magical mentor.

"Oh my darling, I miss you so much," she sighed, then jumped in fright when her daughter gazed up at her.

"Mum?" she asked, voice fearless but wondering. "Is that you? Rose seemed to sense someone tonight, and I prayed it was you."

Excited and eager to connect, Beth tried to make herself known, to become visible or cause some change her daughter could see. Pushing against the shelf, she tried to lift one of the lighter books, but just willing it to happen didn't work. Sighing, she moved over to the bedside table and blew at the candle – but while it flickered briefly, Rhiannon didn't connect it to her. Finally she floated over and put a hand on her daughter's shoulder, squeezing as hard as she could, then tried to run the other hand across her forehead and through her tangled hair. It was no good. Although Rhiannon shivered slightly, and rubbed her shoulder as though she'd felt something, she still kept peering hopefully around the room.

Frustrated and lost, Beth sat beside her and started talking, knowing she couldn't be heard, but needing to say it anyway. "My darling girl, I'm so sorry I left you when I did. You have no idea how hard I tried to hang on. I feel terrible that you have to look after the family during your final school year, when you should be studying. And it breaks my heart that I won't see you go to the ball, or walk down the aisle, or have your own children, or start your career. I failed you, leaving you alone to face all that, and I'm so sorry."

When Rhiannon continued to stare restlessly around the room instead of returning to her writing, Beth hoped the energy and intent of her words was getting through to her, and she clung to that thin thread of hope as she clung to her daughter's hand. She stayed with her, desperately holding her molecules together, until Rhiannon blew out the candle and sank down into sleep. Then Beth sadly disintegrated back into the darkness from which she'd come...

Chapter 2

Into the Water

Rhiannon

Shivering in the freezing wind, Rhiannon wondered if she was mad to be out on this cold dark night as the witching hour approached. Samhain dinner with Carlie and Rose had been lovely, albeit sad, but the girls wanted to do a deeper ritual to mark the potent cross-quarter festival. Now though, as another snowflake brushed her cheek, she was having second thoughts about wandering the midnight streets while the moon waned and ghosts walked.

Just before she was lured home with thoughts of her warm bed, she saw the beam of Carlie's torch approaching, and her friend rushed up to her, teeth chattering but excitement sparkling in her eyes. Giggling, they slipped inside the grounds of the church ruins. It had been built on the foundations of a much older pagan temple, and there was an ancient spring running beside it, which would add the blessings of water to their circle.

The bitterly cold air pierced through their clothes, and they both pulled their thick woollen coats more tightly around themselves as they lowered their heads against the wind and picked up their pace. Finally they stepped within the crumbling stone walls, grateful to be partially sheltered from the wind, yet still open to the sky above them.

Rhiannon filled the chalice the woman in blue had given her with pure water from the spring, while Carlie lit a large pillar candle, secure in its pretty glass lantern from the icy fingers of the wind. Hastily they carved out the boundary of their sacred circle, then called in the elements and the directions before sitting together on the grassy floor. Joining hands over their makeshift altar, they welcomed the god and goddess, then each picked up a black candle.

Hair whipping wildly around her in the breeze, and her hands shaking, Carlie carefully lit her candle from the one between them, then took a deep breath to calm and centre her thoughts before she began her invocation.

> *I call on you Ceridwen, goddess of death and rebirth and the waning moon, on this cross-quarter night that marks the end of autumn and the beginning of the coldness and dark of winter. In your aspect of wise crone and elder, please lend us your wisdom and prophetic foresight, and help us see through the darkness of our hearts and the veils between the worlds to the spirits of our lost loved ones, and let us know they are still with us.*

Then it was Rhiannon's turn. Her hand was much steadier than Carlie's as she lit her candle, and her voice was clear and strong.

> *I invoke you Hekate, woman of the crossroads, goddess of death, and of balance. In this midnight witching hour, in this night of the waning moon, please illuminate the darkness and guide us on our soul journey to the heart of your wisdom, in search of answers from the ones we miss so much.*

A dark shape flapped overhead, and the girls jumped, momentarily jolted out of their ritual mindset. Then, smiling at whatever creature of the night had felt moved to watch over them, they joined hands over the altar. Their voices merged, carrying softly in the cold night air.

> *Deities of darkness and introspection, of the wisdom of the inner mysteries, protect us tonight as we travel to your realm in search of answers, in search of comfort, in search of some glimmer of hope that our parents are still with us. So mote it be.*

Their voices echoed between the stone walls, gradually growing more quiet, then stilling altogether. Finally, their hands still linked, they closed their eyes and went within.

Stumbling blindly, Rhiannon found herself walking along a narrow laneway lined with hedgerows of wild hawthorn. Her feet were bare on the cold ground, and a long blue robe swirled around her ankles. It felt heavy, unfamiliar, and her skin stung where the rough fabric rubbed against it. She was holding a candle, smaller than the one she'd lit in the churchyard, but its golden flame didn't waver in the sharp breeze, and it burned so brightly it hurt her eyes.

Suddenly she tripped on a rock and fell heavily, her palm oozing beads of blood as it scraped along the jagged edge. The physical pain was a shock, and she clutched her hand to her chest as she peered ahead and tried to work out where on earth she was. She felt a flutter of fear at the unfamiliar landscape, but somehow she managed to summon enough courage to pull herself up and walk unsteadily forward.

Then, without warning, the twisting dirt path gave way to a smooth stone surface, and she stumbled again, cursing under her breath. Lifting her candle higher, she saw that she'd come to some kind of building. For a second she paused, then nervously entered the blackness within. It was a relief to be out of the freezing wind, but her heart was racing with apprehension. Bracing herself, she took a tentative step forward – and cried out as the ground fell away and her foot landed in mid-air. Her ankle crumpled under her, and she staggered and almost fell down the three stone steps she hadn't seen.

At the bottom she squeezed her eyes shut, trying to adjust to the darkness swirling around her, and get a grip on her terror. When tiny golden lights flickered against her eyelids, she cautiously opened them. A cavernous stone temple stretched out before her, with high vaulted ceilings, partially lit by hundreds of dancing tealight candle flames. As her eyes became accustomed to the heavy blackness, she saw a large stone pool of deep, dark water right before her, and a smaller one, higher up and to the left, rimmed with more candles. A swirl of incense wove around her, and the sound of falling water overcame her senses, shifting something within her and splitting her apart. She felt vulnerable and exposed, yet strong.

A woman in a dark robe moved towards her, hand outstretched. She inclined her head to Rhiannon, drew her up three stone steps – then pushed her into the deeper, darker pool. Gasping in shock as the ice-cold water surrounded her, filling her nose and mouth, she struggled against the hand forcing her under the surface, wondering why someone was trying to drown her. Flipping over, her eyes opened in terror, and she saw a menacing shadow above her. Then her attention was caught by the sight of her blonde hair trailing out around her, dancing in invisible currents, and starlight twinkling beyond the darkness. Her throat burned, her chest was constricting in panic, and her lungs were about to burst. Fear and anger shot through her, and regret for all she had yet to see and do, until she felt a moment of peace as she surrendered to the thought of death.

Smiling as she closed her eyes, she wondered if she would meet her mother now. But her acceptance was shattered when she was pulled abruptly back up, out of the water. Desperately she gulped in mouthfuls of air, marvelling at how warm her goosebumped flesh felt. Was she so deathly cold it had transformed to heat, or had she been transported to hell, with its terrible burning flames? Confusion swirled through her mind, until she became aware of gentle whispers echoing around the room. Straining with the effort, she peered around, trying to catch hold of them and make out the words.

> *Divine... dive in... die within...*
> *Submerge yourself to emerge from self...*
> *Lose yourself to find your self...*

Her mind let go of thought, and she slipped back under the water, a hand on her forehead. But there was no fear this time. She'd mistaken the intention before. This seemed to be some kind of baptism into a new understanding. *Submerge yourself in order to emerge as yourself?*

Before she could figure it out, she was lifted up and transported to the smaller, higher pool, and she felt the tingle of fresh water falling into the space, falling over her, and the tug of water being drawn out of the bottom of the pool back into the earth. She closed her eyes and leaned her head back, into the waterfall, and her whole world tilted and broke free from its mooring. What was happening? Was the water stripping away layers of her self, or stripping her away from her life? Could she return to the world from this watery realm, or was it a place you went through after death? For a moment she panicked, choking on the water pouring over her and into her, but cool hands lifted her again, and held her safely within the womb of the world.

Relieved, she opened her eyes and gazed out at the candlelight flickering gently on the dark water, the dancing golden flames somehow warming her, body and soul. She felt soothed, and removed, her everyday problems and grief so far away from the pool of calm she floated in. Her mind couldn't comprehend it, this opening to the beauty of the darkness, but her heart was allowing it, was welcoming the tearing asunder of all she had lost, and all she held dear. Content, she closed her eyes and drifted, until a soft voice crooned in her ear.

Wipe away your tears, and unweave your fears,
Rewire, inspire, embrace your desire.
Light your fire and let it burn...

Her eyes snapped open, and she gasped. The mysterious woman in blue was standing in front of her, waist deep in the water. She'd met this mist-wreathed Otherworldly being before, up on the tor, and had been gifted a silver chalice from her at her coven dedication.

"Why can I see you, and not my mum?" Rhiannon demanded, surprising herself with her less-than-friendly, far-from-polite tone.

Brauna smiled. "Beloved, your mother is with you, I promise. And it grieves her deeply that you are still suffering so much over her loss."

"She should have stayed then," she muttered.

"You know she could not," the blue-clad woman admonished. "But the priestess spoke true tonight. Your mother wants you to move forward with your life. And she is very worried about your father. She wants him to welcome love into his life again."

Anger rushed through Rhiannon, warming her inside and out. "What kind of awful betrayal would that be? We will never replace her in our hearts, minds *or* home," she railed. But Brauna laid a comforting hand on her shoulder, and peace enveloped her again.

"Loving your mother the way he did made your father's heart bigger, so it will not mean that he loves Beth any less, or is replacing her in any way, if he opens it to someone new. He has so much room for love in his heart, and in his life, but you will have to help him."

"Me?" Rhiannon tipped back her head and laughed. "Why would he listen to me? Okay, yes, I've let Carlie in, but there is no love in my heart or in my life. And in case you hadn't noticed, by this strange hallucination we seem to be in," she added, gesturing to the darkened cavern around them, "I'm not exactly sane or sensible."

An enigmatic smile settled on the mist woman's face. "Love is coming for you Rhiannon, but you must recognise it, and grant it entrance to your heart, mind and life."

"Knowing my luck, I won't see it for what it is, and I'll drive it away for ever instead of embracing it."

"Look for the raven," Brauna said cryptically. "But for now, allow the power of water to wash away your grief. Let it cleanse and soothe your heart, and strip away what you no longer need."

"Hmm, I thought water was gentle and calming and clearing. Intuitive and feminine. Soft even," she replied, her voice a challenge.

The blue-robed figure laughed, and it wasn't the gentle, calming sound it had been when she'd comforted Rhiannon up on the tor – tonight it held steel and fury, and immense, unbending power.

"It is all those things," Brauna conceded. "But it is also powerful. Water can wear away stone, create and destroy new lands, bury or reveal islands, change the course of rivers. It can alter the physical world, and our inner world. Do not ever mistake gentle for weak."

In the face of the woman in blue's fierce admonishment, Rhiannon's limbs weakened and her body melted away, and she gratefully accepted the dissolution into oblivion.

When she opened her eyes what felt like a lifetime later, Rhiannon was sitting on the cold grass of the churchyard again, and Carlie was gazing at her with concern. She raised a hand to her hair, shocked but relieved to find it dry, and confused about where she'd been and how long she'd been gone. The anger that had gripped her in the icy pool rippled through her, then was gone.

"Are you all right?"

Rhiannon nodded, momentarily incapable of speech, but she saw tears on her friend's cheeks, and wondered where she'd journeyed to while she was in the water temple, being baptised in sacred pools and ordered to let love in. "Are *you* okay?" she finally managed to ask.

Carlie shrugged, and for a moment her face shimmered, the shadows making her look like someone else, someone ancient, with a purple cloak flung around her shoulders. Rhiannon blinked, and the vision faded. She smiled as her friend leaned forward and hugged her. "Thank you for everything you do for me Rhi, for all the things we share. For being you. Our friendship means the world to me."

Laughing in response, Rhiannon tried to explain just how much Carlie helped her too. Their relationship was not one sided, despite what her friend believed. The Australian girl had incredible wisdom, and had taught her so much about herself. She wouldn't even be exploring magic without her to share it with. A shiver raced up her spine. She would be a terrified wreck right now, if she'd come back from wherever she'd disappeared to and been alone out here. It was Carlie who enabled her to hold on to hope through the darkness, not just tonight, out here in the inky blackness of winter, but every day.

She wanted to grill her friend about where she'd gone and who she'd met on her inner journey, but the cold was making her brain hurt, and her hand was stinging from where she'd scraped it on the rock. *Wait, what?* How could her palm be bleeding from a vision?

Panic threatened to tip her over the edge, but Carlie reached out and grasped her arm just in time, calming and soothing her, then suggested that they should head home now to avoid freezing to death. Rhiannon nodded enthusiastically. Physical action was better than driving herself crazy with her thoughts.

Quickly they thanked the elements, the deities and the directions for holding them safe – although she used the term "safe" loosely – and closed the sacred space they'd opened between the worlds. Then they raced back up the laneway to where they had to part, hugged goodbye, and snuck back into their houses and upstairs to the welcome warmth of their beds.

The next morning Rhiannon woke with a shudder. She wouldn't dare admit it, but she was dreading the Samhain ritual at the healing centre that night. It was one thing to mourn her mum at a private dinner with close friends in her own home, safe in the love of her dad and her brother. And working magic with Carlie didn't stress her out, because they were both beginners, both as inexperienced as each other, and patient with their ignorance and mistakes. But to do a ritual with Rose as high priestess, and all the women of her coven – of her mother's coven – made her very nervous. She didn't want to break down again and embarrass herself publicly.

Yet as soon as she entered the ritual room above the healing centre, the enchantment of the night wove around her. Strings of faery lights illuminated the faces of the participants, and black velvet drapes covered the walls, lending a sombre air. Pots of bright marigolds made a circle around the edges of the room, a deep orange cloth covered the altar, which was much bigger than usual, and the rich, heavy scent of patchouli hung in the air, providing a strong bottom note to the lighter scents of cinnamon and pine.

After greeting Carlie, she made her way over to a table piled with orange candles, which their teacher Laura was distributing. Her friend was holding two, but Laura only gave Rhiannon one, before directing her to the slowly forming circle. She wondered what they were for, but there was no time to ask. Suddenly the lights dimmed, their priestess rose from her position in the middle of the room, arms raised skyward, and a hush fell over the room.

Although Rose had looked exhausted and older than her years last night at dinner, Rhiannon watched in awe as she morphed into her high priestess persona. She barely moved, yet with each slow breath she became taller, more imposing, more powerful, as though an invisible cloak of magic was settling around her shoulders.

It never failed to impress her, and Rhiannon's dread fell away as she was pulled into the enchantment. The soothing sensation of being in the water of the sacred temple pool the night before returned, and the memory of it washed away some of her confusion and loss.

Out of the corner of her eye she saw Laura lift her arms to the sky and welcome the element of water, which seemed serendipitous.

*I call forth the element of water and the spirits of the west to
cleanse, consecrate and protect this space during our rite.
I ask the waters of the oceans and rivers and sacred springs,
the lakes and temple pools and holy wells, to wash away all
that no longer serves us and clear our sight.
Please assist us on this night as the veils thin, to communicate
with our lost loved ones and set our hearts alight.
Element of water, welcome.*

Rhiannon gasped at the mention of temple pools, and she suddenly
wondered if her teacher was as gifted with second sight and divinatory
powers as Rose. She'd never heard the spirit of temple pools being
invoked before, and it made her uneasy – until she felt Brauna's cool
hand on her forehead, heard her whispered reassurances, and sensed
her magic enveloping and nurturing her conflicted mind.

A thought niggled at her, and she gazed at Laura with new eyes.
Was she the person her dad could love? She'd been one of her mum's
best friends since they'd met while studying to be teachers, and the
two women had worked together – and woven magic together – for
almost twenty years. Idly she wondered, if her dad was going to
move on at some point, would she prefer it be with a friend of Beth's,
or a total stranger? Would it be too weird to suddenly go from
teacher to stepmother? Her heart rebelled at the thought of anyone
replacing her mum, and anger rose within her. But before she was
consumed by it, she sensed Brauna by her side again, soothing her,
and she managed to turn her attention back to Rose and shake the
idea off. It was *way* too soon for thoughts of a stepmother.

Invisible hands brushed Rhiannon's cheeks and stroked her hair,
and she closed her eyes as the priestess welcomed the spirits of all
those they'd lost. The sensation almost drove her screaming from the
room, but she made herself focus on Rose's words as she welcomed
them to this celebration of the first day of winter, of cold and
introspection... and of the dead.

Last year she'd paid no heed to Samhain, or its modern counterpart
Halloween. Her mother's death had still been recent, and she was
too destroyed by grief and anger and loss to be part of any ritual.

But tonight it felt real, and true – and the intensity of it was freaking her out. Trying to avoid the sadness, her mind wandered back to the possibility of her dad falling for Laura, until she heard Rose's voice in her ear. "Be here Rhiannon, be present."

Her eyes snapped open – to discover that Rose was on the other side of the room with her back to her, not right in front of her. She was making her way slowly around the circle, lighting everyone's candles from the central altar pillar. It was unsettling. How could Rose have even known she was thinking of other things?

Catching Carlie's eye, she saw that her friend was shaken too, her face white, her cheeks damp with tears, and her shoulders trembling. Yet as they smiled at each other, both girls felt instantly calmer and more grounded, and Rhiannon whispered a prayer of gratitude for her friend and magical partner.

Finally Rose reached them, and smiled sadly at Carlie. "For Violet," she said softly, as she lit her first candle. "And for Oliver."

Tears welled in the priestess's eyes as she gazed at her granddaughter, and Rhiannon felt like she was intruding on their pain. But Rose shook her head as she turned to her.

"No sweet girl, you never intrude," she insisted. "Now, let's light this candle for dear Beth." Rhiannon's heart clenched as she finally realised what was happening. People were lighting a candle for the person, or people, they'd lost, then bringing them together in a touching ceremony of remembrance. That's why her friend had two candles and she only had one.

Drawing courage up from the earth, she followed Carlie over to the large altar, which was quickly filling with the candles placed so reverently on it by the ritual participants. *So many lost loved ones.*

Setting hers down in a small silver holder, Rhiannon watched the individual flame flicker then grow strong, and smiled as it became part of the growing spiral of light.

Chapter 3

Bring Me To Life

Rhiannon

"**S**queee!"

Rhiannon let out an excited squeal. She and Carlie were racing up the stairs to school, both tired after three intense Samhain events in two days. But something had woken her up.

"What?" her friend asked, puzzled but amused.

Eyes shining, Rhiannon pointed to the banner overhead. "It's the school ball!" she exclaimed, as though Carlie should know the significance of that event to her. "I wanted to be part of it last year, but… well, you know. Oh, I wonder if they've appointed the organising committee yet? I'd love to do that. How about you? It will involve some after-school meetings, a few weekend days, then probably every Saturday for the month leading up to it."

Carlie shook her head. "Sorry, I promised Gran I'd help in the shop in the lead-up to Christmas. But I can't wait to hear all about it," she offered, grinning at her friend's over-the-top enthusiasm.

Rhiannon pouted for a moment, then shrugged and rushed off to the principal's office to see if she could sign up. Flinging open the door, she came to a halt when she saw three other students hovering around the office manager Glenda's desk.

"Hi Rhiannon," she said with a smile. "Tracy, Karen and Peter are signing up for the organising committee – is that what you're after?"

Regret curled in her stomach. "Am I too late?"

"No, of course not, four is perfect. But the first meeting is on this Saturday, at Smithfield High. Will you be able to make it?"

Rhiannon nodded, then thought fast. She had an appointment in London that day, and was supposed to be catching the train there with Carlie, but she was sure she'd be able to change the date, and knew her friend wouldn't mind making their trip another time.

After confirming the details with Glenda, she hurried off to her first class. And all day she swung between happiness and anticipation, then berating herself for caring. Was it superficial and shallow to be so excited about being part of a social committee, when she'd just been mourning her mum's death so deeply?

Haltingly she tried to explain her fears to Carlie, but her friend just hugged her and told her to go for it. She clearly didn't understand why Rhiannon so desperately wanted to be part of it, but she was supportive as always. Which made her own secret thoughts even worse, because she had to admit that she was jealous of her.

When they'd gone to the Body Mind Spirit festival six weeks ago, not long after they'd cast their love spells, they'd met Rowan, a gorgeous druidic healer and artist, who had fallen hard for Carlie – Carlie who was convinced he couldn't love her because she was too unworthy. It was tough for Rhiannon to have to talk her through her fears, reassure her, convince her to give him a chance, when deep down she wanted Rowan to love *her*, to think *she* was special. She still occasionally stewed over why he'd chosen her friend instead of her. What made Carlie better than her? She'd been into magic far longer than the Australian girl. She was just as smart, and just as pretty. Just as nice, if not more so, and *definitely* more together.

Sighing, she forced herself to stop. This spiral of jealousy and self-pity was doing her no good, and it wasn't worthy of her. She was better than this. *Wasn't she?*

Right, she had to focus on the positives. She really was glad that Carlie had found love, and with a guy who cared so much about her. Besides, Carlie's relationship meant that love was possible for Rhiannon too. That someone as amazing as Rowan could fall for her. She was just getting tired of waiting. A psychic at the festival had told her she would meet a fair-haired guy by Christmas, so there was still time, but it felt so far away, and she was getting impatient.

That afternoon she went home with Carlie, to drink tea with Rose, chat about the ball, and wonder what they could wear. "I think some of your mum's old dresses are still in her room, and some of our old ritual clothes and robes," Rose told her granddaughter. "You should both have a look through them. There might be something you like, or something we could transform into what you'd like, for the ball."

Intrigued, Rhiannon followed them up the stairs to the landing, then towards the front room of the house. It had been Rose's daughter – Carlie's mum – Violet's bedroom, until she'd run away when she was seventeen. Rhiannon's heart ached for her friend and all that she'd lost. Parents, friends, school, home, country. Every time she felt herself wallowing in her own grief, she was reminded that others were suffering worse, suffering more, suffering deeper.

"Sweet girl, it's not a competition," Rose whispered "Someone else's grief does not cancel yours out, or diminish it in any way. You need to let yourself feel all your pain, whenever it raises its head. There's nothing brave or good about ignoring it, or pretending it doesn't count because someone else's is supposedly worse. You must allow all your feelings, and acknowledge them, or you're just bottling it all up and suppressing it, and that's no good for anyone, is it?"

An image slammed into Rhiannon's mind. She was standing on top of the tor in a terrible storm, arms held up to the sky as tears poured down her face, a scream wrenched from her throat while lightning flashed violently from the heavens at her behest. She stared at Rose in shock. Had she put that into her head?

"Just remember what can happen when you try to pretend your grief doesn't exist, when you try to ignore it," Rose pressed. "You must feel it, allow it, express it – otherwise you'll explode again."

Nodding reluctantly, she took another step, then tried not to cough as they entered the dark, dusty room. Faded curtains covered the balcony doors, and there were cobwebs in the corners, complete with a spider. Rose's daughter Violet had left home twenty years ago, and the air of neglect made it clear that no one had been in her room for a long time.

But when the priestess led them across the musty room and opened the closet door, they gasped at the contrast. Inside was a riot of colour – vivid jewel-hued velvets next to sparkling silver sequins and cool blue and green silks, with scarves of every shade imaginable, and countless pairs of shoes spilling out the bottom.

The girls spent hours up there, trying on outfits and dreaming of love, music and magic. By the time Rhiannon rushed home for dinner, a bright red velvet dress embroidered with emerald holly leaves clutched in her arms, she felt much better about everything.

When Saturday dawned, Rhiannon leaped out of bed and hurried to school. Glenda was driving the committee members to Smithfield High for their first meeting, so they could check out the gym and understand the space they had to work with.

For a moment she felt scared. Was she really up for this? Working with three schoolmates and eight strangers, totally out of her comfort zone, with less time for magic and for Carlie? Determinedly she shook off her doubts. It was time she had some fun, and was just a normal student, doing normal student things. Not worrying so much about being sensible and serious, and protecting herself from hurt.

The moment they filed into the staff room, her whole world tilted, and she struggled to catch her breath. Her attention was drawn straight to the tall blond guy at the far end of the table. When he glanced up and their eyes locked, every other person in the room blurred right out, and for a moment it was as though he and Rhiannon were the only two people in the world. Her fingers clutched nervously at the notebook she'd filled with the ideas she'd been brainstorming, and a buzzing sound surrounded her. Butterflies fluttered in her stomach, and she felt her face grow hot.

She was so focused on him that she missed the names of the other students, but his she heard – John – and he was everything she'd imagined when that psychic at the festival told her about the tall, fair-haired and handsome guy who would sweep her off her feet by Christmas. *Oh god, it seemed that her love spell had finally worked!*

When he stood up and shook her hand, her heart rate increased, a stupid grin lit up her face, and she was too tongue-tied to speak. It took her schoolmate Karen jabbing her in the ribs for her to return to the room, to the present, to the situation at hand, and to finally tell him, as her cheeks burned red, what her name was.

With a swoon-inducing smile, he winked at her, then turned back to the group as the students from Maryborough High arrived. "Hello everyone. For those who didn't hear, I'm John McGowan. Thanks so much for giving up your Saturday to come here and check out the location, but don't worry, from now on we'll alternate schools for each meeting, so you won't always be travelling."

Smiling around at each of them, he introduced the other three pupils from his school, Annalie, Lynn and Cameron, then went around the room so everyone else could tell the group their name and school. Rhiannon's voice was barely a whisper as she said hers, and she blushed again as John's gaze fell on her. *What the hell was wrong with her? She had to pull herself together!*

"Now, if you'd all like to follow me, we'll head down to the gym and have a look around there first, then come back here, grab a coffee and get to work," he said.

Trying hard to focus on what they were doing, Rhiannon followed the other students across the grassy school grounds, listening as John explained the facilities, walked them through the school-hall-come-basketball-court-come-gym, then returned them to the staff room.

The walk had done Rhiannon good, and as she slid into her seat she was grateful that her brain was working again. She had no idea what had happened to her, but was relieved that she was back to normal... Well, normal until he turned his gorgeous grey eyes on her again. She'd thought butterflies was just an expression, yet here she was, gazing across the table at a virtual stranger, and *something* was fluttering around in her stomach.

Her mind drifted off on that tangent, dreaming of a whole army of blue-winged creatures swirling around her abdomen just to make sure she was aware of the guy sitting opposite her. Not that they were necessary. She'd never been so aware of another person in her life.

"Rhiannon?" a voice asked, clearly not for the first time.

She stared at John's principal blankly. What had she said? "Theme?"

Her cheeks flamed, but her voice held steady. Thank god she was so prepared. "I was thinking a Yule theme would be great, and really magical. Harking back to our Celtic roots, yet still modern. An enchanted midwinter evening, that kind of thing. A little bit Shakespeare, a little bit pagan..."

A few of the other students nodded their agreement, but she froze when she saw John open his mouth to speak. Breath held, she tried to convince herself it would be okay if he had a different idea, a better idea, but a secret part of her hoped he'd like hers. *Like her.*

"I love that," he said, and she grinned. Even if the rest of the table disagreed, it was enough that he approved. And as it turned out, it was almost unanimous, so they quickly moved on to other aspects of planning. The principal split them into smaller groups, and Rhiannon was overjoyed that John was in hers. They spent an hour brainstorming decorating ideas, musical options and catering choices, and she was gratified that when they made their report back to the main group, everyone loved what they'd come up with.

On the way home she stared out the window, lost in daydreams of John. What was it about him that had made her react that way? How could him shaking her hand spark such a physical reaction in her? And could he really be the boyfriend the psychic spoke of?

Part of her was nervous, almost scared, but another part was thrilled. He was gorgeous. He wasn't older, or a spiritual teacher, like Carlie's boyfriend Rowan, but he'd agreed with all the pagan suggestions she'd made, and was sweet and confident and, well, kind of hot. She wondered if he was into magic, or just liked the traditions of Christmas. Not everyone knew they had their roots in the spirituality of long-ago pagans. Even Christians were enamoured of the festive rituals, so she'd wait a while before she revealed herself to him.

Besides, what would she reveal? She wasn't *really* a witch, not like Rose was. She and Carlie had been to a handful of the priestess's rituals, but there was nothing in them that anyone would find weird, *right*? And they'd started a coven, but it could equally be called a training circle.

It wasn't like they did spells on people or anything, it was more about… Studying? Self-development? Hanging out with her friend?

Argh! How could she already be thinking of throwing in her magical life if this practically-a-stranger wasn't into it? Would she really walk away from what she and Carlie shared together, just to impress a guy? Would she stop going to Rose's rituals, and turn her back on the deep and swirling enchantment she basked in each time? Unweave the love spell she'd cast to draw a boyfriend to her?

Mentally she shook herself. She had to get a grip. She didn't even know him. So he had a pretty face, and a voice that did strange things to her insides, and a touch that felt like jolts of electricity. But was that worth all she'd be giving up?

Abruptly she shook her head, trying to clear away the fog from her mind. She'd just met the guy. Whether or not he believed in magic was irrelevant at this point. Besides, he'd been open to her ideas, had agreed with all of them, and even suggested one of his own before she'd been able to voice it, so there was a good chance he was drawn to the more spiritual side of life. And even if he wasn't, it was unlikely he'd be actively against it. She was imagining problems before there was anything to worry about, and she really should stop.

If only her mum was still here, so she could talk about it with her.

Chapter 4

Light In the Darkness

Beth

The second time Beth became aware of herself, it began with a sucking sensation. Had that happened the first time, and she'd just been too confused to realise? It was so strange, like being pulled towards the hungry mouth of a vacuum cleaner, so fast and strong that she was somehow able to compress herself down to fit through the tiny opening. And then, jumbled and dizzy, she was shot from the soothing darkness she'd been in, out into the glaring light.

Where was she? Who was she? What the hell was going on?

Gazing around wildly, she discovered that she was floating near the ceiling of a large, brightly lit room. Drawing herself together, she raised her eyebrows as she noticed just how dishevelled her clothes were, like she really had been chewed up and spat out by something. With a sigh, she smoothed down the front of her long blue velvet dress, and pulled the sleeves out of the high neckline where they'd become twisted. It had been one of her favourite outfits to wear to school – pretty, but warm and comfortable, and modest enough for teaching social sciences to a bunch of teenage boys.

School. She knew this ceiling.

Rolling over, she remained hovering in the rafters while she studied the room below. It was the staff room of Smithfield High, where she'd been for a few inter-school activities, and there was

Mrs Gallagher, the principal. But who were all the kids around the table? There were more students than teachers, and even the two she guessed were on staff looked completely unfamiliar to her.

Then, with a jolt, she saw Rhiannon sitting amongst them, and swooped down towards her. Why was her daughter in the Smithfield staff room? More importantly, why was *she* here? She'd thought that she was confined to their cottage – wasn't that how hauntings worked? How had she reconstituted herself here? And why?

Awkwardly she drifted above the chair next to her daughter, trying to figure out what was going on. Then every molecule of her beamed. It was the organising committee for the school ball. Rhiannon had wanted to be part of it the year before, although she supposed her mother dying had upset that plan. But Beth soon realised that wasn't the only thing causing her happiness. One of the students was making her blush and stumble over her words.

Intrigued, Beth gazed across the table at the boy with the blond hair and grey eyes. He seemed lovely, his face open and his smile frequent. He listened to the other committee members in a way not all the students did, and he considered each proposal carefully before responding. He was mindful of everyone there, principal, teachers and fellow students, and she liked that.

She also liked the way he was looking at Rhiannon, with genuine affection, and curiosity, and most importantly respect. He was polite when he spoke to her, yet warm too – a wonderful combination from a mother's point of view.

Floating across the table between them, she hovered at his shoulder so she could watch her daughter. It shocked her, in a good way, to see her face like this. At Samhain, Rhiannon had been devastated and grief-stricken, and Beth was terrified that she'd been stuck in a loop of anger and depression since she'd died, with no end in sight. But today Rhiannon looked happy. Shy too, and a little anxious, but alive in a way that showed she was moving forward, that she wasn't condemned to a life solely of misery and pain. That there were moments of light within the darkness. Fire within the freeze.

Watching her cheeks flush and her heart race as she stared into the eyes of an unfamiliar boy filled Beth with joy. Of course she'd rather actually be alive, and be seen, but for some reason she had this opportunity to be present with her daughter, and she would soak up every second of it.

Besides, if she was still alive, she might not even have known that Rhiannon liked anyone. Would she have confessed about her first love to her mother, shared the details, or would she have kept it a secret, unwilling to take her into her confidence? Perhaps there was an upside to being a ghost after all...

Did that mean she was spying on her daughter though? Suddenly it felt a little intrusive, watching her talk and laugh and speak up, when she had no idea one of her parents was in the room. It hardly seemed fair. Beth would never have read her diary, yet here she was drinking in every precious moment like gold, seeing her soul laid bare as she gazed so adoringly at the boy. She sensed her daughter's hope flicker to life when he agreed with her pagan-themed ideas – and Beth was so proud when she suggested it be a magical midwinter Yule Ball, based on the witchy rituals she'd done with Rose.

Rhiannon's face was so expressive, and Beth wondered if the boy could see what she did. See the sparkle in her eyes, the excitement mixed with fear and hope. An ache swept through her as she contemplated how it had been for her daughter, for all of her family, without her for so long. How different would their lives be now if she hadn't died? Would Rhiannon be happier, more confident? Would she have already fallen in love? And what had it done to her husband, to be the sole caregiver for their children? What had he given up or missed out on because she was gone?

There was no way she could answer that, or change the outcome, but she did want to know why she'd been drawn back now, so long after her death. Why not sooner? Or later? Were there rules? Was she supposed to know stuff about her purpose here, about her abilities? Clearly she wasn't stuck in one spot, tethered to her old home – not even to her village, given today's appearance in Smithfield. Was she attached to her three loved ones maybe, able to go wherever her husband or her kids went, somehow made manifest by their yearning for her? And where had she been all this time? Floating in an abyss of darkness? Of nothingness? No feeling, no awareness.

The last thing she remembered was being in that hospital bed, smiling at her beloved, and then... And then she'd become aware, become conscious, on Samhain Eve, as she'd walked up the front path of her cottage as though she'd only been gone a few hours – yet it had been thirteen months. Where had that time gone? Where had *she* gone? And how badly had her family suffered?

When she thought of her sweet young son Brodie, she felt agony like physical blows raining down on her. For a moment she wavered, both her mind, or whatever it was that was making her conscious, and her body, this strange shimmer of a form she'd somehow drawn to her. What was she? A ghost? A spirit? She felt more mist than matter. A wisp of energy trying to shape itself into a woman. How long would it last? Would she suddenly disappear again?

The first time she'd assumed that it was a one-off Samhain gift, that she'd been dragged back to earth because it was the night when ghosts were said to walk, when the veils thinned and the worlds of the living and the dead drew close. And she'd suspected that it was Rose's doing, that the priestess had guided her back as part of her ritual to honour the departed.

Yet here she was, a few days later, in a different place, and a different town, and the only person with even the barest hint of magical knowledge was her teenage daughter, who was completely oblivious to her presence.

Suddenly she felt a blurriness around her edges, a diminishing, and wondered if this was the end. Panic swamped her. She wasn't ready to leave. Desperately she tried to hold herself together, to remain present, but the unravelling continued – until Rhiannon raised her eyes from the object of her affection, and seemed to look right at her. Instantly Beth felt herself solidifying, becoming real, although she couldn't tell whether she was changing physically, or it was just the possibility of it that was making her aware, expanding the boundary of her... soul?

Silently she implored her daughter to see her, to feel her. But then she sensed the boy next to her smile, and Rhiannon's attention returned to him, to his lips, and Beth felt the wanting within her, the tumult of emotion as she tried not to be obvious, as she tried not to hope. Oh goddess, had she contributed to her doubt, the doubt that she was worthy of this boy? She'd been so careful to raise her with confidence and esteem and equality. *Hadn't she?*

Distraught, Beth drifted back across the table and attempted to put her transparent arms around her daughter, to draw her into a hug. When Rhiannon shivered, she whispered words of comfort, words of soothing, trying to calm her, to make her *feel* her. Words she'd whispered so many times over the years. But her daughter couldn't hear her, she knew that. No amount of wishing would make it happen, and she wanted to scream with frustration, to beat her hands on the table, to jump up and down and be seen.

Why could no one see her?

Racking her brain, she tried to think of something to help her communicate with her daughter. A vision rose in her mind of her Book of Shadows, a large old leather book embossed with swirling ivy, bound together with a silver clasp. For twenty years she'd painstakingly written in it, recording her spells and rituals, her study of herbs, crystals and healing, her workings with the moon and the seasons. There were hundreds of pages, some with pictures she'd drawn of herbs or lunar phases, plus a few extra sheets of paper slipped within the covers when she'd run out of room just before she... died. Had the book known when her life would end, and measured it out in parchment pages? The thought chilled Beth, and she focused back on the last time she'd seen it.

After her final ritual, she'd wrapped it in fabric and left it with all her magical supplies in a big wooden chest marked for Rose. If her health had improved, she could easily take it back out and continue writing, but the terror that she would soon die had set in, and she wanted to be sure it ended up with Rose, so she could pass it on to Rhiannon when the time was right. Had the time been right yet? She knew the priestess had gifted her with her own Book of Shadows to begin writing in, so maybe. Shrugging off the despair that was thickening around her, she tried to recall one of her recipes for purification, and for encouraging psychic abilities and the sight.

A Purifying Herbal Bath Blend

This is a wonderful way to cleanse and clear the aura before working any form of divination, and to soothe and release past sorrows so you're ready to focus on your psychic abilities... *Makes five baths.*

1 tblsp lavender, to calm, clear and centre.
1 tblsp rose petals, for love and support.
1 tblsp ground sandalwood, to heal, protect and purify.
1 tblsp rosemary, for protection, purification and relieving fatigue.
1 tblsp vervain, for purification, consecration and inspiration.
1 tblsp thyme, for psychic knowledge, purification and releasing pain.
1 tblsp lemon balm, to calm, cleanse and soothe.
2 cups Epsom salt, for relaxation and drawing out impurities.
½ cup baking soda, to soften the skin.

* Mix all the ingredients together in a wooden bowl, stirring with your fingers to infuse it with your love and energy, focusing on your intent as you work. (It can be prepared beforehand and stored in a jar.)
* Fill the bath with very hot water and pour in half a cup of your bath blend, then let the herbs steep as the water cools to a comfortable temperature. Light some candles, then climb in and soak, allowing your mind to drift as ritual consciousness begins to descend.
* I love seeing and feeling the flowers and leaves swirling around me (just remember to use a strainer when you pull the plug), but if you prefer, you can make a muslin sachet for the herbs, like a giant teabag. Draw a very hot bath, pop in the teabag, half a cup of Epsom salt and a tablespoon of soda, and let it steep while the water cools enough to get in. You can also steep the herbs in boiling water then pour this strong tea into your bath with the salts and soda.
* Herbal baths are healing physically and emotionally. The warm water opens the pores and makes you receptive to the healing properties of the herbs. Lavender, calendula and chamomile relax and aid sleep. Rosemary and eucalyptus are wonderful if you feel congested and need a physical boost. Calendula, comfrey and yarrow make for a soothing and healing bath mix, and are wonderful for the skin. Basil, fennel and eucalyptus are perfect for a refreshing, stimulating bath.

* Next I'll be making essential oil bath treatments, adding a healing blend to a carrier oil such as apricot or avocado oil, then adding a few tablespoons to the bath for a soothing, nourishing experience.
* I'll also try the milk bath Rose mentioned – pour two cups of milk into the water, stir in some honey and some jasmine essential oil, and drift off. It sounds divine, and would be perfect before a love ritual...

A cough from the principal interrupted Beth's pondering of other spells, and she focused back on Rhiannon. But the exercise had reminded her that she should try to connect with Rose again. Ask her to pass on her Book of Shadows to Rhiannon, if she hadn't already, and encourage her daughter to use all the recipes in it that would open up her psychic channels so she could see her mum's ghostly form, or at least sense her presence.

Or should she find a psychic medium, someone who communicated with the dead for a living? Maybe Rhiannon wanted so desperately to see her that she was blocking her intuition, and doubting anything she encountered as simply wishful thinking. Perhaps it had to be a message from a stranger, someone who'd never met her, for her to believe. Then she remembered that she'd somehow managed to slip into Mike's dream, so she could try that with Rhiannon too.

But all this hoping and wishing was too much for Beth. Not knowing what else to do, she kept her diaphanous arms wrapped around her daughter, then relaxed and let herself go. And felt herself dissolving, her outer awareness slipping beneath Rhiannon's skin, wrapping around her bones, sliding into the cells of her blood and the beats of her heart. She could no longer see, but oh, she could feel. And her daughter was filled with excitement and guilt and attraction and turmoil and hope and fear and wonder. Could she have sensed her mother after all? Or was it all about this boy?

Just as Beth thought she might be able to communicate with her daughter, to think her thoughts directly into her brain or her heart, she heard a roaring sound, and the vacuum sensation pulled her out of the blood and bones she was meshed with, then picked her up and threw her about, like an autumn leaf in a sudden storm. Dizzy, she felt herself being torn apart and flung to the four directions.

Chapter 5

Otherworldly Gifts

Rhiannon

"Rhiannon!"

She jumped at the sound of her name, jolting back to the present, and her surroundings. The car had just pulled up out the front of their school, her classmates were piling out, and Glenda was smiling at her from the front seat.

"Are you okay lovely? You were a million miles away."

Blushing, Rhiannon nodded. "I'm fine, just preoccupied with planning things for the ball."

"Do you need a lift home?"

Clumsily she opened the door and scooped up her bag. "No, I'm good, but thank you for taking us today. I'll see you on Monday."

And she fled. Despite her embarrassment at being caught daydreaming about John, she was happy, and had to push down the giggles rising within her in case they turned into full blown hysteria. But as she left the school grounds, she couldn't keep the grin from her face, and she floated along the pavement in a daze. Was this butterfly-filled shimmery sensation love? Recalling the day Carlie had run into Rowan up on the tor for the first time, and how she'd acted right after that, she decided that maybe it was.

She felt excited-shy-hopeful-scared-giggly-nervous-yearning all at once, plus a bunch of other emotions she couldn't identify. She just felt full. Picturing John's kind grey eyes, his sweet smile, the warmth on his face as he'd spoken to her, she laughed with joy. Would she burst with all these feelings running through her?

Abruptly she changed direction. She couldn't go home now and talk to her dad and her little brother – they'd think she was crazy, blushing and babbling about some boy. Better if she let her excitement spill over with Carlie. She'd understand what she was feeling, and it was so wonderful that they could talk about boys together now. Picking up the pace, she tried to calm herself down so she wouldn't seem *too* flustered, but her brain was awhir with hopes and dreams. John must be the cute blond guy the psychic had seen for her.

Carlie seemed a little on edge when she opened the door, and Rhiannon felt guilty that she'd ditched her for the day. Silently she vowed that she would make it up to her.

Rose smiled when they entered the kitchen. "Hello sweet girl. You two are so adorable – spending the whole day together, then still wanting more time with each other at night."

What? Confusion swamped Rhiannon, but she quickly recovered her composure. "Well, we figured we should do a bit more on the assignment," she said, motioning to the messenger bag on her shoulder, before shooting daggers at Carlie.

"I'm not complaining! I'm so happy that you both have each other," the priestess said, then ushered them upstairs with promises that she would bring them tea and shortbreads soon. They climbed the stairs in silence and collapsed on the floor in Carlie's small room, backs resting against her narrow single bed.

"So I'm guessing you didn't tell Rose about my change of plans today, and you went to see Rowan instead," Rhiannon stated, her disapproval clear. She'd been so excited at the thought of sharing her news about John with her friend, but now she didn't want to. Now she wanted to keep it to herself. Carlie didn't deserve to know.

Her friend nodded, but didn't defend herself.

 "Be careful with your lies, Rose isn't stupid," Rhiannon snapped, but then she saw the look on Carlie's face and her voice softened. "What happened? Did he hurt you?"

"No," she said, then faltered. "Not really…"

Looking embarrassed, Carlie haltingly revealed her story. She'd gone to see Rowan, who had been due back the night before from teaching a spiritual retreat in France. But his car had broken down on the drive home, adding hours to his journey, and he'd still been asleep when she arrived. He'd told her to come to bed with him, which made her nervous, but he actually had meant to sleep.

Rhiannon smiled. "That doesn't sound so bad. He would have been beyond exhausted after his trip."

Carlie blushed. "Well, we slept for a while, but then I woke up to him kissing me, and trying to... I don't know, go further."

"Oh my god! Did he force you to –"

"No!" Carlie insisted. "He tried to convince me for a bit, but he finally stopped."

"And will he keep trying to convince you until you give in?" Rhiannon demanded.

"I don't know. I do feel guilty though. I mean, isn't that what you're supposed to do when you love someone?"

Rhiannon gasped, horrified. "Of course not, you're supposed to respect your girlfriend or boyfriend's decisions, to wait until they're ready, no matter how long it takes."

"I know, and he does, he's usually really good about it..."

"Don't you dare let him pressure you into this!" Rhiannon said, voice fierce. "And don't make excuses for him. Any guy who thinks that behaviour is okay should be avoided at all costs, no matter how sweet he appears to be the rest of the time. Believe me, I know."

The anger in her words, and rushing through her body, shocked Rhiannon. Where had it come from? Why was she so upset? Nothing had happened, and Rowan was a good guy. Kind, gentle, supportive...

"I won't. And he won't," Carlie assured her, and she seemed calmer now, and more certain of it herself. "But that's not the worst thing that happened," she finally admitted, and Rhiannon's eyes widened.

A stunningly beautiful woman had turned up, kissed Rowan hello, then remarked on how quickly he'd replaced her. So now Carlie was feeling insecure all over again, worried that she wasn't his only true love, upset that she didn't know any of his friends, and suddenly not as trusting about the time they spent apart.

Rhiannon tried to reassure her, but her heart wasn't in it. And really, how could she know what he got up to when they were apart? When he was teaching, with all those women who flocked around him. Uncharitably, she thought Carlie was being selfish. Why did it always have to be about her? *Her* boyfriend? *Her* dramas? Maybe that wasn't fair, but she'd been so excited to confide in her about John, yet now she wanted to keep it to herself. It was too precious to reveal like this, too important to be derailed by an unrelated issue.

As if sensing her lack of interest, Carlie reached over to her bag and gently pulled out a parcel wrapped in green velvet. "I have something for you," she said with a smile. "I'm sorry, I was so preoccupied with... everything else... that I forgot about it."

Rhiannon's eyebrows lifted in surprise, all thoughts of Rowan – and her own swirling anger – driven from her mind. She held out her hands for the mysterious velvet-wrapped bundle. "You saw her again? When? Where? What did she say? Which one was it?" *God, how come Carlie had all the magical encounters?*

"It was the woman in green. I saw her this afternoon. I was in a strange mood when I got off the bus, too scared to come home and face Rose straight away, because she would no doubt pick up on it, so I thought I'd climb the tor, and see if I could gain a sense of perspective from being at the top," Carlie said wryly.

"Instead, I somehow wandered into the mists and found myself weaving around the lower slopes, amongst the apple trees, far from the path to the summit. And Brianna suddenly emerged, and talked to me for a little while, saying to trust and have faith. Then she handed this to me, and said to give it to you, because you'll know which one of us has need of which object."

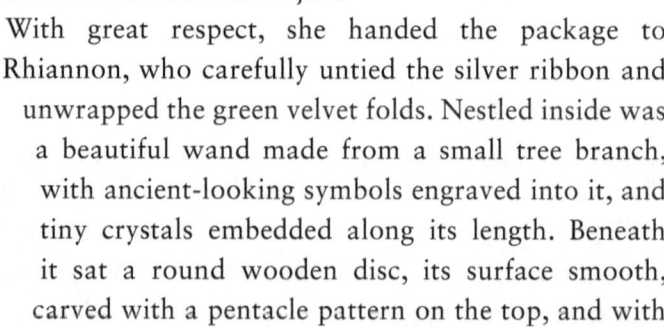

With great respect, she handed the package to Rhiannon, who carefully untied the silver ribbon and unwrapped the green velvet folds. Nestled inside was a beautiful wand made from a small tree branch, with ancient-looking symbols engraved into it, and tiny crystals embedded along its length. Beneath it sat a round wooden disc, its surface smooth, carved with a pentacle pattern on the top, and with a large rose quartz crystal set in a hollow in its centre. Both were breathtaking, and both exuded an air of deep magic.

"Earth and air," Rhiannon said, awe in her voice. Then she panicked. How could she decide who should have which ritual piece?

Nervously she picked up the pentacle and held it to her heart, hoping she could connect with the objects in some way. She felt a sense of peace from it, and strength. Smiling, she put it down and picked up the wand – and gasped as a deep thrumming energy pulsed from it, sending a jolt of power up her arm. She could hear a murmur of voices, of words, as she held it. Visions danced through her mind – fae creatures of the forest, of nature… and of her, they whispered. *What did that mean?*

Closing her eyes, Rhiannon took a deep breath, then scrunched up her nose in concentration. Again the voices spoke, crooning to her of love and belonging, of nights up on the tor under the stars, of being loved so intensely, and held so gently, in strong arms. John's? With a smile and a sigh of relief, she buried her head in his chest, surprised that he was here with her, but so glad. Until a light touch on her arm dragged her back to the room, to the present, and away from him. She blinked, dazed and confused. Putting the wand down, she stared around her and tried to focus. It felt as though her mind and spirit were no longer in her physical body.

What had happened? Her hand hovered over the two ritual objects, torn. She desperately wanted the wand for herself. From the second her fingers had grazed the tip of it, the magic had been so powerful, so instant. Was that selfish though, to choose which one they'd each have based on her own greed? To give Carlie the one she didn't want? What if it was a test?

Oops! Her friend was gazing at her, eyebrows raised in question. How long had she been silent? "They'll both connect us to nature and the elements," she said quickly.

Then, with only a small twinge of guilt, she handed the pentacle to Carlie. "This wooden disc was made from a piece of oak, from a tree that had fallen, rather than being chopped down," she explained, surprised, and filled with wonder, that the fae beings, *or something,* had somehow imparted that to her.

"Oak is considered the king of the forest, and is revered for its size and great age. It represents courage, strength, stability and endurance, which will certainly be of use to you. It's also good for divination and inner reflection, for connecting you to your inner knowing and your authentic voice. And of course the rose quartz is there to amplify your feelings of self-love, self-healing, self-esteem and compassion to self," she added, and as she said the words she felt a softening towards Carlie, a wave of emotion that swelled within her, and made her feel more patient and forgiving.

"The pentacle is used by witches as an amulet and symbol of protection, and this piece can be used to represent earth on our altar. The shape can also be traced in the air, with an athame or wand, or even just your finger, to invoke the elements and the directions in ritual. In many traditions the lower left hand point of the star represents earth, the lower right represents fire, the upper left air, the upper right water, and the topmost point spirit."

Rhiannon watched her friend tracing over the pentacle pattern as she listened, and reminded herself just how much the poor girl had been through. Surely she could cut her a little slack. So she'd taken advantage of her change of plans to see her boyfriend, and was feeling insecure about some glamorous woman. Would it kill her to offer some reassurance? To reflect back the love and groundedness of the crystals and symbols they'd been gifted? Her heart expanded as she thought this, and she was glad that her earlier annoyance had dissipated. Besides, it wasn't like *she'd* never lied to her parents. The night before her mother died, she'd told them she was staying at her friend Debbie's – but had snuck out to meet Debbie's brother instead.

Carlie smiled as she took the ritual tool and held it to her own heart. "Thank you," she said softly, as she placed the pentacle in her lap, bit into a biscuit and sipped her tea. She radiated a sense of peace and security that had been missing when she'd arrived, and she was glad her friend was benefitting from the magic of the pieces too.

Finally, barely able to contain her excitement, Rhiannon picked up her own new ritual piece, and it felt so natural, so much a part of her. Gazing down at it, she marvelled at its beauty. It looked like an extension of her hand, an elegant part of her.

"It's an elder wand," she told Carlie in reverent tones. "It can be used to represent air on our altar, can direct energy in spellcasting, and also carve out a ritual circle, the sacred space between the worlds. The elder tree is considered the queen of the forest, and it has a powerful feminine energy, holding the wisdom of the crone within it. It represents renewal and regeneration, aids in emotional transformation, offers protection, and can help deepen visions and visualisation exercises."

As she spoke, Rhiannon traced the symbols carved along its length, and heard the whispers again. Then she softly touched the small amethyst crystals embedded in the branch and the moonstone at its tip. Energy zapped through her, and she felt a rush of warmth, wonder and wisdom envelop her. "This means we have our four ritual tools – the chalice for water, the athame for fire, and now the pentacle for earth and the wand for air. It seems that we have friends who want to encourage our magic."

The gifts had cheered them up and brought the two girls closer, and Rhiannon focused on that, and the strengthening of their bond. They spent the next few hours planning rituals they wanted to perform and things they wanted to study on upcoming coven nights, until they both started yawning, and were shocked again by the time. Hugging her friend goodbye, Rhiannon tiptoed downstairs, careful not to wake Rose, and quietly let herself out.

As she headed home through the midnight dark, she thought about the beautiful elder wand in her bag, and slipped her fingers inside to reassure herself it was still there, and to seek the comfort of its immense, intense, yet gentle power.

And when she fell into bed that night, the wand placed close to her on the bedside table, she was smiling. The joy of meeting John combined with the magic of the wand, and her dreams that night were filled with love and wonder.

Chapter 6

Queen of the Witches

Rhiannon

Monday was the dark moon, and Rhiannon woke up with a shiver of dread. Although she'd smoothed things over with Carlie the other night, and left happy, she was disturbed by how angry she'd become, and uncomfortable with how she'd reacted. The last thing they needed right now was the introspective energy of this moon phase. The extra push to see the darkness within.

She still didn't know why she'd been so lacking in sympathy when her friend had revealed what had happened with Rowan. Instead of offering comfort and reassurance, she'd jumped to the most dramatic conclusion and turned on Carlie, belittling her, making her question her judgement, and suddenly acting like Rowan was some kind of predator. Even if her worst suspicions about him were true – and she was pretty sure they weren't – she could have handled it much better. Much more kindly. Her reaction made no sense to her.

As she slipped on her school uniform, she was determined that she and Carlie would ride out the darker lunar vibrations together today, in preparation for the energy and beauty of tomorrow's new moon. For whatever reason, she'd over-reacted. She would apologise, reassure her friend, and they'd move on.

Relief coursed through her when Carlie greeted her with a smile and they headed off to class together as usual.

"I just remembered that today is the dark moon, which explains my weird dreams and silly paranoia about the mystery woman," Carlie whispered as they sat together in history. "I know Rowan loves me, and how close we are, so this afternoon I just have to let him explain, and we can move on. It was probably just a friend's wife or a co-worker or something, and I flipped out and ran off without letting him introduce us. I'm such an idiot!"

"You're not an idiot. But you're right, I'm sure there's a logical explanation," Rhiannon said in soothing tones.

When the final bell rang, Rhiannon wished her friend luck then headed to the staff room for a quick committee meeting. It was just her and her three classmates today, preparing for tomorrow's proper get-together, when the students from the other two schools would travel to theirs. She was so excited that she would see John the next day that she barely listened as Karen, Peter and Tracy put forward their ideas, nodding absent-mindedly to whatever they suggested. Glad when it finally ended, she raced off, already daydreaming about the boy she was so eager to see again.

But the smile slid from her face when she saw Carlie sitting forlornly on the front steps of the school. Rowan had obviously stood her up, and Rhiannon's heart ached for her friend. She sat down next to her and slipped an arm around her shoulder.

"I'm so sorry…"

Carlie wiped her eyes and tried to put on a brave face. "Silly me, huh, thinking I could date him, that he could really love me. That a silly, naive schoolgirl could ever be enough for him."

Rhiannon made comforting sounds, but her anger had returned full force. Why would a guy bother being with someone if he didn't really want to? Why had he been leading her friend on? Why not end things and save them both the heartache? Why start in the first place?

"I guess it's just hard, with him travelling so much, and meeting so many women, women who clearly adore him, to know if you can trust him," she said, her voice sharper than she'd intended.

"I suppose you'd never really know what he got up to while he was away, or who he was with. And it's weird – he's a healer and a spiritual teacher, yet he's not honourable with his word."

"What do you mean?" Carlie gasped, shocked at the harsh words.

Rhiannon was surprised too. Until the other day, she'd adored Rowan, even been jealous that he loved her friend. Why wasn't she defending him, offering suggestions? There were plenty of reasonable explanations – it could be car trouble, a work issue, *something*. She watched Carlie deflate even further, and felt bad. Not bad enough to stop her character assassination though. "He's unreliable, dishonest, unfaithful, disrespectful, arrogant, misogynistic..."

Finally she managed to rein herself in and halt the barrage of criticism. "What are you going to do?" she asked.

Laughing bitterly, Carlie shrugged. "What can I do? He chose the other woman, *woman* being the operative word, so I should retreat gracefully I guess. What other option do I have? Still, it means I'll have more time to help Rose in the shop, more time to study, and more time for our magical work. I have neglected that a bit. I'm sorry."

Rhiannon smiled reassuringly. "Rose will love that, and so will I. But I feel terrible – I have to go home now and look after Brodie, because Dad has a meeting tonight. Will you be okay? Do you want to come over tomorrow after my committee meeting gets out? We can do our new moon ritual, and you can sleep over – we can stay up all night chatting and eating cookies and moaning about boys – personally I reckon they all suck." Of course she didn't think that, not now that she was obsessing over John, but her friend didn't know that.

Carlie smiled, not the biggest or most joyful smile, but it was a good attempt. "That would be really nice."

"Great. Now, shall I walk you home? You're not going to wait any longer are you?" she asked, the disapproval clear in her voice.

"No, let's go."

As they left the school, Rhiannon felt guilty again. Reminding herself she was so out of sorts because of the dark moon, she changed the subject, determined that not another mean or discouraging word would pass her lips. And she'd do a ritual later tonight, to work on releasing this strange anger she seemed to be drowning in.

When they reached Rose's cottage, Rhiannon hugged her friend and promised her everything would be fine, then headed off to pick up her little brother and entertain him for the evening. After she'd fed him, bathed him, put him to bed and read to him, she went up to her room and lit four black candles, placing one in each of the four directions. Even that small action was soothing, and she felt peace descending on her as she prepared.

Using the beautiful elder wand she'd been gifted, she carved out her space between the worlds, lit some sandalwood incense, then closed her eyes and began her invocation.

Dear Hekate, goddess of death and rebirth, and the dark.
Help me banish my jealousy and fear, and ignite the spark,
Of understanding, patience, balance and healing,
And show me the reason for all I am feeling.
Queen of the witches and of the night,
Help me release my anger to the approaching light.
Guide me as I look within my heart,
To discover what I need my subconscious to impart.
Reveal my hidden truths and what lurks inside,
And strip away the emotions I've tried to hide.
Allow me to see in my black-candle flame,
What I've bound and who I blame.
With love, honour and respect I invoke you,
To aid me in my quest to see what is true.
Through your wisdom and insight help me attune,
To the wisdom and introspection of this darkest moon.
So mote it be.

Opening her eyes, Rhiannon stared into the candle flames, and felt herself sinking down into the deep waters of that strange temple pool she'd been in at Samhain. Water lapped against her chest, and she gritted her teeth and fought through the overwhelming urge to panic. Trust, she repeated over and over like a mantra, like a life raft, and finally her breathing slowed, and her panic receded. *Like water.*

Her alarm returned with a crash when the flames rose above her, and she cowered before their size and heat. Smoke filled the room, writhing in long, sinister, darkened tendrils, reaching out for her, before it thickened and coalesced in a grotesque dance.

Heart racing, Rhiannon looked on in horror – which escalated to terror when a woman appeared within the blackened fog then stepped towards her, arms outstretched, face twisted with... *something*.

"Hekate," she whispered, fear hollowing her voice.

"Rhiannon." Her name from the lips of the goddess was a deep rumble, as though dragged from the depths of the earth. "Are you ready to really see, to really become aware?"

A shiver ran up her spine, and she recoiled from the vision before her. What did she mean, was she ready? What could she possibly be not seeing, not aware of? And why wouldn't she want to know? Of course she was ready. *Right?*

As she tried to form the word yes, and discover what she needed to know, a knock on the door made her jump. Turning towards it, she broke eye contact with the enigmatic figure in the flames.

"Rhiannon?"

Damn! It was her dad, home from his meeting. She glanced at the clock, and was shocked to see that three hours had passed since she put Brodie to bed. How long had she been in that temple pool?

"Are you okay?"

She gazed back to the middle of her sacred circle, to the eerie black-clad figure within it, but she was gone. The candles flickered as if in a breeze, but that was the only sign that anything... anyone... had been with her tonight.

Sighing, she blew out all but one candle, hauled herself to her feet, switched on her lamp and opened the door.

"Hi Dad. How was the meeting?"

His eyebrows furrowed in consternation. "I've been home for hours. I was in bed, but something woke me. I thought I heard you talking to someone."

He tried to peer around her, into her room, but the light from the lamp was dim, and she was blocking the doorway.

"I must have called out in my sleep," she offered. "Sorry."

Her father frowned, taking in her school uniform. *Oops.* She tried to think of a reason why she wasn't in her pyjamas, but he had shrugged and turned away from her before she could come up with anything.

"As long as you're okay. Get some shut eye darling," he muttered, and shuffled back to his room, still half asleep.

Nodding, she hurried to her altar space and quickly farewelled the goddess, unwound her circle and extinguished the final candle, letting the darkness descend. She fell onto her bed, still fully clothed, and tried to calm her breathing once more. Her mind whirred, and she peered nervously into the corners of her room and the shadowy places beside her dresser. Had she really invoked the goddess tonight, into physical form? Was that possible? Even Rose just invoked the essence of the goddess in her rituals, channelling the power through her own body. But she'd seen her, right in front of her, solidifying from the darkness of the smoke. She'd heard her deep and ancient voice.

And if she had somehow brought her through, made her physical, would she be angry to have been disturbed? Hekate was no sweet and innocent deity of love, light and protection, she was Lady of the Night, of the Mysteries, of Death. Not someone you wanted to bother with trifling human problems. But scared as she was that she might have displeased her, Rhiannon did feel some comfort that the goddess had spoken to her, even if she had been interrupted before she could impart her message. Would she return?

She didn't find out, because soon the scent of sandalwood had lulled her to sleep, and she smiled as she saw herself getting out of Glenda's car at Smithfield High for one of their committee meetings. Excitement bubbled within her as she followed the path to the staff room, but it was taking so much longer than usual to get there, the way twisting and turning each time she thought the door was in sight. When a hand grasped her shoulder she jumped, and twisted around in panic – to see a tall, dark-haired guy leering down at her. She stared up at him in fear, and tried to get away, but he dragged her from the path and pulled her roughly into his arms, smashing her head up against his hard, broad, suddenly naked chest. Her breath came in ragged gasps as she struggled against him, but he crooned her name, his voice unnervingly familiar.

"What are you doing? What do you want?" she cried out, trying to disentangle herself from him. But he just smiled at her, lust blazing in his eyes as he looked her up and down, gaze lascivious, breath hot on her face. His hand reached out for the collar of her shirt, determined to rip it apart. Just as she opened her mouth to scream, his features blurred, then changed, and he turned back into John, her grey-eyed, blond-haired crush. And he was reaching out his hand to her, smile wide, face welcoming. He led her away from the pain, away from the fear, and they wandered hand in hand through a field of flowers, chatting about their lives, their families, the things they wanted, and aspired to. Relaxing at last, she let him draw her down onto the grass, and they sat cross-legged, facing each other, continuing their conversation and laughing at all they had in common.

After a while he left to get them coffees, and she smiled as she awaited his return, so happy they were talking together, away from their classmates, and getting to know each other. When a shadow fell on her she looked up, hand outstretched for the drink he'd brought her – except it wasn't John, it was the other guy, the one who wanted to hurt her. He crouched next to her, ripped her shirt open and forced her down onto her back in the long grass, then pulled off his own shirt and lay on top of her, his weight pressing down on her, his body hot and heavy against hers. She thought she would faint from the fear, but suddenly he was being pulled off her, and John pushed him away, far from them, and gently lifted her up and held her close.

"You saved me," she said, voice a whimper, and her eyes filled with wonder and surprise.

"Of course," he replied, and slowly reached across and wiped the tear from her eye, before gently kissing her forehead. She felt so safe, so respected, so honoured with him. So right. Gazing up at him, she marvelled at his kind face, his kind eyes, and the promise they held.

"I'll protect you Rhiannon," he whispered. Relief flooded her, and her heart opened up to him as she felt the sincerity of his words. Somehow she knew he was speaking the truth, that he cared about her, and wouldn't let anyone hurt her.

When her alarm went off, she woke with a smile on her lips, and a desperate desire to return to her dream. Although she couldn't remember the details of it, she knew it had been about John, and that he was even more wonderful than she'd imagined. She couldn't wait to see him for real that afternoon!

Getting through the school day was tough. Rhiannon was so impatient, and all her classes dragged on interminably. She daydreamed through most of them, her mind drifting off to how she'd felt wrapped in John's arms. He'd been so strong, so confident, so caring and protective – everything she wanted in a boyfriend. She prayed he felt the same for her, and wondered if she'd snuck into his dreams too. Occasionally a shiver would ripple up her spine as the vaguest scrap of some dark memory tried to take hold, but she shrugged it off. If she'd dreamed anything else, she didn't recall it, and her mind was happily filled with visions of John.

She longed to talk about him with Carlie, to confide in her so she could share her excitement, but her friend was so sad about Rowan standing her up that she couldn't rub salt into her wounds. Besides, part of her was thrilled to have a secret. And really, what was there to say right now? *There's a cute guy on the planning committee, who I barely know but seem to have fallen for? I've been dreaming about him, yet he probably hasn't spared me a thought?* It wasn't much of a story, since their "relationship" only existed in her head, and her dreams. As she drifted off into another imagining, she was relieved that Carlie was so preoccupied with her own sadness that she hadn't noticed Rhiannon was wearing lipstick and mascara today.

During the last class, her mood swung from excited to scared and back again, and when the end-of-day bell finally rang, she shouted a hurried farewell to Carlie, promised to see her later that night for their coven meeting, then rushed off to the staff room. She was the first one there, so she sat, tapping her fingernails on the table impatiently, then trying, and failing, to relax. When Karen, Tracy and Peter strolled in, she said hello but didn't join their conversation, too anxious to pay any attention to them.

After what felt like hours, but was only twenty minutes, the first person from the other two schools arrived. She held her breath as the other students filed in, and her heart didn't beat normally again until John entered the room, the last to do so. He grinned at her as he took the chair opposite her, and she blushed bright red. Surely he didn't know how she felt about him? How did she feel about him? This was so weird. How was she supposed to act?

"How have you been Rhiannon?" the object of her affection asked, and she stared at him in wonder, tongue-tied again. Karen rescued her once more, elbowing her in the ribs to break the spell.

"Fine," she managed to stammer, embarrassed by her lack of eloquence. "Um, I've been checking out recipes for the ball, so that's been fun. How have you been?"

His brilliant smile made her tummy flutter, and his voice did funny things to her brain. "I've been researching some bands that could play –" he began, eyes alight with excitement, but her school principal brought their meeting to order then, and they had to turn their attention to her. It didn't matter though. She loved it every time John spoke, and her heart beat a little faster whenever he cast his grey eyes in her direction.

When they paused for a coffee break he approached her, and they chatted for a while. He was lovely – but it took several moments for Rhiannon to get over her disappointment that he was so lacking in affection. *Patience*, she cautioned. While she felt as though they were already together, thanks to their incredible dream intimacy the previous night, to him she was simply a student he'd just met.

Time rushed by, and before she knew it John and his schoolmates were saying farewell. Reluctantly Rhiannon headed home – it was coven night, and she'd promised to cheer Carlie up. Of course all she wanted to do was rave about John, but she would hold her tongue in deference to her friend's heartache. Sighing with disappointment, she set up her room for their ritual, then waited. And waited.

Hmm, had she been so distracted by John that she'd forgotten their plan? Was she supposed to be going to Carlie's place? But no, she'd definitely invited her over, and she was going to stay the night so they could bitch about boys. Not that Rhiannon was anti-guys. She giggled, and threw herself on her bed, imagining being with John.

But as the clock ticked out a half hour, she started getting annoyed. After another thirty minutes passed, worry about her friend replaced that. Was Carlie okay? She assumed that Rowan had turned up and somehow made things right with his girlfriend, but a small part of Rhiannon was scared that something had happened to her.

She felt so helpless. She couldn't go over to the cottage and find out, because if Carlie was reuniting with Rowan, she was probably using Rhiannon as an alibi, which made her furious. But if something had happened to her friend, and she was lying in a ditch somewhere, shouldn't she alert someone? Her mind raced, from anger to worry to fear to annoyance and back again, until her little brother barrelled into her room and told her dinner was ready.

So she shook off her concern and headed downstairs, losing herself in time with Brodie – hanging out, laughing, then helping him with his homework. By the time she got him off to bed, she was so exhausted that she passed out in her school uniform again.

When she saw her friend in class the next morning she looked nervous, and Rhiannon was torn between sympathy and fury. Carlie greeted her shyly, and Rhiannon stared at her for a long moment, eyes assessing, before sullenly echoing her hello.

"Please don't be mad at me," Carlie implored her. "I know you're upset that I didn't stay over, but I'll make it up to you, I promise."

"Oh my god Carlie, I'm not angry at you, I'm worried about you. I didn't know what had happened to you when you didn't come over last night, but I couldn't exactly pop by Rose's and ask her, since I was probably your alibi again," she snapped.

"For god's sake, I don't want to be your fall back plan, and I don't want to be part of your lies. It's not fair to me, or to Rose. I thought you were better than that, but it seems that your growing deceit doesn't bother you – it appears to be as natural to you as breathing now, which is disappointing."

Carlie gasped, shocked by the force of her animosity. "Gran was teaching last night, and didn't get home until after I did, so don't worry, I didn't have to lie to her," she retorted. "And I don't want to deceive anyone, ever. I am really sorry that I let you down Rhi – I didn't plan it that way, it's just that Rowan was waiting for me yesterday, after school, and I figured he deserved the chance to at least explain what had happened."

"So I take it you're back together, and everything is wonderful again – until the next time of course," Rhiannon said sarcastically.

"What was his excuse for treating you so badly on the weekend, and for standing you up the other day?" she demanded. "And, more importantly, how could you just forgive him?"

"Because I love him, and he loves me, and because he explained everything, and it was all just a misunderstanding," Carlie said, her tone defensive. She was beginning to sound a little annoyed too.

"His mum arrived on Sunday to stay with him for a few days, but she got really sick the next day and he had to take her to hospital. They were there all afternoon and into the night, and she was scared, so he couldn't just leave her to see me. She was released the next day and is feeling fine, so he came to meet me straight away – he was waiting for me yesterday when school ended, with a beautiful bunch of flowers, and he was really apologetic."

Rhiannon rolled her eyes, but motioned for her to go on, so Carlie explained that the mystery woman was Rowan's manager Jay, not some worldly second girlfriend, which she would have known if she'd stayed around and let him explain.

"That's great, but what about how bad you felt being compared to a 'real' woman – as you described her – and what about that whole forcing you to have sex thing?" Rhiannon demanded.

"That's not fair Rhi, he didn't force me to have sex – nothing actually happened. And he's mortified that I felt pressured in any way. He'd been dreaming about me, and then he half woke up, and I was lying in his arms, so..." she paused, blushing deep red.

"He stopped the second I asked him to, and he knew straight away that I wanted him to back off. And he's finally convinced me that just being together is enough for him – it's my paranoia that makes me feel as though I'm not enough, that I'm not doing enough. It's not his fault. So you don't have to worry about me, I'm fine. We're fine. He feels terrible about that morning, and he promised it wouldn't happen again."

"That's what they all say," Rhiannon muttered.

Chapter 7

Written In the Cards

Beth

The whirlpool pulled at Beth, the tugging sensation she was gradually becoming accustomed to, and she allowed the molecules that seemed to shape her coalesce, and her mind to struggle upwards towards the pain of awareness. The place she'd appeared in this time was unfamiliar, and dimly lit, but she felt the heat of a candle flame and pushed herself towards it, seeking its warmth as well as its illumination.

Gazing around the dark space, she saw a woman with long black curly hair, a colourful scarf around her head, and gold hoop earrings. She was sitting at a small table, polishing a crystal ball, then shuffling a deck of tarot cards. *Why on earth had she been drawn into a carnival tent at a village fair? Where the hell was she?*

Movement behind her made her spin around – then freeze. Rhiannon was ducking into the tent, eyes wide with curiosity and hope. "Hello," she said nervously. "Um, they told me to come to you?"

Beth swooped over to her daughter's side, overjoyed to see her. Somehow she must have conveyed to Rhiannon that she should find a psychic to try to connect with her mum.

The psychic looked happy too. "Of course dear, just take a seat here. I'm Miranda." As she accepted several pound notes, Beth realised why the woman was so joyful. *Oh, please don't be a fake!*

After offering the deck of cards to Rhiannon to shuffle, the woman took them back and placed the first ten on the small table, face down, in a Celtic cross formation. When she turned the first card over, she frowned. "Oh sweet child, there has been great sadness in your life."

Rhiannon nodded reluctantly, and Beth felt her own enthusiasm waning. That could apply to pretty much anyone.

"Your mother died," the psychic continued. Rhiannon looked startled, and Beth's ghostly form straightened as her interest was piqued. Maybe she was genuine after all.

Miranda smiled, as though she knew what her client had been thinking. "Yes, everyone has faced sadness at some point, but not like this, not like you. You're too young to have lost your mum."

Excitement coursed through Beth. Finally she'd be able to get her own message to her daughter. Laughter bubbled up within her, and she tried to get the woman's attention. She waved her hands. She called out. She flew over to her and fluttered in front of her face, so she would have to see her. She even shrieked "boo" in her ear. But there was nothing. No reaction. No idea she was there. What kind of medium was she, if she couldn't see the client's departed loved one hovering right in front of her?

Distraught, she turned back to her daughter, and saw tears sparkling on her lashes. "Is she okay?" Rhiannon whispered. "Does she know how much we miss her?"

"Of course she knows," the psychic said glibly. "And she's fine. Very happy on the other side, and no longer in pain, so you should be glad for that."

But Rhiannon didn't look at all glad, and started crying at the woman's words. Beth was outraged. How could she say something like that to a young girl? No one was going to be glad a parent was

dead! And how did she know anyway? Beth didn't even know where she'd been for the past thirteen months – she could have been writhing in torment for all she knew. And now? Whatever this strange... existence... was, she wasn't happy, she was tortured. Her heart was breaking over how devastated her

husband still was by her passing. Her mind was shattered by her grief at leaving her two young children to grow up without their mother. Why would anyone be glad about that?

"But I miss her so much," Rhiannon sobbed, and Beth floated over to her and tried to hold her, tried to comfort her, growing more and more frustrated that her transparent form could not be felt.

Miranda took Rhiannon's hand. "My dear, of course you do. That's completely normal, and you'll always miss her – it's a sign of how much you loved her – but it will get easier."

Rhiannon sniffled, unconvinced.

"I have a message for you, from your mother."

Instantly Beth's attention swung from her daughter back to the psychic. How on earth was she going to relay a message from her when she didn't even know she was in the room with them? Or did she? Was she just testing her?

Determined, Beth sprang back into action. She darted right at Miranda, fast, but the medium didn't flinch. She waved her arms again, then shouted in her ear. Nothing. Finally she squeezed her eyes shut, then pushed herself up against her, trying to melt into her, become a part of her blood and cells and bones like she had with her daughter, yet the woman remained oblivious. Beth screamed, so loud she thought people in neighbouring tents would come running, but neither Rhiannon nor the psychic blinked.

Devastated, she thought about dissolving back into the nothingness, too depressed to remain there and listen to whatever stuff the woman was going to make up, but she couldn't leave Rhiannon. She didn't know how long she'd be able to be with her, how long she could remain in this strange state she was in, so she had to make the most of it while she still could.

"She wants you to know how much she loves you, and will always love you," Miranda began.

Beth huffed.

"She's so sad that she had to leave you before you'd grown up, fallen in love, started a family. And she's sorry about that. She feels as though she failed you."

Wow, way to lay a guilt trip!

"But she loves you so much, and she trusts that you are strong enough to cope without her. That you will make her proud, no matter what you choose to do with your life."

Beth groaned. Of course she would be proud of her daughter – no one had to be paid to come up with that platitude. Disappointed, she switched off from the woman and gazed instead at her daughter, committing every expression to memory, in case her time here ended without warning. But she was brought abruptly back into the moment when she sensed Rhiannon stiffen.

"There's something painful you're trying to keep buried," the psychic ventured, then broke off. Rhiannon stared at her, eyes narrowed, and shook her head.

"Oh wait! I'm getting a message about a friend of yours, a warning of sorts. She's with a violent man, someone who professes to be spiritual, but who can't handle her independence, can't handle her light. He will try to destroy her. You must tell her that he will hurt her if she stays. You can't allow her to be with him, without at least trying to reveal what he's like. You can't keep this secret – it will haunt you forever. You must listen to me."

Rhiannon stared at the woman, speechless and clearly confused, but Beth shuddered. This was aimed at her. She'd felt guilty for the last twenty years that she hadn't warned Violet about Andrew, the shaman who'd convinced her to run away from home. She'd wanted to, but it was complicated. She was falling for Violet's boyfriend Mike, so she was conflicted, and Andrew had threatened to destroy her if she didn't keep her mouth shut, a threat she knew he was capable of carrying out.

"I don't know what you mean," Rhiannon said. "My best friend is dating someone a little older, but he's wonderful, and so kind."

"And yet you've had doubts about him," the psychic retorted, and Rhiannon blushed.

"It was just a misunderstanding, they figured it out. He's really lovely, and he'd never hurt her. Couldn't it be someone else?"

Miranda shook her head. "It's your new friend, your sister of the heart, and she's also suffered a loss." Her voice was firm, unwavering. "This man is dangerous. He's older than her, a shaman, a mysterious weaver of dreams and lies, who can dazzle people and keep them on their toes, keep them off-balance, so his own darkness remains hidden. He will break her heart and cause her deep pain – he'll hurt her in a way she won't be able to recover from."

Part of Beth was aware that her daughter was distressed, was starting to believe unwarranted evil of Carlie's boyfriend, but she knew the psychic meant Andrew, not Rowan. Meant Carlie's mum Violet, not Carlie. Meant *her*, Beth. It was her fault, the pain Violet had endured, and her excuses for not warning her about the shaman were just a self-preservation instinct she'd decided was more important than her friend's wellbeing. Pain ripped through her, and ripped her apart, until she lost all sense of time and place.

It was a familiar voice that brought her back from the abyss this time. "Rhiannon darling, are you ready?"

A sigh of regret shuddered through Beth as she felt herself becoming aware again, but she smiled when she saw Anne in the psychic's tent. Her mother-in-law had been a pillar of strength to her from the day she'd met Mike, offering enough love and support to make up for the yawning absence of it from her own cruel parents. She'd been such a comfort to her when Rhiannon was born, and a beacon of calm and wisdom that had soothed her own pain and helped dissolve her fears about what family meant.

Why was Anne here though? Where were they? Curious, she followed Rhiannon and her grandmother out of the tent into the chilly grey afternoon, pulling the long dark coat she was suddenly wearing tightly around herself. Midwinter was coming, and night was falling earlier, especially in the small northern village Anne and her husband William called home. Rhiannon must be visiting them for the weekend, so hopefully Mike and Brodie were here too.

Excited, Beth floated alongside Rhiannon and listened to her talking to her grandma. A worry within her unknotted as she realised her daughter still had people close to her, family close to her, and she was grateful to her husband for keeping that relationship strong.

When she saw Mike greeting his mother and his daughter, she smiled, still as deeply in love with him as she'd always been.

She had a beautiful evening, sitting in the empty chair at the dinner table as her little family talked and laughed around her, then joining them in the living room as they had coffee and cake, and more conversation. But later, as they all got ready for bed, she was torn. As much as she wanted to curl up with her husband and spend the night with him, she knew it was Rhiannon who needed her tonight. So she kissed her husband and her son as they drifted off to sleep in the narrow twin beds in the guest room, then shimmered downstairs to where her daughter lay on the couch, blankets pulled up to her chin against the cold, and tossing and turning in frustration.

"God, Mum, I wish you were here!" Rhiannon cried out, and Beth felt a new crack in her heart. Helplessness enfolded her as she floated towards her daughter, trying so hard to wrap her arms around her, to be felt, but making zero impression.

Rhiannon sat up in the darkness, and lowered her voice to a tortured whisper. "The psychic said you're with us in spirit, and that you're out of pain, and... not unhappy... and I really hope that's true," she said. "But I need you here in body, because she was also talking about Carlie, and how Rowan will harm her. And yes, I'm still angry at her for standing me up last week, but I would hate her to be hurt in any way. I'm not sure she'll believe me though – she'll probably think I'm making it up to pay her back. What do I do?"

Distraught, Beth stroked her daughter's forehead. She couldn't believe the parallels between their lives, and she thought she might explode in frustration. How could she let Rhiannon know that the psychic was talking about Violet, Carlie's mum, not Carlie? That she meant Beth should have told Violet, not Rhiannon should tell Carlie. She'd described their tragic, long-ago situation to a tee.

Then she froze, and pain and regret threatened to swallow her whole. "There's something painful you're trying to keep buried." That's what Miranda had said, before she became fixated on the Violet thing. In a devastating flash, Beth was dragged back to the night before she'd died. While sorting out herbs in her kitchen, she'd suddenly been overwhelmed with a premonition of danger.

"Rhiannon," she'd blurted out – just as there was a knock on the door. Fear rushed through her as she hurried to answer it, scared that her daughter was sick, or worse. So she was shocked to see Rhiannon's friend Debbie standing on the doorstep. Debbie whose house Rhiannon was supposed to be staying at that night. Debbie who didn't look at all upset or worried.

"Hi Mrs Stark. Is Rhi here?" she'd asked, so nonchalantly. "I just wanted to borrow her history notes, because I was off sick today."

"I hope you're feeling better now," Beth had replied, trying desperately to keep her voice level as her knees buckled beneath her. Grasping the door frame, she'd watched Debbie say yes, then raise an eyebrow in question. "Oh, I'm sorry. Rhiannon is out with her dad," she'd managed to stammer. "I'll remind her to take everything you need to school tomorrow, is that okay?"

Debbie had nodded politely and left, and Beth had somehow made her way back to the kitchen, where she clung to the bench to keep from falling. She tried to return to her premonition, to force it back, but her fear was blocking her. Impatiently she pulled a jar of herbs down from the top cupboard, lit the burner on the windowsill, and threw a handful of the pungent leaves into the dish. As the herbs burned, she inhaled the cloying smoke, drawing it as deeply into her lungs as she could, then closed her eyes and focused again on her daughter's face. The image was blurry at first, but then it sharpened, and she almost passed out in sheer terror.

Rhiannon was standing in the woods, shivering as the brisk wind left her naked flesh goosebumped, and the light of a candle cast long shadows across her body. Then Beth gasped in horror as she saw a man with her, skyclad as well, a predatory gleam in his eye.

Her limbs turned to water, but somehow she found the strength to grab a coat, slip into the boots near the back door and race outside. Before she was even conscious of her plan, she was running down the street, turning onto the path into the woods, and praying she would find her daughter before... Her mind recoiled from all the possibilities, and she pushed herself onwards, ignoring the stitch in her side, and the light-headedness that threatened to leave her unconscious on the forest floor. Her doctor had warned her not to exert herself, not to exercise too strenuously, but her child was in grave danger, she could feel it in her bones, and so she pressed on.

Just when she thought she would collapse with exhaustion, she saw the flicker of candlelight up ahead, and desperately increased her pace. It looked like she'd made it just in time. As she staggered into the clearing she heard a thrashing in the underbrush, and realised that whoever had been with Rhiannon had fled, leaving her with the remnants of their ritual, and alone to face whatever approached. *Charming.* In twenty years of witchcraft, she'd never cursed anyone, but if this man had hurt her daughter, he would feel her wrath in ways she couldn't even find words for right now.

The young girl had her back to Beth, and was hastily pulling a black velvet cloak around her trembling body.

"Rhiannon," she said, placing a hand on her shoulder.

Her daughter screamed as she spun around.

"Darling, it's just me."

"Mum?" she gasped, mouth open in shock. "What are you doing out here?"

"I could ask you the same thing," Beth replied, trying to hide her anger as she drew her daughter close and held her shaking body in her arms. "Are you okay? What's going on? Honey, you must be so cold," she added, as Rhiannon's cloak slid open and revealed that she was naked beneath it.

Naked. It turned out that the man – Debbie's older brother – had convinced Rhiannon he could help her work a spell to save her mum's life. And after grooming her for weeks, tonight was the night, when he'd insisted they had to come together within the sacred circle as the god and goddess did, in order to power the spell. Which was a fancy way of saying she had to have sex with him.

Beth didn't know how far it had gone, and part of her didn't want to. It would destroy her if her sweet, innocent daughter had been assaulted within the sacred circle of magic and ritual that had meant so much to her for so long. She had her suspicions, but Rhiannon was so freaked out at the time that she could barely speak, and Beth had decided to be patient, that she wouldn't press her to talk about what had happened until she was ready.

Her daughter needed the healing of sleep and distance before she would be able to process whatever had occurred. And Beth was ashamed to admit that she hadn't been ready to hear it either – she would need to process it too.

Now, thirteen months later, in this faraway cottage, her heart wrenched with pain. She'd planned to suggest, the following morning, that if Rhiannon wanted to see a counsellor she would go with her, or at least organise the appointment and take her there, if she needed to do it alone. While it would hurt her to be excluded, it was more important that her daughter feel safe.

But the next day she had died, and it seemed Rhiannon had buried all her pain and anger over the incident, overwhelmed by her grief at losing her mother. Which was understandable, of course.

Now though? It sounded like Rhiannon was finally becoming aware of it again, the trauma resurfacing, yet Beth couldn't help her. Couldn't reach her. Who would her daughter go to for help? There was no way she'd confide in her dad, even though he would be wonderfully understanding. And right now didn't seem the best time to bring it up with Carlie, given their arguments over Rowan.

This was the biggest failing of Beth's life, bigger even than her inability to help Violet. Having the premonition of her daughter being assaulted, but not getting there in time to save her. Vowing to help her deal with the aftermath, then dying before she could.

Was this her great unfinished business, the reason she'd returned to her family from beyond the grave, in ghostly form at least? Was she supposed to find a way to help her daughter heal from this awful incident? But if so, how? She was so insubstantial that she couldn't make Rhiannon feel her arms around her, let alone direct her to a counsellor. She was so translucent that a medium who claimed to see dead people didn't know she was there while she hovered right in front of her face.

The pain and frustration built up until her heart broke apart, and she allowed herself to succumb to the weightless, lifeless darkness where she could not exist for a while...

Chapter 8

Dreams and Wishes

Rhiannon

Knock. Knock. Knock.

Sighing, Rhiannon headed downstairs to let her friend in for their coven night. After the long weekend at her grandma's she'd been off school sick for the last two days, so she hadn't seen Carlie since last week, when they'd argued briefly over Rowan. Which made what she'd be telling her tonight even harder.

Nervously she opened the door, but Carlie was smiling, and only seemed concerned that her friend had been so unwell that she'd missed school. "Are you okay?" she asked, worry in her voice. "Are you sure you feel up to doing a ritual tonight?"

Rhiannon returned her smile. "I'm fine. I stopped throwing up at lunchtime today, so I'll be back at school tomorrow. And don't worry, I'm not contagious."

"I'm so glad. And I've got so much news, I've been dying to see you," Carlie said, as they headed upstairs and settled on the bedroom floor with their Book of Shadows and pens.

"Me too. You have to break up with Rowan, he's really bad news," Rhiannon burst out.

Just as Carlie said: "He really does love me! I've finally been able to accept it!"

Shock registered in green eyes and blue.

"Why?" Carlie gasped.

"What?" Rhiannon stammered.

The girls stared at each other. "You first," Carlie said icily.

Rhiannon hesitated for a moment, trying to decide how best to word it, then she poured out her heart, anxious and regretful, but determined. She shared the beautiful messages she'd received from her mum first, and there was pain in her eyes as she spoke, and the desperate longing for the messages from the psychic to be true.

"That's brilliant Rhiannon, but what does that have to do with Rowan?" Carlie asked sharply.

"Well, then she said that my best friend is in danger, and I have to make sure she breaks up with her boyfriend." There was challenge in her tone, and in the tilt of her jaw.

Carlie smiled, relief clear on her face. "Rhi, she doesn't know Rowan, or me. She's never met either of us, or come into contact with us, so she couldn't know anything about us. You don't even know Rowan that well, so she couldn't be picking stuff up from you about him. Besides, maybe she meant Debbie or Sue."

"I wish it was that simple, believe me. I don't want it to be you, but she was so specific. It was my newest friend, my sister of the heart, the one who had just suffered a terrible loss. And it was definitely Rowan who was dangerous – an older man, a shaman, a mysterious weaver of dreams and lies, who can keep his own darkness hidden. The psychic said he'll break your heart, and cause you deep pain. Hurt you in a way you won't be able to recover from."

Looking like she'd been slapped, Carlie took a deep breath before finding her voice. "If I could go on after losing Mum and Dad, and thinking for so long that I'd killed them, I can cope with any pain," she said coldly. "But she's wrong, in that part at least. He's not dangerous, he's the kindest, gentlest person I've ever known. I trust him with my heart, with my life, and with myself, body and soul."

Rhiannon shook her head, refusing to listen despite her friend's assurance. "I don't want it to be true either, but I'm more concerned about your safety, and you should be too."

Defiance flashed in Carlie's eyes. "I can't believe you'd just blindly accept this. You know the psychic at the Body Mind Spirit festival was totally wrong during my reading, and she was world-renowned, so why not this one too?"

"You should have heard her. She was so clear, so certain."

Carlie sighed. "I know you want to believe it all because of the messages from your mum, but this part of the reading not being true doesn't take away from that."

They kept arguing, both getting more and more defensive, and more and more upset. Then finally Rhiannon snapped. "I just don't trust Rowan. He's so much older than us – don't you think it's weird that he wants to be with a schoolgirl?"

"So this isn't even about the psychic," Carlie said flatly. "You don't *really* think I'm good enough for him, even though you insisted I was. I'm not spiritual or worldly enough for him, is that it?"

Rhiannon winced and shook her head. "No, of course not. You know I don't think that. He's lucky to be with you. But he's bad news. I know you don't want to hear this, but I can feel it in my bones about him. I just don't want him to hurt you," she insisted.

Carlie glared at her. "Don't you see Rhi? He's not the one hurting me, *you* are!"

Before it could go any further and they both said something they'd really regret, Mike interrupted them with cups of tea and biscuits. Reluctantly they agreed to a truce and began their magical working – starting with a cleansing and space clearing ritual to defuse the tension and negativity. But Rhiannon knew Carlie hadn't forgiven her for her cruel message, and she was starting to wonder why she had believed the woman so readily. Rowan was a great guy, kind and considerate and good, so what was it about him that made her willing to believe he would destroy her friend? Or was it something about *her* that made her willing, some belief she held about men in general, totally unrelated to Rowan?

Her thoughts darkened, but her mind shied away from the shadowy path it wanted to go down, and she forced herself to return her attention to their ritual. The past was the past. No need to revisit that. She had the future to focus on, and John to dream about. A secret smile crept across her face, and for the next few hours the girls lost themselves in ritual and magic. And when Carlie finally went home, Rhiannon fell happily into bed, desperately hoping to dream of John again.

The rest of the week yawned out ahead of her, slowed by her eagerness to see John in real life. She'd missed the previous Saturday's committee meeting because she was at her grandma's, then John missed the mid-week one for a dentist appointment, so Rhiannon couldn't wait for the weekend. There was a sense of urgency to her desire, because she needed to figure out whether she really did like John, or it was just the idea of him she'd fallen for, encouraged by the frequent romantic dreams he starred in. In her mind it felt like they were already dating, yet she knew her perception of him was based almost solely on her dreams and fevered imaginings, rather than the few times they'd actually been in the same room together and spoken to each other.

She hoped her night-time dreamscapes were a result of their few short, real-life interactions, that her subconscious was somehow seeing deeper within him during their meetings, and picking up on his unspoken reactions to her. But it was also possible that it was all in her head, fuelled by the first psychic's reading about the tall blond guy who would sweep her off her feet, and her wishful thinking.

Every night she dreamed of him, which only increased her infatuation. In one they were dancing together at the ball, and it felt so right to be wrapped in his arms. In another he was holding her hand as he led her into a cafe then sat drinking coffee with her and talking for hours. Later he was shepherding her up the steps of what she assumed was his house, to meet his family.

She woke from that one feeling a deep yearning for her own mother. Then she blushed. Her subconscious clearly wanted her to be with John, yet it was possible – even likely – that he hadn't spared her a single thought since the last time they'd seen each other. He might even have a girlfriend already. She would have to be careful when she finally saw him. She didn't want to seem too eager, too over-familiar, too stalkerish. There was even a chance she'd invented her own passion for him, and would be horribly disappointed when she got to know him better. But she doubted that.

When Saturday finally dawned, she was the first one down at the school, eager to be off. Glenda arrived next, and surprised her by giving her a hug. "How are you feeling today lovely, and how's your dad going?" she asked, her voice kind.

"He's okay I guess, busy at work, but he seems to be coping," Rhiannon replied, puzzled by the question. Then she stared at the office manager, and finally twigged. She looked different in her work clothes, with her hair in a bun, but now she thought about it, had she seen her at one of Rose's rituals?

Glenda laughed, but it was kind. "You're wondering if you've seen me out of school, right?"

Embarrassed, Rhiannon nodded.

"I dress a little less corporate when I'm working magic with Rose, but yes, you would have seen me at a ritual. I don't get there as often as I used to, because I've been looking after my adorable granddaughter, but I was part of the circle with Laura and your mum." Her voice quavered a little, and Rhiannon was touched by the emotion she displayed. "I'm so sorry you lost her. Beth was such a gorgeous, loving person. It's not fair that her life was cut short."

They heard voices coming along the path, and Glenda hugged her again, then quickly wiped her eyes. "You're so much like her Rhiannon, she would be so proud of you," she whispered, then turned to greet the other students so they could head off.

The closer they got to Maryborough High, the more excited – and anxious – Rhiannon became. What if she suddenly realised she didn't actually like John? What if he totally ignored her? What if she was tongue-tied again and made a fool of herself? And oh god, what if he had a girlfriend? Maybe she should try to make friends with Annalie and Lynn, the two girls from his school, and suss that out... Although what if it was one of them?

By the time they filed into the staff room, she'd worked herself up so badly that she felt nauseous. And she was so preoccupied with not throwing up that she almost missed John looking up and smiling when she entered the room. Unfortunately someone was already seated to each side of him, so even if she'd managed to summon up her courage to sit with him, she was too late.

"Hey Rhiannon," he said, and her cheeks coloured, mortifying her, while her voice deserted her. Finally Karen nudged her in the ribs, and she managed to squeak out a hello.

As she pulled up a chair, the Maryborough principal explained that they would be breaking into smaller groups to start work on the decorations, and would be separated from their own classmates, since the point of the ball was to foster inter-school relationships.

When he called out their names, Rhiannon was happily surprised that she was in John's group. And once she got over her nerves, she was delighted to find that conversation between them flowed smoothly. They kept it light – hobbies, favourite school subjects, bands they liked – but she was so relieved that she was keeping up her half of the dialogue, and that he seemed happy to chat to her, that it felt like the most important conversation she'd ever had.

Time flew, and before she knew it they were back in the car and heading home. She was staring out the window again, trying to remember everything he'd told her, store interesting facts away, when Karen broke into her thoughts.

"I think John likes you," she teased, and Rhiannon blushed.

"No he doesn't," she protested, while secretly hoping it was true.

"Maybe he'll ask you to the ball," Karen suggested. "Or do you already have a date?"

Rhiannon shook her head. "Nah, I'll just go with Carlie. How about you?"

Her classmate raised her eyebrows. "Well, I wouldn't be surprised if John asks you, since he smiles a *lot* when he's looking in your direction, and you were talking together for ages. But I'm hoping Luke will ask me, how cute is he!"

Tracy joined the conversation then, agreeing that Luke was cute, and Rhiannon left them to it, gazing at the green fields slipping by and tuning the girls out so she could daydream about John. *Oh, she hoped Karen was right!*

Chapter 9

Moon Magic

Rhiannon

No matter the frustrations in their friendship, magic still bound the girls together, so on Sunday afternoon Rhiannon headed over to Carlie's as planned. There was a moment of awkwardness as they greeted each other, but it melted away in the warmth of the kitchen as Rose brewed a pot of fragrant tea and shared the deeper meaning of the approaching winter solstice. The girls baked cakes and pies to test them out for the ritual, diving into the mystery of the sabbat, and realising again how much recipes were spells that could lift the mood and create change.

At school on Monday things seemed to be back to normal, and Rhiannon breathed a sigh of relief when Carlie didn't mention Rowan. Maybe her friend had come to her senses and decided to end things with him, although she didn't have the courage to ask. She didn't want them to fight any more. Besides, she was too busy raving about the school ball committee, and trying not to drift off into daydreams of John and his gorgeous grey eyes.

"Rhiannon!"

She jumped in surprise. *Oops.* Had Carlie asked her something?

"Earth to Rhiannon!"

Guiltily she looked at her friend, and raised an eyebrow in question. "Sorry! Um, what did you say?"

Carlie laughed, seemingly not offended by her vagueness. "I was wondering what we should do for tomorrow night's full moon. Since it coincides with our coven night this month."

"Oh yeah, it does. Shall we do our ritual up on the tor at the moment it becomes full?"

Her friend nodded enthusiastically. "That would be great. It's full just after 3am though, right, so we'll have to meet about twenty to?"

Rhiannon nodded, and happily agreed to the plan. But when her alarm screeched at her at 2.30am, she had second thoughts. Grumpy to be woken up in the middle of the night, she thumped her clock off and burrowed back into her cocoon of blankets. It would be freezing up on the hill, and all she wanted to do was snuggle up in the warmth of her bed and drift back to sleep. She couldn't stand her friend up though, even if she deserved it.

Forcing herself out from under the covers, she shook off that thought. It was petty and mean, and it would be cruel to let Carlie battle the frosty winds on her own. Besides, it would be magical up on the tor tonight, out in the elements and at one with the wildness of nature. As long as there wasn't a storm. They still made her nervous, even though she'd hadn't seemed to control the weather or cause lightning flashes or a thunderstorm for a while now.

Quickly she shrugged off her pyjamas and dragged her long green velvet dress over her head, then slipped two jumpers and her warmest coat over the top, finishing with her hand-knitted scarf. As she contemplated the dodgy rows of stitches, she smiled. She and Carlie had painstakingly knitted them as part of one of their new moon rituals, and she liked the homemade texture. She also loved the enchantment she'd felt while working on it, and she sensed it now as she wound it around her neck three times.

It had been a revelation when Rose imparted to them the magic that existed in ordinary things. How you could bring a sense of the sacred to every aspect of your life. It wasn't limited to the major festivals of the year – enchantment could be found in the smallest and most mundane acts. Growing plants, creating art, cooking meals, crafting objects to use in your everyday life. Every action could be a ritual. Every word could be a spell.

Tiptoeing downstairs as quietly as she could, she managed to avoid tripping over Buster, who was curled up in the warmth of the kitchen, before creeping out the back door and through the garden to the tor path. The golden moon illuminated her way forward, and she whispered a prayer of thanks for its beauty and the light it shed.

A shivering Carlie greeted her at the base of the hill. Her teeth were chattering so loudly that Rhiannon could hear them, and she grinned at her friend, who was even more rugged up than she was. They had far milder winters in Australia, and she sympathised with her struggle against the English cold. She wouldn't have blamed Carlie if she'd stood her up tonight, choosing her cosy bed over their wild magics, but she was glad she hadn't.

Tentatively the two girls climbed to the top of the tor. They didn't speak, but it was a companionable silence, a shared recognition of the sacredness of the ritual they would soon begin. While they usually laughed a lot and chattered non-stop when they were together, they treated their coven time with great reverence, and took it very seriously. So their walk to the summit was almost a meditation, as they opened their senses to the world around them.

Looking skyward, Rhiannon took in the white clouds glowing overhead as they raced across the sky, pushed by the cold wind, and smiled as she watched the tiny stars twinkling after their cover passed, before being hidden again when the next clouds came over.

Overshadowing all of that was the beauty of the full moon and the peace of the dark night. Rhiannon's heart lifted as she stepped out the boundary of the circle, moonstone-tipped wand held up to the sky to channel the lunar energy and carve out their sacred space between the worlds. It was a liminal place atop the tor, located as it was between land and sky, and in this moment being balanced between dusk and dawn. There was so much magic in these intersections of elements and timings.

While Rhiannon completed the circle, Carlie lit a white candle in a tall glass holder, then ignited a lavender smudging bundle from the flame and swept it around the two of them. Then Rhiannon placed her wand on the altar in the east, to symbolise air, and positioned her chalice in the west to represent water. Her friend arranged the small silver god and goddess statues her grandmother had given her in the centre of the altar, with her pentacle in the north to symbolise earth, and a small gold candle next to her athame in the south to represent fire.

Feeling calm and centred, Rhiannon picked up the small bottle of richly scented essential oils she'd blended earlier – jasmine, lemon, sandalwood and vanilla – and anointed her friend with a drop between her brows. Then, moonlight sparkling in her green eyes, Carlie took the bottle from her and repeated the process.

But as the oil touched her skin, Rhiannon felt blackened shadows descend around her, and a shiver of nameless dread snaked up her spine. For a split second she was standing in the darkness of the woods, and someone was about to –

"Rhiannon." It was only a whisper, the faintest sigh, but Carlie's voice reached out to her and held her safe, guiding her back from the nightmare she'd been slipping into, and returning her to their sacred circle. To the space between the worlds where they were protected by magic, by moonlight, and by the power of their friendship.

Shaking off the fear, Rhiannon smiled at Carlie, took a deep breath, then raised her arms to the brilliance of the golden lunar orb.

Moon goddess, we welcome you to our circle tonight,
And ask that you lend us your light
and your strength on this beautiful night.
Fill us with your energy and intuition, your wisdom and sight.
Please help us know what it is that we need to know,
and see what we must see.
Fill us with love and patience, and honour us with your beauty,
and all the potential and promise you hold within you.
And please help show us what and who we can be.

Then it was Carlie's turn, and Rhiannon gazed at her with awe as she welcomed the element of fire, and its strength and passion; the element of water, and its emotion, intuition and balance; the element of earth, and its powers of grounding and security; and the element of air, and its insight and focus. She marvelled at her words, and her conviction. It wasn't that long since their first magical working, when both of their voices had been shaky with nerves, and they'd stumbled over what to say and how to say it.

Now her friend looked like a goddess, calm and cool, the golden moonlight flooding her face and illuminating her with an eerie, magical glow. Rhiannon's thoughts drifted back to her night in the temple, on the eve of Samhain, and the golden light on the water of the pools there, but her attention jerked back to the present when Carlie took her hand. She blushed, embarrassed to have been caught with her mind so far away. Her friend smiled though, looking as spaced out as she felt, and they turned their faces to the sky, and to the great golden ball of light that bathed them in its magical glow.

"When the moon is at its peak, so our hearts' desires we seek," they called in unison, and Rhiannon felt a surge of energy envelop her, coming as much from the ground beneath her as from the moon in the sky above her. Overwhelmed for a moment, she inhaled deeply and focused hard to stay present, to stay in her body, before they gracefully sank to the ground.

Spellbound, she stared up at the moon. The inky black of the sky stretched out like velvet across the heavens, sprinkled with stars that twinkled and glittered diamond-bright. And in the centre was the deep golden glow of the lunar orb. Usually it shimmered above them in cool silver tones, but tonight, for these precious moments before the cloud cover would hide it again, it was gold. Luminescent. Inspiring. Enchanting. There was a warmth to the light that spilled down over them.

She stared at Carlie, at her face lit from within by her own magic, and from without by the moon. The golden shimmer was like a halo around her friend. Then she closed her eyes and went into her own heart. She had spells to cast, and magic to work.

When the moon is at its peak.

Rhiannon smiled. That time was now.

So my heart's desire I seek.

She stifled a giggle, not wanting to disturb her friend or break her concentration, as she admitted to herself that this month her desire was not cerebral or magical, it was all for John. Each time she saw him she liked him more and more. He seemed so sweet, so lovely. So different to everyone at her school. And he seemed to like her. Well, she hoped he did. Or was he just being polite?

Oh god! If only she could ask someone about all of this. It was times like these that she most missed her mum. Her father was doing his best, but she couldn't ask him about boys, she would die of embarrassment – and so would he. And she couldn't bring it up with Carlie, since relationships weren't really on their chat list right now. Although she was probably selling her friend short.

Focus. There was no point worrying about things she couldn't change right now. But she *could* send a wish out on the moon to John, and pray that he would feel her thinking of him, perhaps become aware of the moonlight sneaking in his bedroom window in the pre-dawn dark. Her cheeks flamed red at the image of him in his bed. It seemed a step too far to be imagining that just yet.

Struggling to swallow the laughter that her train of thought was causing, Rhiannon opened one eye and peeked at Carlie. And was instantly sobered. Her friend, who she'd thought wasn't taking their magic seriously, had her head bowed and her eyes closed, her posture revealing strength and confidence as she journeyed within.

She had to get a grip. At the full moon they meditated on their goals for the coming month, examining what was working and what was not, and releasing the things holding them back. What was that for her? Acknowledging that her mind was on a one-way track tonight, she allowed herself to think of John – he was her desire after all. So what stood in her way to being with him, to developing their friendship beyond the cordial colleagues they were at their school meetings? Her shyness when she tried to speak to him for one. Her lack of courage in approaching him, in always leaving it up to him to start the conversation. And her fear that he would reject her if she dared speak her heart.

Just as she decided to shake it all off and end her ruminations, Rhiannon felt a presence beside her, and a cool hand on her forehead. A jolt of energy vibrated through her, into her mind then down into her heart, and she sat up straight, her thoughts suddenly clearer, calmer. There was no rush. No need to be stressed. She would see him in a few days, and she could speak with him then, even sit next to him, if she hurried into the room rather than lagging back, too scared she would look obvious to be brave and take action.

And she should enjoy the journey, the mystery, the lack of clarity. Enjoy the butterflies in her tummy when he looked at her, the tingles up her arm when his hand brushed hers. Enjoy the innocence and the friendship and the sense of all things being possible.

"Yes, beloved. Enjoy every moment, every glance, every ounce of anticipation. The dreaming is all part of it, the wishing is its own joy and pleasure. Be patient. Stay connected to your truth. And take it slowly as you lower your guard and open your heart."

Fighting the impulse to open her eyes and see who was speaking to her, Rhiannon nodded, knowing as she did that the voice spoke truth, and that it was time to return to the present, and to her partner in magic. She felt such a strong connection to the earth, to the moon above, to the spirits of the land and its people, and to Carlie. Whatever pettiness lay between them over Rowan, she cared about her deeply, and she couldn't blame her for wanting to be with him, since here she was, longing for a guy she barely knew.

Gently opening her eyes, she saw that Carlie was miles away too, and she placed a hand on her arm, slowly, not wanting to alarm her if she was still coming back into her body.

"Are you okay?" she asked, worry in her voice as she saw tears trembling on her friend's lashes.

Carlie nodded and smiled back at her. "Just feeling it all," she whispered. "The beauty of this night, of the moon, of the connection we have between us." She gestured above her, around her. "I never felt this back home. Not because I couldn't feel it there – I'm sure I could have if I'd known about it. But Mum hid all this from me, and from herself it seems, and now it feels like there was always a part of me missing, a piece I didn't even know was lost. I don't know how Mum could have lived that way, could have given all of this up. What could have happened to her, to throw this away?"

A sharp pain pierced Rhiannon's heart at the thought of their lost mothers, but she knew how blessed she was, to have been able to share rituals and magic with hers. Not enough, nowhere near enough, but still so much more than her friend had.

Carlie smiled, brave again, and stood up to farewell the quarters, to thank the moon goddess for being part of their ritual, and to close their sacred circle. Once that was done, and the swirling energy had been released, they drank elderflower spring water and ate full moon cookies to ground themselves back into the real world.

They sat together on a blanket on top of the sacred hill, the candlelight dancing between them, flickering so prettily, and casting shadows that were great pools of mystery. For a moment Rhiannon wanted to dive in and submerge herself in the waters, but a blast of bitter, icy wind woke her up with a start, and she pulled her coat tighter and wound the scarf in another loop around her neck. As cold as it was though, they didn't want to walk back down to their beds, back down to the real world, just yet. While they remained up on the tor they felt a part of the magic of the earth, and of the universe. Out of step with the normal, mundane world they usually inhabited. And they didn't want that to end.

But eventually their yawning became more frequent and their shivering more intense, so they slowly gathered their ritual pieces and blew out their candles, letting their eyes grow accustomed to the dark. As they carefully placed each foot on the path back down, Rhiannon felt a shimmer of the magic they'd woven surround her, and when she hugged Carlie goodbye at the bottom of the hill, she felt such love for her, and gratitude for all that they shared.

Chapter 10

A Constellation of Tears

Beth

Hours later – or was it an eternity? – Beth felt the air stir around her, then realised she *was* the air. She was that insubstantial mist that she'd felt before, back when she was alive, when she had a body. Up on the tor, under the light of the moon, under invisible stars. Had she felt this blurring before, this wondering whether she was real or a dream? A construct of her own mind, or someone else's?

Urgently she tried to draw the molecules of air into herself, into being. Could she find a spark of... something... and somehow ignite that spark into fire, into flame, into light? Into the physical? Star light, star bright. Wasn't everyone made of star dust? Gazing around wildly, she saw that the stars were at her feet. Was she part of a constellation of stars made manifest? Or a constellation of tears wept from the eyes of her loved ones?

And was that where she needed to be in order to become? Would she coalesce into some kind of form if she was with them? With an extreme act of will, Beth started to draw in her surroundings. To inhale the strength of the stars overhead and beneath her, and the moon that was in her heart. Or was it her heart?

She felt ripples in the fabric of the universe, in the fabric of herself. Sensed the depth of the heavens, of the oceans, and of herself. She was out of her depth. She wanted to drown in her memories, float away on a sea of darkness and pain and regret. Yet she was here now, for goddess knows how long, and she had to find the strength to keep trying. Had to find a way to communicate with her daughter, and with her beloved husband.

Pain crackled through her as she wondered whether she was still his wife. She missed him so much, missed their long conversations, the messages they left each other in the steam of the bathroom mirror in the mornings, the notes slipped into lunch boxes or briefcases, to find throughout the day. Had anyone ever loved someone the way she had loved Mike? The way she *still* loved Mike? And had anyone ever been loved the way she had been loved by this sweet, gentle, strong and caring man? He'd never thought he was special, never thought their love was out of the ordinary, but she knew it was. It was the kind of love that was written in the stars, burned into the heavens, shot across the sky in the flame of a dying star. Not everyone had that. Not everyone had the imagination to love that fully, to fall so far and so wide and so deep.

She was drowning in darkness, loss and pain – until there was a rushing sensation, and a dizziness, and a sudden crash into a new awareness. In the blink of an eye, she was back in their kitchen, where Mike was sitting at the bench, a notebook in front of him, a pen in his hand and a frown on his face. Had she been drawn back to him by the force of her hope? Or was it the strength of his wishing?

From her perch in the beams of the ceiling, precariously balanced, feet swinging beneath her, she watched him. When a tear splashed onto the page in front of him, she swooped down and hovered just above the bench in front of him, agony shooting through whatever there was of her, vibrating in a way that should have been impossible in her ghostly state, yet was happening. And the torment was consuming her.

Abruptly he looked up, eyes wild and searching.

She froze, terrified he would see her, then doubled over as her molecules shook with laughter. That was what she wanted, wasn't it, for him to see her? What on earth was she doing here, back on earth, if not that?

"Beth?"

It was a whisper wrenched from the depths of hell, from the shattered ruins of his soul, and the raw pain broke her into a million tiny pieces and dispersed her out into the atmosphere, into the ether, into the blackness from whence she'd come.

She didn't know how long she'd been gone before she started to reform, reorganising her cells, drawing together and becoming solid. As solid as a ghost could be, anyway. Her husband's shoulders were shaking, his head fallen onto his folded arms, and she could see the defeat in every sharp angle of him. Floating towards him, she tried to hold him, to hug him, to be felt by him. A shiver rocked through him, but he didn't lift his head. Hopelessness seeped out of him like water.

Frustration made her vibrate again, but she forced herself to be calm, to maintain her form. Gingerly she laid herself over him, like her priestess cloak, trying to protect him, to shield him, to love him. And then she felt herself sinking into him, surrendering her sense of self as she merged with him.

Alarm threatened to split her apart again, to scatter her back into the air, but she wouldn't let it. And then she shut off her mental musings and focused solely on the physical. She became aware of the pumping of his heart, of the movement of his blood cells as they tumbled around. Dizziness swept over her again, and she felt herself disappearing, but she held on tight and willed herself to remain. Peace settled over her, and she felt the elasticity of his tendons and the strength of his muscles, the stretching of his skin over his bones.

Dazzled, she reached out her awareness, questing deeper, and wondering whether it was his heart or his mind that needed her attention. Her love. Her healing. Or maybe she should just dissolve into him, become part of him, and remain within him forever? That was the goal of romantic love wasn't it, to merge your selves, your souls, your very beings? Happiness consumed her, and she felt the rightness of her decision.

Until the front door suddenly slammed shut. Mike's head jerked up, and she exploded out of him, expelled from his body, smattered, and scattered, all over the kitchen. The shock startled her back into awareness of herself, and a deep sense of loss at being separated burned within her, just as she'd begun to feel a part of him.

But as he turned towards the doorway, he paused and looked around the room again, eyes searching, and she was breathlessly, brilliantly certain that he knew she was there. Before he could say anything to her though, Rhiannon walked in and captured his attention, so Beth drifted over to the bench and sat on Mike's stool, gazing down at the notebook he'd been contemplating.

My darling Beth,

Wherever you are, please know that I still love you more than anything, and I always will. That I miss you with a heart-searing, mind-destroying intensity that has left me a broken shell. A broken man, who still seeks you out in any crowd, on any street, so real do you feel to me even now.

My love for you still burns with the strength of a thousand suns, with the magnitude of every golden moonbeam that illuminated you as you slept beside me. You still are, and always will be, my world.

Don't worry though, I haven't descended into the depths of insanity, although there are those who may argue that point. I am functioning, if you can call it that. I get the kids up in the morning and off to school. I go to work, and go through the motions – just enough to keep my job, yet not enough to distract me from my pain, from the gaping hole in my heart, the wound that consumes my soul.

When you first left me...

The words blurred in front of her, and she drew in a great, gasping, shuddering breath. She hadn't left him! She hadn't wanted to go! Did he really blame her for leaving? Think she'd had any choice in the matter? Her head spun, and she felt herself rippling at the edges again, tearing apart at the seams. Should she just let go? Surrender this strange grip on existence and melt back into the nothingness from which she'd come? Being here was so hard. So painful.

She wanted to be near her family, wanted to make sure they were okay, but it was destroying her to see their pain. And if Mike really thought she'd left willingly, had wanted to go, there was nothing she could do to reassure him, and that was a thought she couldn't bear.

With a supreme act of will she drew herself together again and looked back at the notebook.

When you first left me I felt you around me, holding me at night, pushing me onwards through my day, steadying me when I was about to fall. And for a long time, you remained. I felt you at the breakfast table, untangling the chaos as we each tried to get out of the house. I felt you during the day, strengthening me in my lowest moments, comforting me when colleagues made thoughtless remarks. I felt you when I crawled into bed at night and pretended I was sleeping.

But a few months ago, you started to fade, to become quieter, to be with me less. I wondered if you were mad at me, or tired of propping me up – or whether, a year after your death, you were moving on somewhere else and were no longer able to, or allowed to, be with me. Maybe they – whoever and whatever they are – only allow one year of comfort, one year of connection, and then you are swept away?

Beth stared at the words swimming before her eyes, bewildered. Had she been around him all that time? In the endless stretch of nothingness before she'd become aware? In the blackness of the yawning abyss of her numbness, of the absence of herself? Or had he willed a presence into being to soothe his heart, to help him through the day? That was nice, she supposed, if he'd been able to imagine her with him, comforting him in his pain, the way she would have done if she could.

Or had it been someone else? A burning hot whoosh of jealousy swept through her. Had Violet been here, easing his pain, when she couldn't do it herself? The thought made her uneasy, but she wouldn't be surprised – Rose's daughter had been the kindest girl she'd ever known. The most considerate. The most giving of herself and her time. Could she have gotten a pass from... wherever they existed, in that place outside of time and reason... and abandoned her own beloved to help Mike through his grief? She didn't know how she felt about that. And yet, that couldn't be it. Carlie's grief had been new, her loss recent. Violet couldn't have been with Mike a year ago.

Reassured on that score, a new panic gripped her. Panic that she could be snatched away at any moment and returned to the nothingness. Worse than pain, worse than fear, worse than jealousy, worse than guilt, worse than regret – the absence of *anything*. She returned her gaze to the page before her...

And then at our Samhain dinner, I felt you again. At first I thought it was Rose who had brought you, calling you to us for the night, for that magical time when, so she told us, the veils thin and our lost loved ones are able to return. We set a place for you at our festive table, along with ones for Violet and her husband Oliver, and Brodie was wonderful – you would have been so proud of him, the way he filled your glasses with punch, and spoke to Carlie about you.

That's a whole other story of course, the one where Rose discovered a few months ago that Violet had been alive all this time – but had just died. And that she'd had a daughter, Carlie, who for some reason had no idea of Rose's existence – until, on the death of both her parents, she was sent across the ocean to live with a stranger. Yes, after all this time, Rose has a flesh-and-blood granddaughter! My heart breaks for her that she knows now that Violet is dead – but I am so happy for her that she has Carlie. Not a replacement, never that, but someone to love and cherish none-the-less.

But I digress. The important thing, the only thing, is that I still feel you now my darling, three weeks after Samhain, right here in this kitchen, hovering above me, touching my shoulder, diving directly into my heart...

Could you really be with me? After all this time? I hope so. I pray to any god or goddess I think will listen. And I know that I shouldn't, that I'm supposed to move on, but I can't. I love you too much for that.

I want you back, or I want to join you. I can't bear to be alive while you are not. And yet as much as I want to... cease to be here... I have to remain for our children, who still miss you every day, in their different ways. Not that I'm much good at that either. That's why it should have been me who died, not you, because you were always the strong one. The capable one. You would have coped so much better than me, recovered so much better than me, would have helped our kids so much better than me.

That is perhaps the cruellest blow, that it was you and not me. That poor Rhiannon and Brodie are stuck with me and not you. And I hate it, that I have to live on without you, into some interminably lonely future, alone and yearning for you for the rest of my life.

Why can't you be with me Beth? Wherever you are, why can't you come back here, in whatever form you are in? I need you, so desperately. Please my beloved, give me a sign. Something. Anything. Just let me know that I am not totally and utterly bereft and alone.

Relief crashed through Beth when she got to the end, because every word he'd written was breaking her apart, and she couldn't bear any more. It wasn't true, that she would have handled bereavement better than him. She didn't know why he thought that. She could feel his pain, she knew how dark and deep and wretched it was, but she would have been the same. She *was* the same.

Trying to pull herself together – the mist-like molecules of her strange transparent reality if not her physical self – she stared again at his words. Then jolted in shock when she saw a fat tear land on the opened page, right on the word *sign*. As the letters blurred around their edges, she froze, then shot back up to the ceiling in panic. What the hell was that? *She* had created a tear? *How?*

Mike stopped talking to Rhiannon and spun around and stared in her direction, as though he'd heard the sound of her tear splattering onto the paper.

"Beth?"

The pain in his voice was even more heartbreaking than his words, and she quickly fled upstairs, away from him and his intensity and his bare naked pain. For a while she drifted aimlessly in the corridor, letting her thoughts skim and dance but never settle, too freaked out, and too sad, to want to feel, or explore, or wonder what on earth she was, and what it meant. But finally she heard her husband's sad and broken footsteps on the stairs, and she followed him into their room. His room, she supposed it was now.

Seeing the look of agony and anguish on her husband's face as he stared at their wedding photo on the dresser cut her deeply. It had been such a beautiful day, and the sudden memories were making her dreamy, and languid, almost joyful – then furious at the injustice of her being ripped right out of the perfect life they'd shared. It wasn't perfect by anyone else's definition perhaps, but it had worked for them, and their kids.

Absent-mindedly she brushed her hand across her cheek, trying to wipe away invisible tears – and jerked in surprise. Her wrist was enclosed in white lace.

What?

Chapter 11

Rhiannon

"It's finally here! It's tonight!"

Rhiannon squealed with excitement as soon as Carlie opened the door. She'd skipped school that day to be at the venue with the rest of the committee to set up for the Yule Ball – decorating, getting the food sorted, overseeing the band's soundcheck – and chatting to John as often as she could manage to steal a moment. Now she was back at Carlie's so they could get ready together, psyche themselves up for the night ahead, and catch up on their news.

They'd barely seen each other over the past three weeks. Rhiannon had been so preoccupied with the planning meetings, and her growing feelings for John, that she'd neglected her friend. It hadn't helped that Carlie missed school the day after their full moon ritual to be with Rowan. Apparently it was because his mum had been rushed to hospital, but they were supposed to do their history presentation that day, so Rhiannon had been mad at her. And her anger made her feel less guilty about spending so much time with John. Well, with all the committee members. She still hadn't worked up the courage to let him know how she felt, although her blushes and giggles and foolish comments in his presence might have given him a clue.

But she was looking forward to hanging out with her friend tonight. She'd actually missed her. And they were already having more fun than she'd expected, with Carlie swept up in her enthusiasm. They played music and danced around the room, laughed and joked as they did each other's hair and make-up, then finally slipped into the outfits they'd chosen from Violet's dusty wardrobe.

The vivid red of Rhiannon's dress suited her perfectly, and the way the soft velvet flared out around her hips and swished around her ankles when she moved made her feel elegant and grown up, a sensation accentuated by her blood red lips and dark, smoky eyes. And to top it off, the embroidered green holly leaves at the hem and neckline transformed her into the Holly Maiden who symbolised Yule, adding a magical element that she loved.

Carlie was dressed as the Snow Queen, in a long white floaty gown that contrasted beautifully with her glossy curls and deep purple lips. Now they were almost ready though, she was starting to look nervous. "You won't leave me on my own for too long will you Rhi?" she implored her. "I know you have to do a bit of committee stuff, but we'll be able to spend most of the night together, won't we?"

"Of course," Rhiannon said, reassuring herself as much as Carlie. "And I can't wait. It will be so nice to hang out together and have fun. Relaxing, dancing, chilling out – no homework, no planning meetings, no coven research, no boys. Just us, having a good time."

Guiltily she thought of John, and her desire to be with him, but that was just wishful thinking. Nothing had happened, despite her hints, so she was looking forward to spending time with Carlie and restoring their closeness. Snow was falling as they pulled on their coats, picked up their masquerade masks and ran down to the bus stop, but it couldn't dampen their spirits. They laughed with their fellow students, and Rhiannon hoped the magic of the Yule Ball would reinvigorate their friendship. They were coven sisters after all...

Of course the moment they entered the wonderland of the ball, Rhiannon's entire focus was on seeking out John, but she reluctantly forced her attention back to Carlie, accepting her compliments on the event with a smile. The gym did look amazing, even better than she'd imagined. They'd transformed it from a bare, draughty room, devoid of warmth or character, into a magical faerytale realm, with rich red and gold drapes covering the brick walls, a huge golden chandelier casting light and shadows from the high ceiling, and tiny twinkling faery lights strung everywhere.

A beautifully decorated pine tree stood in one corner, weighed down with tinsel and red and gold streamers, and giving off a crisp, invigorating scent. Silver stars hung from the boughs, and more faery lights were looped around it. Along one wall, tables groaned under the weight of colourful Yule-inspired party foods, alongside bowls of spicy fruit punch filled with cinnamon sticks and orange slices. Just one of the many recipes of Rose's that they had used.

Rhiannon turned back to her friend, eyes shining with joy. "Yeah, it turned out pretty well didn't it? And now I just have to check in with the committee," she said, then blushed.

Carlie stared at her. "Hey, what's going on?"

"Well, John is on the committee too, and I really like him," she admitted, suddenly feeling shy and unsure of herself.

"Wait, what?" Carlie gasped. "Who's John? Why haven't you told me about him? Is he nice? Oooh, which one is he?"

"He's the tall fair-haired one over there, dressed as the Oak King. He's from Smithfield High, and he's really sweet. We talked a bit at the meetings, and he's so smart and funny and kind, but he doesn't like me like that," she explained, eyes downcast. "I don't think he noticed I was a girl, to be honest."

"Oh Rhi, how could he not notice you, you're adorable!" Carlie said. "And you look so beautiful, so radiant. Plus you match – did he know you were coming as the Holly Maiden?"

"I'm not sure, but yeah, I guess we do." A shiver of excitement ran through her, at the possibility that he had dressed as the pagan Oak King to mirror her outfit. "But what about you?"

"I'm fine, honestly," Carlie insisted. "Now go and say hello to him before someone else does."

She didn't need to be told twice, and quickly made her way across the room.

"Hi Rhiannon, you look beautiful," John said warmly, and she melted at the compliment, and the way his eyes had lit up at her approach.

"Thank you," she replied, mouth dry and tummy dancing with butterflies. "You look fantastic too. The Oak King, right?"

A broad smile crossed his face. "I'm so glad you figured it out. I remembered the story you told in one of the meetings, about the Holly Maiden and the Oak King, so I looked him up. See, I was listening to all your talk of Yule," he grinned.

Her heart filled with hope. Maybe he did like her! Desperately she tried to think of something to say, to keep the conversation going, but she was tongue-tied again, and the more she panicked, the less capable she was of coherent thought. *Oh goddess, not now! Please make me eloquent and sparkling and fun.* But a silence fell between them, and she realised he was nervous too. Taking a deep breath, she willed her mind to work, or at least her mouth.

"Um, do you want some punch?" she managed to ask.

Just as John spoke too. "Um, would you like to dance?"

They both laughed, and the tension between them lifted.

"I'd like that," she said, and he led her onto the dance floor.

Rhiannon was shaking with nerves, and terrified that she'd step on his feet, but after the first song she calmed down a little. At first he seemed anxious as well, but they were soon moving together in a surprisingly harmonious way.

Time fell away, and for the next hour they danced, still shy in the slower numbers, but becoming more comfortable together with each song. Eventually she started feeling guilty about Carlie though, so she made her excuses to John, determined to be a good friend. But as she headed over to where she'd left her, she saw that she was talking to a really hot guy dressed as the Stag King, with antlers on his head and an intricate mask covering his face, and pale leather pants and no shirt. She almost went straight back to John, then thought she should at least say hello, in case Carlie was praying she'd return to rescue her. But before she could reach them, the guy took Carlie's hand and led her onto the dance floor, and they were swallowed up in the sea of swirling dresses and elaborate costumes.

Relieved, Rhiannon returned to John and lost herself in the thrill of the music and his strong arms around her. In his warm breath on her ear when they talked, and his firm hand on her back as he guided her to the table for a glass of punch. She couldn't believe how long they'd been hanging out together, and how attentive he was. She'd dreamed of this night from their very first meeting, but it was exceeding all her expectations.

Suddenly the music stopped, and two of the principals stepped up to the microphone. They wished everyone a merry Yule, and congratulated everyone for getting on so well with students from different schools. Then they thanked the organising committee for their hard work, calling out their names, and Rhiannon blushed with pleasure. She looked around for Carlie, who caught her eye and waved at her from across the room, then gazed pointedly at John and gave her a thumbs up. Relief washed over her, knowing her friend was okay with being abandoned.

"Now, it's time to announce the Winter Queen and the Sun King," said one of the principals. "And this year it makes us very happy that they are from different schools, furthering the ties we've been hoping to forge in the wider community. These two have the most fitting costumes, being the Snow Queen and the Stag King. So, Carlie Parker from Summer Hill, and Paul Vickers from Smithfield, please come up."

Rhiannon was worried the attention would be too much for Carlie, who stood frozen in shock as the spotlight was angled on her. But Paul took control of the situation. He grabbed her hand, kissing it as he bowed low over it, then led her to the stage. The Maryborough principal shook Carlie's hand and placed a diamante tiara on her head, while their principal handed Paul a gold-plated crown, which he wrapped around his upper arm and squeezed closed, so it sat like an ancient Celtic armband on his impressively muscled bicep.

Then he swept Carlie back onto the dance floor and began the next dance. They were soon joined by all the other couples, including Rhiannon and John, and the whole room seemed to shake.

After another break for some punch, Rhiannon gazed around the room, wanting to introduce John to Carlie, and to meet the guy she seemed to be having fun with. Maybe she'd stop seeing Rowan if she met someone else. Someone younger, less worldly, more appropriate. She cringed inwardly at her assessment, since she'd admired Rowan for so long – then she became frantic when she couldn't see her friend.

Excusing herself to John, she wandered through the smaller room off to the side, then, not seeing her there either, made her way outside. Shivering, she wiped a snowflake from her cheek, and was about to step back into the warmth of the gym when she saw Carlie leaning against an oak tree in Paul's arms. She smiled. Definitely promising!

"Carlie," she called out as she walked towards them, and had to repeat herself, so lost was her friend in the embrace of the guy she'd just met. "I couldn't find you. Are you okay?"

Carlie broke away from the guy and nodded happily.

"And you must be Paul," Rhiannon said, turning to her companion. But it wasn't a new guy, it was Rowan. She stiffened as anger coursed through her. A small part of her was relieved that Carlie hadn't been cheating on the guy she'd professed to love, but mostly she was furious that he'd snuck in to a high school dance. He smiled at her, complimented her outfit and congratulated her on the success of the night, but she wasn't listening.

"I can't believe you'd come here. How dare you? And what about Paul? Does he even exist? Why wasn't the school principal suspicious when you were crowned prom king?" she demanded. "You haven't been to school for years."

"Paul's a family friend, and when he told me he was sick and wasn't coming tonight, he offered me his ticket. I figured it would be simpler to just say I was him – with the mask nobody noticed. I thought it would be easier on everyone."

"Easier on *you* perhaps," Rhiannon spat. "What's Paul going to say at school when he finds out that he was not only crowned Sun King, but that everyone saw him making out with Carlie?"

"That's a small complication, but I'm sure he'll live it down – he might even be happy about it. I notice you weren't upset when you thought Carlie was cheating on me with Paul though," Rowan said, and sighed. "Anyway, it's more than two weeks until school goes back, so most people will have forgotten." His arms tightened around Carlie's waist. "But I'm not here to cause trouble. I just came to see my beloved, and tell her how much I miss her."

Rhiannon rolled her eyes. "Missed having sex with her you mean. I saw you two out here," she shouted.

Carlie was shocked out of her silence. "It's not like that. We were just talking."

Rhiannon laughed, a cruel laugh.

"And yes, we kissed once. But Rowan just came here to tell me how much he loves me, before he leaves to go to the retreat."

"Love? He wouldn't know the meaning of the word."

"That's not true!" Carlie retorted, tears in her eyes.

"Rhiannon, please," Rowan said softly, calmly. "Carlie's right, I came here because I love her, and that's the simple truth. But I don't want to cause any problems, especially tonight, because this is your night. So I'll go now, but please believe me that I adore your friend. And know that you can't scare me off just because some little old lady who's never met either of us warned you I was bad news."

Shock swept through Rhiannon, that he knew, but Rowan ignored her. He turned to Carlie, cupped her face in his hands and gave her a long, sweet kiss. "I love you baby, hand on my heart, and I will never hurt you. I'll see you soon." And he faded away into the night.

Rhiannon turned to her friend to berate her, but paused when she saw the pain on her face.

"How could you do that?" Carlie whispered, her voice more sad than angry.

"I'm just looking out for you."

"No, you're not. If you cared about me at all you'd know how happy he makes me, and how much he cares about me."

"He doesn't care Carlie. Remember the reading I had – the woman said he was bad news, and that he would hurt you, physically and emotionally. And remember Dad's stories about your mum's shaman guy too – I want to protect you from all of that."

"No you don't, you're just jealous that someone loves me. You're too shy to ask John out, so you want me to be miserable too."

Rhiannon gasped, and Carlie paused in her outburst, before holding up her hands in surrender.

"I'm sorry Rhi, I don't want to hurt you, but you have to butt out of this one. I've seen Rowan a lot lately, and he really does care about me. He's never pressured me, and he won't. He came tonight to give me a present, look."

She held out her hand, and Rhiannon was shocked when she saw the beautiful ring sparkling on her finger. "It's a friendship ring, a token of his love – his words, not mine. It's a herkimer diamond, and he has one too. It means we are bound together, and it's a promise that we'll always return to each other, even if something – or *someone* – tries to part us."

Rhiannon didn't want to believe her friend, yet she felt less certain of her stance now, and more impressed. "I'm sorry, I really am. But it would kill me to see you hurt, because you've been through so much."

Carlie tried to smile, but it was a struggle. "I know, and I'm grateful for that, but you have to realise that you are actually the one who is hurting me. You have to trust me."

"I do trust you, I swear, I just don't trust him."

"Rhi, we've been through this."

Before they could say more, a teacher called out to them to come inside before they froze to death. John was standing at the door too, and Rhiannon hesitated, wanting to be with him, but wondering if she should continue her conversation with her friend. But Carlie shook her head fiercely at her, motioned for her to go with John, then turned her back on them and walked into the crowd.

"Is everything okay?" John asked softly, and she smiled at the look of concern on his face.

"It's all fine," she said, and took his hand. "Dance?"

They stepped into the sea of students, and she surrendered herself to the music, and to the warmth of his body against hers when they accidentally touched. She pushed Carlie from her mind – she would go and see her tomorrow, and they could sort it out then. For now she was here with John, and she wanted to be in the moment, to not miss even a second of this closeness by worrying over her friend.

Finally the last song was announced, and Rhiannon's heart beat faster. It was a slow, sweet love song, and John drew her into his arms and held her tight, all his earlier nervousness forgotten. Her butterflies returned. Then he leaned down and kissed her, and she stopped thinking, stopped wondering, almost stopped breathing.

It was the perfect kiss. Gentle and respectful, but sure too. There was none of the hesitation or shyness they'd felt around each other over the past six weeks, or even earlier tonight. His lips were soft yet the kiss was firm, and a shudder rocked through her as he drew her closer, and held her tighter. When her body slammed against his, fire ignited in her blood and desire swamped her.

In answer, his lips became more demanding, and she let out a low moan that made his fingers bite into her shoulders while he tried to pull her even closer. Her knees buckled, but he had her gripped in strong arms, and she loved the feel of them around her. She wanted the world to stop, and the kiss to go on forever.

It took one of his friends elbowing him in the ribs and making comedy kissing sounds for them to realise the music had stopped, and people were filing out to the buses. Rhiannon blinked, trying to get her bearings, and John looked just as disorientated. She felt shy again, and thought about fleeing, but John turned his back on his mate and took her hand.

"Don't go," he whispered, his breath ragged, and she thought her heart might burst with joy.

Reluctantly she turned to look for Carlie, and caught a glimpse of her dress as she walked out the door. Shrugging, she stuffed the twinge of guilt down. Her friend knew she had to stay back to clean up, so it wasn't like she was ditching her, right?

Rhiannon had been totally dreading the clean up, but now she was excited because it meant she could spend more time with John. And when a few of the other committee members offered lame excuses and left them to it, she laughed. More time for them to talk, and to laugh, and to snatch stolen kisses. They did all their chores together, stacking the chairs, dismantling the tables, and sharing the washing up while the others busied themselves elsewhere.

When a slow song came on the radio, John took her hand and spun her around the room, then held her close and kissed her again. Fireworks exploded behind her eyelids, and she almost broke the kiss because she was smiling so widely. When someone opened the kitchen door they sprang apart, but it was Glenda, who beamed at Rhiannon, then told her they had to leave soon to drive home.

Reluctantly, Rhiannon started to say goodbye to John, but he wasn't ready for the night to end either. "She'll be out in a minute, we just have to stack the last of these clean dishes back in their places," he said to Glenda. "Is that okay?"

Glenda winked at Rhiannon then left them to it, and John lifted her chin so he could gaze into her eyes. "Thank you for a beautiful night. I've been dreaming about it, about us, but I didn't think you liked me," he confessed. "I thought you were just being polite when we talked at the meetings."

"Oh my god, how could you not know? I thought I was so obvious," she said, then grinned. "I'd been hoping you would invite me to the ball, or at least dance with me, but tonight was beyond my wildest imaginings. I had such an amazing time."

He leaned in and kissed her forehead. "I'd been wanting to ask you out for a while, but I always lost my nerve. And I've been wanting to kiss you since the moment you walked into the hall tonight."

Giggling, she stood on tiptoe and kissed his cheek. "I've wanted to kiss you all night too," she admitted, and his face lit up with relief.

"I guess I should go though, I can't miss my lift." She sighed, but made no move to leave, and he took her hand again.

"I was wondering," he began, then paused, blushing. "Um, well, there's a Christmas concert here tomorrow afternoon, well, in town, and I was wondering if you'd like to come with me?" he finally blurted out, nerves making his voice unsteady. "Or we could do something else?"

Joy bubbled through Rhiannon. "I'd like that," she whispered. "What time should I meet you?"

"Is one o'clock okay? I'll be at the bus stop, waiting for you."

Delighted, she nodded, kissed him again, hard, then raced off to meet Glenda and her fellow students for the drive back to Summer Hill. She ignored Tracy and Karen as they chattered over her about their night, sitting silently between them, reliving each one of John's kisses. She couldn't wipe the smile off her face.

Chapter 12

Love and Anger

Rhiannon

Stretching luxuriously, like a cat, Rhiannon woke with a smile on her face and a heart bursting with excitement. Last night had been perfect. Everything, from the way John had looked at her when she walked into the hall, held her as they danced, and spent most of the night by her side, had surpassed her wildest dreams. And the way he'd looked for her when she went outside to find Carlie, then pulled her into his arms during the final song and gently kissed her, driving all thoughts of her friend from her mind. So perfect.

She hugged the memories close. It sounded like a stupid cliche, but when they'd slow danced together in the darkened kitchen, she really had felt like a faerytale princess, like a winter goddess, in her swirling red dress. In the warmth of his arms she'd felt safe, secure, protected. It wasn't boring safe though – she was so excited when he leaned down and pressed his lips to hers, and desperate for him to keep kissing her. Sweet kisses. Soft kisses. Respectful kisses. Passion-laced kisses. Her lips were still tingling from all his kisses.

It had been a wrench to be parted in the early hours of the morning, but it wasn't for long – he'd invited her on a date this afternoon, and she'd eagerly accepted. It meant standing Carlie up for their Yule ritual, but she wasn't impressed with her friend right now, so maybe it was a good thing. Maybe she needed to spend some time with someone else, and her impatience with Carlie would subside. Even now she couldn't muster the anger she'd felt last night. All she could think of was John, and the magic of what she was feeling. Surely love was the most fitting way to celebrate Yule.

She gasped. *Love?* Burying her head under her pillow so she wouldn't wake Brodie, she let the fit of giggles bubbling up in her throat out, smothered by cotton and feathers, and allowed her mind to wander again. When she finally slept, she dreamed of a tall blond boy with his hand in hers, bringing her a mug of hot chocolate, guiding her around a skating rink, swirling her around the ice under the sparkling night sky, then pulling her close and kissing her for hours. And soon she'd be with him again!

Then her mood darkened. She would be letting Rose down if she didn't go to the Yule celebration tonight, or help prepare this afternoon, and she regretted that. There was also a twinge of guilt that she'd be deserting Carlie for one of the most important rituals of the magical year, because their coven was important to her, and she'd really been looking forward to this sabbat. And after she'd been so mad at Carlie for missing a single coven meeting last month, surely it was even worse to ditch her for a major ritual, and for a boy she barely knew no less.

Trying to flip from guilt back to righteous indignation, she focused on Rowan. She'd been so furious that he showed up last night. So angry when she saw him kissing her friend so passionately under the oak tree, and looking so damn hot. A shiver of desire ran through her now as she recalled how sexy he'd looked, shirtless, muscles rippling, one hand in Carlie's hair, one around her waist, pulling her closer, crushing her up against his hard naked chest... Had it been the incredible passion burning between Carlie and Rowan that had made her so desperate to kiss John?

No! She hadn't been jealous of what they had, she'd been annoyed that he turned up to a school event, and mad that her friend hadn't broken up with him after she'd told her about the psychic reading. So she was entitled to spend the solstice with her own boyfriend, right?

Rhiannon grinned. Was he her boyfriend? It was so soon – yet it wasn't like she'd only met him last night. She'd had a thing for him since the first committee meeting, and they'd slowly been getting to know each other during the six weeks in between.

Oh god, he'd kissed her! As angry as she was with her friend, she couldn't wait to tell her the good news. Her love spell had finally come to fruition, and she was so excited.

And despite everything, she knew Carlie would be too.

Nerves shot through her as she stood at the door to Rose's cottage. What was she going to tell Carlie about John? Would she be mad at her, for being so nasty to Rowan? He had seemed genuine when he said he was just desperate to see Carlie before he left for his retreat. And while she'd doubted him last night, she knew he did love her friend. The gorgeous ring he'd given her was proof enough – not that she needed that to know it was true. Deep down she was happy for Carlie, and she hoped her friend would be happy for her, despite the standing-her-up-tonight thing.

Footsteps sounded in the hallway, then Rose opened the door. Rhiannon blanched.

"Sweet girl, hello! Come in. You're early for the Yule preparations."

"Oh, no, I just came to see Carlie, to chat about last night, and see how she is," she faltered.

"Wasn't she well last night either?"

Puzzled, Rhiannon racked her brain. Had Carlie been sick last night? Or was it a cold from kissing out in the snow? "She's sick?"

"Nothing terrible, just not feeling great, so she said she might do her Yule ritual with you tonight, rather than come to the big one," the priestess said. "But how are you? Did you have a good night? Carlie said you did an amazing job, and it all looked really beautiful."

A smile lit up Rhiannon's face, and Rose's eyes twinkled knowingly. Oh god, could she read her mind? Know that she'd been kissing a boy, in public? Sometimes she hated how easy she was to read.

"It was awesome. So much fun, and so magical. But I guess I should go up and see how Carlie is..." And pasting a smile across her face, she followed the priestess up the stairs.

Rose bustled into Carlie's tiny bedroom, kissed her goodbye, wished them both a blessed Yule, then hurried off to the healing centre to prepare for the solstice ritual. Rhiannon stood in the doorway, nervous again. Her friend didn't look thrilled to see her, and for a moment she was worried that she wouldn't let her in. But after a long, awkward pause, Carlie relented.

"Come in silly," she said with forced cheer. "I hope you didn't have to stay too late last night cleaning up." She paused as Rhiannon blushed. "Or was it a good thing that you had to stay back, because you got to talk more to John?"

Rhiannon's cheeks went a deeper shade of red.

"And he asked you out?"

Rhiannon shrieked with excitement, ecstatic that she could finally share her news. "Yes! He invited me to a Christmas concert they're having in his village this afternoon."

"I'm so happy for you," Carlie said, and she sounded genuine. "So what's he like?"

Relaxing, Rhiannon moved into the room, perching on her friend's bed and grabbing her hands in excitement. "He's so lovely, and apparently he'd been wanting to ask me out too, but he wasn't sure whether I liked him, or was just being polite when we talked."

"Yeah, being polite can be a bitch," Carlie joked, and some of the ice between them melted.

Rhiannon raved about John, and her night, and how much they'd talked together, and danced. "And during the very last song he kissed me!" she gasped, eyes shining with joy.

"What was it like?" Carlie asked, voice flat now.

"Well, we were both a bit shy – I'd wanted to kiss him all night, and he told me later that he'd wanted to kiss me all night too. But we finally did, and it was lovely. So gentle, so sweet." She smiled, and her eyes had a faraway look as she relived the beautiful moment, oblivious to Carlie's discomfort.

"So you're going to see him today?"

"Yes! I mean, if that's okay with you?" For a moment Rhiannon was worried her friend would guilt her into staying, and she realised how desperately she wanted to be with John. "I thought you'd be doing the ritual at the healing centre," she added hopefully.

Carlie didn't look thrilled about it, but she nodded. "Of course it's okay. And although you've kept him a secret from me, I've thought for a while that you must like someone. And this is a great time to go and see him – to discover whether you still like him in the cold light of day," she teased.

Rhiannon smiled, and raved about John, and the ball, until her mood sobered and she took a deep breath, uncomfortable again. "Look Carlie, I'm really sorry about what I said last night."

"It's okay," she muttered.

"It's just that I worry about you," she blurted out. "I know you think you love him, but you're too young to commit to anyone. He's so much older than you, and... my god, he's so... well, I mean –"

"He's so what?" Carlie demanded, glaring at her.

"Well, he's a guy, a hot-blooded, grown-up guy, as everyone noticed last night with that outfit he was wearing, or not wearing. So he's going to want to have sex with you. If you haven't already –" Rhiannon broke off.

Carlie looked angry, yet she sounded dangerously calm. "Not that it's any of your business, but no, we haven't. He hasn't pressured me at all, he's happy to wait until I'm ready, no matter how long that takes. He actually likes talking to me, as surprising as that might sound to you," she said, sarcasm making her voice bitter.

"I don't mean that, I promise," Rhiannon said sadly.

Carlie shrugged, but she was defensive now. "He's twenty-three. That's only six years older than me. Grandpa was ten years older than Rose, and they were very happily married."

"But it's a lot right now," Rhiannon argued, and she felt herself getting angry too, even though she knew there was something not entirely rational about that. "You're in school, and he's travelling the country teaching, meeting hundreds of women who no doubt throw themselves at him. I'd hate for him to hurt you, especially with what your mum went through, with the older shaman guy who treated her so badly."

Fury flashed across Carlie's face. "How dare you talk about my mother? You didn't know her, and you don't know what happened between them."

Tears trembled on her lashes, but her voice was fierce. "He was the first man she really loved, and she never regretted any of it."

Pain crossed Rhiannon's face, and shock, at her friend's response. Carlie's mum Violet had been in love with her father Mike long before she'd met the shaman – they'd been childhood sweethearts with plans to marry.

"I'm sorry, I shouldn't have said that, of course she loved your dad," Carlie said, voice contrite. "It's just that Andre was her first grown-up relationship, and she loved him deeply."

"How do you know all this?" Rhiannon broke in suspiciously. "You can't twist it around now to try to justify being with Rowan. Dad said the shaman treated her really badly, and was jealous and possessive."

"Sandy found Mum's diary in a safety deposit box, and sent it to me a couple of weeks ago."

Rhiannon couldn't mask her surprise. "You never told me that. Did it answer any questions, like why she ran away?"

Her friend shrugged. "I haven't finished it yet. I'm saving it, savouring it, trying to make it last so I can feel close to her for longer."

That made sense. Rhiannon totally understood why Carlie would want to string the diary out – she was the same with her mum's Book of Shadows. Each page was a new discovery about the mother she'd lost, the mother who was still surprising her, a year after her death, with new depths and shadows and strengths. Slowly the anger drained from both of them, and they sighed at the same time, then looked up at each other and smiled.

"We shouldn't be fighting," Rhiannon said softly. "It's the festive season, the time for family and friends, and forgiveness. I just care about you, that's all. And I'm here if you need me."

Carlie nodded, then rubbed her hand across her face to wipe away her tears. The ring Rowan had given her the night before caught the pale light creeping in the window and sparkled a rainbow onto the wall, and all the anger Rhiannon had felt earlier rushed back.

"I just don't trust him!" she said. "And I'm only saying this because you're my best friend, and because I care about you – otherwise it would be much easier if I didn't say anything. But that reading I had was so clear, and according to her visions, he's going to leave you heartbroken, and physically beaten as well."

Fresh tears appeared in Carlie's eyes. "Just go. Go and see John, and have a great time with him."

"Please think about it," Rhiannon insisted. "Rowan is a bad influence on you, and you don't need that. You need to focus on school, not skip classes to be at his beck and call. And you said you wanted to help Rose in the shop, but instead you're lying to her, sneaking around, bringing him into her house to do god knows what behind her back."

Carlie stared at her, speechless with shock, but Rhiannon was on a roll now, and she couldn't make herself stop, even if she'd wanted to. "You don't turn up for our coven meetings, you take me for granted, and you expect me to back up your lies or provide an alibi for you. I don't think I can be around you, and watch you ruin your life. Watch you betray me, betray Rose, betray yourself – become someone you don't want to be. Please, you *have* to break up with him. Otherwise I just... I don't think I can be your friend," she cried. And she stood up and fled down the stairs.

Even as she stumbled her way to the door, Rhiannon knew she'd gone too far, knew she hadn't meant all that, but something was triggering her, making her feel angry even when it seemed illogical. Rowan really loved Carlie, and it wasn't fair to expect her to break up with him just because her best friend demanded it.

She was shocked that she'd uttered such a stark ultimatum, and already wanted to take it back. Her friend had looked devastated by her harsh words, and she knew she should run back upstairs and hug her, and apologise, and promise that she hadn't meant it.

But she didn't.

Chapter 13

Beth

Peering down at her ghostly self, Beth gasped. She was wearing her wedding dress. The first time she'd become aware of herself as a ghost, she hadn't paid any attention to her clothes, them being so irrelevant to her existence, or lack thereof. But when she'd appeared in the school staff room she'd been in an outfit that she'd often worn as a teacher, and now she was clad in the long white flowing dress she'd married Mike in.

She laughed. It had *partly* conformed to the wedding tradition, although it was more hippie-boho than bridal-magazine-cover material, which would have horrified her mother. Fortunately, the haughty Patricia hadn't been invited, so it wasn't an issue. It was *her* special day, hers and Mike's, and they wanted only loved ones to be there celebrating with them.

Beth had sewn the dress herself, with Rose's help, and it featured coloured ribbons stitched into the bodice, to represent the sabbats, and the circle of magic that was so important to her.

Now her hair was out too, as it had been then, hanging in loose golden waves down her back, with the crown of ivy and flowers Laura had woven for her resting on her head. And her feet were bare, since she and Mike had dispensed with shoes for their ceremony, which took place in the green meadow at the bottom of the tor rather than in a stuffy church. It had been so beautifully romantic, and for Beth, so long lacking love, it was a dream come true.

She and Mike wrote their own heartfelt vows, and Rose created a touching ritual that so perfectly evoked the love they shared. The priestess had shed a few tears, and Beth wondered now how she'd felt seeing *her* walking down the aisle to Mike, when she'd always thought it would be her daughter Violet doing that. The daughter she hadn't heard from since she'd run away three years before.

Mike's parents had been there, smiling proudly, and holding Beth so close and so tight, overwhelming her with more parental love than she'd ever experienced. His mum Anne had welcomed her into their family so genuinely, so generously, and had always been such a wonderful part of her life.

And her sister Jenny, so long a stranger to Beth, had come down from Scotland to help her celebrate. Spending time with her reminded Beth of her first date with Mike, which had taken place at Jenny's wedding. Not that it had *really* been a date, that was just her wishful thinking. But since Beth had been living in France for a year prior to her bridesmaid duties, and London for a year before that, she'd had no one to attend with. It was Violet who suggested that Mike escort her, lending her boyfriend for the occasion.

Giggling, Beth remembered how she'd pretended they were a couple, as Mike accompanied her up the aisle, sat with her during dinner, then danced with her all night. But he was just being a good friend. And he'd stayed just a good friend, even after Violet dumped him and started dating someone else, then disappeared forever. The mystery of Violet's leaving, and Beth's guilt over it, had convinced her it was impossible for them to be together, and for a long time she resented Violet for breaking Mike's heart, then running off in such a way that they'd always wonder if she would one day come back to reclaim her childhood sweetheart.

Just before Violet left home, Beth had cast a spell on Mike to make him love her, to bind him to her. A spell of desperation and desire. Alone in the woods on a dark moon night, she'd woven a dark kind of magic, a magic Rose would never have condoned, never understood.

Gods and goddesses, hear my plea,
Bring my greatest wish to me.
With my blood I bind his soul,
With our love, both become whole.
Mike and Beth, both true of heart
In love forever, till death do us part.
So mote it be.

And it had worked. It was only her death that had parted them. Only her death that had released him. *Although clearly it hadn't released her yet.* But the memory of the spell had plagued her all her life. She always wondered if that was what made Mike love her. Whether he'd been with her of his own free will.

That was why, after casting the spell, she pulled back from him. She didn't push it, didn't pressure him, instead biding her time, forcing patience. She'd actually given up altogether when, a year later and almost to his surprise, Mike asked her on a real date, and steered their friendship from its innocent beginnings into the dangerous waters of love.

He didn't think it was dangerous, when he finally realised he loved her – he was just surprised it had taken him so long to figure out. But Beth, who had long held herself back, masked her feelings and denied her heart, took a while to unwind and unbind her wild nature.

Once she did though, it was explosive. They became everything to each other. Loved so wide and deep and desperate. Unleashed a passion so long repressed, that in the early days she wondered if they would burn themselves up with their smouldering desire.

Nervously she tested him, cursing herself as she did, but so desperate to know that it was what he really felt, and not just her spell. When she asked a priestess they met on their travels – for she could never, ever ask Rose – the woman laughed, and told her the magic of her spell had been intense and instant and red-hot with desire. That he had felt it, and wondered, but that it had loosened its grip and dissipated a few weeks later, in the shock of someone leaving and Beth's own lack of action. That anything he felt after that was all of his own choosing. *She* was of his choosing.

Yet she couldn't quite bring herself to believe it. And so, a year after her spellcasting, she returned to the woods, stripped off her clothes and bared her self again, body and soul, wanting to ensure the universe knew she was releasing anything that bound Mike to her unnaturally, that only real, genuine feelings were acceptable.

She encountered a strange mist-wreathed woman in red there that night, all flashing eyes and glittering danger, who terrified her as she grilled her, then took pity on her and confirmed that the spell's power had worn away mere weeks after she cast it.

Still she always wondered, despite Mike's reassurances, despite the priestess, despite the strange Otherworldly being, despite every oracle reading she ever did for herself. It wasn't until one morning in the local hospital, after she'd been in labour all night and Mike held a baby Rhiannon in his arms and gazed up at his wife with such total love and devotion, that Beth allowed the ghost of Violet to finally fade away.

Now she wondered if Violet had ever spared her a thought over the years. Rose's daughter had opened her heart to Beth the first night they'd met, and they'd instantly become close friends. She'd welcomed her into her magical circle, and even into her relationship with Mike, inviting her out with her, as well as on their dates. Whenever Beth asked why, Violet laughed and told her she had all the time in the world to be alone with him.

But just a few months later Violet ran away from home, seduced by the violent, awful man Beth had known about but not warned her friend against. Had Andrew told Violet that he'd dated Beth before her? Had she cursed her when she realised his true, cruel nature? And had she kept Mike in her heart all the years after, or blocked out her past entirely?

Learning that Violet had only died a few months ago confused Beth. She was devastated for Rose, and angry at the wayward daughter who had left her mother in the hell of not-knowing for twenty years. Yet she sensed there was a deeper story there, that it hadn't been her choice to leave the way she did. That her escape was desperate and last-minute, and that while ultimately she'd found love and had a daughter, she had once been in more danger than Beth liked to contemplate, since it was all her fault.

Now, twenty years later, it was so strange to watch her own daughter becoming so close to Violet's daughter. To see the girls, who looked so much like their mothers, working magic with Rose, the way she and Violet once had. What did it do to the priestess, to be part of it? How much did her heart hurt at the memories? Desperately Beth hoped that the comfort Rose had found with this hitherto unknown granddaughter went some way to balancing the pain of finally knowing her daughter was dead.

God, what a mess she'd made all those years ago. If she'd stayed in Paris instead of going home for Jenny's wedding, would Mike and Violet have eventually returned to each other? Would Vee have outgrown her fascination with Andrew and remained in Summer Hill, working with Rose in the healing centre, performing rituals with her, and marrying Mike and bringing up their children steeped in the magic she was so filled with? It confused her that Carlie knew nothing of this magic, because it had been so much a part of Violet, a natural expression of her heart, of her personality. How could she have turned her back on it all?

And what about their daughters? Would Carlie or Rhiannon have been Violet's daughter, or hers? Or would the two girls never have existed? Fiercely she rebelled at that thought. No, it had all turned out the way it should. Carlie and Rhiannon were both meant to be, and to be here. And if it was her own death that had bonded them, she would not regret being taken from the world. She just wished she could help her darling husband move forward with his life.

Beth shivered as she contemplated how awful her life would have been, how empty, if she hadn't returned to Summer Hill for Jenny's wedding. God knows she hadn't wanted to. She'd been happy in Paris as the nanny to two sweet young girls, dating a supposedly wonderful man, and at peace with the fact that she was despised by her parents and estranged from her sister.

But when her boyfriend Andrew proclaimed his love for her, then abruptly disappeared back to London, Beth accepted her sister's invitation, thinking she would meet up with him while she was in England so they could reconcile.

In the end she didn't need to track him down though. He appeared, in the guise of a shaman teacher called Andre, and promptly fell in love with Violet – at times, it seemed, just to spite her. Yet she recovered from her heartbreak, soothed by her friendship with Mike and Violet, her growing love for the magic she wove with Rose, and the surprising realisation that she and her sister could be dear friends, now they were no longer living under the oppressive cruelty of their parents.

It was her sister who told Beth she would end up with Mike. Jenny claimed she'd known from the moment he held the rings during her own wedding ceremony that he would one day marry Beth, and that he would heal her broken soul the way her husband Josh had healed hers. He would love her, and transform her, and see her.

And for twenty years he had done just that, making her the luckiest woman alive. Now that she was dead, remembering just how magical their love had been was leaving her in the worst kind of hell. So finally she allowed the agony of her broken heart to shatter her entire being into a million little pieces.

Chapter 14

Stolen Kisses

Rhiannon

Slamming Carlie's front door shut behind her, instead of going back in to apologise, Rhiannon rushed home to get ready. She was so eager to see John. This was her first-ever proper date, and butterflies were dancing in her stomach. She couldn't wait to kiss him again, which was such a strange, unfamiliar feeling, and see his eyes as he gazed at her without pity, without knowledge of the tragedy that defined her to everyone else she knew.

She loved that he saw her as just a normal girl. She wasn't the one whose mum died, the student afflicted by grief, the one to be pitied, and have allowances made for them. She knew people meant well, but she didn't want to be defined by her loss. To be known for what she didn't have. To be followed by sympathetic gazes and avoided because people felt uncomfortable around her. To hear excuses for not being invited somewhere, because her friends no longer knew how to talk to her, or were scared they'd say the wrong thing, or accidentally do something to upset her. When really, them ignoring her was what hurt the most.

She wanted to be known for herself. For her personality, her achievements, her quirks and faults and strengths. She didn't want to be treated better than anyone else, or be given special dispensation. She didn't want to be treated worse either.

It made being with John so wonderful. He didn't know yet, so he wasn't walking on eggshells around her, tiptoeing around her feelings. He didn't mention his mother then panic and freeze up, too scared to continue. It was liberating.

Of course it had been different with Carlie, because she'd lost her mother too, and her dad. It was the first thing that bonded them – their shared misery and loss, their mutual understanding of the pain and isolation that came from being suddenly cast in the tragic role. Overnight, friends struggling to talk to you normally. Overnight, suddenly feeling so much older, so much more tired. It was exhausting, the constant need to reassure others, to put on a brave face so they didn't feel bad. To make them feel less discomfort. To make them not feel bad. Always worrying about protecting them.

On the bus trip over to John's, she lurched from sheer terror to joyful anticipation and back again, with nausea alternating with dizziness. As they pulled up in his village, she wondered if she should stay on board and go back home. What if he didn't like her in the harsh light of day, without make-up and a pretty dress? What if he'd just been swept up in the excitement and romance of the night?

But when the bus stopped the driver gestured at her to get off, so she grabbed her bag and clamoured down onto the street – to find John waiting, looking just as unsure as her. He handed her a bunch of flowers with a sprig of holly in the middle, then awkwardly hugged her, and she smiled with relief. Thank god, he was just as anxious as she was, which endeared him to her even more.

"I wanted to come and get you on my own, so you weren't scared off by my pesky little brothers from the moment you got here," he said shyly, then took her hand. "Is this okay?"

"Yes," she whispered, voice faint with nerves. "And thank you, I'm glad we have a few minutes alone. I just... well, I wasn't sure if you'd still feel the same about me today."

He grinned. "Do you mean do I still want to kiss you?" And he leaned in and did just that, pulling her close and almost lifting her off her feet.

Relieved, she kissed him back, then broke away from his embrace. "I don't want to embarrass you, if you know people around here," she said reluctantly, but John shook his head.

"I don't mind if everyone sees us," he declared, and she felt herself lighting up from within at the pride in his voice. Throwing herself back into his arms, she kissed him with more enthusiasm. She didn't know how long they would have stayed like that, locked together, joined by lips, hands and hearts, but soon she heard a shrill voice calling John's name. He laughed and drew away from her, but not in a way that made her think he was ashamed to be seen with her.

"And speak of the devils," he sighed, and introduced his two younger brothers. They were adorable, like mini Johns.

"Eww, you were kissing a girl," shouted one.

"That's gross," cried the other, letting out a high-pitched laugh. Before Rhiannon could react, one of them grabbed John's hand and the other hers, and dragged them off down the street, to the town square where the concert was about to begin.

"Sorry," John mouthed over their heads, but she shrugged. It was nice to be included, to be seen as someone with a blank slate. She wasn't the poor tragic motherless girl here, she was just a girl, and she liked that.

Her nerves returned as they approached John's parents, but they greeted her warmly, and she managed to say hello, and stutter out her name, before her voice gave out. This whole situation was so strange to her. So far out of her comfort zone.

"Coffee?" John asked after the first carol was sung.

She nodded in gratitude and relief. "I'd love one."

Taking her hand again – which sent another thrill of excitement coursing through her – he led her over to a cosy cafe that was pumping out an endless conveyor belt of hot drinks to go. Steam curled upwards in strange patterns from each cup, and she was entranced by the mist-like quality and the sense of possibility swirling around her. John ordered two coffees, then handed one to Rhiannon to warm her hands while he paid.

"Should we get one for your parents too?" she asked, even though she hoped he'd say no. She didn't want to hurry back.

"Nah, we don't have to return just yet," he replied with a grin, and offered her a cookie. She smiled back, and he leaned over and kissed her nose, which made her crinkle it, and him laugh. "I'm so glad you could come today."

She was too, and while part of her thought she should be worrying more about her situation with Carlie, she thrust it to the back of her mind and focused all her attention on John. This was her first date, and she was determined to be totally present for every second of it.

"You looked serious for a minute there," John said. "Is this okay? Would you rather go back to my family? Safety in numbers and all?"

"God no!" she burst out, then giggled. "Sorry, not that there would be anything wrong if we did, but it's nice to be on our own for a bit." And she summoned her courage, stood on tiptoe and planted a kiss on his cheek.

Relief crossed his face, and he slung an arm around her shoulder. "Shall I give you the grand tour of Smithfield then?" he asked, and they wandered off, meandering over the cobblestoned laneways, peering into festive shop windows and going past the church he went to every Sunday with his family.

As they walked, they chatted about school and little brothers, and about their resolutions for the new year – he wanted to save up for a three-month European adventure after he graduated, and she said she wanted to be more patient. Really she wanted to deepen her magical practice and be brave enough to lead a ritual, but she was hesitant to admit that. John had been fine with the ball's Yule theme, had dressed as the Oak King to her Holly Maiden, but the idea of real witchcraft might scare him off, especially as he'd just told her his mum was very religious.

There was plenty of time to share that later, when they felt more comfortable with each other. For now she was happy to walk hand in hand with him through the snow-dusted village, slowly getting to know him, smiling ecstatically whenever he stopped to kiss her, and soaking in the festive spirit of the afternoon.

For a while they watched the performers from the other side of the square to his family, then he took her hand and led her back to the cafe, and inside to a cosy corner booth at the back of the room.

"Ready for another coffee? Or something else? Sorry, I can drink coffee all day, but don't feel pressured by my addiction."

"Another coffee would be great," she grinned. "My best friend drinks tea all day, so whenever I'm with her, that's all I have."

"She won't make you coffee?" he asked, shocked.

Her cheeks reddened. "I'm sure she would if I said I wanted one, but when we first met I had tea, and I've never told her otherwise."

"Shouldn't she notice? Think to ask you?" John asked.

"I don't know, I always make tea when she's at my place too, so I guess it's my fault... But wait, let me give you some money," she offered, as he stood up to order.

"No, it's my treat, you came all this way," he said, and she was happily surprised by the gesture. As he headed to the counter though, she felt shame seep into every pore. *What was wrong with her?* She wouldn't let Carlie know she preferred coffee, yet she had no problem demanding that she dump her boyfriend, or else.

"Hey, what's up?" John asked, sitting down and taking her hand.

She shook her head. "Nothing, I'm just really happy that I came today. Thank you for asking me."

For another two hours they chatted, drank more coffee and ate cake, then she reluctantly said she had to catch the last bus home. He held her hand as he walked her to the bus stop, and she loved the emotional connection the physical connection created – she felt like she was floating along the darkening streets. The sun set at four o'clock at this time of year, and the last rays had already disappeared as they wandered slowly together, their breath fogging in front of them like an enchanted mist, the faery lights on the huge Christmas tree casting a twinkling glow around them, and the decorations of the shop windows making the village look like a faeryland.

She half expected one of the women of the mists to appear in front of them, to take her hand and offer her advice, or a gift. *Or a warning.* Out of the corner of her eye she imagined she saw the edges of a swirling ruby cloak, and worried about what the red-clad woman would say to her. Would she tell her to be kinder to Carlie?

She shivered, and John drew her closer to him and kissed the top of her head. The tenderness of the gesture brought her back to the present, and she threw off the dark thoughts swirling around her mind and leaned into him. For right now, in this moment, she was going to focus on this sweet boy and all the new feelings he was stirring in her.

A small hand on her shoulder shook Rhiannon awake the next morning, and she rolled over and groaned. She'd been dreaming of John, of being enfolded in his warm, comforting arms, and being kissed even more passionately than they had in real life.

"What?" she snapped, grumpy that she couldn't see him today.

"Come on Rhi-Rhi, wake up!" her little brother cried. "Nanna and Pop will be here soon, and we have to decorate the tree before they arrive. You've been putting it off because of your school meetings, but they're over now, so come on!"

Hearing the hurt in his voice, she shrugged off the remnants of her dream to focus on him. "I'm sorry buddy, it has been really busy. But you're right, now is the perfect time to do it. I'll just get dressed, and be down in a minute."

"No, come now," Brodie whined. "You'll go back to sleep if I don't get you out of bed right this second. Your pyjamas are fine."

Laughing, she dragged herself out from under her cosy quilt and followed her brother downstairs, where their dad was frying eggs, making toast, and already pouring her a coffee.

"So, how was your date?" he asked, wiggling his eyebrows at her.

"Dad!"

Sheepishly he grinned. "I'm sorry. But I don't know how it all works. Am I allowed to ask you about it? Or are parents too old to understand the complexities of modern courtship?"

He laughed, but Rhiannon saw the pain and fear in his eyes, and knew how much he was missing his wife. This should have been her responsibility, the awkward dating conversations, the advice. Then she noticed the panic he was trying to hide.

"It was fun Dad," she said, determined to be generous, to share something with him, to make him feel at ease. "He's really lovely, and sweet too – you have nothing to worry about, I promise. We just drank coffee, and watched the concert, and both of his parents were there, as well as his two annoying little brothers," she said, turning to Brodie with a grin.

This time she caught the relief on her dad's face, and was glad to have reassured him, but she felt a sadness and longing too. What would happen if it progressed beyond the hand holding and kissing stage, and she needed to talk to someone? Clearly she couldn't confide in her father – he'd blanched at her drinking coffee with a boy – and she would be way too embarrassed anyway. She knew Rose would be happy to discuss delicate matters and give advice, but she couldn't talk to her about boys – she was like a grandmother to her.

Which left Carlie. Not that she knew much about romance either, but she supposed they could figure it out together. She really wanted to confide in her friend about John, to share every detail, but she'd just made it perfectly clear she didn't want to hear a word about Rowan. Didn't want her to *be* with Rowan. God, what a mess. She really must go and sort it out today. Reassure her friend that she hadn't meant that cruel and stupid ultimatum.

A knock on the front door interrupted her reverie, and she sighed with relief. It was her grandparents Anne and William, and she greeted them warmly. They'd been a big part of her healing last Christmas, when she'd almost let it pass her by in her grief-stricken state. It took Brodie thinking she didn't like him any more to jolt her back to life on Christmas Eve, and reluctantly agree to head north to spend a week with their grandparents. A week that had slowly brought her back to the world.

Now, Anne swept into the house in a cloud of cinnamon and lavender, dispensing festive cheer and hugs. And it wasn't long before she'd made everyone coffee, whipped up a plate of choc-chip cookies, and shepherded them into the lounge room to decorate the tree. In an hour that was done too, the scent of pine adding warmth to the room and cheering them all up, and the twinkling faery lights making Rhiannon smile as she remembered her date with John.

"You look so much happier darling," her grandma said in a quiet moment, and Rhiannon was surprised that the comment didn't offend her, or make her feel defensive. For a long time she'd thought she wasn't allowed to be not-sad, that she would have to spend her whole life actively missing her mother. Which she did, and always would, but she'd finally stopped feeling guilty when there were occasional moments of joy.

The idea of guilt made her think of Carlie again, but she tried to shake it off. She would take back the ultimatum as soon as she saw her, but she did want her to think about her relationship with Rowan, and what it was costing her, and making her do, and the person it was turning her into. Then she recalled John's kisses, and wondered if she would give him up without a fight if her friend didn't like him. She supposed if Rowan really did make Carlie happy, it wasn't up to her to stand in the way. Ugh. The quandary was hurting her head, so she was relieved when William came back inside with a sack full of presents, and placed them under the tree.

"Pop, that's crazy! I'm too old to get presents," she began, but Brodie came tearing into the room then.

"Did you say presents?" he squealed. "Are they for me?"

Anne laughed. "A lot of them are for you, but you'll have to wait until Christmas morning," she teased. Brodie pouted, but still threw himself down on the floor and started peering at gift tags and picking up boxes and shaking them, curiosity lighting up his face.

"How long is it until Christmas?" he asked finally, hopefully.

"Just a few more days buddy," Rhiannon said, amused. "But it's still Yule, so you can open this one from me."

Brodie practically tackled her to the ground when she grabbed it off the mantelpiece for him, and she laughed and allowed herself to sink into family time, appreciating how far they'd all come since last Christmas, when her mum's death had been so new and raw. She still missed her desperately, and her heart ached when she put on Beth's favourite festive songs, and tried to figure out how to make the pudding she'd always baked. But she realised, with a shock, that in this moment she was actually happy.

Chapter 15

I'll Tumble For You

Rhiannon

It was only December 23rd, but Rhiannon woke up even more excited than if it was Christmas Day, because John was on his way over. She was nervous, since she had to entertain him, and she didn't want to bore him, but her eagerness was winning out. After rushing through a bowl of cereal and a large mug of coffee, she took off for the bus stop. Thank god their grandparents were staying with them, or her dad might not have been so amenable to her disappearing for another whole day.

Snowflakes swirled around her as she huddled in a shop doorway, but when John raced down the steps of the bus and scooped her into a hug, her shivering immediately stopped. Taking his hand, she showed him around her village, before they gave up on the icy chill and hid out in her favourite cafe, drinking hot chocolate – her treat this time – and raving about school, their classes, and what they planned to do once they graduated.

John was going to follow in his father's footsteps and be a pharmacist, working with him after university then taking over the business when he retired. Rhiannon told him that she wanted to be a grief counsellor, which made her think of Carlie again, since it had been her idea. "I'll be studying with my best friend," she said, and there was sadness in her voice.

"Why on earth do you want to do that for a career? Wouldn't it be totally miserable and depressing?" John asked. "I don't think I could listen to people going on and on about the person they'd lost, it would depress the hell out of me."

Her cheeks flushing with embarrassment, Rhiannon tried to change the subject, but John held up a hand. "Wait, why did it make you sad to tell me that?" he asked. "And why would you want to do that for a job?"

Sighing, she stared down into her mug. "My mum died," she finally whispered, as she tried desperately to stop the tears forming. "A year ago. And it was hard to deal with..."

Awkwardly John stood up and moved around to hug her. "I'm so sorry. My god, you must think I'm such a jerk," he said. When he sat back down, he took her hand, maintaining their connection. "I can't even imagine losing one of my parents. You're so brave."

She shook her head. "Nah, I'm not brave. And I was a total mess for months. My friend Carlie is brave – she lost both her parents, then got sent to the other side of the world to live with her only relative, one she didn't even know she had. She lost her whole family, her home, her friends, her school, her country even..."

Another wave of guilt swallowed her up, and she stammered to a stop. She'd just threatened Carlie with losing another friend, or giving up her boyfriend. How could she have demanded that a girl with so little give up any more of what she did have? She really had to go and make it right with her.

Tomorrow.

"Is that your friend who was making out with the guy outside at the ball?" John asked, and she heard the contempt in his voice.

"It was her boyfriend, she didn't just meet him that night," she said defensively. "And I over-reacted. I panicked that I'd get into trouble if they were discovered, because he wasn't a student, so I was kind of nasty to her, and to him."

"I can't imagine you would ever be nasty Rhiannon, you're so sweet," he replied, and she almost swooned at his faith in her. She wanted to believe that so badly – she didn't want to be the mean friend, the uncompassionate friend, the unforgiving friend. But even more pressing right now, she didn't want John to think that of her, so she couldn't confess what she'd done. She'd just have to sort it out with Carlie. Tell her how sorry she was, and that she took her cruel words back.

Forcing a smile, she tried again to change the subject. "Tell me about your friends," she said, and John took the hint and regaled her with tales of him and his two best mates, their weekends in Wales mountain climbing, and the backpacking trip around France they wanted to do in the next holiday break.

Rhiannon's face lit up. "We had a few family holidays in France. Mum loved it there. She backpacked around Brittany after she left school, then lived in Paris for a while, and adored every minute of it. In fact she loved it so much she almost didn't come home for her sister's wedding, which is where she met Dad. It's funny to imagine those parallel lives we could have had, isn't it. Would I even exist if Mum hadn't returned to England? Or would I be French, with a different dad and a different personality? So many possibilities, and potentialities..." She paused. "Sorry, listen to me rambling on. Would you like another drink?"

"I'll get this one."

Shaking her head, she picked up her bag and quickly stood. "No, you came all this way today, so it's my turn," she teased.

He grinned. "Ah, beaten by my own logic. Fair enough, I'll have a coffee. Thank you."

They talked for hours, losing track of time as the moments flashed by in the cosy atmosphere of the cafe, with its roaring open fire and festive candles drenching the room in a nutmeg, ginger and cinnamon haze. Then all of a sudden it was dark outside, and John had to rush off for a festive dinner with his family, and Rhiannon realised she should have already been home and helping her grandma cook their Christmas feast.

"I'm sorry I have to run, I've had so much fun with you today," John said, and Rhiannon was relieved, happy and excited all at once.

"Me too."

He pulled her into his arms, and she melted into them. He was so tall, so strong, and she loved the way she fit against him. "I know tomorrow is Christmas Eve, but would you want to meet up?" John asked shyly. "Our local cinema is screening some Christmas movies. *Love Actually, Miracle On 34th Street, The Holiday*... If they're not too soppy for you?"

She laughed and shook her head. "That would be really nice."

As the bus pulled in towards them, he leaned down and kissed her. "Can you be there by midday?"

Nodding happily, she kissed him back.

"I really am sorry about your mum Rhiannon. And you'll be an amazing grief counsellor."

Beaming, she kissed him once more, then watched as he climbed aboard, already impatient for the morning so she could see him again. Carlie would have to wait an extra day. Besides, she hadn't come to see her either, right?

Snow glistened on the side of the road and icicles dripped from the trees, as Rhiannon gazed out the bus window on her way to see John the following day. She felt a brief twinge of guilt that she wasn't at home spending time with her grandparents, but they had Brodie to fawn over, and he would love the extra attention.

When they passed a car on the side of the road, its front smashed in where it had skidded into a tree, she shuddered. She hoped everyone was okay. How awful to have such a terrible accident today – to be spending the festive season in hospital, or worse, losing someone. Christmas was hard enough when you were grieving. How much worse if it was all so fresh.

She was distracted from her morbid thoughts as the bus pulled in to John's village. Peering nervously through the window, she was relieved to see him waiting for her, and overjoyed that his face lit up when he caught sight of her. She hurried down the steps to the pavement, and he scooped her into a hug.

"Perfect timing," he grinned. "I've already got the tickets, so we can go right in."

The warmth of the movie theatre wrapped around her as they entered, and she loved how sweet John was, holding her hand, buying their coffee and popcorn, and introducing her to one of his friends when they ran into him in the lobby. It was such a relief that he didn't pretend he hadn't seen the guy, or snatch his hand away from her and act as though they weren't together.

When the first movie started and he casually slung his arm around her shoulder, she snuggled happily into him, and couldn't wipe the grin from her face. This was what she'd always imagined dating would be like, but she'd never experienced it, so she hadn't been sure. She supposed she should be more patient with Carlie. If being with Rowan was anything like being with John, she could understand why she gave him some leeway.

As the credits of the second movie rolled, John leaned over and kissed her, then spoke above the noise. "I was wondering if you'd like to go ice-skating? They've set up a rink for the week, which is very cool, no pun intended."

Rhiannon gulped. She'd never been ice-skating – but she was so excited that he didn't want their date to end just yet that she couldn't say no. "That sounds like fun," she began, voice only a little shaky. "Except I've never done it before, and I don't want to hold you back." Stumbling and tumbling around the ice while John sped gracefully off on his own didn't sound quite as enticing as their movie marathon, and she was scared she'd fall over and make a fool of herself. Then she remembered her dream of them gliding on the ice hand in hand, and nodded with more enthusiasm.

John stood up and took her hand, pulling her gently to her feet. "You won't slow me down, I promise, and it's not too difficult. I'd love to show you how, but only if you really want to."

"Okay, I'd love to," she blurted out, before she could change her mind. Oh god, would she regret this? A broken leg wouldn't be much of a Christmas present. But they had a wonderful time, John clutching her hand tightly as she anxiously took her first steps, and not letting go even when she'd figured it out and become more confident. And when he kissed her, out in the middle of the ice, not caring who saw them, her heart melted. She couldn't believe how happy she was.

It was even better when they took off their skates and went back to their cafe, Rhiannon falling into the red velvet booth they'd sat at last time, glad her shaky legs could rest. They talked and laughed, and ordered food, then more coffee – until the waiter came over to say they were closing, and they would have to leave.

"Oh my god, it's not really nine o'clock is it?" she gasped. "I think I've missed the last bus home!"

"You just couldn't bear to drag yourself away from me, could you?" John grinned.

Rhiannon blushed. That was true.

"I'm kidding. I wouldn't have let you go anyway. Why do you think I had so many activities prepared? I didn't want you to get bored and want to leave me." And he leaned over and kissed her again – until the waiter returned, and cleared his throat.

"Sorry," Rhiannon said sheepishly, and quickly grabbed her bag and headed for the door.

John was still laughing when they tumbled out onto the freezing cold pavement, his breath emerging in puffs of condensation in the icy air. "I didn't mean to embarrass you," he said softly. "And don't worry, I'll be able to borrow Mum's car and take you home. But I mean it. I've loved spending all day with you."

"Me too," she admitted, grateful that she wouldn't have to get an expensive taxi or call her dad. Her spirits rose as John took her hand again and led her up the hill to his house, and she was thrilled when he invited her inside.

His parents weren't impressed that he'd missed Christmas Eve with his little brothers, but his mum smiled at Rhiannon and wished her a wonderful festive day for the morning, then handed over the car keys with an admonishment to John to drive safely. Rhiannon shuddered as she recalled the car wreck she'd seen on her way over. Yes, they would take it easy.

When they pulled up at her house half an hour later, she turned to John with a sad smile. She didn't want to say goodbye. "Thank you so much for bringing me home, and for the wonderful day."

"You're welcome," he replied, as he cut the engine then leaned over and kissed her. For long blissful moments they lost themselves in each other, the darkness and silence of the night swirling around them, comforting, concealing. Then Rhiannon saw her porch light go on, and sighed.

"I guess you need to get inside, but I want to see you again soon," John said. "I know we both have family stuff tomorrow, but shall I come over on Boxing Day?"

Rhiannon grinned. He looked so hopeful, and she was so glad he was as keen as her. "Yes!" Her voice was a squeak, and he laughed and kissed her again.

"Merry Christmas Rhiannon," he said, and gave her a small, brightly wrapped package. She smiled and dug around in her bag, then handed him one too. Thank god she'd bought something for him, just in case. They were so new, she hadn't been sure.

"Merry Christmas," she echoed, then kissed him quickly and leaped out of the car with a hurried "see you soon". She would die of embarrassment if her dad came out to see why she was taking so long, but she couldn't wipe the smile off her face.

Racing up the front steps, she opened the door as quietly as possible and crept inside, trying not to draw attention to herself. Her dad heard her though, and came out from the kitchen to talk to her, but she just waved and headed for the stairs.

As soon as she made it to her room she closed the door and jumped up and down, unable to contain her excitement. Her grin was so wide she thought her face might crack. Finally she threw herself across her bed and ripped off the paper from John's present, then smothered a laugh. They'd bought each other the same thing, the new book they'd been discussing at the last planning meeting, and a red felt stocking with a holly leaf stuck to it, filled with the dark chocolate she loved so much. Her heart raced as she gazed at the holly leaf. It was a symbol of them and their meeting. Of their first dance, and their first kiss.

It felt like a sign of good things to come...

Chapter 16

Everyday Magic

Beth

It was the scent of pine that drew Beth back this time, and she smiled as she saw her son sitting on his grandma's lap, munching on cookies and drinking milk, and trying so valiantly to stay awake.

"But I want to see Santa this time," he was telling Anne, and Beth's heart ached with the pain of missing him, as well as gratitude for her mother-in-law for being here for her family now that she couldn't.

"He's not going to come until you go to bed though," she argued, and Brodie's sweet face furrowed in concentration, considering this new information.

"Okay," he finally conceded. "Will you read a story with me first though Nanna? Rhi-Rhi's not home yet."

Beth's heart melted as she watched Anne lead Brodie up the stairs, help him brush his teeth, then wrangle him into his pyjamas and grab a book from the shelf beside his bed. She was amazed by how much her son's reading and comprehension skills had improved over the past year, which made her teacher-self proud, but her mother-self fill with longing and regret.

Her attention was diverted from the cosy night-time scene when Mike hurried in the front door, in a swirl of snowflakes and icy wind, arms filled with brightly wrapped gifts. As she swooped down the stairs and hovered around him, he arranged them all under the sweet-smelling pine tree, then made his way out to the kitchen to start work on the Christmas treats she used to make. It was bittersweet to watch her husband poring over her handwritten recipes, his finger tracing over the looping scrawl, a tear now and then falling into the bowl of chocolate cake mixture he was stirring for the Yule log, the puffed rice, cherries and white chocolate he was transforming into a White Christmas slice, and the cinnamon and nutmeg-laden cookies he was decorating to look like reindeers and snowmen.

The kitchen smelled heavenly from all the spices, and Mike seemed momentarily content in the warmth of the fire and the haze of his activity, dreamily moving around the space as the clock ticked hypnotically in the corner. When the front door opened two hours later, he was startled back to the present moment. Wiping his hands, and his eyes, he shuffled out to greet Rhiannon. But she just waved guiltily and raced upstairs to her room before her father could question her, face glowing with excitement, and sparkles of electricity dancing on her skin. Beth stared at her in amazement, startled by the effect. They looked like mini streaks of lightning. Intrigued, she floated upstairs in her daughter's wake. Was it passion she was exuding, in these tiny jolts of fire?

Quickly she passed through the closed door to Rhiannon's room. Once this ability had terrified her, but aside from the slightest jarring she barely noticed it now, let alone was alarmed by it.

The young girl was on her bed, tearing open a gift, eyes bright with elation. And as she sat gazing at the book and the red stocking in her hands, smiling joyfully, Beth was shocked to realise how much Rhiannon had grown up in the year she'd been away, and her heart broke for Mike. He would struggle with the dating issue, with questions that made him squirm, and would miss his wife even more. She had to find a way to help him.

When Rhiannon stood up and moved over to her dressing table, Beth leaned over her shoulder, marvelling at her flushed cheeks and radiant eyes, and the grin she couldn't keep from her face. She was so thrilled her daughter had found love, or at least companionship, at last. She'd sacrificed her social life while her mum was sick, then been in no fit mental state to find a boyfriend while grieving her death. So this new development seemed like a great step forward – she just wished she was alive so she could share the excitement. She longed to know all the details – what the boy was like, and what they did together, and how her daughter felt. But when Rhiannon opened her journal, Beth floated away from her, not wanting to spy as she spilled her stories of love and the drama of her emotions onto the page. Strange enough that she could hover here, invisible, and observe her. Reading her diary would be crossing a line.

When she heard her husband's footsteps on the stairs, Beth left Rhiannon to her happy dreams and drifted down to her old bedroom, curling up around her beloved and trying to dissolve herself into his very being. Just before he fell into sleep, she felt a prickle of disquiet, as though someone was watching her. She gazed around the room in panic, then laughed at herself. She was the only ghost in this house.

It was a dog's bark, followed by an excited squeal, that woke Beth and Mike the next morning. She shimmered back to awareness from the depths of a beautiful dream, where she'd been on holiday in Iceland with her husband. They'd never been there, so she wondered if her subconscious had chosen it for its bare, barren beauty and isolation. Whatever the reason, they'd been alone together, just the two of them, on a passionate, romantic second honeymoon. Now her husband's secret smile as he slowly shook off sleep made her wonder if they'd dreamed the same dream.

"Beth," he sighed, voice a whisper of love and longing.

Putting her arms around him, she was shocked to feel more solid and substantial than she had before. His sharp gaze at the exact spot she was lying filled her with hope, but the next bark dragged his attention away, and he sighed and forced himself out of bed.

Regretful as she was that their night together was over, a smile tugged at Beth's soul, and she floated down the hallway to Brodie's room – then froze when he came tearing out, his dog yapping excitedly at his heels, and ran right through her. She doubled over, confused by the physical wrench as he'd slammed into her. That hadn't happened before.

Quickly drawing the wisps of herself together again, she turned to follow – then felt another shock of sensation as Rhiannon emerged from her room, laughing at her brother's enthusiasm, and walked right through Beth too. What did it mean? Was she becoming more solid, more real? Would she one day be able to communicate with her family properly, be heard by them, even seen? A shiver of excitement rushed through her as she recalled the tear that had fallen from her eye when she read Mike's letter. *Oh goddess, please let her be able to tell her loved ones she was okay, and that they needed to move on.*

After taking a moment to compose herself, Beth made her way down the stairs in her family's wake, and was caught up in the flurry of activity. Anne was brewing coffee and flipping pancakes at the stove, her husband William was heating up some milk for Brodie to ward off the chill in the air, and Rhiannon had followed her brother into the lounge room as he impatiently rifled through the stack of presents, begging his dad to let him open some.

When Mike pointed to the huge stocking with Brodie's name embroidered on it that was hanging from the mantelpiece, he squealed gleefully, making his sister laugh. "Is all that from Santa?" Brodie asked, and Mike mumbled vaguely in affirmation.

Beth shivered with amusement. They'd had many discussions about Santa over the years, arguing over how long you should lie to your kids, the impact of scaring them with threats of no gifts if they were naughty, and whether some stranger should get the credit for the gifts you spent so long choosing. It was Beth who had argued for keeping Santa for at least a few more years, based on her love of Christmas and all its traditions, and it made her love her husband even more that he'd kept up the facade.

Drifting off into memories of past festive seasons, Beth felt warmed by all the beautiful moments they'd shared, and it took her a while to realise that Rhiannon was staring right at her. Or through her? Gazing in her direction at any rate. But before she could try to make herself noticed, Anne called them in for breakfast, and everyone piled into the kitchen, Brodie with his favourite new toy clutched under his arm, and Baxter jumping around his feet. Rhiannon offered a few words of grace – part spell, part prayer, part well wishes to her much-loved, much-missed mother – then they all dug into the pancakes, stealing apple slices from each other's plates, teasing each other, trying not to spill the maple syrup, and laughing.

It was a scene of such beautiful, normal, everyday chaos and magic, and Beth was overwhelmed. Part of her was sad they were moving on with their lives without her, but she was also relieved. At the Samhain ritual six weeks ago she'd been devastated by how broken her family was, but today they appeared less crippled by their grief, and more capable of moving forward. Brodie was genuinely happy to have his family around him as he opened his presents, Rhiannon was lit from within thanks to the excitement of her first love, and Mike was, if not thriving, at least coping.

Desperately she hoped it was her presence that was helping them heal. Wanted to believe that despite them not seeing her, on some level they were responding to her soothing hand on their forehead and her whispered words, her arms around them at night while they slept, when she shared their dreamscapes and tried so hard to let them know she was with them and would love them always.

But while the bigger part of her was glad to see their progress, it made her nervous too. If she helped them heal, would she no longer be any use to them? Would she disappear back into the nothingness of her lost year, her existence blinking out as though she'd never been? Snuffed out like a candle flame that was no longer required to guide her family through the darkness?

And yet she remained, as they finished their breakfast and trooped back to the lounge room to open their gifts. Stayed through lunch and afternoon naps. Was present as Rhiannon washed up, helped her grandma with dinner, then took Brodie outside to play in the snow for a while. Was an extra guest at their festive table while they ate dinner and reminisced over past years and long-ago memories, and shared stories that included her.

When Beth was still there at midnight, she wondered if that meant she would be able to stay with them always. Or was there some unfinished business she was yet to fulfil?

Chapter 17

Rhiannon

"**R**hiannon, come and sit down."

Her dad's voice was the first shock as she stumbled into the kitchen the morning after Boxing Day, still half asleep and wrapped in the beautiful dream she'd been having of John. His voice was stern, sharp and sad, which confused her, and had a touch of... *Anger*? He hadn't sounded like this since the day he'd confronted her about not going to school in those weeks after her mum died. Dread crept up her spine. What could she have done to upset him? Was he annoyed at all the time she was spending with John? Perhaps disappearing all day yesterday to be with him had been too much.

But when she saw his face, her heart clutched in fear and she collapsed into a chair. She knew instantly that he wasn't mad at her – but that something was deeply wrong.

"Dad?" It was a whisper, panic choking the words in her throat.

He just stared at her, horror etched across his face, and evident in his posture.

"Dad! What's wrong? Is Brodie okay?" *Where was her brother?*

"He's fine, your grandma took him down to the park."

Relieved of her most immediate fear, she nodded and took the cup of coffee he offered her. Thick and black, she noticed, with no honey. Not how she took it. What the hell was going on?

"It's Carlie," he finally said, and Rhiannon dropped the mug in terror. She felt the boiling liquid splash her, but didn't register the heat. Heard the cup smash into jagged shards on the floor, but didn't care that it might cut her.

"What happened?" she gasped, and felt her breath become short as panic overwhelmed her. "And Rose –" She couldn't get the words out. Because she knew Rose couldn't handle another loss. It was just too awful to bear.

"Rose is fine. And Carlie is okay. But apparently she had a boyfriend…"

"Oh my god, Rowan. What did he do to her?" she shrieked, body trembling with fear and fury.

Her dad stared at her, brow furrowed. "Do to her? Nothing." He paused, suspicion flashing through his eyes, then pulled himself together and continued. "He died."

"*What?*" She sank down further into the chair, visibly shaking. "What happened?"

"His car ran off the road in the snow and hit a tree. He died quickly, not that that's much consolation."

All the colour drained from Rhiannon's face, as a vision of the crashed car on the side of the road when she'd gone to see John flashed into her mind. "When?"

"Five days ago."

"Five *days*?"

Her friend had been suffering all this time, while she was off having fun, kissing John, seeing romantic movies, falling in love. Not sparing a thought for Carlie, because she knew there would be time later to make up for ignoring her, for threatening her, for trying to take something from her, when she'd had so little to start with. And now she *had* lost it, permanently. Lost the guy who had loved her so much. Why hadn't she run back up the stairs and rescinded the ultimatum as soon as she'd uttered it? Or gone over and apologised the next morning, or the morning after that?

"How is she?"

Her dad shrugged. "As distraught as you would imagine. Rose has been terrified, that's why she asked me to go over yesterday. Carlie collapsed into her bed when it happened, and hadn't got up again. Hadn't said a word. Hadn't noticed that Christmas came and went. Hadn't eaten anything..." Pain filled his eyes as his gaze drifted to the window, and Rhiannon knew he was remembering his wife in her final days, wasting away, unable to eat. Remembering his own total collapse after she died.

"Did you manage to... Did you get through to her?"

"I finally convinced her to get up and eat half a piece of toast – but I had to threaten her with Rose's health to get through to her. And then it was like she saw her for the first time, like she hadn't noticed just how much older Rose seemed in her fear and worry."

A pang of guilt hit Rhiannon. Rose had been part of their Christmas every single year she could remember, but this time she hadn't even thought about her. Hadn't taken a gift to her, hadn't wondered if she had plans for Christmas dinner. Not only had she stood the priestess up for the Yule ritual, but she'd ignored her on Christmas Eve, too, eager to be with John again. On Christmas Day she'd used her grandparents as an excuse to avoid Rose and Carlie. Even yesterday, Boxing Day, she'd run off to be with John again, spending every minute with him and neglecting her family and friends.

Her eyes filled with tears, her heart filled with regret, and guilt bubbled up and swallowed her whole. The last thing she'd said to her friend was that she had to break up with Rowan or else – and now he was dead. She knew she would be the last person the grieving girl would want to see right now, but there was no one else.

Her chair scraped loudly then crashed to the floor as she abruptly stood up. "I have to see her."

"Um, love, not today. She's not ready to see anyone."

"But it was days ago. She must be going crazy with grief."

Mike looked embarrassed. "Darling, she's not ready to see... *you*." He winced on the last word, and she felt a sharp pain in her heart. She deserved it though. She'd been a terrible friend.

Righting her chair but leaving the broken mug where it was, Rhiannon stomped upstairs to her room and threw herself on the bed. No wonder Carlie hadn't come to see her. She'd justified her own absence because Carlie hadn't got in touch with her either, but really she'd just wanted to be with John. She'd thought she could make up with her friend any time, tell her she was fine with her dating Rowan. But it was too late. And now that she knew the awful truth, and all she wanted to do was race over and comfort her, she had to deal with the fact that Carlie didn't want to see her.

Sadly she couldn't blame her.

A wild storm raged all night, and Rhiannon tossed and turned, restless and drifting. Guilt and anxiety were like a weight pressing her down into the mattress, into the earth, and sleep eluded her as the thunder rolled and lightning crashed outside her window.

As soon as a sliver of pale grey dawn sky lightened the darkness, she gave up and forced herself out of bed. She'd hoped the knowledge of Carlie's loss was only a nightmare, that when she woke up it would just be a crazy memory, but somehow she knew it was the truth.

Before she could change her mind, she dragged the clothes she'd been wearing the day before off the floor and over her head, tucked her long hair up into a beanie, grabbed her warmest coat and slipped outside. She shivered in the icy wind, but she was determined, and in moments she was at Rose's door and knocking quickly, before she lost her nerve.

"Sweet girl," Rose said sadly, as she opened the door and ushered her through to the kitchen, which was warm but empty. Where was her friend? "Tea?"

Rhiannon stared at her, momentarily confused by the question. "Um, sure. But I came to see Carlie..." She broke off, unnerved, when the priestess just stared at her. "Dad told me... about Rowan. Is she –?"

For a moment Rose seemed to shrink, to crumble under the grief she'd experienced in her own lifetime, and the suffering she was trying to help her granddaughter through now. Would this be the final straw that crushed her? Was it all her fault?

"Ah, Rhiannon," Rose said softly, then sighed. "Don't make this about you."

A fiery blush rushed into her cheeks, that the older woman could read her mind so easily, know her thoughts. She wanted to flee, to get away from Rose's sad, defeated eyes, and the shame, and blame, they made her feel as she wilted in their glare.

"Is she okay?" she persisted. "I just need to know she's okay... Well, that she will be okay."

The priestess glanced right through her, making Rhiannon shiver again, before pouring two cups of tea from the pot and leading her to the kitchen table.

"She's devastated, and it breaks my heart that she's already mourning another loved one, so soon after losing her parents," Rose finally said. "But there's something else distressing her, something I can't see, can't figure out, and so I don't know how to help her."

Rhiannon sighed, then took a deep breath, and a sip of her tea, and tried to force the words out. "It's me," she whispered. "That's why I feel so bad."

The priestess gazed at her, eyes steely, and questioning. "Why would you feel bad?"

Cringing inwardly, Rhiannon screwed up her courage and leaped in, before she could censor herself or try to make excuses for her behaviour.

"Um, well, Carlie was dating someone... An amazing guy, who absolutely adored her –"

"I know Rowan," Rose interrupted. "Well, I knew him."

Rhiannon's mouth dropped open in shock, and she gripped her cup of tea, trying not to drop it – or squeeze it so hard that it broke in her palm. *What?* Part of her objection to Carlie being with Rowan was that she was seeing him behind Rose's back. "She told you about him?" Why hadn't her friend let her know?

"No, Carlie wasn't ready for that, but he came in to the shop before the solstice to tell me. I'd met him a while ago at a healing course, and seen him a few times since then, and he was always lovely. He said he'd been dating Carlie for three months, and wanted me to know how he felt about her, and that I could trust her with him."

"Did Carlie know you knew?"

Rose shook her head. "Rowan said she was worried about what I'd think, especially given her mother's past, so I thought I'd wait, and let her tell me when she was

ready. He just wanted to impress upon me how much he respected her, and that he was taking things slowly. That he would never hurt her, and he loved her deeply. Knowing that was enough for me."

Rhiannon hung her head, feeling awful, but Rose reached out across the table and touched her hand, and she felt peace and reassurance flowing into her. "What is it sweet girl?"

"I was so nasty to her, telling her what a bad person she was for sneaking around, and taking you for granted. That she was ungrateful and selfish, and a total disappointment."

A wrinkle creased the priestess's forehead, and Rhiannon wanted to erase it, wanted to make her stop looking at her like she'd done something bad. Yet she had done something bad. She'd hurt her friend.

"So I need to tell her how sorry I am, how much I regret trying to interfere with her relationship..." She broke off, conscious that the more she spoke, the more stupid she sounded. What *had* her problem with Rowan been? Her breath started coming faster, and a pit of guilt opened up in her stomach, thick and bubbling, making her nauseous. She couldn't meet Rose's eye, so she stared at the table instead, at the scratches on the surface she knew so well from study sessions and coven nights. "I should go," she said, voice a wisp.

"She wrote you a card," Rose said suddenly. "Before he died." And she disappeared into the lounge room, while Rhiannon sat frozen, not sure she could cope with whatever Carlie had written to her. But when the priestess returned with a red envelope she took it with a shaking hand, then sank down in her chair and turned it over and over. Fear added its poisonous heat to the guilt clawing at her belly, and she swayed a little, overcome with dizziness. The last thing she wanted to do was unseal the envelope and look inside, especially with Rose sitting opposite her. But the sooner the better, right? Rip the band-aid off instead of playing with it?

Weighed down with dread, she forced herself to open it and slide the card out. There was a woman on the front, holding a chalice like the one she'd been gifted on their coven dedication night, and she smiled despite herself as she realised it was an illustration of the woman in blue.

Steeling herself, she began to read.

Dear Rhiannon, sister of my heart,
I went to see Rowan today, and I broke up with him, because
of the ultimatum you gave me. But I've been thinking about it
every moment since, and I know that I made the wrong decision.
I will not choose between you. I love you both. I choose you both.

I appreciate that you are concerned for me, and I'm grateful
that you care so much, but please know that there is nothing to
fear. Rowan loves me, and he will never hurt me. I know this in
my heart, in my mind, in the very bones of my body. And
there's something I learned from my mother today – Rowan is
my Oliver, not my Andre. He is the man who makes me more,
not the one who diminishes me. He is my beloved, and being
loved by him has healed me in so many ways. I hope that when
you come to know him as I do, that you will see us together and
recognise how much we love each other. And I want you to
know that he has always honoured you, and your importance in
my life, even tonight, even when I told him I had chosen you.

Another thing I learned from Mum – if Rowan didn't want
to be with me, he wouldn't be. He doesn't gain anything from
it – it would be so much easier for him if he wasn't with me, if
he didn't have to sneak around, and wait for me to finish school
before he can see me, if his girlfriend had a car and was free to
travel with him, if she didn't have a curfew, if she wasn't too
scared to tell her grandmother about him...

But he loves me despite all that. He loves ME. I love him so
much, and I love you too. I hope one day you'll be able to see in
him what I see, be able to spend time together with us both like
we did at the festival. And I hope you won't carry out your
ultimatum, because I would be devastated to lose you. You are
the sister of my heart, my dearest friend, and I value you and
want you in my life.

Much love, Carlie xx

Shock stabbed through Rhiannon and she doubled over, like she'd
been kicked in the stomach. Desperately she tried to suck in oxygen,
but all the air had been knocked from her, and the room was bereft

of it too. It was so much worse than she'd thought. She'd blamed herself, feeling terrible for giving Carlie the ultimatum – but she hadn't thought she would actually do it! When she'd seen her last, the day after the ball, when she'd stood her up to spend the afternoon with John, she'd assumed Carlie had just stayed in bed, disappointed in her friend, but not doing anything about it. Yet she must have gone to see Rowan while Rose was running the Yule ritual.

She turned tear-stained eyes to the priestess. "It really is my fault she's so sad," she sobbed. "The thing you couldn't see – I told her that if she didn't break up with him, she couldn't be my friend. That she had to choose between us."

Rose gazed at her calmly, weighing up what she'd said, what she felt, no doubt what she sensed. But she stayed silent.

"This makes me the worst friend ever, the worst person! How could I have been so cruel? And how will she ever forgive me?"

"Perhaps she won't."

Rhiannon jerked back, as though she'd been slapped. "What?"

A flicker of sadness crossed the older woman's face, and she took Rhiannon's hands. "You are only responsible for your actions, your emotions, your reactions. You are only responsible for, and have control over, your half of a relationship. Yes, you can apologise to her, and try to make it up to her. And she probably will forgive you. But I can't speak for her. It will be up to her if she forgives you – and even if she does, whether she wants to be friends with you any more."

A tear splashed onto the table, and Rhiannon realised it was hers. "Should I even bother trying?" she asked, voice angry and defeated.

"It takes a brave person to admit they have done wrong, and a strong person to attempt to redress things, and I think you have both those qualities. And whether or not she can move on and continue being your friend, it will mean a lot to her to know you regret it, and are remorseful, especially now when she's lost so much again."

Heart breaking, Rhiannon stood up to leave, but Rose took her hand. "What I still don't understand is why you thought she should break up with him, if he was as wonderful as you've said."

Gutted, she fell back into her chair. She wondered the same thing. "I had a psychic reading, and she told me I had to convince my friend to break up with her boyfriend before he hurt her, physically and emotionally..." She sighed. Why had she so blindly accepted that? "And there was an incident, but it was just a misunderstanding apparently. Yet I just couldn't let it go."

"I think that's about something else though, no?" Rose asked. "Something deeper, more personal. Something not about Carlie at all."

Waves of heat then freezing cold rolled over Rhiannon, and she stared blankly at the priestess, before finally summoning enough energy to shake her head. "I have to go," she whispered. "But could you tell Carlie I came by, and that I'm so sorry, and remorseful, and all those other things you said?"

And she fled.

As she ran, the storm broke again. Rain poured from the sky, thunder roared overhead, and a flash of lightning landed in front of her, so close she couldn't believe her clothes weren't burning. Her emotions bubbled through her and out, spilling from her eyes as tears, from her mouth as a breathless, rasping roar of pain.

Once home, her hand shook as she tried to fit her key in the lock of the front door, so desperate was she to hide in her room, and she almost screamed in frustration before it finally swung open. Desperately she raced up the stairs, needing to hide from her dad, her brother, her grandparents. Needing to be alone. Slamming the door behind her, she threw herself on her bed, and the tears that had been trickling down her cheeks turned into full-blown sobs.

Time passed as she drifted in and out of awareness, trying to escape into her dreams, to escape the storm raging outside, but always being beckoned back to the harsh reality where she'd broken her best friend's heart – and where she'd suffered her own horror, a horror she couldn't begin to face. She flinched away from it, and allowed herself to drift away in the violence of the storm.

Her father tried to talk to her, tried to lure her downstairs for dinner, for ice-cream, for a movie, but she shouted at him to leave her alone, and threw pillows, and jumpers, and finally a book at him, before he sadly left her alone, and she fell into an uneasy slumber.

Chapter 18

In A Different Light

Rhiannon

W eak sunshine pierced the clouds and crept in Rhiannon's window, forcing her bleary, bloodshot eyes to reluctantly open. The world felt harsher today, sadder, and a wave of exhaustion settled around her heart. How could life be so cruel? How could Carlie have another person torn away from her? And how could she herself be so damaged?

Her mind recoiled from that dark thought, and she turned wearily to see what time it was – then swore. John would be here any minute, yet for once she wasn't excited. She didn't want to have to hide her feelings, but she didn't want to bring him down either, and bore him with her problems. And she wasn't quite ready to admit what had happened, what she'd done. Maybe he would pull her out of this melancholy state though, for a while at least. Distract her from the storm of guilt and recrimination.

When she heard a loud knock downstairs she leaped into action, dragging on a dress and scooping her hair into a knot on top of her head. Rubbing roughly at her eyes, she flew down the stairs and wrenched open the door, squinting in the grey glare.

"Hey there," John said, leaning in to kiss her.

She squirmed away, embarrassed that she hadn't brushed her teeth yet. "I'm so sorry, I have to stay here and look after my brother for a couple of hours, is that okay?" she asked nervously. "I feel terrible that you came all this way…"

John's laughter cut her off, and he followed her inside. "That's absolutely fine. I've been looking forward to meeting Brodie anyway," he called out, loud enough for him to hear. Sure enough, her little brother came barrelling down the hallway, then pulled up short in front of the tall blond stranger.

"Hi, I'm Brodie," he declared, holding out his small hand with a confidence that surprised Rhiannon. "You must be John, Rhi-Rhi's first boyfriend."

Oh god! Her cheeks turned beet red, and she wished the floor would open up and swallow her, but John took it all in stride.

"I hope that I'm her boyfriend," he said, with a wink and a smirk. "Am I?"

For a moment she was puzzled, until she realised they hadn't actually talked about their relationship status. A goofy grin spread across her face. "Yes," she said, before losing her nerve. "Well, um, if you'd like to be?"

"I would indeed. Now Brodie, what did you have planned for us today? Is there a movie you'd like to watch, or a book we can read, or do you have a new Christmas game we can all play?"

As her little brother rushed off to the lounge room to grab something for them to do together, John smiled at her. "Hey there girlfriend," he said, and it sent a shiver up her spine. She was someone's girlfriend!

"Are you okay? You look a little upset." Then he pulled her into his arms and kissed her before she could reply.

"Eww!" Brodie cried as he returned. "None of that thanks! Now come in here John, I've set up the game!"

Laughing, John followed Brodie into the lounge room while Rhiannon slipped upstairs to brush her teeth and wash her face, and smudge some concealer under her eyes to try to hide the evidence of her distress. Then, feeling a little more human, she brewed coffee for her and John, poured a glass of milk for Brodie, and arranged a plate of choc-chip cookies. There was nothing wrong with biscuits for breakfast, right? Forcing a smile, she sprawled out with the boys beside the Christmas tree, joining in their board games and making an effort to throw herself into their child-like fun. And for a while it was the perfect antidote for her emotional turmoil.

She was impressed with the way John talked to Brodie, asking him questions, making jokes with him, and including him in their conversation. Maybe it helped that he had two younger brothers, because he never spoke down to him, or seemed annoyed by his presence, which made her like him even more.

Later, while she made lunch, John flipped through comic books with Brodie, then the three of them settled back on the couch to watch a movie. When her brother dozed off, John reached over and took Rhiannon's hand, and she smiled as their fingers intertwined. It was nice to feel this closeness with someone, to feel understood, and cherished. And it made her feel a little braver. She'd been worried about what to reveal when he finally asked her what was wrong, but now she was looking forward to the support, to sharing her burden, and to him drawing her into his strong arms and comforting her.

So she was surprised when he leaned over and started telling her, in great detail, about the previous day's football practice, then raved about the camping trip he was going on with his mates, which he was leaving on tomorrow.

Disappointment washed over her when John revealed that he wouldn't get home until the night before school began, so she wasn't even sure when she'd see him next. She tried to convince herself it would be good for him to be with his friends, since she'd been monopolising his time of late, but why hadn't he mentioned he was going away before? Was it a last-minute decision because he was sick of her? And it hurt that he'd noticed she was upset when he arrived, yet hadn't waited for her to reply then, and hadn't asked her about it again. Did he not care about her as much as she'd thought?

"It's going to be so much fun. There's always a big party at the lake on New Year's Eve, with kids from all over coming for the bonfire, and lots of alcohol on hand, and a band or a DJ, and fireworks and kissing as the countdown to the new year begins." He laughed, until he noticed Rhiannon's pained expression.

"Oh, don't worry babe, I'm not planning on kissing anyone this year," he said hastily. "But what will you be doing to celebrate?"

Rhiannon took a deep breath, trying to calm herself down. One, she'd assumed she'd be spending it with her boyfriend, either at his place or hers. And two, what did he mean he wasn't *planning* to kiss anyone? Was he trying to say he *wouldn't* cheat on her, or that he wouldn't set out to, but it could happen "accidentally"?

When he touched her hand, she focused back on him. "I thought we'd be doing something together, but I guess I'll go to the New Year's ritual at Rose's healing centre," she blurted out, then instantly regretted it when she saw his face scrunch up in... *disdain?*

"What is that?"

"Carlie's grandmother runs really lovely ceremonies. I guess it's a kind of positive thinking thing – we'll all gather together, sum up the year just gone, think about our intentions for the new year, share them, then celebrate a little. Cakes and ale, that kind of thing."

"Ha, that sounds cool. Like a Viking bash," John said.

Rhiannon stared at him, puzzled, but before she could put her thoughts into words Brodie woke up, and they started another game.

When John left to start packing, he said he'd send her a postcard, and asked if she would come over to his place on the Saturday after their first week of school. She nodded helplessly, dismayed that she wouldn't seem him for two weeks, but unable to voice it without sounding churlish. He still kissed her as passionately goodbye as usual though, so she closed her eyes and surrendered herself to the feeling, and tried to convince herself she was over-reacting.

When she glumly crawled into bed that night, Rhiannon lay awake for ages worrying about whether John's feelings for her had suddenly lessened, and trying to make sense of his reaction to her mentioning Rose's ritual. Was it disdain on his face when she said that word? And where had Vikings come from? For a while she forced her attention to Carlie, cursing herself for the ultimatum she'd issued as well as her failure to make it right before tragedy struck. But then a vision of John kissing some other girl around a campfire rose up in her mind, and she wanted to scream.

Finally she gave up on sleep and dragged herself out of bed, wrapping a thick cardigan around her shivering shoulders. Rifling through a drawer, she found a card, then curled up on her window seat and began the painstaking process of writing a letter to her friend.

Dear Carlie,

I don't even know where to begin, other than to say I am so deathly so deeply sorry for your loss. It seems the cruellest blow of all, after you've already lost so much.

I know how much Rowan loved you, and how devastated he would be to have caused you more pain, and I know he wouldn't have wanted to hurt you in this way. (Maybe that's what the psychic saw, that he would hurt you by leaving you dying.)

And I know now how wonderful he was, to have gone to talk to Rose, to reassure her of his love for you, until you got brave enough decided the time was right to tell her about him.

And I know how amazingly kind he was, how patient with me, how generous in sharing his knowledge with us, and how desperately, magically, he loved you.

Most importantly, I'm so very, very sorry for my part in your sadness, for not supporting you in your decision, and for not trusting you with your heart, and your faith in your beloved, when I couldn't see it.

It hurts me worst of all that I haven't been there for you now, when you've most needed a friend...

She paused, with no idea what to say next, no clue how to comfort someone, and no willingness to admit her own guilt. If Carlie was too angry with her to be friends, nothing she said would help, and if she wasn't, she didn't want to give her any more reasons to feel that way.

I'm so sorry Carlie. I hope you can forgive me, I hope you can accept my apologies and let me in, let me be there for you. I hope you can believe that it's better late than never, and that you don't turn your back on me forever.

All my love, Rhiannon xx

Sighing, she placed the card in the envelope, then thought about what kind of gift she could get to go with it. Pulling out her mum's Book of Shadows, she flicked through to the section on herbs and herbal healing, then skimmed through the neat handwritten listings until she found what she was looking for – a selection of flowers and their meanings.

Rosemary for clarity and remembrance.
Daisies for playfulness and joy.
Daffodils for hope and rebirth.
Geraniums for love and comfort.
Violets for loyalty and protection.
Foxglove for confidence and communication.
Hyacinths for apology and the asking of forgiveness...

That was the one. Deciding to go by the nursery in the morning, she slipped back into bed and finally fell into a deep, exhausted sleep.

The next morning she almost lost her nerve, dragging her feet over breakfast, then happily playing with Brodie for hours, before her dad gave her a stern look and asked if she had somewhere to be. Wishing she'd never told him her intentions so she could put it off again, she grabbed the card she'd written and headed out to look at plants. For a while she lost herself in the beauty of the colours and the heady scent of the flowers, trying to inhale a sense of peace and serenity. But finally she stopped procrastinating and picked up the pot of hyacinths, then slowly, reluctantly, made her way to Carlie's.

When Rose answered the door and shook her head, then told her that Carlie still wasn't ready to see her, Rhiannon was a little put out, but mostly relieved.

"Um, what's the best way to let her know I'm sorry?" she asked, feeling forlorn and rejected as she shivered on the doorstep. "How can I convince her to forgive me?"

The priestess sighed. "Sweet girl, this isn't about you. Don't put yourself into the narrative, don't make it about what you did or didn't do, and don't make her feel as though she needs to comfort and reassure you. Whether she forgives you, or not, is not the most important thing right now. This is about her grief, her loss, her love torn away from her. The love that was helping her heal from her previous loss and pain."

Feeling thoroughly reprimanded, Rhiannon nodded stiffly and gulped down the tears that were forming.

"When you do talk to her, just listen," Rose continued. "You have to put your own guilt aside – it's not up to Carlie to help you with that, you'll have to do that on your own. Don't burden her with your feelings, just listen to her. Be present with her pain. You don't need to solve it for her or make her feel better – nothing can do that right now. Just be her friend."

Straightening her spine and squaring her shoulders, Rhiannon took a deep breath, then forced a smile. "You're right. I promise I'll do that. In the meantime, will you give her these for me?" she asked, thrusting the card and brightly wrapped pot plant into the priestess's hands. Then she fled, before she embarrassed herself further.

Rose was right, she had to get over herself. Why was she crying? She hadn't just lost her boyfriend forever, she was just grumpy because she wouldn't see him for two weeks. Carlie was devastated, yet all *she* could think about was everyone else making her feel better about herself. Sadly she wouldn't blame her friend if she never spoke to her again, but she wanted her to at least know she was sorry. That she'd tried to make amends.

And she hoped she'd be able to see her before school started in a few days, so they could make some kind of peace. She didn't want Carlie to feel like she was on her own when they went back. And she wasn't sure how her friend would cope – especially as everyone would be asking about the hot guy she'd been dancing with at the ball, the one she'd been crowned Winter Queen to his Sun King with. The one everyone at school would remember crushing her to his naked chest in the heat and passion that was so clear between them.

When she got home, her dad was eager to chat, so she tried to dredge up some enthusiasm to reply to his questions about John's visit. She couldn't tell him she was annoyed he was going away, and put out that he hadn't cared that she was upset, and scared he was going to get drunk and kiss some random girl. Not so soon after she'd revealed she was dating for the first time. So soon after John had declared them boyfriend and girlfriend. Instead she focused on how lovely he'd been with Brodie, and how generously he'd included him in everything, and she felt herself softening towards him.

It was a relief when her dad steered the conversation to the magic she wove with Carlie and the rituals they attended. He hadn't asked much about them before, but over Christmas she'd admitted she had her mum's Book of Shadows, which Rose had given to her at Beth's behest, and had been shocked by how much comfort he seemed to gain from the revelations about his wife. She'd shared with him just how knowledgeable her mum had been on the magical path, discussed some of the metaphysical subjects she'd studied – much of which he already knew – then revealed the outlines of some of the rituals Beth had performed, and glimpses of spells that she'd worked.

Not the one she'd cast on her future husband of course. Rhiannon had been shocked when she'd read about *that* spell in the huge, ancient-looking book. It had really challenged her image of her mother, to read about her secretly acquiring arcane knowledge, then sneaking out into the woods one dark moon night to enact a sex magic rite, naked and exposed to the elements, baring her soul – and her body – to the goddess and to her own desires.

Her sensible school-teacher mum had definitely had a wild side, which while surprising, did fit with the stories she'd occasionally told of her travels through France before university. Backpacking with friends old and new, camping under the stars, going to festivals and full moon circles, bartering work for food, and shelter when it rained.

Her dad knew most of the stories, and had smiled proudly at them, but she suspected he might not take it quite as well if he knew that Beth had worked the deepest kind of magic – magic Rose would not approve of – in order to win his heart. She still didn't know how she felt about the revelation that her mum wasn't quite as sweet and innocent as she'd always imagined, but it was intriguing.

As Brodie stole their dad's attention for a while, Rhiannon stewed over her own situation while she started making dinner. Why was she suddenly starting to doubt John's feelings for her – and hers for him?

And perhaps more importantly, why had she fallen so deeply for him in the first place? Was his strange reaction to the idea of Rose's ritual forcing her to see him more clearly, without the enchantment of the Yule Ball, and the words of the psychic who'd promised her love with a tall blond guy by Christmas ringing in her ears? Because if her other psychic had been wrong about Rowan, and Carlie's had been wrong about her migraines, had she just wanted to believe that John was the boyfriend who had been foretold? Had he just been in the right place at the right time?

Was there someone else in her future?

Chapter 19

Heroes and Villains

Beth

A shiver crept up Beth's spine as she floated above the stove in her old kitchen. She was watching longingly as Mike and Rhiannon made dinner together, but for a split second she'd sensed something else here with them, and she stared nervously around the room. Was someone keeping tabs on her? Watching her as hungrily as she watched her family? Another ghost in her orbit? But who would want to waste their eternity with her?

Rhiannon's laughter brought her back though, and she shook off her uneasiness and returned her focus to where it belonged. It touched Beth deeply to see her husband and their daughter sharing their magical recollections of her. As Rhiannon sliced vegies for the salad and checked the pie in the oven, she told her dad about some of the rituals Beth had done over the years, which she'd read about in her mum's Book of Shadows. She carefully omitted the spell her mum had cast on her dad though, which made Beth giggle.

Seeing Rhiannon's shock as she'd read about that long-ago love spell had been amusing – and more than a little mortifying – and Beth thought it was sweet that she was keeping it from Mike in an effort to protect his memory of his wife. If only her daughter knew about the sex magic they'd created together, outside in the woods, up on the tor, on moonlit beaches and sun-drenched river banks.

Sex magic that had helped them heal old hurts, and conceive their two children, and show, over and over again, their deep and desperate love for each other.

When Beth had worked her love spell that long ago night in the woods, she'd vowed that she would enact the Great Rite with Mike, and do it properly, in the body, flesh to flesh, the way it used to be done. Not placing an athame in a chalice as a symbolic representation of the ritual, as Rose did, but tearing each other's clothes off so she could lead him naked into the sacred circle and raise energy and power through real sex. Passionate, earth-bound, galaxy-exploding sex.

That was the way it had been done in the past, high priest and high priestess embodying the god and the goddess and joining together in the sacredness of sex during the ritual, blessing the lands with their physical bonding, and balancing the energies of their coven, their village, their whole country if need be. And Mike had always been a very willing participant. A shiver of desire shot through Beth now, and she sighed in frustration. The etheric plane wasn't anywhere near as satisfying as the physical one had been.

But while the memory of their many erotic nights together filled her with joy, it also reminded her of that spell, of her selfish desire to turn Mike from his beloved Violet and choose her instead. And her never-ending guilt when it had worked.

She hadn't *really* meant to do it. She was just so hurt when her boyfriend Andrew turned up as the teacher of a psychic development class and fell for Violet. Violet who fell right back. At first Beth had just felt sorry for Mike, watching his childhood sweetheart being wooed away from him by the charming older man, the spiritual guru who unscrupulously entrapped and manipulated her. She'd been angry at Violet for stringing Mike along, and, to be honest, for luring Andrew away from her.

When she threatened to reveal his secrets to Violet – his two-timing, his violence – he blackmailed her into silence, then sweetened the deal by helping her cast the love spell on Mike. Did that make her as bad as him?

When she was diagnosed with cancer, she'd wondered if she'd brought her illness on herself. Was it karma for coveting another girl's boyfriend? For using magic for personal gain? It was even worse after she got sick, when Mike started having nightmares. At first he wouldn't tell her about them, but one night he cried out Andrew's name, and woke up with tears rolling down his face. And finally he broke down and confessed that he'd gone to the shaman all those years ago, and begged him to leave Violet.

The intervention hadn't worked though, and Andrew had threatened Mike – claiming that if he came between him and Violet, he'd curse him so that every woman he loved would die by their fortieth birthday. Chillingly, that had happened. Beth had died the morning she turned forty.

Yet Mike hadn't come between them. Violet had run away to be with Andrew, just like he wanted, so no curse could have been, should have been, activated. Which made Beth blame herself even more, and feel guilty about what she'd done in the past, as well as how she felt now. Because of more concern to her than the curse was the fact that her beloved had tried to get his high school sweetheart back. Interesting, that she was still bitter about that, so long after the event. But no one likes being the back-up plan.

Not that Mike ever made her feel that way – it must have been her guilty conscience, trying to punish her for the spell she'd cast, the information she'd buried, the secrets she'd kept. Which made her wonder if her illness, and her early death, was her fault. Was she being punished for her treachery?

Now, Beth reached out a hand to her husband, but it passed right through him. She tried again, but there wasn't even a hint of substance to her being. A few days ago she'd felt herself solidifying – forming a tear, experiencing the wrenching impact when her kids walked through her – but now panic turned her to water. Was she slipping away? Would she cease to exist? Why did her physical dimensions seem to vary so much? Was it when she wallowed in guilt that she became more ghostly?

Her guilt *had* grown as the years passed, despite her husband's constant reassurances, making it easy to think her diagnosis was karma finally rebounding on her. But she'd spent her whole life trying to make up for that one spell, that one bad choice. She was a better, kinder person, more patient than came naturally, and definitely more considerate, as a result. Hiding her selfish streak, denying her instinctive unwillingness to help others, and being sweeter and more compassionate, because she felt so guilty. But did good deeds count if they were done for personal gain, for balancing out her ledger?

She'd confessed her crime to her husband, not long before she died, hoping for absolution perhaps.

"I'm so sorry Mike, that I was never the woman you really wanted. I know I was always your second choice," she'd whispered in the dark of night, when secrets slipped more easily from the tongue. "And that's okay, that's always been okay – that's all I deserved."

"Oh my darling, how can you say that?" her husband had demanded. "You are my true and forever love, the only woman I've ever given my heart to, fully and without condition. The only woman I'll ever want."

"But I'm not Violet," she'd said, voice choked with pain.

"And I'm *glad*. Darling heart, she was my childhood love, before either of us even knew what love was, or who we each were. You are my true love Beth, you always have been." Then he'd stared at her, suddenly stricken. "Have I made you feel like that?"

"Of course not, you've been the perfect husband," she'd insisted. "You *are* the perfect husband. I've just felt bad all these years, for stealing you away from her, for tricking you into being with me."

His brow had furrowed, but his voice was firm. "Darling, that's not what happened."

So, summoning up her courage, she'd finally admitted her darkest secret. "I cast a love spell on you," she'd sobbed, then looked up in consternation when he laughed.

"No spell was needed to make me love you Beth."

"But it was," she'd protested. "I don't even know how genuine Violet's feelings were for Andrew..."

He'd laughed again then, and assured her that they most certainly were – but that even if Violet had changed her mind and returned to him, he wouldn't have taken her back. "Darling Beth, don't you see? It's you. It's always been you. *You are my true love.*"

She felt the same rush of warmth now as when he'd said it while she was alive – and noticed that her translucent self had become a little more solid. Was it love that made her form stronger, and guilt that made it weaker? Were they the two opposing emotions?

And how do you judge a life? Is it the sum total of the things you did, the jobs you worked, the people you knew, the impact you had? Were all the bad things you'd done subtracted from your final score, and balanced out by the good, or did one poor decision wipe it all out? Did a life even count, if you didn't do something noteworthy with it? Were you judged on the good that you did, or only on the bad?

Was she a hero or a villain? Her beloved husband and their two sweet children would say she was a hero – brave, kind, strong, courageous, filled with love and empathy. People always saint the ones they lose, and Mike had always seen the best in her. It was what she'd loved so much about him. But surely Violet would think otherwise. And if Carlie or Rose ever discovered her secret, they might think she was the devil incarnate.

Beth sighed. Rose knew. Well, she knew Beth knew something, anyway. When her daughter left home in mysterious circumstances, the priestess had implored Beth to tell her anything she knew, but she couldn't. Or wouldn't. It wasn't like she had any idea where Violet was, so she wasn't really lying. But could she have found out, if she hadn't been so desperate to keep her own secret? To protect herself from people's scorn at her selfish act?

Mike had felt guilty too. When Violet had fallen in love with the shaman while she was still Mike's girlfriend, she'd begged him to pretend they were still together, because she didn't want her mum to know. It had pained him so much to lie to Rose, even when it was just that small, supposedly inconsequential lie. And he hadn't understood why Violet wanted the deception, but he couldn't refuse her.

A few weeks after she disappeared, he'd admitted to Beth that Violet had shared with him a tarot reading Andrew had done for her, which claimed her father would die if she didn't leave home and move to the city with him. Mike had told her how ridiculous that was – even *he* knew the cards would never say that – and she'd agreed to talk it over with Rose. But clearly she hadn't.

As if drawn by this conversation, or the lake of guilt they were drowning in, Rose had come into the cafe where they were having lunch, eyes red from crying, body frail from the double tragedies she'd endured. In a broken voice, she'd begged them to tell her anything they knew, no matter how small, about where her daughter was, or why she'd left.

Mike had looked at Beth, eyes pleading with her for silence, and of course she'd complied. She didn't want to get him into trouble. She knew how much he loved Rose, and how devastated he'd be if he earned the priestess's wrath, which he would if she discovered he'd been deceiving her. Even though it was all Violet's fault. She had forced him to pretend they were still dating while she was off with Andrew, even though it nearly destroyed him. How could their friend have left them in this position? Deserted her parents? Disappeared without a word?

Yet Violet had been lying to everyone for a long time. Had only admitted to Beth just before she left that she'd been dating the shaman for much longer than she'd let on. She must have run off to London with him, but surely she would let her mum know where she was, and how she was, any day now.

As soon as the priestess left, Mike slumped in his seat. "Oh god, why didn't I press Violet about it? Why didn't I tell Rose

she'd broken up with me back when it happened?" he wailed.

"You did that for Violet, because she begged you to."

"This is all my fault," he whispered.

The anguish on his face tore at Beth's heart, and she desperately wished she could ease his pain. Well, ease his pain without making him hate her, which is what would happen if she confessed all that she knew. She stared at him, losing herself in the tears trembling on his lashes, then feeling her own heart hurt in reaction to his. It was more important that she ease his torment than he like her.

As his shoulders slumped lower, she took his hand, her eyes imploring him for understanding while she tried to gather the courage to speak. "It's not your fault, it's mine," she finally said. His eyes jolted up, and he gazed at her with growing horror as she revealed that Violet had been dating Andrew for several weeks before she left. "I didn't know though, she only told me just before she disappeared. But maybe I should have told Rose?"

Mike had taken her hand, right there in the cafe, not caring that people thought he'd only just lost his beloved. "You are so sweet Beth, and so kind. You were just being a good friend to her. And it wouldn't have changed anything, if I'd known earlier."

Groaning inwardly that he thought so much more of her than she deserved, she asked hesitantly if they should mention Andrew to the police. So they went down to the station and told the officer what they knew. He thanked them and put in a call through the psychic development school, but Andrew claimed he had no idea where Violet was, and hadn't seen her for a month.

Relieved that they'd at least told someone, Beth and Mike continued their lives, their friendship slowly deepening. For the first six months after Violet left, they still talked about her whenever they spent time together, but finally she receded from their conversations, and frequented their minds less often.

And when Beth and Mike married three years later, the priestess treated her as a daughter, without suspicion, and Beth slowly lost her fear that Rose would somehow realise what she'd done, and see her secret heart, see her sin branded across her face.

Since she'd become aware she was a ghost though, Beth had pondered the reality of good and bad, heroes and villains... heaven and hell. If those realms did exist, she had no idea which one she'd end up in when this strange half-existence ended. But she realised now that you couldn't walk into the light without going through the darkness – it's what made the light so precious.

Chapter 20

Out of the Darkness

Rhiannon

Almost a week passed before Rhiannon felt brave enough to face another rejection. So when the last Friday of their school holiday dawned, she forced herself to try again. She didn't want them to be like strangers at school. Carlie would need her support, and she wanted to be there for her. Prove she was a good friend.

Shivering, from the cold and her nerves, she knocked on the door of Rose's cottage. She heard footsteps, then the door was wrenched open and Carlie was standing there, face carefully blank. They stared at each other in silence for what felt like ages, Rhiannon trying to imagine the emotions her friend was feeling. Anger, panic, grief, caution, despair, depression, defeat. For her part, she was alternating between worry, guilt, sadness, sorrow, pity, regret… and fear that the door was about to be slammed in her face.

"I suppose you should come in before you freeze to death," Carlie finally said, voice stiff. Rhiannon smiled, relieved, and followed her out to the kitchen, hovering around her as she put the kettle on, but it didn't seem that Carlie was going to say anything else.

"I'm so sorry," Rhiannon finally blurted out. "For your loss, for not being there for you, and for pressuring you in any way." Her smile slipped, and she reached out to her friend, trying to hug her, to connect with her, to bridge the strange awful distance between them. Carlie let herself be held for a moment, then wriggled away on the pretext of fussing with tea leaves and cups.

"I came by a few times…" Rhiannon began tentatively.

"I know. I just, I couldn't talk about it. I can't talk about it. And you were so great about my parents, and so kind to me, I just…"

"You just couldn't understand how I could be such a bitch?" Rhiannon asked flatly, and Carlie looked startled by her honesty. "I've gone over this so many times, replaying each scenario, trying to work out why I reacted the way I did, what drove me to give you such a cruel ultimatum. You have no idea how sorry I am."

Rhiannon watched her friend closely, saw her surprise smooth out to acceptance, then switch back to anger. She winced. No doubt remembering her awful demand. "I admit that I could have acted better, I could have been more understanding. But I panicked. I put my own issues on you, and let my jealousy and insecurities colour how I saw Rowan. Please forgive me."

Handing her a mug of tea, Carlie nodded reluctantly then sat down in the breakfast nook. As Rhiannon joined her, she flashed back to John's comment about how she should tell her friend she wanted coffee instead of tea. Not that this was the time.

"I'm really sorry you had to go through it all on your own too. Not that I would have been your first choice to grieve Rowan with," she added, trying for a flippant tone but not quite pulling it off.

"It's not like I have many options – it's basically you and Rose, whether I like it or not," Carlie replied, then blushed. "Sorry, that came out wrong."

Rhiannon shrugged. "You deserve a few free shots at me."

But Carlie shook her head and changed the subject, asking about her father and brother, and how things were going with John.

"Christmas was nice, just a quiet one with Brodie and Dad, and my grandparents. I think it will always be hard for us, without Mum," Rhiannon said, and Carlie nodded. They both grieved.

"And John is still lovely," she added cautiously. "I've been over to his place a few times now, and he's come to mine. Brodie has loved having something to tease me about, but it's going really well. I really like him…"

She broke off, noticing Carlie's distress just as she started wondering whether she did still think he was lovely. The silence drew out between them, becoming strained and uncomfortable. Rhiannon took a big slurp of tea, swallowed hard, then inhaled deeply.

"So, are you ready for school on Monday?" she asked, trying to make conversation, then rolled her eyes at the question. God, this was excruciating. This was the girl she'd shared everything with – grief, magic, hopes, dreams – yet she suddenly had no idea how to talk to her. She wondered if she should give up and go home.

"As ready as I'll ever be," Carlie finally said, making an obvious effort to engage. "On the plus side, no one even knew I was with Rowan, so no one will ask me about him or get all weird and quiet around me. But that makes me sad too, because it will seem as though he never existed."

Rhiannon winced. "Um, hon? It's a small village. Everyone will know your boyfriend died, even though they didn't know him, but they'll be respectful. And they all knew you were with someone, because they saw you lost in each other while you danced together at the ball, and being crowned Winter Queen and Sun King. Which, if it helps, means there will be lots of photos of you together."

Carlie's eyes misted with tears, and Rhiannon felt awful for bringing it up. "Of course they think his name is Paul, and that he went to Smithfield High," she added wryly. Carlie smiled too, trying to put on a brave face, but they were both relieved when Rose strode into the kitchen and sat with them to drink tea and chat about the next sabbat. There had been enough emotional intensity for one day.

S now was falling as Rhiannon hurried to Carlie's place so they could walk to school together on Monday morning. Her friend's eyes were full of dread, and she took Rhiannon's hand gratefully and let her guide her up the steps. They had different classes first, so Rhiannon dropped Carlie off at her room then rushed across to the science lab, making it just before the teacher.

Taking her seat, she looked with mild curiosity at the new boy who'd come in with him. He was tall and sporty looking, with wavy blond hair, and a tan that made him look like he was from Australia.

It was summer down there right now, rather than the bitterly cold winter they were suffering through. Wherever he was from, he was pretty cute.

"Good morning everyone, I hope you had a good break."

"Good morning Mr Harris," the class chorused.

"I want to introduce you to Jake Mattherson, who's come all the way from Australia."

"Hi Jake!"

"He'll be here for the rest of the school year, so please make him feel welcome. Jake, you can sit there," he said, and the stranger folded himself into the seat in front of Rhiannon, offering her a cheeky smile when their eyes met.

She couldn't believe he really was from Australia, and couldn't wait to tell Carlie. It would be a great excuse to start talking to him too.

When she got to history, she slid into her seat next to Carlie and gave her a quick hug, then their teacher Laura came in – well, Ms Henderson, but she was part of Rose's ritual circle, so it was hard for them to remember to call her that. She was followed by Jake, and Rhiannon elbowed her friend sharply in the ribs.

"He's cute isn't he! He was in my biology class just then," she said with a grin.

Carlie stared at her, unable to mask her shock.

"I'm sorry," Rhiannon whispered, instantly guilt-stricken. "Way too soon for that."

Laura introduced Jake to the class, telling them he was from Australia, but was staying with his grandfather in Summer Hill while his parents spent six months in Africa doing aid work. Rhiannon wasn't the only one who found him fascinating, judging by the whispers of "he's so hot", "he looks like a surfing champion", and similar sentiments that echoed around the room.

"Do you know him Carlie?" one of their classmates asked.

Rhiannon rolled her eyes. "Australia's a big country Dave," she snapped, knowing her friend didn't want any attention on her.

"Carlie's from Sydney, and Jake is from Perth, which is on the other side of the country," their teacher explained. "That's thousands of miles apart, right?"

Jake nodded, then tried to catch Carlie's eye, but she was concentrating on her books. He looked happy when he was paired with her for their major term assignment though, and Rhiannon was glad her friend might have an ally from back home to get to know.

At lunchtime she tried to bring the conversation around to the new boy, but Carlie was surly and disinterested. Until she got suspicious. "Oh no, what are you thinking? I know that look!"

Rhiannon tried to look innocent, but failed miserably. "So, Jake huh. Quite the hot guy, no?"

"You seriously think I'm looking at any guy right now?" her friend demanded, horrified.

"Didn't say it had to be you looking."

"But what about John? I thought all was well with your solstice beloved?"

Torn between a sigh and a grin, Rhiannon nodded, unwilling to think about her growing relationship doubts. "Carlie, please, neither of us has to date him, I'm just making an observation. Namely, that he's a good-looking guy, and seems really sweet. Can't two friends gossip about the cuteness of a hot new boy at school?"

There was a cough close to them, and Rhiannon looked up in panic, worried she'd been overheard. Even worse, overheard by said new boy. She groaned. Jake was standing at their table, holding a tray of food, with an adorable smile on his face. Recovering quickly, she managed to introduce herself and Carlie and invite him to sit with them, and he dropped down into a chair gratefully. In the face of her friend's lack of interest, Rhiannon found herself desperately making small talk, tripping over her tongue as she tried to shape words. What was wrong with her? Carlie's amused glance revealed that she was finding her behaviour a little weird too. Why was she was so nervous around this guy?

I n their last class at school the following day, Rhiannon sneakily passed a scrap of paper to Carlie, then watched her unfold it carefully and peer at the words.

"Coven meeting tonight?"

A wave of sadness washed over her when she saw the look of panic and caution on her friend's face. But something finally made her scrawl yes in reply, so Rhiannon risked another furtive note.

"Your place or mine?"

Rolling her eyes, Carlie put the slip of paper in her pencil case, unwilling to risk their teacher's wrath by continuing the note passing, then turned and pointed at her friend.

"Great," Rhiannon mouthed – then froze when Mr Stephens cleared his throat.

"Ms Stark, is there something you feel you'd like to share with the class?" he thundered.

Blushing, she shook her head and said no, and apologised for interrupting. Then she studiously kept her eyes on her school book, trying to avoid catching Carlie's eye in case they started giggling and couldn't stop.

When the bell rang, she raced home to set up her room, nervous that the energies of the night's dark moon might be too much for Carlie. The dark moon was all about introspection, reflection and banishing the darkness, and she wasn't sure that was where they should dwell right now. She suddenly wondered if pushing for them to have a coven meeting tonight had been wise.

By the time Carlie arrived and she ushered her up to her room, Rhiannon was panicking. "Dad's at a meeting, but he sends his love. He's been really concerned about you, and about Rose," she babbled.

Carlie smiled, a rare smile. "Thank him for me, please. He's so kind. I can see why Mum loved him so much."

"Did she though?" Rhiannon asked, before she could bite her tongue and keep the words from spilling out. Her friend stared at her, puzzled by her challenging tone, so she tried to clarify. "He's been talking about her recently, and he seems to think that she hated him, and that he failed her in some way."

Carlie gasped, shocked. "Not at all! Mum cared about him deeply," she insisted, then paused, her discomfort obvious. Rhiannon grimaced. It was weird talking about her dad's long-ago relationship with Carlie's mother – it felt disloyal to her own mum, and she could only imagine how strange it was for Carlie.

But before she could apologise and change the subject, her friend continued speaking. "Mum felt that *she'd* disappointed *him*, treated him badly, and that she no longer deserved his friendship. She felt so bad for hurting him, and even though she realised later that she'd been manipulated into losing touch with him, she was still so angry with herself for letting him go."

Rhiannon stared at her, curious. "How do you know that?"

"It was in Mum's diary, the one Sandy sent me. She regretted hurting Gran and your dad more than anything – she said that he'd been so kind and supportive to her, so sweet and caring, but she was too stupid to see it. Although she did mention that she hoped he would find much-deserved happiness with a lovely girl called Beth," Carlie said, and they both smiled at the reference to Rhiannon's mum.

"Also, I know it myself, from what I've experienced and what I've seen," Carlie continued. "Your dad has been so wonderful to Gran all these years, and he's helped me too. It was him who finally convinced me to get up and eat something on Boxing Day, to stop worrying Gran, so please let him know that. And let him know how much Mum, Gran and I all appreciate him."

She paused again, trying to summon the courage to keep speaking. "I understand that it's hard for you to hear him talking about my mum, but I think it's just because he's such a kind-hearted man, and cares about everybody."

"I know, and it doesn't bother me any more, I promise," Rhiannon said softly. "I'm just sorry that Dad has lost both of his great loves, and we've both lost our mums. It's not the kind of kindred spirit thing I wanted to share with you."

Carlie smiled wistfully. "It doesn't seem fair, that's for sure." She gazed around the room, taking in the small altar between them on the floor, and Rhiannon took the hint. It was time to move on.

"Do you want to do a ritual tonight, or would you rather we do some study, or just talk?" she asked. "It's the dark moon, so, I don't know, is that too intense?"

Carlie shrugged, still not sure herself. "I guess I've gotta get back on the horse some time, right?" she said, then groaned at the cliche.

Rhiannon nodded. "Was Yule the last working you did?" she asked cautiously, as she sank down onto one of the big purple cushions in the centre of the room. It looked like Carlie was going to cry, and she felt awful for upsetting her, but she was impressed as she watched her friend gather her strength and steel herself against the pain.

"Yes, the last group ritual I did was with Rowan that night. And it was so beautiful. So powerful and magical. Oh, and..." she began, then trailed off. Rhiannon watched as her friend's eyes grew unfocused and a shutter came down, making her expression blank, before a strange sense of peace settled around her shoulders. Then she blinked, and shook herself. "And that was the night I met Jasmine too," she finally murmured.

Rhiannon gazed at her in confusion. She was pretty sure her friend had been thinking of something else, but she didn't want to pry. Besides, she had no idea who Jasmine was, which must have been clear from her expression.

"Oh, you don't know any of that yet do you? Jasmine was at Rowan's retreat. I ended up sitting with her at dinner, and she looked like she'd seen a ghost when she saw me. When she told me her name, I realised why – I'd been reading Mum's journal on the way there, and she'd mentioned a woman named Jasmine who'd tried to help her get away from the shaman, despite being in his circle and risking his wrath by befriending her."

Rhiannon was rapt, and eager to know more, so in the end they didn't perform a ritual or cast a spell, they just talked. About their mums and their experiences of magic, which they were slowly beginning to piece together from the Book of Shadows each had kept, which had found their way to their daughters. About good boyfriends and bad. Rhiannon was shocked by the awful physical and mental abuse Violet had endured in that relationship, and she cried when Carlie revealed that the shaman had smashed Violet into a glass table, as that psychic at the fair had seen – it had been a past event of what had already happened to her mum, not a future vision of something Rowan was going to do to her.

Rhiannon was mortified that she'd got that so wrong, and tried to split Carlie up because of it. Her heart also broke at the pain her friend's mum had suffered.

"Oh god, Dad would just die if he knew. He suspected that man had been cruel, but I can't believe just how terrible it was," she said, voice thick with tears.

Carlie nodded grimly. "Dad found her one day, battered and bleeding, and helped her escape." Then she made a visible effort to lighten the mood. "Mum really did get her happy ever after, eventually."

The door downstairs banged shut, and Carlie jumped. "It's just Dad," Rhiannon said softly. They looked over at the clock on the bedside table, and were surprised to see it was already 10pm.

"I'm so sorry," Carlie said. "I've taken up the whole evening! But I do actually feel a little better for having shared it all with you, so thank you," she added. "I guess I should get home though – I still have a fair bit of homework to do for the morning, and I imagine you do too."

Rhiannon rolled her eyes. "Yeah, a little bit. But thanks for tonight, it's been really nice. I've missed you."

Carlie hugged her then ran down the stairs, and Rhiannon smiled as she blew out the candles and closed the circle she'd cast. She was glad they'd ended up just talking all night, because she felt closer to her friend after they'd shared so much. Confessions seemed easier wreathed in sandalwood incense and candlelight, and the introspective energies had bonded them closer together.

The rest of the week passed quickly, in a blur of history projects, homework, and a surprise test. Since Carlie had been paired up with Jake for their history assignment, he spent a lot of time with the girls, sitting with them at lunch and accompanying them to classes. Carlie was immune to his charm, but Rhiannon liked talking to him, and found his Australian accent and sweet, summery vibe intriguing.

Finally Saturday dawned, and she was on her way to see John. She'd half-heartedly offered to cancel to spend time with Carlie, but her friend had insisted she go. And she was glad, because she needed to see him, and figure out if she still felt the same way about him. Although she knew it was irrational, since he'd planned it before they began dating, she was resentful that he'd gone away, and even worse, that he hadn't seemed to care that they wouldn't see each other for two weeks. And while she hardly dared admit this even to herself, she really liked spending time with Jake. Hopefully that was just because she missed John though, and today would remind her of all the things she loved about him. Well, liked... *Oh god, how did she feel about him?*

When her bus pulled in to the village, John was waiting for her with a bunch of flowers. Relief coursed through her as she realised she really was happy to see him. She'd been worried that she'd exaggerated her feelings for him, carried away by the romance of the ball, but it was real. As soon as she jumped down onto the pavement he scooped her up and spun her around, then his lips found hers and she laughed as she kissed him back.

"How was your camping trip?" she asked, as she tried to catch her breath. "And your first week back at school? How are your brothers?"

John grinned, then kissed her nose. "One question at a time! Besides, that's not the most important thing. Did you miss me? Because I really missed you. And I'm so glad you came over today."

"I did miss you," she conceded, and felt a thrill as he took her hand and led her down the street to their favourite cafe. Scooting into their usual booth, she gazed happily at the flowers while he ordered their coffees, then sighed with pleasure when she took a sip. She still hadn't told Carlie she'd rather drink coffee than tea, so she was savouring this strong, frothy one.

For a few hours they talked, conversation coming easily. They filled each other in on their first week back at school, and the surprise test they'd both had foisted on them in maths. They shared what they'd done for New Year's Eve – Rhiannon's far less exciting than his, since she'd spent the day cooking with her grandma, then stayed in with Brodie, while John had been at a music festival with a bunch of teenagers he'd been camping with. And they reminisced about the ball, and chatted about whether they would nominate for the summer dance committee.

John had also done a tour of their closest university, where he would go for his pharmacy degree. Rhiannon stared off into the distance. She and Carlie had planned to visit the same university soon, to find out about their grief counselling course, yet given her friend's recent loss, she knew it would be better to wait a bit. They preferred that students not have had a personal bereavement in the prior year, since it could make the course too intense. But they'd deal with that when they came to it. Today was for hanging out with John, having fun, and not worrying about the future, or the slight strain that still remained in her friendship with Carlie.

"Are you okay?" John asked softly, and she snapped back to attention, gazing into his kind grey eyes. "You looked like you were miles away."

"Sorry. It's just... oh god, I didn't even get a chance to tell you. Carlie's boyfriend died in a car accident just before Christmas, although I didn't find out for several days because we'd had a bit of... well, a misunderstanding I guess, and, um –"

Sympathy flashed in his eyes, and he took her hand. "You're feeling bad because you were with me, right? You didn't see her earlier because I was taking up all your time?"

She shook her head, but her blush gave her away.

"Oh Rhiannon, you have no reason to feel guilty. Even if you had seen her sooner, it wouldn't have changed the outcome, right? And she might have needed to be alone for a little while anyway, to try to process her feelings."

"That's true. She didn't even talk to her grandma for the first few days," she conceded. "And I'm the last person she would have wanted to see anyway..." She broke off, unwilling to let John know about her ultimatum.

His hand moved to her face, and he tenderly stroked her cheek. "You're there for her now, I'm sure," he said. "But wow, it really blows my mind that you've lost your mum, and Carlie lost both her parents, and now her boyfriend. I haven't lost anyone close to me, not even my grandparents. I don't think I'd be able to cope."

She was saved from having to reply when the waiter brought them another round of coffees, and she sipped hers slowly, trying to focus on the swirls of steam, the chocolate sprinkled on top, and the soothing aroma that always grounded her and made her feel better.

"Thank you," she whispered. "And I'm sorry I brought the mood down. Tell me more about your university visit. Will you be commuting, or living on campus? Do you have any friends doing the same course?"

Over lunch they talked more about their future plans – not getting too specific about whether they had a place in each other's, but not discounting the idea either – then headed off to see a movie, eat popcorn and sneak kisses in the dark. By the time Rhiannon was heading home in the misty gloaming, she felt so much better and more positive about herself and her relationship.

Chapter 21

Rhiannon

When Carlie rolled her eyes a second time at lunch on Monday, Rhiannon paused in her endless stream of chatter. "Oh no, I'm so sorry, I've just been raving non-stop about John, haven't I," she admitted sheepishly. "That's totally insensitive of me."

Carlie shrugged. "It's fine, I promise. And I already told you, I don't expect you to be miserable and not see your boyfriend just because I can't see mine."

Rhiannon winced.

"I'm not being sarcastic, I'm serious. And I'm not being a martyr either. I want you to be happy, and I'm glad you're happy with him. To be honest, I was beginning to think you liked Jake a little more than someone with a boyfriend should."

"Oh my god, of course not!" Rhiannon shrieked. Then she laughed. "Although he is really sweet, and pretty cute too."

Carlie smiled. "Yes, he's a lovely guy, and I'm glad he's our friend. But that's all he is, all right?"

Rhiannon nodded, then laughed again. "Speak of the devil…"

Jake bounced over to them and pulled up a seat, and the three chatted about their weekends, and how incredibly cold the two Aussies were finding the bitter, snow-filled winter. As they began talking about television shows she'd never heard of, and making jokes she didn't understand, Rhiannon drifted off into thoughts of John, and how warm she'd felt in his arms, in the cafe with him, and as he'd held her hand while walking her to the bus. Hmm, maybe tomorrow night she and Carlie could cast a love spell, to strengthen her bond with John, and help bind his thoughts to her in the days they were apart. Help bind her own thoughts to him, and banish her doubts.

But when she got home from school that afternoon, her dad had other plans for her coven night.

"Hi darling, I hope you had a great day," he said, as he poured her a cup of coffee.

"It was okay."

"Um, I'm sorry to do this to you, but it's Brodie's play tomorrow night, and unfortunately I have to work late. Would you be able to meet him after school and help him get ready for it, then stay for the performance?"

Rhiannon pouted.

"I know it's your night with Carlie, but it would mean so much to your brother, and to me."

Reluctantly she nodded, annoyed that she'd miss a night of magic, and she was still grumbling when she started cooking dinner. But when Brodie heard she'd be at the play, his excitement was so genuine that she was swept up in it, and she apologised to her dad for not seeming happier about it when he'd asked.

"I understand," he said, washing the dishes while she dried them. "I know you have a lot more family duties and commitments than everyone else your age, and I really appreciate everything you do. Your mum would be so proud of you." His voice cracked. "And I *am* so proud of you."

Rhiannon smiled, touched by his words. And seeing her brother on the stage the next evening, dressed up as one of the little pigs for the story of the Big Bad Wolf, then as a pirate in the song and dance number, filled Rhiannon with love and warmth. There *were* times she resented the extra chores and the extra responsibilities, but moments like this were precious, and she actually felt sad for her friends who hadn't bothered coming along to support their younger siblings, or who didn't play with them on weekends. Tonight had shown her just how fast Brodie was growing up, and she vowed to never become so busy with her own life that she missed out on being a big part of his.

Her heart melted to see him chatting to his friends while they got ready, and blossoming confidently on stage. Her little brother had been through so much, lost so much, and she worried sometimes that he would forget their mum – or be so scarred by her absence that he couldn't function. But he was a bright, engaged kid, his painful shyness from a year ago gone, and she was further reassured when his teacher approached her at the end of the night to let her know how well he was doing socially and with his school work.

As they walked home hand in hand, jackets pulled tight against the chill in the air, Rhiannon realised how much she was enjoying talking to Brodie and listening to his enthusiastic chatter, and she was touched by how much he liked being with her.

The following night, after she'd done the dishes and tucked her brother into bed, Rhiannon closed her bedroom door and pulled out the wooden chest she kept her ritual tools in. Laying one hand on the candles and the other on her jars of herbs, she battled her indecision. Magic always had consequences, and spells had to be worded very carefully to avoid them backfiring. Love spells were especially tricky, and she'd been fascinated, yet slightly horrified, to read her mum's long-ago spell to make the man she loved fall for her. It had worked – they'd eventually married and had Rhiannon and Brodie – but Beth had written in her Book of Shadows that she regretted the spellcasting. That she'd always wondered whether her husband had loved her freely, or just as a result of her magic.

So Rhiannon knew she had to be careful. Cautious. She didn't want to bind John to her, she just wanted him to know how much she liked him, and for him to like her back. For their doubts about each other when they were apart to disappear.

A jolt of energy flashed up her arm as her hand brushed a black tourmaline crystal. *Protection.* For herself or for John? She breathed deeply, centring herself. The voice inside was calm, clear. *Both.*

Okay then. Lifting out two pink candles and sitting them in their ivy-carved holders, she anointed them with jasmine oil and placed them on the floor in the middle of her room. Then she unscrewed the lid of one of the glass jars and strewed dried pink rose petals in a heart shape around them.

Next she placed a piece of rose quartz along with the black tourmaline within the circle of petals in the north, to represent earth, as well as love and protection. Then she sprinkled some ground patchouli root on a charcoal disc in a censor in the east, to embody air, and the energy of love. In the south, a small orange tealight candle symbolised fire, and passion, and to finish she poured a few drops of water into a clay shell in the west, to hold the power of water.

Once her tiny altar was complete, she visualised a sphere of white light enveloping her and forming the sacred circle of protection around her, then lit the incense and the candles, and dabbed a drop of jasmine oil on her forehead. Inhaling deeply, she felt its sweet scent ground her, and a sensation of comfort and peace surround her.

When she spoke, her voice was soft yet strong.

Elements of nature, and of the earth,
Allow my beloved to see my worth.
Reveal my emotions to him while we're apart,
So he will know the depth of my heart.

A warmth spread through her chest, and from the corner of her eye she saw tiny sparkling lights dancing around her. She blinked, then rubbed her eyes, but they remained, and she smiled as she felt tingles up her spine. The tangible sensation of magic never failed to move her.

With great reverence she farewelled the elements, closed the circle and packed away her ritual tools, then climbed into bed and dropped gently and smoothly off to sleep. All night she dreamed of John. He was holding her close, smiling down into her eyes, and reassuring her that he cared about her, and that their days apart did nothing to dim his feelings for her.

She woke the next morning smiling and feeling relaxed about everything, so she was able to get through Thursday and Friday at school without fretting over their relationship, or boring Carlie with her endless questions and tortured ponderings.

The feeling of enchantment and power was still with her on Saturday when she caught the bus over to meet John, so she was full of excitement instead of apprehension. And when she banged on his door, he answered almost immediately, like he'd been watching for her, and seemed just as keen to see her.

"How are you?" he asked, dragging her inside then pushing her up against the door without waiting for an answer. His lips found hers, his tongue plunged into her mouth, and he pressed his body against hers, hard, knocking the breath right out of her and forcing her arms around him.

Her eyes widened in surprise. Had her witchy working done this? Had she accidentally used red rose petals instead of pink, inspiring lust and desire rather than innocent love? Had her chant somehow gone beyond a lack of doubt to a lack of restraint?

"Hi Rhiannon. How are you today?"

His mother's voice shocked her into action, and she wriggled out from beneath John, cheeks scarlet, mortified to have been caught like this. What had their passion-fuelled embrace looked like to his super-religious mum? She glanced at John, but he just grinned at her as she blushed and tried to get her breathing under control.

"Um, I'm good," she finally managed to gasp.

"Coffee?"

"Please!" she blurted out, and eagerly followed his mother through to the kitchen. She needed a moment to process how she felt about the new intensity of John's kisses.

"Are you over the winter weather too?" Mrs McGowan asked, as she poured out the thick black brew and pushed a jug of milk towards Rhiannon. It took her a minute to figure out what the abrupt change of subject was about.

"Absolutely. I'm so keen for spring to get here, and all the energy of new growth and new beginnings. It's been a tough winter."

His mum gazed at her, puzzled. Oops, too much information. Quickly she fixed her coffee, and one for John, then carried them out to the lounge room.

"Thanks," he said, taking a sip and gazing at her with an ardour she didn't remember seeing before. Did he always look at her that way, and she just hadn't noticed? Or was she simply reading too much into his expression, overly paranoid because of her spell?

"What did you want to do today?" John asked. "I was thinking we could go out for lunch first, then come back here – I got that movie we were talking about last week, so we could watch it later?"

That all sounded normal enough. "Perfect."

Gulping down her coffee, Rhiannon took the cups back out to the kitchen, said a quick goodbye to John's mum, then followed him out the door. He took her hand as they walked to the cafe, and once inside they caught up on their week, and homework and friends, and talked again about the summer dance – all the usual topics. And he seemed to be back to his regular self as they ate burgers, shared chips and drank milkshakes. Relief swept over her. Perhaps she'd misinterpreted his over-enthusiastic greeting.

Once back at his place, John made them coffee, popped some popcorn, and grabbed a big woollen blanket. Snuggling up under it on the couch, they started watching the movie, and Rhiannon relaxed into the cosy warmth, caught up in the magic of the story and the soothing feel of John's hand in hers.

"Sorry to interrupt, but I'll see you both later," his mum said from the doorway. "I'm off to pick your brothers up from soccer, then we'll be shopping for the afternoon before we meet your dad."

"No worries. Bye Mum," John said.

"Thanks for having me Mrs McGowan."

"It's always lovely to see you Rhiannon. Take care." And she headed out the front door in a cloud of perfume.

John turned to Rhiannon and grinned. "Alone at last."

She smiled at him, then turned back to the TV screen, but John reached out a hand to her and drew her back to face him.

"I've missed you so much. I wish there was another school ball to plan, so we could see each other more often, spend time together during the week." And he leaned in and kissed her.

A shiver of desire rippled through her, and she kissed him back, the movie forgotten as he held her close, peppering her cheeks and her neck with kisses, his hands in her hair, around her shoulders, drawing her closer until they were melded together under the heavy blanket.

As John's breathing quickened and his kisses became more forceful, Rhiannon drew back, flustered. He opened his eyes and smiled at her, while his hands moved to her shoulders, caressing her, holding her tight. For a moment she froze, as a vague memory of other hands, other heated kisses, overtook her, but she gazed into John's clear grey eyes and forced herself to shrug them off. And slowly she returned his kisses.

Her stomach tightened and butterflies danced within her when one of his hands found its way under the blanket, and under her shirt. His cold fingers burned her warm flesh, then slowly heated up as they drew circles around her bellybutton, around her waist, then down to her hip. And all the while his lips remained on hers, gentle but insistent. Unrelenting.

Rhiannon's cheeks flushed with want, and she wriggled her body against his until her arms were around his broad shoulders, exploring the muscles of his back. She smiled as goosebumps covered his skin wherever her hand touched him, and when he deepened their kiss she went with it, liking the heat that burned between them, and the way she seemed to be melting against him.

Dimly she was aware of the touch of his hand as it grew more intense, more demanding. She felt him caressing her hip, stroking her tummy, then slowly moving lower. Her breath caught. She waited anxiously, trying to calm her breathing, but when his fingers began to slide under the waistband of her jeans, she yelped in surprise, and jerked back, away from him.

Eyes dazed, John gazed up at her. "Rhiannon," he breathed, voice raspy as he tried to pull her back into his arms and trap her lips under his again.

But she pushed against him, overwhelmed and a little panicked.

"I have to go," she cried out.

"Wait," he implored. "We can just finish the movie."

They turned to the screen, but it was blank, the movie long over, and the player shut off.

"I'll see you soon," she said, as she grabbed her bag and headed for the door.

"Can I still come over tomorrow?" John asked desperately. "I really miss you."

She smiled despite herself. "Um, yes, of course. I'll see you then."

And she ran.

As the bus headed back to her village through the early dusk, confusion swamped her. Had she wanted him to stop? Or go on? Was she just scared of his parents coming home early and catching them, or scared of him and his fervour? And was it all simply the result of her spell backfiring, and accidentally making him desire her more than usual, or were his feelings true?

God, now she had an inkling of how her mum had felt all those years, wondering if her relationship was real, or fuelled by magic.

And what was she so scared of anyway? They'd been dating for a month, and had been friends for weeks before that, and she was seventeen. She was a grown-up, a woman, capable of love, and sex…

So why had she run out on him? She thought back over their afternoon, her lips tingling as she recalled his passionate kisses. Closing her eyes, she replayed the rest, squirming as she remembered the feel of his hands on her body, visualised the flush of his cheeks and the desire in his gaze.

It had felt so good. *He* had felt so good. And she really liked him, and knew he liked her. But was she ready for their relationship to become physical? And why was the very idea of it terrifying her?

Chapter 22

Gardenias for Growth

Beth

Golden light from the full moon was spilling into the bedroom as Beth became solid again. Was it the shining lunar orb that had brought her back this time? As the clock ticked seven o'clock, she heard Brodie's laughter snaking up the stairs to her, and caught the hum of voices as Rhiannon and Mike crashed pots and pans and ran the hot water while washing up together after dinner. She sighed. The bliss of ordinary family life. That's what she missed the most.

The sweet scent of the huge white flowers in her hair wove around her, making her smile. Gardenias represented love and purity, love and marriage, love and protection, but they were also a symbol of secret love. She recalled the vase of the fragrant blooms she'd kept in her room while pining after Mike, and the hope their aroma had given her while she waited for him to recover from Violet's loss.

Lifting a hand to her head, she imagined she could feel the softness of the petals, then she gazed down curiously to see the golden-brown dress she'd loved so much swirling around her ankles. And although she'd usually worn silver jewellery, tonight she had a rose gold chain around her neck, with a large crescent moon pendant resting heavily on her chest.

Oh! She knew this memory, this night. It was a ritual at Rose's healing centre, before Violet had broken Mike's heart, before she'd disappeared forever, back when the two girls had been friends, the way their daughters were now.

On that long-ago evening, Beth had got ready with Violet at her place, the small but cosy, welcoming cottage that was so different from her own larger, colder house. They'd danced around the room as they played music, brushing each other's hair, and weaving the beautiful blooms into garlands they pinned into their long flowing locks. Then they'd raced, hand in hand, into the village, the mists winding and twisting around them as they passed, glittering in the last rays of sunset, cooling their cheeks, and making them feel as though they were the only two people on earth.

As they neared the park they'd slowed down, then without having to speak, or ask, slipped inside and wandered onto the path. The trees had cast strange shadows in the approaching twilight, and the fog thickened around them the deeper within they walked.

"Wait, did you see that?" Beth asked suddenly, gripping Violet's arm as a tremor of fear rushed through her.

Violet turned inquisitive eyes on her friend. "What is it? Don't tell me you can see Brauna?"

A strange hunger filled Beth, and while she had no idea who or what Brauna was, had never heard the name before, she felt safe next to Violet, and ready to leap into the magic of whatever the priestess's daughter had in mind.

In that moment a woman stepped out of the mists, a long midnight-blue cloak hanging from her shoulders, and whirling around her as though it was a thing alive. A thing more real than she was. Beth's heart thudded, yet a sensation of peace surrounded her, enveloping her in warmth and comfort.

"Beloved," the mysterious figure said, her voice a whisper, a memory, a cocoon. She stepped forward and took Beth's hand, making her shiver. Who – or what – was this being?

"I am whatever you need me to be," she crooned. "I am the Lady of Water, the woman in blue. I am the sigh of your emotions as you push them away and deny them."

Confusion clouded Beth's mind, making it hard to think, hard to focus. "But –"

Tinkling laughter swept through the trees, and in an instant the woman had enfolded Beth in her arms, her embrace unexpectedly soothing. The fragrance of the flowers in her own hair mingled with the earthy, woody scent that radiated from the blue-robed being, and the combination made Beth feel instantly connected to nature as well as every living thing around her.

"I know you have suffered child. You have been hurt by your family, and hurt by the one you thought was your beloved, but I am here to tell you there is a greater love coming for you, along with the love of the family you will create around you, the people you will choose to give your heart to, and want to spend your life with."

That sounded nice, but it all felt so far away. Beth was struggling to cope with being back in her childhood home, living under the same roof as her cold, cruel mother and emotionally absent father. And while she was becoming a little closer to her estranged sister, whose wedding was the reason she had temporarily returned, it was killing her inside to see herself through her mother's eyes – see her failure, and the disappointment she clearly was to everyone.

"Try to release your anger, and the sense of injustice that is burning you up. Focus on the positive. On the friendship you have right here," the woman said, indicating Violet, who was standing frozen beside them. Had the blue-clad figure somehow stopped time? What on earth was happening?

"Focus on the magic you are beginning to feel," she continued. "On the sense of potential and possibility that is swirling around you, which I can see, and the priestess Rose can see. Things will work out as you wish, once you accept all of your self, and all that you can be. Have faith."

It took Beth a while to realise that the sigh she heard, which sounded as though it came from deep within the earth itself, had come from her own lips. It was a sigh of relief, that someone knew her heart, and a sigh of hope, that she could escape the misery of her own family and dream a better one into being.

She looked up, to press for more details, but the woman was no longer there. Had she ever been there? Or was she just a hallucination? A feverish wishing for a better life? "But –"

Eyes wild, she turned to Violet, squeezing her arm in alarm. "Who was that? *What* was that? Or... was she even there? Did you see her? Hear her? Or am I going crazy?"

Her friend smiled, but there was envy in her eyes, and yearning. "What did you see?"

Head spinning, Beth tried to focus, tried to remember, tried to put it into words. "A woman dressed in blue, who seemed real, and yet she was all misty too. She appeared to embody the earth, or all the elements really, including water." Pausing, she tried not to laugh, worried that she was on the edge of hysteria and would never be able to stop once she started. "She had a message for me, and it was so comforting, so beautiful, and yet... she isn't even real!"

She started to tremble as horror rushed through her. Clearly she was losing her mind, thinking she was conversing with a being no one else could see. But Violet put a hand on her shoulder, bringing her back to the present, back to her physical surroundings, to reality.

"You're not going crazy Beth, don't worry," she said kindly. "Not everyone sees her, but for those she has a message for, apparently she can take physical form, human form."

"What!?" Beth jerked backwards, releasing her friend's arm and slipping from her grasp as her eyes widened in fear. She'd been joking about her not being human. "I don't understand."

"Well, you know how Mum calls in the elements and the directions as well as the god and the goddess at the beginning of our rituals?"

Beth nodded. She adored Violet's mother Rose, and desperately wished she'd been lucky enough to be the priestess's daughter, to have grown up accepting magic and spirits and beings out of time.

"It sounds like this was one of the women who embody that essence, kind of like the spirit of nature I guess. Or the embodiment of an aspect of the goddess."

It was too much for Beth. "I... um, oh god, I don't know. Seriously, am I going crazy? This can't be real. Did you plan this?"

Violet's laughter sounded like the woman's, sweet and high. It could have been part of the bird song, part of the wind. "Of course not silly, how could I?

Brauna comes to those who need her, not at anyone's bidding. I've never seen her, I've just heard about her." She paused for a moment, and a look of deep sadness, almost betrayal, crossed her face.

"Anyway, I guess we should head down to the healing centre – the ritual will be starting soon. You're welcome to call one of the quarters if you'd like to, to connect more deeply with water, and the west. With your Lady of Water?"

Shaking her head, too shy and uncertain to even contemplate that right now, Beth tried desperately to get her mind around it all. It felt too strange, too crazy, to be real. And yet, wasn't that what Rose's rituals were about? Connecting with nature, with the elements, with your own inner heart? Maybe the figure had just been a projection of her own dreams, her own doubts, her own mind – a hallucination of sorts. That made way more sense.

"Okay, let's go." As she took Violet's hand and let her guide her out of the trees and back to the safety of the physical footpath, Beth filed away the memory of her strange encounter under wishful thinking and a yearning for real magic. And yet as Rose invoked the goddess that night, then guided them through a ceremony of enchantment and power, a tiny part of Beth was waking up, was beginning to wonder. Could the flutterings of hope she felt be true? Could there be another layer to this world, another dimension she would be able to tap in to?

What she experienced in that temple space with Rose was unlike anything Beth had ever felt or experienced. She'd been to church with her family as a child, but it had washed over her without touching her spirit. Knowing that her parents went only to be seen, to be social, stripped away some of the mystery, and the disconnect between the Christian ethos they espoused and their cruelty to her and others just made her angry. She'd always longed to feel the spiritual connection others felt in church, but it wasn't until her first ritual with Rose that she finally found it.

She was so grateful to the priestess for allowing her to stay within her circle, of women and of magic. Even after Violet ran away, Rose welcomed her, never judging her, always embracing her, even when she started dating, and eventually married, the man the priestess had thought her own daughter would wed.

And Rose had become a dear part of their family, a kindly grandmother figure to Rhiannon and Brodie, and a maternal one to Beth. Rose had performed her wedding ceremony, and had no doubt had to do her funeral too.

Tears welled in Beth's eyes, and she was shocked to see one drip onto the floor. Poor Rose. She had buried far too many people, lost far too much. Then pain shot through Beth at the awful reminder that she was dead. That the priestess had lost another one. Not that she'd *forgotten* she was a ghost, but the beauty of the moments she was so grateful to be reliving was making it even harder to deal with the knowledge that she no longer existed, in the physical realm at least. And that she might disappear from even this strange half-life at any moment.

Movement and a flash of gold from the corner of her eye made Beth spin around in panic. Was something following her? Seeking her out? Suddenly she was terrified that something wanted to lead her away from the living and deposit her somewhere... *other*. And she realised this wasn't the first time she'd felt unsettled, felt a presence other than herself. How had she managed to disregard it until now? And what was it?

The first time it happened she'd been lying in bed with Mike, cuddled up against him as she tried to soothe his tears, hold him safe, provide some comfort in his grief. She'd felt a prickle of disquiet, but had dismissed it immediately, too focused on her husband to worry about something feeling out of place.

And it had happened again recently, now that she thought about it, when she'd been in the kitchen, happily watching her husband and daughter chat while they made dinner together. For a moment that night she'd become aware of something amongst them, a presence perhaps, yet she'd ignored it then as well, far too caught up in the warmth she felt in the company of her loved ones.

But this was the first time she'd seen something. Now it was becoming clearer to her, more solid, even though it dissolved away into nothingness the moment she turned to face it, to try to catch it, to communicate with it. What was it? What did it want with her? Uneasiness stole over her, and she felt haunted, and hunted.

Fear made her heart race. She wasn't ready to leave her family, not for a second time. She still needed to be here, to know that they would be okay without her.

"Who are you?" she whispered. "What do you want from me?"

Silence greeted her, silence and the scent of gardenias, wafting in through the open window, lulling her into memories of love and friendship and enchantment.

"Please, you can't take me yet," she implored. "I need more time. Time I didn't have before, when I would have been able to actually help. Are you the one who took me then?"

Laughter from downstairs reached Beth, and broke her concentration. The feeling of someone else – something else – being with her faded, and she became aware that she was alone again.

Alone.

She broke down and wept.

Chapter 23

Passion and Power

Rhiannon

"Sorry!"

When Rhiannon knocked her coffee mug over and the hot liquid splattered across the table and started dripping onto the floor, her dad looked up abruptly from his newspaper.

Swearing at her clumsiness, and the burn on her hand, she grabbed a cloth to clean up the mess.

"Are you okay darling?" her dad asked.

Nodding impatiently, she scrubbed at the table and floor, then sank back into her seat and finished her toast.

"Did you want to come to the winter fair with me and Brodie today? We'll be leaving soon."

"I can't, I have that assignment to finish, and John is coming over for lunch."

Her dad looked at her shrewdly, and she couldn't keep the tell-tale blush from her cheeks. She was still confused by what had happened the day before. And was swinging wildly between anxiety over seeing him again, and wishing she'd stayed on his couch with him and given herself over to their passion.

"Don't worry, he knows I have to get my homework done. And he has loads too."

"I'm not worried darling, I know you'll be sensible. It's just that –"

Whatever he'd been planning to say was interrupted when Brodie came tearing into the kitchen, calling out for more toast. Rhiannon breathed a sigh of relief. She was so not ready to have *that* conversation with her father.

Once her brother and dad had left, she jumped in the shower then pulled out her homework, determined to get some done before John arrived. But she couldn't concentrate. Her thoughts kept straying to the way his lips had felt on hers, how desire had heated her body when he'd deepened the kiss, the tingling she'd felt as his hands moved ever lower from her shoulders, to her stomach, to her hip, to…

Throwing herself down on her bed, she gave up on her assignment and thought about what she would do when her boyfriend arrived. Should she take him out to a cafe, where they would be safe from each other, or stay in and have lunch at home, where they both risked giving in to the desire that had consumed them yesterday? If only she knew what she wanted. Whether she was ready. And if he was the one to go there with…

When John knocked she was no closer to a decision, and her heart started racing, whether in anticipation or fear she wasn't sure. Quickly she rushed down the stairs and threw open the door – and as soon as she caught sight of him, slouching nervously on the verandah, she dragged him inside and kissed him.

"Hello," he said when she finally allowed him to pause for breath. "It's good to see you too."

Rhiannon blushed and ushered him through to the kitchen. "Coffee to warm you up? Your cheeks are so cold!"

"I could think of better ways to warm up," he said, raising one eyebrow and smirking at her.

Oh god! What should she do?

"Aren't you hungry?" she asked as she filled the kettle.

As soon as she'd switched it on, John grabbed her around the waist and spun her around. "Very hungry," he almost growled, his voice low and husky in her ear as he pushed her up against the bench. Then he pressed his lips to hers and drew her into his arms.

Rhiannon shivered, part fear, part desire, as her body seemed to fit so neatly against his.

"So, wanna see my room before we eat?" she blurted out, before she could think it over and second-guess herself.

His eyes became deep pools of want as he nodded, and she took his hand and led him up the stairs.

At the threshold of her room she paused, uncertain again, then she took a deep breath and marched inside.

"Hey, we don't have to do... anything," he said gently. "We can take it slow."

Rhiannon shrugged. "But I really liked kissing you yesterday. Didn't you like kissing me?"

His grin was slightly lopsided, and he nodded. "Of course. But I don't want to rush you, rush us. You don't have anything to prove."

A flash of anger that she didn't understand shot through her, but she shook it off and went over and sat on her bed. John stood in the doorway, looking unsure, and for a moment she wavered. Then she remembered how it had felt when he'd held her so tight yesterday, and she stood up and sauntered over to him.

Sliding her hands under his shirt, she felt warmth and energy rush into her as her palms slid along the hard muscles of his chest. When his eyes widened in surprise then pleasure, she ripped his shirt off and threw it over her shoulder. He gasped, and looked conflicted for a moment, but when her nails pressed into his flesh, he smirked and crushed her body to his. Then he angled her towards the bed, and before she knew it they were lying there together, him propped up on one arm to keep his weight from squashing her.

For a long time they just kissed. He was cautious with his hands, and gentle with his kisses, and she began to relax into it. But soon their kisses deepened, and she felt herself responding to his touch, her whole body on fire. Forgetting her shyness, she let her hands roam over him, loving the hardness of his chest, the strength of his arms, and the weight of him as his body pressed down on hers. When he slipped her t-shirt over her head she didn't stop him, and she liked the way his eyes darkened with passion as he gazed hungrily at her.

Gingerly his hands caressed her shoulders, then as he became more confident of her reaction, he dropped his head and kissed her neck. She shivered, then moaned softly when his tongue traced a path from her lips down to the hollow of her throat. As his teeth grazed her flesh, she thought she would melt away to nothing, so she focused on the heat of his hands through her bra, then trembled when his thumb slipped beneath the fabric, cool as it traced circles on her hot skin. She gasped, and he increased the pressure, groaning as his whole hand pressed against her.

A jolt of heat shot through her when he reached around to unhook her bra. She tried not to giggle, that it took him a while – she was glad he wasn't too practised at the manoeuvre. Then it was on the floor along with her shirt, and she stopped thinking altogether, consumed by the sensation of their bodies pressed together, the contrast of fire and ice doing strange things to her.

This time when his hand slid lower, she surrendered to the sensation. Her awareness had shrunk down to three points. His mouth, hot and wet on her skin; one hand, kneading her flesh then becoming butterfly light; and the other caressing the flesh of her stomach, which tightened in reaction to each stroke of his fingers.

"I love you," she murmured.

His body stiffened for a moment, then he relaxed, and continued kissing and caressing every part of her.

Senses blurring, she raked her nails up his naked back, while her other hand twisted in his hair as she pulled him closer to her. He cried out, and she pulled away, scared that she'd hurt him.

"Sorry," she whispered, embarrassed, but he looked up at her and grinned, eyes clouded with want.

"Don't stop," he groaned, then his lips found hers again, and she kissed him back with an abandon she'd never felt before. They were skin to skin, heat to heat, but she wanted to get even closer to him, to be even more consumed by the white-hot lust she was drowning in. Her breathing was ragged, her body burning up wherever he touched her. When his lips left hers she whimpered, desperate for them to return, but then they scorched a trail of fire down her neck that was almost better, while his hand slid under the waistband of her skirt and moved lower.

When he pulled back she felt bereft, and as he stared into her eyes, she knew she must look just as dazed as he did. He raised an eyebrow in question, and Rhiannon hesitated for only a moment before she nodded.

Drugged with desire, she arched her back and pressed her body upwards to meet his – just as a door slammed downstairs and her dad called out her name.

She swore, then moaned in frustration as John leaped away from her, as though their heat had suddenly scorched him. A chill rushed over her skin, and her body felt naked, deprived, without his touch. But the panic she felt when she saw they'd left her door open quickened her pace. She fumbled for her t-shirt and pulled it over her head, then finally located her bra and pushed it under her bed with one foot. She was trembling, but again she didn't know if it was from fear or desire, or some strange mix of the two.

"I'll be down in a minute!" she yelled, eyes darting wildly around the room as one hand raked through her hair, trying to tame it, while the other smoothed down her quilt in an attempt to erase any evidence of their passion.

Finally she looked up at John, embarrassed that they'd almost been caught, and devastated that they'd had to stop.

He stared at her, eyes still glazed. "God, I want you so bad."

She blushed, then laughed as she realised he'd lost one of the buttons on his shirt when she'd ripped it off him. She slid it under her bed too, then John leaned in and kissed her, his tongue forcing its way into her mouth, and sending another ripple of lust through every inch of her body.

"Next time," he sighed.

She nodded. "Ready?"

"Oh, I'm ready," he said, pressing his body against hers and warming her in an instant.

"Me too," she said sadly. "But not for that. Ready to face Dad?"

"As I'll ever be."

Regretfully she pushed him towards the door, ran a hand through her hair again, then led him downstairs.

"Hey Dad," she said as casually as she could. "John was just offering some help on my assignment."

"Hi John."

"Hello Mr Stark."

Rhiannon tried to hide her laugh. She'd never seen John look so uncomfortable. Nor her dad for that matter.

"Darling, unfortunately I got a call from work almost as soon as we got to the fair, so I have to go in to the office for a while. Can you watch Brodie this afternoon?"

"Sure," she said brightly, but inside she was screaming in frustration. Oblivious to what she was feeling, her dad picked up his briefcase and hurried out.

"You kids behave," he threw back over his shoulder. Rhiannon's cheeks flamed, and John sounded like he was choking, before he turned it into a coughing fit. Before she could reply, Brodie ran in and threw himself at her with an enthusiastic hug.

Then he dropped his arms and turned to her boyfriend. "Hi John," he said, his voice so innocent after the passion that had drenched theirs just five minutes ago.

John stammered out a reply as Rhiannon busied herself with the kettle again.

"Coffee?" she asked. "And have you had lunch Brodie?"

"No, Dad got the phone call just before we ordered. Could I have a sandwich please?"

"Of course." She glanced over at John. "Hungry?"

"You have no idea," he muttered.

She placed a hand on his chest. "Yes, I do." Her voice was low, and just as frustrated as his.

"John, will you come and play a game with me while Rhi-Rhi makes lunch?" Brodie asked.

"Sure buddy, let's go." When Brodie turned away, John kissed Rhiannon, hard, then headed to the lounge room.

Sitting on the couch together this time was torture, and a lot of sighing went on throughout the afternoon. Thankfully her dad returned just before John had to leave.

"I'll walk you to the bus stop," Rhiannon said, and practically dragged him out of the house. They hurried through the village hand in hand, then clung to each other in the shelter of the bus stop while they waited. Their kisses were deep, and desperate, and when the headlights of the bus swept over them they both swore. It was going to be another week before they saw each other again.

"I'll miss you so much," Rhiannon said, still holding his hand while he moved towards the bus.

John leaned down and pressed his lips to hers. "It's been fun. I can't wait for this to continue," he said with a grin. "Good luck with getting your assignment finished!"

And he was gone. Rhiannon stared at the retreating tail lights, shocked. *It was fun.* Not: "I'll miss you," or "I love you," just: "It's been fun." All the excitement leeched out of her, and an icy chill stole over her, body and soul. Was he only interested in her because he thought she'd sleep with him?

At dinner she was quiet, preoccupied, and although her dad tried to reach her, to discover what was wrong, she just mumbled vaguely then headed upstairs the minute the dishes were done.

Restless, she threw herself onto her bed, peering up at the ceiling and trying to divine answers in the patterns of the moonlight playing out across the smooth surface. It didn't help though. And she wasn't even sure what was upsetting her most – the disappointment of being interrupted, or the idea that she had been prepared to go all the way with someone who didn't seem to like her as much as she'd thought. And now that she was questioning him and his motives, she was even more uncertain of her own feelings.

Oh no! Her whole body flushed with embarrassment as she remembered that she'd told him she loved him – and he hadn't replied. His body had stiffened slightly, so he must have heard her. He just hadn't said it back, even in the heat of passion, because he obviously didn't feel it.

And if John didn't really care about her, was she just one of many? Had it not been as meaningful for him as it would have been for her?

Now all her past uncertainties were rearing their ugly heads again, just when she'd decided to trust him, and cut him some slack over his New Year's trip. God, had he had sex while he was away, getting drunk and partying with all the girls he'd known from previous years?

Why was it all so hard?

Chapter 24

Letters of Love

Rhiannon

After tossing and turning all night, Rhiannon was no closer to a conclusion – she was just tired, and frustrated that she wouldn't see John until the next weekend. Would she spend the whole week obsessing over how he felt about her, how far they'd gone, and what would have happened if her dad hadn't come home?

She couldn't really talk to Carlie about it either, since she'd been less than understanding when her friend had broached the topic of sex regarding Rowan. And Jake was with them at every break, sitting with them at lunch, walking them to class. It was pretty clear that he liked Carlie, and Rhiannon thought they would make the ideal couple. They were both kind and sweet and smart, and both living with their grandparent. They were from the same country, and were the same age too. She'd always worried that Rowan was too old for Carlie, but Jake was kind of perfect.

Hmm, maybe at their coven night this week they could do a summoning of a loved one spell or something, to see if Carlie could open her heart to someone new. And Rhiannon could try to understand her relationship, or lack thereof, with John.

But on Tuesday morning their history teacher announced they'd all be doing a presentation the next day on where they were up to with their research project. Panic broke out, since no one had started their home study sessions, so instead of working magic with Carlie, Tuesday afternoon saw Rhiannon on the bus out to Dave's farm to begin their assignment.

It wasn't fair. Not only did they have to miss another coven night, but she had to travel miles to work with her annoying partner, while Carlie got to walk to Jake's place and hang out with their mate. She wished she'd been paired with him, but she couldn't really begrudge her friend the easier ride. She did want all the details though.

"So, how was your night with Jake?" she asked at lunch the next day, wiggling her eyebrows suggestively.

Carlie stared at her in confusion. "What do you mean? We did some research, I had a cup of tea with his grandad, then I walked home and had dinner with Rose."

"But he's nice, isn't he?" Rhiannon pressed.

Carlie shrugged. "I guess so, why?"

"And he's cute, right?"

This time her friend glared at her. "Do you want me to ask him out for you?" she asked, her frustration barely contained.

"Don't be daft, I've got John," Rhiannon said, ignoring how forced her laugh sounded. "I was thinking of you. Maybe the four of us could double date or something? Jake does seem to really like you, like, *like* like you. And you're both Aussies, so you have lots in common. Half the time I don't know what you're talking about when you're raving about things from back home."

"Seriously Rhi?" Carlie snapped. "The love of my life just died, or have you forgotten about that? The funeral was only three weeks ago. I'm not sure if you remember him? His name was Rowan, and you used to think he was really amazing." Sarcasm dripped from each word. "He helped us with our assignments, and took us to festivals – and he respected you as my best friend perhaps more than he should have, if you can seriously ask me this."

Rhiannon shrugged and blundered on, despite the warning note in her friend's voice. "I know Carlie, and I get it. But you'd only been together for a few months, so you need to keep a bit of perspective. I don't mean you should be totally over him already and never think of him again, or try to forget how important he was to you, but life goes on. You can't put your whole life on hold and act like a widow at seventeen," she said.

"Surely I'm allowed to grieve for a few weeks though?" Carlie retorted, voice cold.

Rhiannon mustered a smile. "I'm sorry, I guess this is coming out wrong. I just don't want you to punish yourself for something that isn't your fault, or feel that you have to deny yourself happiness and friendship, or a new relationship, because he died. I don't mean to offend you hon, I promise."

Frustration radiated from Carlie. "I'm glad you're not *trying* to offend me, but I don't know how to be any clearer – I don't want to date anyone right now, so there's no point going on with this. Why don't you tell me how Brodie is, or how it's going with John, and let this subject drop?" she insisted.

Chastened for the moment, Rhiannon finally took the hint. "Brodie's going really well, I'm so proud of him. And it's going well with John, I really like him." She spoke fast, to hide her uncertainty and disappointment. "Actually, we're thinking of going to see a band on Saturday night, if you want to come. You could ask Jake."

Carlie rolled her eyes in exasperation.

"I meant as friends, so you'd have someone to talk to while I was with John, and so you could meet my boyfriend properly, okay? But don't exaggerate the impact of your loss too much. I know you think you really loved Rowan, but there's a chance you would have broken up with him a few months from now, and dealt with it all then, and then you would have moved on, met someone else. And later you would look back and think your time with him was a nice teenage romance, one of many," she said, blundering onwards.

"Death can add more weight to a relationship than what was truly there," Rhiannon continued. "Like, someone having a nasty ex-wife to deal with is one thing, the guy can move on and date again, and the new girlfriend doesn't feel threatened, but being a tragic widow with a sainted dead wife is a totally different story, and is so much harder for someone new to deal with."

Carlie glared at her. "I'm guessing you're not *trying* to upset me as much as it sounds like you are?"

"Geez, you're so sensitive," Rhiannon griped, even as she realised she was giving her friend a hard time to avoid thinking about her own romantic problems.

Blinking in surprise, Carlie took a deep breath and tried to respond calmly. "Let me be clear. The guy I love just died in a tragic accident. He'd told his manager he wanted to travel less so he could spend more time with me. He was helping me heal my grief at the recent death of my parents, which, you know, is still pretty hard to deal with, and he loved me deeply. I can't just 'get over it', no matter how much I want to. And I really thought you would understand this. You've lost someone close to you, you know that it's hard to cope with, and that it's impossible to go on like nothing happened."

"You can't compare losing my mother to losing your boyfriend," Rhiannon said indignantly.

"I'm not Rhi, god! I'm just asking that perhaps you could be a little more understanding, and try to hear me when I say that I need some time to process my grief and loss, to get over the guy I loved so much – and that finding someone else to date is really not at the top of my list of priorities."

She sighed impatiently. "I can't even look at another guy, let alone want to go out with anyone. And seriously, someone being Australian – from the other side of the country no less – is not really a reason for me to date them."

"I'm sorry Carlie, I do understand that it's hard for you," Rhiannon said, tone conciliatory. "And I'm sorry about the way my words came out – I didn't mean to be insensitive, or to upset you in any way. I guess I just hope that soon you'll be able to look at your relationship slightly more big-picture, and put it all in context. You hadn't been with Rowan that long, and... well, you know, if something happened to John now, I mean it would be awful, and I'd be sad, but I'd get over it."

"Please stop," Carlie said sharply, voice thick with pain and unshed tears. "I really can't talk about this anymore. And wow, maybe you should have a think about why you *wouldn't* be a mess if your boyfriend died. What's the point of being with someone you're not in love with? Who you wouldn't miss if, heaven forbid, something happened to them? And how can you even talk about him like that?"

Then, face showing her horror, she picked up her bag and ran outside, away from her friend and her awful judgement.

Rhiannon sat at the table alone, wondering what had just happened, and what had made her say all those awful things. And would she really not care if something happened to John? Carlie was right, if she didn't love him she was wasting her time, and his. And she definitely shouldn't be sleeping with him if that was the case. If only her mum was still here to talk to...

The next day Rhiannon didn't see her friend – they had no classes together, and Carlie must have gone home for lunch, because she couldn't find her in the cafeteria. But maybe that was best, it would give her time to cool down. Give them both time to cool down.

On Friday, Rhiannon, Brodie and their dad took the day off and left early to drive up to see her grandparents for the weekend. She had a wonderful two days with them, but managed to convince her father to head home early on Sunday morning, ostensibly to get some homework done – but really so he could drop her in Smithfield so she could see John. Her dad wasn't even mad at her for the deception, just happy that she was opening herself up to someone, so she didn't have the heart to tell him how conflicted she felt over the relationship. But she was hoping that seeing John again would help.

Unfortunately though it was a frustrating afternoon – his brothers were with them, so they couldn't really talk, and the answers she'd hoped to find just by seeing him didn't magically appear. On top of that, there was a shadow hanging over her that she couldn't ignore. She was uneasy about how she'd left things with Carlie, so she finally made her excuses and got the bus home.

But once she was standing cold and breathless at Rose's front door, she suddenly had no idea what to say. Before she could turn around and leave, the door swung open and Carlie was gazing at her, looking surprised and a little anxious. Which was fair enough. They hadn't spoken since Wednesday, when she'd told her friend to hurry up and get over Rowan.

"Oh, it's you," Carlie said, not sounding exactly overwhelmed with enthusiasm.

"Um, hello," Rhiannon began, voice shaking a little with apprehension. "I just got back from Nan and Pop's, and I was wondering if I could join you for a cup of tea or something?"

For a moment she wasn't sure her friend would agree, but finally Carlie relented. "Come in, we were just about to make a fresh pot."

Relieved, Rhiannon followed her towards the warmth of the kitchen – then stopped abruptly when she saw a tiny black kitten weaving around her friend's ankles.

"Oh, this is Luna," Carlie explained, a smile transforming her face. "Luther brought her home for us to look after. You can pat her if you like. She was terrified of us at first, but she's friendly now."

Rhiannon slid down to the floor and cautiously held out her hand. The kitten looked over at Luther, who inclined his head in what seemed to be approval, because the curious little kitten stepped closer to the new arrival and let herself be patted for a moment, before racing back to Carlie and hiding behind her legs.

"She's adorable," she said. "And she clearly loves you already."

"I think that's why Luther brought her here," Carlie said. "To give me something to love, something to be responsible for, something to want to hang around for."

As Rose tried to hide her emotions by busying herself with the tea, Rhiannon felt ashamed. She really hadn't been there for her friend when she'd needed her, but she would change that. Filled with purpose, she went over to pat Luther. "You're a very wise cat," she said, sinking onto the floor next to him. "Thank you for caring for my friend when I was too stupid to do it myself."

The girls talked to Rose over cups of tea, about school, the seasons, and the upcoming Imbolc ritual. Then the priestess headed off to the healing centre, and the girls were left alone together. Feeling awkward, Rhiannon wondered if she should leave, but Carlie turned to her with a smile. "I'm going to move in to Mum's old room, so do you want to give me a hand? Or just chat while I do it?"

"Sure, I can help, if that's okay," Rhiannon said hesitantly. "But I can go home if you'd rather do it on your own?"

Shaking her head, Carlie stood up, holding Luna close to her heart, and led the way upstairs. "You can help me go through Mum's clothes if you'd like. Gran said we can keep what we want then take the rest down to the homeless shelter, so maybe that would be a good first step. I'm sure there are some people in need of extra coats and jeans right now. And maybe we'll find something to wear to the Imbolc ritual next weekend."

Watched by the cats, the girls chatted as they tried on clothes, keeping a few things each, then folding the rest and taking them to the shelter. They headed back to the cottage for hot vegie soup and fresh warm bread, then Rose made herself scarce, sensing they still needed to talk. It was awkward, but Rhiannon eventually screwed up her courage and spoke, face contrite and voice shaky with nerves.

"I'm so sorry about the other day, I really am. Everything I said came out wrong, and I wasn't being fair to you, or honouring your grief. I of all people should know there's no timetable for healing, and simply being told to snap out of it is worse than useless. Please forgive me," she implored.

Carlie hugged her. "I'm sorry too," she said. "And I can't expect you to understand how I'm feeling, because I never told you just how much I loved him, or how close we had become, since I was scared of upsetting you. I played down our feelings for each other because I knew you didn't approve –"

Rhiannon tried to interject, but Carlie shook her head. "It's not a criticism of you, I'm just explaining why I didn't share everything about Rowan. And I realised that I told you about the one time I thought he was cruel, but I never told you how easily it was resolved, or that it was my own misunderstanding, not his actions, which caused the problem in the first place. He was always so kind and sweet and protective of me, and never did anything to hurt me. I just let my insecurities run away with me, which was unfortunately the bit I confided to you," she admitted.

"So I feel awful that I misrepresented him to you, because that wasn't fair to him. And it means I can't blame you for thinking badly of him, because I didn't tell you I'd been wrong about him that day. And I never told you how amazing he was to me, how deeply he cared about me, how kind he was." She paused, trying to get her emotions under control.

"And I feel terrible that I left you thinking he wasn't good for me, because that meant you didn't like him, and led you to make that awful ultimatum," she said, her face creased with bitterness.

Rhiannon blushed. "I'm so sorry about that."

Taking a deep breath, Carlie wiped away a tear. "Anyway, I can't change the past, I can't erase my regrets or what they wrought, but maybe I can help you understand how I felt, how I feel now, and show you why I'm still so devastated."

Curious, Rhiannon watched her friend go to her school bag and tentatively lift out a package tied up with a red velvet ribbon. "Someone suggested that showing you these letters and cards from Rowan, and the one I wrote to him but didn't get a chance to give him, might help you see why it's so hard for me to just get over him."

She didn't hand them over though, and Rhiannon felt awful as she saw the indecision and fear on her friend's face. She wondered who had suggested it, then decided that was the least important thing right now. Tentatively she leaned in and placed her hands around the package. "I'd be honoured to read them, and don't worry, I'll guard them with my life," she whispered. After a long moment, Carlie reluctantly surrendered them.

They both jumped when Rose came in to put the kettle on, and Rhiannon carefully slipped the letters into her bag then made her farewells. It felt a little voyeuristic, but she couldn't wait to get home and read them. Her dad and brother were asleep, so she tiptoed upstairs, threw herself onto her bed and untied the red ribbon...

And fell into an avalanche of emotions, switching from jealous to ecstatic to moved to confused to desire-filled and desperate, then to yearning and depressed and envious and compassionate, and back to jealous. Then guilty for being jealous of a girl whose love had been taken from her so tragically.

Tears ran down her face as she struggled to read the final two cards. The one Rowan had written to

Carlie after she broke up with him – at Rhiannon's insistence – which was so full of love, understanding and patience. And the one Carlie had written for him, but never got the chance to deliver.

My Sweet Soul Mate and Beloved,

I'm coming to see you in the morning, first thing, to tell you how much I adore you, and beg you to change your mind, but I wanted to write it down too, hoping that you can feel every word I write as I write it, feel me thinking of you, feel my arms around you, feel my love. I want you to know, no matter what happens, how much I love you, how much I will always love you.

I hope it's not just wishful thinking, but I can feel you with me right now, your lips on my hair, your voice in my ear, whispering your love across these miles that separate us, telling me you've changed your mind.

I want to apologise to you my love – finding out that it was my father who treated your mother so badly shook me to my core, but please know I am nothing like him. I barely knew him, and what I do know of him, what I've learned recently, I despise.

I know we haven't been together all that long, in some people's eyes, but it feels like forever, and it will be forever. I fell for you in the dreams we shared before we ever actually met. I was smitten the moment you walked up to my stand at the festival to have your painting done. And I fell hopelessly in love with you that first morning we spent on the tor, as I held you in my arms and we watched the sun rise, as we sat by the stream together and just talked, just held hands.

Every day I'm away from you hurts me physically – you are the missing piece I'd been searching for, and once found I couldn't bear to be apart. You make me feel whole.

Your love has made me a better, kinder person, with more depth than I ever imagined possible. My mum was right, she realised it even before I did, that I am more myself when I am with you, that you have helped me recognise my light and encouraged me to shine it. I feel like we're meant to be together, that we're destined for each other. Whether we were together or not in a past life means nothing, because we are together now, and that's all that matters.

I don't want to keep us a secret any more. I want the whole world to know how much I love you – our friends, your grandma, my students. How could anyone be upset by how much I love you? How could that hurt anyone?

Because I love you Carlie, and I will fight for that love. I know you long for me as much and as deeply as I love and long for you, and I know we can figure out a way to make this work. I will never give up on you, on our love, and I will be there with you soon, to tell you all of this in person.

Until then my precious beloved, my sweet goddess, know that I love you, and I always will.

Forever yours, Rowan xx

Dear Rowan, my Sweet Beloved,

As soon as I left tonight I knew I'd done the wrong thing, made the wrong choice. Because I love you. And I choose you. I want to be with you. That's the truth of it, and anything else is superfluous. How I deal with Rhiannon, when I tell Gran about us, they're just details to be worked out. They don't affect the only thing that actually matters – the fact that I love you.

I'm going to come and see you in the morning, get the first bus back so that I can tell you all this myself, but I want to write it down too, right now, in this moment that I choose you, because I'm sure you will feel it. I'm sure you will know it deep in your bones, in your heart, in your soul, and you will feel my arms around you until I can be there in person to tell you, to hold you, to love you. I can feel your arms around me too, I'm sure of it – I can feel your love, and I thank you with all my heart for your forgiveness.

I deeply regret the pain I caused you, caused both of us, tonight. I let other people's opinions cloud my judgement, and allowed someone else to make a decision for me. And I'm sorry, *so sorry, for thinking for even a second that you could be anything like your father. I know you're not. I feel that in every cell of my body, every beat of my heart. And I am not my mother, though I love her dearly. You and I are not fated to walk the path of our parents, but to forge our own path, our own destiny. Lives entwined, souls in harmony, hearts as one.*

I choose Rhiannon too, and I hope that one day soon you'll both see in each other what I see. She is the sister of my heart, and I value her highly and deeply – but you are the love of my life, and I will not give you up for anyone or anything.

You have opened my heart to love, after I thought it would be closed forever. I thought I was unloveable, unable to love, unworthy of being loved, but your patience and compassion have transformed me. Being loved by you has made me blossom, has given me the courage to let my light shine, has made me a better person. Your mum got it wrong – it is you who has changed me for the better, not the other way around. You have transformed me. You have healed me, in so many different ways, and I am so grateful to you.

I will love you forever,
        Your Carlie xx

The words of grand and sweeping love blurred on the page, and the salt on Rhiannon's lips was as bitter as her heart. What she had with John was nothing like this. Even in her confusion, even as she tried to give him the benefit of the doubt, she knew she was settling, since it was clear that she could have so much more. Devotion. Adoration. Passion. Fireworks. True love. Soul mates throughout time.

Her heart ached for Carlie's loss, yet she was also envious of the love she'd experienced. She knew she would happily suffer the pain her friend was in now, to have had even the short time of true love that she'd experienced.

She sighed. She felt even worse now, that she'd been so impatient with Carlie. Had told her to stop being overly dramatic and just get over it. That she hadn't been with him long enough to feel such grief. If only Carlie had shown her earlier, she wouldn't have doubted

Rowan's love for her. Yet the letters had gained added poignancy by his death, the immensity of the love expressed more powerful because it was cut so devastatingly short.

No wonder her friend didn't want to date the first guy who expressed interest in her. Rhiannon's heart broke for her friend's loss, and now she understood her fear that she'd never find another love like it. Had Rowan spoiled Carlie for relationships forever? Would he spoil Rhiannon for relationships? How could she settle for John, when she'd discovered there was this?

Knowing what was possible, how deeply a person could be loved, was putting what she had in perspective. She'd been having fun with John, and she'd loved the early days when he didn't know her mum had died. She'd even, in some strange way, enjoyed the drama of her sex dilemma, but she didn't see herself with him once school ended. The thought shocked her, yet she knew it was true. They had different views of the world, their plans for the future didn't intersect, and she didn't feel able to share her spirituality and magic with him, which she had to admit was a deal breaker.

While she'd tried to pretend it didn't matter, reading these letters, seeing just how much Rowan and Carlie had shared, of themselves, and of magic, left her bereft. She wanted a boyfriend she could go to rituals with. Someone she could weave magic with. A person she could bare her soul to.

Tracing a finger over the words of love, she read each letter again.

And desperately wanted a love like this.

A love like Carlie's.

A love like her mum and dad's.

Chapter 25

Beth

onight when Beth became aware of herself, she was clad in casual, loose-fitting black pants and a long top she hadn't worn in years. Peering down from her perch in the rafters, she saw Mike sitting alone on the couch, flipping through a photo album with tears in his eyes. Swooping to his side, she settled next to him, her heart aching when she saw the pictures he was looking at. Now her clothes made sense. This was what she'd been wearing on the plane when he'd whisked her off to Paris and proposed.

ights twinkled below them as the plane began its descent through the night-time clouds. The whole city was spread out in a glittering arc, a magical wonderland, and Beth felt her heart skip a beat.

"It really is the City of Lights," she grinned, excitement and awe in her voice.

Mike squeezed her hand. "It's beautiful." But he was looking at her, at the flush of joy that was making her face so radiant and her eyes light up.

She squirmed under his gaze. "You're not looking at Paris." She pouted, although she was secretly pleased.

"I'm looking at something far more breathtaking."

It should have sounded corny, but it didn't, and she was amazed all over again that he saw her this way. She still had trouble believing that this kind, sweet man could love her, even now, a year after he'd finally confessed his feelings for her. Thanks to his patience, she was slowly beginning to accept it though. Well, most of the time.

Feeling self-conscious, she leaned in and kissed him, then turned back to the window, dragging his attention with her. "I've never seen it like this, from the air," she whispered. She'd arrived by train the first time, in the chill of midwinter, cold and broke, after six months backpacking around the French countryside. Despite having no money, she'd loved it instantly – but oh, to have seen it first like this!

"It's incredible! And I can see why people call it the City of Love too – it's so enchanting!"

Mike looked relieved, and she suddenly realised he was nervous. Why? What on earth would she not be loving about a romantic week away together in Paris? Or was he scared she'd want to stay if she returned to this place she'd once loved, leaving him and the village behind? Was this some kind of test?

It was two years since she'd lived in the French capital, and a wave of longing had washed over her when he'd surprised her with this trip. There was a time that she'd envisioned herself living in this romantic city forever, separated from her awful parents by a language barrier and a body of water, allowed finally to be fully herself, free of perceptions and old wounds.

Yet as the plane began its descent, she realised that she'd found all of that with Mike. It wasn't a geographical location she'd been yearning for, it was a state of mind. Being given the freedom to be truly herself. Being with someone who saw her inner heart, her inner doubts, her inner fears – and loved her anyway. Without judgement, without conditions. She almost laughed. The answer to her searching was a person, not a place.

Driving through the late-night streets, past charming buildings and across the darkened waters of the Seine, Beth felt an incredible lightness of being. She didn't miss it like she'd thought she would, didn't regret leaving it like she'd feared. It was beautiful, but Paris felt like a stranger to her now. The feeling of belonging she'd found with the man beside her, the roots she'd already laid down in the village she'd hated for so long, finally sunk into her bones.

"Thank you," she whispered, her heart in her eyes, and her voice. Mike squeezed her hand and beamed at her, and she hoped he could feel all she was feeling, all she was realising. If this trip had been a test, he had definitely won.

When the taxi pulled up in a narrow street, a sleepy doorman ushered them out of the vehicle and into a small, dimly lit lobby. In halting English he told them the floor number, pointed to a rickety old metal screen, then handed them a key. Always the gentleman, Mike picked up her small suitcase and led the way to the quaint, slightly nerve-racking elevator, which creaked and groaned, but finally deposited them on the top floor. Then he opened the door to their room, and stood back to let her enter first.

Dropping her bag in surprise, she ran across the wooden floor in delight. Their apartment was tiny, just big enough for the double bed, a small table with two chairs, and a bar fridge set against one wall next to a sink with a small square of bench boasting a kettle, two tea cups, and a glass jar filled with tea bags.

But none of that registered to Beth, as she pulled back the billowing curtain that only partly shielded the moonlight pouring in, and gasped. It wasn't a window but a glass door, which opened out onto the smallest balcony she'd ever seen. The size was irrelevant though, because she could see all the way to the Eiffel Tower. Breathless, she turned back to Mike, eyes shining, and threw her arms around him.

"Thank you," she said again, although words seemed inadequate. Taking his hand, she led him out to the balcony, her body pressed against his partly as there was little room to move, but also because she craved his physical presence. His arms came around her, and she leaned back into him as she gazed out over the rooftops of the City of Love.

For a moment she closed her eyes, revelling in the feeling of safety and comfort his closeness gave her. As she stood there in the sweetly velvet midnight air, she was suddenly, dramatically, sure of her place in the world. And it wasn't in a foreign country amongst strangers, it was by this patient man's side.

"I love you Mike Stark," she whispered, turning away from the sparkling lights of the Eiffel Tower and burying her head in his chest. How had he known, that this was exactly what she needed to finally lay the ghosts of her past to rest?

"I love you Beth Bishop," he replied, voice thick with longing.

Standing on tiptoes, she reached up a hand and caressed his cheek, and as she gazed into his eyes, she saw her future. She saw the vision that the strange gold-clad woman of the mists had gifted her after she returned home, of herself in a long white dress with a diamond ring on her finger. Saw herself holding a baby in her arms with her beloved beside her. And she felt the strength of this man who was holding her tight, and knew beyond a shadow of a doubt that he was her present and her future.

An icy wind swept over them, and Mike gently stroked her hair, tucking a loose strand behind her ear. She shivered, although it wasn't from the cold. It was from love, and desire.

"Oh darling, you mean the world to me too," he said softly, as though he'd read her mind. "You *are* the world to me."

Floating in the light of invisible stars, on a tiny balcony overlooking centuries of art and culture and literature and history, Beth thought her heart might overflow, all the emotions within her too great to contain. She hoped Mike could see them, or feel them. Did he know just how much she loved him? Had seemed always to love him?

The corners of his mouth curved upwards in a smile, and he nodded. Then he let her go.

She swayed, confused and suddenly cold and vulnerable. Had he seen something else in her eyes? Decided she wasn't worthy of him? But he drew something from the pocket of his coat, then drew her down to the tiled floor of their tiny, intimate space.

"Darling, I had the perfect moment all planned out, the perfect speech in my head, but the fact is, every moment with you is perfect.

And seeing you out here, silhouetted against the Paris skyline, against the shining lights, yet content to turn your back on it all to look at me with such wonder..." He paused, inhaling deeply as he tried to get his emotions under control, then gazed into her eyes, into her heart, into her very soul.

"Will you marry me Beth?"

She gasped, and stared at him in shock. Surprise washed over her, along with joy and gratitude, and her eyes sparkled as she nodded her acceptance, unable to find her voice through the tears that were choking her. But she tried.

"Of course," she stammered. "I'd love to!"

Beaming, Mike took her hand and gently slid the ring onto her finger, where it fit beautifully, the small diamond drawing in all the light of the surrounding neighbourhood. Then a teardrop splashed onto her hand, and he gazed up at her, concerned, as her face paled, a jewel-like tear slid down her cheek, and her eyes darted away from him – to the sky above, to the corner of the building she could see to their left, to the dusty tiles they were kneeling on.

"My love, what's wrong?" he asked urgently, fearfully.

She wanted to break down in tears and cry all night, to be left alone out here to sob her heart out, to sob her guilt and unworthiness out, to the blackness drawing down around her.

"Beth!"

She looked up at the man she adored, and saw the love he had for her shining from his face, from his eyes, from his heart. Then saw the pain and fear her silence was threatening to wipe it all away with.

Swallowing her own feelings and stuffing them back down, she forced a smile. "I'm sorry, I didn't mean to cry," she whispered. "I would be honoured to be your wife, and I am so happy, so thrilled." This time the smile did reach her eyes, and Mike finally relaxed.

"I love you more than anything. I've loved you for a long time, perhaps longer than I should have. I just can't believe that you could love me as much as I love you!" she cried, then threw herself into his arms and burrowed her head into his chest.

Strong hands held her close and stroked her back, so soothing that she eventually managed to get her emotions under control.

Sensing that, Mike drew back slowly, and held her face in his hands. "I have never loved anyone the way I love you," he said, voice soft, and tender.

"But Violet..." she managed to choke out.

A flash of anger rushed through Mike, but it was quickly tempered by a wave of sadness. "There's only you and me."

"But this is forever. What if she comes back one day?" she asked, voice small, and scared.

Mike recoiled as though she'd slapped him. "I'm devastated that you could think that, that you could doubt me, and doubt my love for you."

"It's not you I doubt, it's me," she croaked.

"Oh Beth, darling, if Violet had never left, I would still want to marry you. And if she came back, I'm sure she'd be delighted that we fell in love. She cared about you too, even before I did. Darling, you have no need to feel insecure, or guilty, or unsure of my feelings, or of our love. It is you I want to spend my life with. You I want to have children with."

Finally his words penetrated through her layers of protection, and she held the vision of her with the baby in her arms close to her heart as she looked up, face radiant.

"I want that too," she said shyly, and Mike sighed with relief.

From across the dark waters the sound of a church bell echoed, and Mike scooped her up in his arms, carried her carefully inside and lay her on their bed. "We should probably get some sleep, but I did call ahead to order some champagne, if you'd like to make a midnight toast to our future?"

Beth nodded happily, and scooted up so she was leaning against the ornate wrought iron headboard. Their room might be small, but it was beautiful, old-world-charming yet immaculately clean, with romantic touches in the lamps, the dresser drawer handles, the billowing curtains and the bedding.

As Mike retrieved the champagne from the bar fridge, she thanked the gods she hadn't ruined this perfect moment with her insecurities. It wasn't fair to her beloved, to make him keep proving his love for her.

Her jealousy might have been understandable for a few months, but no longer. When Mike's childhood sweetheart Violet had dumped him then run away from home, Beth had been too scared to let him know how she felt about him. But that was two years ago, and he'd proved his love for her over and over again since then. Intellectually she knew that if Violet returned now it would change nothing between them, so she had to stop making Mike suffer for her own guilt and insecurity.

Glancing down at the sparkling diamond on her finger, she felt a weight lift from her shoulders, and from her heart. This was perfect. He was perfect. And she would spend her whole life trying to be worthy of him.

He handed her a drink and settled down on the bed next her, and she finally relaxed, allowing the wonder and romance of the occasion to overtake her. She was in Paris, engaged to the man she loved, and they were drinking champagne out of vintage tea cups in this perfect little garret room overlooking the city of love. It was a dream come true, with the man of her dreams. Draining her drink, she crawled across the bed and kissed him. Their passion ignited, and they didn't even notice when Mike's cup wobbled off the bed and rolled onto the floor, spilling champagne on the carpet.

The next morning Beth awoke naked, in a tangle of sheets, and stretched languidly. Peering up at Mike, she snuggled into his chest, and smiled when she felt him stir beneath her.

"Hello Husband-To-Be," she purred, and he grinned and dragged her into his arms.

When they emerged hours later onto the street below, desperate for coffee, they held hands as they gazed around them. In the mid-morning sunshine it still looked as enchanting as it had the night before, all cobblestoned pavements and quaint restaurants, with newspaper stands and flower shops adding colour and character.

The scent of coffee, sugar and pastries drew them into the closest cafe, where they feasted on croissants and ordered several rounds of short blacks. No milky cafe au lait today, after she'd spent the night too excited, then too... busy... to sleep for more than a moment here and there.

Biting into a chocolate-filled pastry, she saw Mike's sheepish gaze on her, and raised an eyebrow in question. "I hope I didn't ruin things, asking you last night," he said reluctantly. "I had it all planned out in minute detail – I was going to propose up at the Sacre Couer at sunset, us all dressed up instead of crumpled and travel-weary, with champagne and strawberries, and a lot more fan fare."

She leaned across the table and kissed him. "It was perfect," she whispered in his ear, her breath hot on his cheek, and she grinned when she felt him blush. "It was truly the perfect moment, I promise. A tiny part of me had wondered what I would feel, being back in Paris. Whether I would find remnants of the girl I had been as I walked down the boulevards. What memories would emerge of the hopes I'd had. If I would discover that I'd missed it, that I'd given up some part of myself when I didn't return to this city, to this life."

His face fell, and she reached over and squeezed his hand. "But I didn't. As I gazed out over the rooftops, I had the most incredible epiphany, that home for me is with you, wherever that is. That the girl I was, the girl I am, is within me, not without. And a fierce, possessive part of me was so relieved that you asked me then, in that moment when it was just the two of us. Alone together, in the beautiful dark."

Then she raised an eyebrow suggestively. "Is it wrong that I want to be alone with you again right now?" she asked, voice husky, and she saw the passion ignite in his eyes to mirror her own. When the waiter came over with their bill, he grinned. "Jeunes mariés," he laughed. They looked up at him, puzzled.

"Honeymooners," he said in sweetly accented English. "Can't keep your hands off each other."

Beth laughed, delighted, and dragged Mike back to their room.

Hours later, as the sky began to darken, they got dressed again and headed out to explore. They were in Paris after all, and Beth had so much to show him.

Chapter 26

Flame of Inspiration

Rhiannon

It was a struggle for Rhiannon to drag herself out of bed on Monday morning, because she dreaded having to face Carlie. Last night she'd read Rowan's letters over and over, falling more deeply in love with him and his beautiful heart each time, and finally understanding the depth of her friend's pain. What Carlie and Rowan shared was so precious, so surprising, so huge and all-encompassing. To have been loved so deeply by someone – especially someone as amazing as Rowan – blew her mind. She'd misjudged him so badly. And now she couldn't even remember why, which was embarrassing. Had it been pure jealousy?

As she waited out the front of school for Carlie, she tried to push her guilt down, and pull herself together. When her friend approached, she raced over and hugged her, as her eyes filled with tears.

"Oh Carlie, I can't tell you how deeply sorry I am. For not understanding how much he loved you, for not trusting you when you told me how wonderful he was, and for belittling your grief and telling you to get over it."

Her friend shocked her by smiling. "It's okay, you didn't know," she said gently. "I should have told you sooner."

But Rhiannon shook her head. "No, this is on me. I should have had more patience. I should have asked you. I should have trusted you. And last week, I should have listened to you about Jake and stopped tormenting you. Can you forgive me?"

The bell rang, and Carlie took Rhiannon's hand and led her up the school steps towards history. "Of course. Life really is too short. Now come on, we can't be late for Laura's class. We don't want her telling Gran we've been slacking off."

Knees weak with relief, Rhiannon collapsed into her seat the moment they got to history, feeling a huge weight lift from her. At lunchtime she gave Carlie back her letters, but they didn't get the chance to talk about them because Jake pulled up a chair and sat with them. Maybe that was okay though. Maybe they could just move forward now, with her new understanding and compassion.

The following night was coven night, and the girls had decided on a practical lesson, helping Rose and her circle prepare for the upcoming Imbolc ritual at the healing centre. As she stood in the doorway, on the threshold of the sacred space, Rhiannon felt the magic envelop her, and the energy reach out and touch her heart.

It reminded her of Rowan and the healing his love had given Carlie. But he'd not only been kind and respectful to his girlfriend, he'd always honoured Rhiannon and her importance to Carlie – despite her being a selfish angsty bitch to him. Even when she uttered that stupid ultimatum, Rowan didn't pressure Carlie to choose him, or to dump her friend. Not that she would have blamed him if he had.

And Carlie was such a good friend that she'd actually agreed to her ridiculous demand, breaking up with Rowan because she valued their friendship above her own happiness. She was just glad that in the end Carlie had realised she shouldn't have to make such a decision, and had refused to choose between them.

If only she hadn't issued that cruel ultimatum – then stood Carlie up for their Yule ritual that night – her friend wouldn't have gone to see Rowan at his retreat, wouldn't have ended things with him... and he wouldn't have been driving over on solstice morning to beg her to take him back. *Oh god!* If she hadn't forced Carlie's hand, would Rowan still be alive? Her blood ran cold, and her face froze with fear. Did her friend blame her for Rowan's death?

Before she could break down in tears, Rose appeared at her side, and drew her into her arms. "Lovely Rhiannon, stop torturing yourself, please. She doesn't blame you – in fact she's only just beginning to stop blaming herself. But it's in the past now. Don't beat yourself up over past actions, past words – just be the friend for her now that you wish you had been. She's still fragile, and she needs you now more than ever. So get over yourself, okay? Snap out of it, and be the young woman I know you're capable of being."

Tears stung Rhiannon's eyes, but they were tears of gratitude for the wise priestess. "I will, I promise," she whispered. "Will you tell Carlie I had to go though? There's something I need to do."

Fleeing the healing centre, she ran home and started searching through old spiritual magazines, newspapers, online articles and blogs for anything she could find on Rowan. Carlie didn't have many physical things to remember him by, so this was something practical she could do, to show she'd meant every word of her apology.

She stayed up all night, consumed by her mission, and by the time she had to leave for school, she had a folder overflowing with interview printouts and newspaper clippings, with photos of Rowan and Carlie dancing together at the Yule Ball, eyes full of love, and even a few snaps of the three of them at the Autumn's End festival, when Rowan had arranged tickets for the girls and spent the whole time carefully including Rhiannon, despite clearly wanting to be alone with Carlie. He'd always been a good guy.

It was a struggle to get through school the next day on zero sleep, but the look on Carlie's face as she flicked through the folder Rhiannon had created for her made every minute of exhaustion worthwhile.

The sun peeking through Rhiannon's window woke her early on Saturday morning, and she smiled. She loved this time of year. Early February marked the beginning of spring, when icy winds gave way to gentle sunshine and warmer breezes, and the first snowdrops waved their delicate petals. It was the perfect day to spend with Carlie and Rose in the witch's cottage, getting ready for the spring festival of Imbolc. The ritual wasn't until the following night, but Rhiannon found the preparation just as enthralling.

First they ground herbs, sewed dream pillows and blended gorgeously scented incense. Then, while Rose regaled them with stories and legends about the sabbat's traditions and significance, they baked foods that held the energy of the season. Choc-orange poppyseed cupcakes and trays of sunflower and sesame seed sprinkled Bridie's bread, since seeds symbolise growth and fertility and evoke the energy of new life and new beginnings. Mini lemon cheesecakes and individual pots of baked custard, as dairy foods are also a strong part of the seasonal theme, the latter flavoured with ginger, cinnamon, nutmeg and other spring spices. Once everything was in the oven, they paused for lunch, then blended an Imbolc tea crafted from chamomile, nettle and violets that they poured into little gauze bags for the participants to take home.

When the evening drew in and the sky faded to black, the silver-haired priestess taught the girls how to weave Bridie Crosses, the traditional fire wheel symbols of the goddess, from stalks of wheat, so they could hang them around the house and in the ritual room. Then they made candles for the ceremony, half of them white and the other half pale blue, to embody the innocence and purity of Imbolc and represent the cleansing power of the element of fire. Some were for the ritual, but Rose also wanted to gift each person another one, along with their tea, so they could continue to weave the magic of the season when they returned home.

On Sunday night, as the sun prepared to set, Rhiannon and Carlie wove wreaths of snowdrops and primroses for their hair and slipped into their long velvet sabbat dresses, then climbed the stairs to the ritual room. Reverence and enchantment enveloped Rhiannon as she stood in the doorway, breathing in the mystical fragrance of incense and gazing at the rows of blazing candles set within the beautifully decorated space. She didn't know how Rose achieved it, but you could always feel the magic long before the ceremony begun.

As they greeted their teacher Laura, Rhiannon saw her friend stiffen. Following her gaze, she saw Jake standing in the doorway with his grandfather Richard, looking lost, awkward and apprehensive. She tried not to laugh as she remembered that the other night, when Jake was at Carlie's to work on their assignment,

Rose had invited him to stay for dinner – then told him he and his grandfather were welcome to come to the ritual. Carlie hadn't been thrilled by either invitation, but now she smiled politely and went over to shepherd Jake and his grandfather inside and into the circle.

Finally the lights dimmed, and a hush fell as Rose gracefully stood up from behind the central altar. It always gave Rhiannon chills to see the etheric mantle of the priestess settle around her shoulders, and to feel the power and strength that emanated from her, a physical thing.

A gasp beside her broke her focus, and she turned, catching the look of wonder on Jake's face. It plunged her into memories of her first ritual, three years ago, when she'd attended a public sabbat with her mum. Although she hadn't understood much of what went on, she'd been amazed by Rose's transformation from kindly grandmother to awe-inspiring priestess of the goddess, and she'd felt a shiver of fear at how like a warrior woman from ages past she had seemed.

Standing next to Jake, his grandfather was staring at Rose with surprise and admiration. Rhiannon grinned as she caught Carlie's eye. Apparently Mr Mattherson had been a bit sceptical of Rose's interests in the past, but tonight he looked thoroughly enchanted.

Forcing herself to pay attention to the ritual, Rhiannon watched, spellbound, as Rose invoked the god and the goddess, drawing their essence down within her. She felt the magic weaving around her – then anxiety washed over her as Rose beckoned the girls forward. Taking a steadying breath, she picked up the basket of candles she'd crafted and reverently paced around her half of the circle, touched by the sense of camaraderie and connection as each person whispered a blessing to her as she handed them their beeswax creation.

A sad smiled tugged at Rhiannon's heart. At the Samhain ritual three months ago, they'd lit candles to honour the dead. Tonight they were lighting candles to honour the present and the future, to make a wish for new love and new beginnings. Awestruck, she watched while Rose lit her own candle and stated her intentions for the coming weeks as the wick caught and the flame shimmered. Then the priestess offered her candle to Laura so she could light hers as she made her own wish, and on the golden flame went, rippling around the circle as each person used its spark to light their own candle and speak their own wish or dream.

Rhiannon's heart raced as the flame moved around the circle towards her, worried her voice would shake. First it reached Carlie, who whispered her wish so quietly that only Rhiannon heard it. "Sweet goddess, or the universe, or whoever is listening, please help my heart to heal, and to one day open again, without walls, without fear," she murmured, then turned to her friend and offered the flame to her.

Nervous, Rhiannon spoke just as quietly, not ready to reveal herself so deeply, yet swept up in the magic of the night and the power of the group's sharing. "Dearest Bridie, thank you so much for my remaining family and my friends. I am so grateful for all of your blessings. My wish tonight is to someday find a love like Carlie and Rowan's, and to feel worthy of the depth and the joy of it."

Once everyone's candle was alight, forging a vibrant ring of fire, the last person lit the pillar candle on the altar from their flame. This would hold the energy and intent of the group, and they could light it at future rituals to reinforce the magic they were weaving. And at home they could each light their own candles when they needed strength or just a reminder of the magic of their wishes.

Next Rose had them sink to the floor, candles in hand, then her rich voice led them into a deep guided meditation.

Tonight we celebrate Imbolc, the first day of spring, which marks the return of light and warmth to the land, and to our own hearts. It is a time of hope, renewal and fresh starts after the barrenness of winter, and the chill it brought not just to the earth, but to our very souls.

Energetically Imbolc is a time of awakening, rebirth and re-emergence. Nature fills with life force and begins to quiver with the energy to grow again, and we too emerge from the introspection of winter, shaking off our lack of motivation, and re-engaging with the world. This makes it the perfect time to sow the seeds of what we want to achieve in the coming month, and the coming year, so we must be very clear about what that is, and what our intentions are.

On this night we honour Bridie, the maiden goddess of fire, inspiration and creativity. She symbolises achievement, knowledge and healing, and can be your muse as you take action to manifest your desires. Feel her presence as you stare into your flame, and focus on the spark within. Let its heat thaw the frozen parts of you, the space that holds your feelings of self-defeat, stagnation and resistance to change and growth, so you can release them. Feel its warmth filling your heart and your mind. Become aware of the power of fire...

For a moment Rhiannon actually felt the heat on her face, felt the whoosh of flames around her, and she opened her eyes and stared at Rose in alarm. The priestess turned and caught her eye, and smiled serenely. A wave of calm enveloped her until she felt safe again. When she offered a tiny smile in return, Rose continued with the meditation.

Now, close your eyes, and allow your mind to reach out ahead of you. See yourself walking along a gentle forest path, the darkness illuminated by the candle you hold, and by the light within you. Drink in the moonlight dancing through the branches overhead. Soak up the starlight twinkling down on you.

There is a well before you, the edge ringed with candles spilling light onto the dark surface. Kneel down and take a sip of this pure water, and feel its essence permeating every cell of your body. This is Bridie's sacred well, and it has the power to inspire, enchant and heal you. Gaze into its inky depths. If you see images, make a note then let them go. This is the time to clear old energy and old emotions so the new can thrive. To release pain and guilt so love can fill you.

With a jolt, Rhiannon opened her eyes again and peered at the priestess, who was staring right at her once more. Was the guilt she felt so obvious to Rose that she was singling her out within the ritual? Or did everyone here feel guilty about something? Suddenly there was a comforting hand on her shoulder, a soothing touch, and the peaceful sensation returned. Then she heard a whisper: "Beloved, let it all go. Release your guilt, so you can move forward." Was it Rose? Was it one of the Otherworldly women? Or something else?

Snapping her eyes shut, she slumped forward a little, then almost screamed when the hand returned to her shoulder – and she "saw" a woman in a long red dress sitting opposite her, on the other side of the well, with flames rising from her outstretched palms. *Bridie?* From a distance she heard Rose's voice continue with the meditation.

Breathe in, inhaling the wisdom of this moment. You are accessing your own truths, your own knowing, connecting with the great potential that resides within you, which you are usually so quick to dismiss. If Bridie is sitting with you, ask her any questions that need answers. Don't worry if you can't hear her reply right now, just trust that she will make the answer known to you when you are ready to hear. It may be woven into a dream tonight, it might come in flashes of inspiration that you experience over the coming days, it could be revealed when you are offered guidance or help from someone else. Be open to receiving your answer in whatever form it takes.

Rose's voice faded as Rhiannon felt herself drowning in the dark pools of black that were the woman's eyes. She shivered, then forced herself to concentrate again on the priestess's words.

Now gently start to return to your body, to your self, and to this room. Know that even when you blow out your candle tonight, you are not blowing out the light. It is within you, growing each day as the wheel of the seasons turns towards the light. Imbolc brings new energy, new beginnings, a new way of seeing, awakening a new force within you. And you can continue working with this magic at home. Light your candle each evening and stare into its flame as you focus on what you are working towards and the actions you need to take. Breathe in strength and resolve, and remember the magic in this moment, right here, which is within you always. Then, when you feel ready, blow out the candle, sending your desire out to the universe.

After several moments of silence, Rhiannon opened her eyes, and saw others slowly returning to the present, looking as dazed as she was. Carlie squeezed her hand, and she realised she had tears running down her cheeks. Yet she felt good. Calm.

Clear. As though she really had let go of doubts that had been weighing her down.

Before she could get her head around it, Rose announced a spiral dance to wake everyone up and get their energy swirling again, and Rhiannon grinned as she joined a line of people weaving in and out of the circle. Grabbing a bewildered Jake's hand, she pulled him along with her, the steadily increasing rhythm ensuring everyone was soon totally back in their body. Then, as laughter rang out, Rose turned the mood serious again, and began a healing spell that they all contributed to, then sent outwards over the land.

As the ritual wound down and the deities, quarters and directions were farewelled, Rhiannon glanced over at Jake and his grandfather, worried it might have been too weird for them. But their eyes were full of wonder, and she sensed an expanding around them, as though their hearts were opening up. The moment Rose closed the circle, Richard went to speak to her, and Jake rushed over to the girls.

"Oh my god, I had no idea anything like this existed!" he gushed. "Do you do this often? Is it always so amazing? I feel like I have electricity rushing through my veins, waking me up in a way I've never felt before. And Pop loved it too..."

He broke off, and they all looked over at Richard, who was speaking to Rose, a wide smile on his face. "I think I saw a few tears too, which is a good thing. I know how much he misses Nan, but he's bottled it all up. It felt like something was loosening in him."

Rhiannon stared hard at Jake, surprised by his eloquence and empathy, and he laughed, as though he knew what she was thinking. "I don't think I've noticed anything like that before, or been able to put it into words. But something about tonight really affected me. I think it opened me up too, not just Pop."

He beamed at the girls – then started to sway. Quickly Rhiannon led him over to the table laden with all the treats they'd baked, and ordered him to eat before he passed out. "Any time you weave magic, you have to eat something afterwards, to ground your energy back into the real world, and your spirit back into your body."

Jake looked a little puzzled – then he swayed again. Rhiannon grabbed his arm. "We mean it," she said sternly. "Eat!"

Chapter 27

Rhiannon

Jake's enthusiasm hadn't waned the next day. At lunchtime Rhiannon had to wave her hand in front of his face to get his attention. "Earth to Jake!"

"Oh, sorry!" he said, eyes focusing on her and Carlie. "I was off in another world, a magical world, still thinking about last night. Your grandmother is amazing Carlie, it was like she became someone else, so wild and strong and powerful, yet so welcoming and nurturing too. I've never seen anything like it."

He broke off. "Um, you'll probably both think I'm crazy, but I swear I could see golden strands, like electricity almost, running between each person, connecting all of us, all different widths and different intensities of sparkle. God, I know that really does sound insane. I'm sorry, I'll get over it soon, I promise. It's just... well, I just loved it so much."

Carlie smiled. "You're not crazy Jake, I see it too. It's like a giant web or something, all sparkling and golden, running through the room. The connection between you and your grandfather was the thickest – it was so strong, so vibrant. The love you share is very clear."

"Really?"

Nodding, Rhiannon interjected. "I don't see it so much as sense it, and my heart felt so full when I looked at you and your grandad.

Your relationship is just beautiful, and he adores you. You being here has really given him a new purpose, much like what Carlie's arrival gave to Rose."

Jake beamed at them. "You can really see and sense those things?"

"It sounds like you can too," Carlie said.

"Is there a way to practise it, or develop it? Is there any way to get better at it?"

Rhiannon was saved from replying when one of the guys came over to grab Jake for training, but she was filled with excitement at the idea of inviting Jake to join their coven. It would be fascinating to have some masculine energy, since magic was all about balance, and there was that whole power of three thing people talked about. It was supposed to make your magic bigger, more powerful. To juice up your spellcasting and push you to improve. Maybe their magical practice would evolve with new input.

And he was so lovely. It would be fun to hang out with him every week, outside of school. And he could probably provide a male perspective to their friendship too, balancing things out, as well as helping them magically.

"Should we invite Jake to join our coven?" she asked Carlie. "It seems he's really interested in learning, and you said he's been working hard on your assignment, so he wouldn't be slack. And it sounds like he'd love to join us."

Carlie shrugged, unconvinced. "I'm not sure... I mean, we shouldn't feel obligated – we can lend him some books and head him in the right direction for his own study, and just invite him to the public rituals. And maybe he'd rather find someone more experienced to teach him anyway. It's not like he asked to join our coven."

"True," Rhiannon conceded. "But I don't think he knows we have one, so how could he ask that? I'm sure he'd be more than happy if we wanted to help him. And it would be pretty awesome to have the power of three..."

Carlie stared at her. "You like him, don't you?" she asked, eyebrows raised in surprise, and her friend squirmed a little.

"No, of course not, he's just a really sweet guy..." she began, but her flaming cheeks gave her away.

"Oh my god Rhi, you do!" Carlie said, a grin splitting her face. Then she frowned. "But what about John? I thought you guys were really happy?"

"We were. We are," Rhiannon muttered.

"What's wrong?"

"Nothing's wrong, not really. It's just hard because we don't get to see each other very often. I mean, we talk, but we're running out of things to say. And we see each other on weekends, but I can't help but notice that there are times he'd rather be with his mates. And to be honest, often I'd rather be with you. And if I really liked him, I probably wouldn't feel like that, would I?" she asked.

Carlie shook her head. "I'm not sure – Rowan's the only boyfriend I've ever had, and we know how that ended."

"But don't you see, it's because of Rowan that I don't feel satisfied with John," she wailed. Seeing the pain on Carlie's face, she quickly backpedalled. "Sorry, I don't mean that the way it sounded. It's just that ever since you showed me the letters you wrote each other, I've wanted more. I want someone to love me like Rowan loved you, and to be with someone who I love as much as you loved Rowan."

A vision of John casually telling her they wouldn't see each other for two weeks, and not seeming to care, flashed into her mind, followed by the awkward silence when she'd told him she loved him, and the far-from-romantic: "It's been fun," after they almost had sex.

"He's a lovely guy, but I'm not desperate to see him when the weekend comes around – I like seeing him, don't get me wrong, but I want someone to feel the way Rowan felt about you, about me. To be that smitten, to want to be with me every minute, to hurt when we're apart. Rowan was cutting his work back because it took him away from you –"

"Jay wasn't real happy about that though," Carlie sighed, but Rhiannon ignored her and continued.

"But that's so romantic. You were prepared to make sacrifices for each other, because you loved each other so much. And I guess I've just realised that I don't feel that way about John. We really like each other, and we enjoy hanging out together, but I can't imagine he'd be especially devastated if we broke up." She blushed. She'd assumed their intimacy meant he loved her, and it hurt to realise that it was all just a bit of fun to him.

Carlie touched her hand, sympathy and surprise in her expression.

"Perhaps even more importantly, I want someone to love *me* – the real me, the magical me – to understand how important this part of my life is. Someone who'll inspire me on my magical path, like Rowan did for you. I want a boyfriend who'll come to rituals with me and share this aspect of my life, but John has no interest in anything remotely spiritual, and I have no interest in going to his football matches, which is what's important to him, and which I should care about, surely, if I was a good girlfriend? I guess that's why the idea of Jake is so appealing – he's interested in all this too."

Carlie smiled. "So what are you going to do?"

"Argh, I don't know. I don't think I realised until this exact moment, telling you, that this is how I actually feel. I hadn't questioned my being with John – or whether I even wanted to be. But now it kind of sounds like I should break up with him, doesn't it?" she asked, eyes pleading for answers, for reassurance.

"I'm so sorry Rhi, I don't know what to say – I'm not the best person to ask about this kind of stuff. But is it just because you think Jake is cute and he came to a ritual that all of a sudden you're not sure about John, or is it separate to that? Like, if Jake wasn't around, would you still be happy with John?"

Rhiannon sighed. "That's no help, that's just even more questions with even less answers," she said, pouting at her friend.

"What do you need help with?" Jake asked, suddenly reappearing and sliding back into his chair opposite Carlie. She started laughing, while Rhiannon blushed furiously, and sent a desperate signal to her not to say anything. But Carlie either didn't understand, or chose to ignore her.

"Well, we have a friend who's been dating someone for six weeks, and they get on really well, and have a nice time together, but it's not that desperate romantic love that people dream of, you know?" she began, with a side-long glance and a grin at Rhiannon.

"And this friend is wondering whether they should stick it out, because maybe the love will grow over time and they should just be patient. Or should they break up with the person now, even though there's nothing really wrong in their relationship, so that they're both free to find someone better for them, that mystical soul mate who'll inspire them to write poetry, and make them want to become more than they are, to fulfil all their potential, and be all that the person sees in them, even if they can't see it themselves yet."

The bell rang before Jake could reply, and they all hurried off to their next class, but the following one was history, and the three of them sat together as usual. And to Rhiannon's embarrassment, Jake turned around and stared right at her.

"So, I was thinking about what we were talking about earlier, and I think your friend probably should break up with the guy. Which is just my opinion of course, but if you're not in love with him, maybe you should end it, so he can find someone who'll love him as he should be loved, and you have the space in your life for someone you could potentially love to fit into."

Rhiannon blushed, but nodded, aware that her friend was staring at her intently.

"In fact, I've been thinking about what you were saying before Carlie, and it made me ponder my own life too. My girlfriend and I decided we'd try the long distance thing, but our conversation at lunch made me realise that I don't miss her as much as I probably should. And it's the same as you Rhiannon," he said, letting the pretence that they were talking about someone else drop.

"I really like her, and I'm sure if I was in Perth right now we'd still be together, but I've realised today that she's not the love of my life, so it's not fair to her to make her wait for me, and turn down the possibility of her meeting someone who really does adore her. She's a wonderful girl, don't get me wrong, but she doesn't make my heart sing like in the movies – and she certainly doesn't make me want to be more than I am, or inspire me to be all that I could be, like you said Carlie." And he looked at her with so much love that Rhiannon felt a physical pain in her chest. A longing. Why did the good ones always fall for her friend?

Sighing, she opened her books. Still, maybe Jake was right – whether or not there were any other potential love interests, was she wasting her time with John, and wasting his time too? And had she just become excited at the possibility of dating someone *like* Jake, not Jake himself – someone who would make magic with her? Someone as spiritual as Rowan?

Yet she had to admit that she'd never actually asked John if he'd come to a ritual with her, she'd just assumed he wouldn't. She knew how religious his parents were, she'd seen all the bible verses in their house, and walked past the church John went to with them, and that made her nervous. But maybe she had to give him a chance.

Terror filled her as she contemplated revealing her magical self to him. Could she be brave enough? Did she have the courage to be vulnerable, to show him her true heart and see what he thought of it? To be rejected after that would be awful, humiliating, but what was the alternative? To hide her real self just to keep the peace? And was it fair to him to not give him the credit for being strong enough to accept her, pointy witch's hat and all? Maybe he would surprise her...

When Rhiannon swept into Carlie's candle-lit room the following night, she smiled at the sense of magic already present. It was a powerful night for their coven working, since the earth was swirling with the energies of the sabbat as well as the dark moon. They'd planned their own Imbolc observance, a ritual of forgiveness, new beginnings and moving on, and it was the perfect time to let go of the darker emotions they'd been battling – resentment, guilt, bitterness – and banish them for good.

Soft light flickered from every corner, from tall pillar candles as well as spirals of tealights in small coloured-glass holders, and incense burned from a wrought iron censer on Carlie's dressing table.

"Wow, it's beautiful," Rhiannon said, eyes shining in the candlelight. She sat down on a cushion on the floor and gazed at the altar Carlie had set up. Each time they met they seemed to have something new to add to it, and she loved how it was growing alongside them as they grew on their magical path. Yet there was an object missing, which wasn't like Carlie.

"I thought tonight we should focus on fire," Carlie said. "The fire of the Imbolc flame and new beginnings, and the fire that can burn away pain and regret, and leave only what is pure and good behind."

"That sounds really great, but you don't have fire on the altar," Rhiannon replied, embarrassed that she had to point this out. Her friend had never forgotten an element before. Smiling mysteriously, Carlie placed a small wrought iron cauldron in the centre of the altar space, the size of a teacup, then handed a long parcel wrapped in red velvet to Rhiannon. "A gift for you," she said simply.

Rhiannon raised her eyebrows. "Really? Another one?"

"Really," she giggled. "The woman in red this time, Aideen. Do you know what that name means?"

"Fire."

"Of course," Carlie said, laughing.

As excited as Rhiannon was to have another gift from their Otherworldly friends, it also made her sad. Was she really so awful that they would go to Carlie alone instead of to both of them? To not even speak to her, and give her a chance to explain her actions?

"Hey," Carlie said, breaking into her thoughts. "I've been dying to know what's inside. Come on, unwrap it so we can see what it is! I have an idea, but I'm not sure I'm right."

Bursting with curiosity now, Rhiannon untied the ribbon and opened the parcel, then smiled. On the top was a small wrought iron tealight holder, with a vanilla-scented candle nestled within it. She laughed as she lit it and placed it in the south of their altar.

Carlie grinned too. "Lucky guess huh? Otherwise you might have thought I'd forgotten the fourth element."

Oops! She *had* assumed that. She turned back to the parcel. Inside were two elaborate wrought iron candle holders, both wreathed in sculpted metal ivy leaves, one with a sun on it, and one with a moon. Two tall candles, one silver, one gold, lay beneath them, so she placed the silver one in the moon holder and the gold one in the sun holder, then positioned them on the altar too, one on either side of the cauldron. That must have been their gift to Carlie. Both gifts of fire.

A small folded note fluttered down to the floor, and she unfurled it and read it aloud.

My dearest Rhiannon, here is some light to illuminate your own light, when you feel that you are drowning in darkness and cannot see what others see in you. Please trust yourself, and your worth.

Tears started to well in her eyes. How could a woman who'd never met her know how she would feel tonight, when apparently she'd given Carlie the gifts two weeks ago?

As Rhiannon lit the candles, a sensation of peace descended around her. She inhaled the sweetness of the incense, smiled as she heard Carlie's cats Luther and Luna exhale in their sleep behind her, and felt joy and such a deep sense of connection as she looked at her friend and magical partner. Carlie was right, they didn't need Jake joining them, didn't need anyone. Their Power of Two was perfect just as it was.

"Now, how shall we begin things tonight?" she asked.

"I thought we could write down the things we want to let go of, then burn them in our Imbolc fire," Carlie replied, waving her hand over the cauldron in the centre of the altar, which was filled with sabbat herbs. "We can harness the spirit of the dark moon to burn away our regrets, extinguish our bitterness and release all the stuff we want to get rid of. Then we can use the energy of fire and the Imbolc flame, and the approaching new moon, to ignite our new passion and purpose, and make our own fresh start."

"That sounds perfect." Rhiannon sighed. "I really am sorry."

"I know you are. And I'm sorry too."

"Why are *you* sorry?"

"I've been sad and angry, and full of the injustice of it all. I'm sure I haven't been all sweetness and light to be around."

"You've been fine," Rhiannon said softly. "And I'm glad you called me out on my awful behaviour. You needed a friend and instead you got a jealous harpy, someone who wanted you to get over such a heartbreaking thing in an instant, just so I didn't feel uncomfortable. I'm really sorry. I was selfish to harp on about how you should just 'get over it', as though you can simply flick a switch and turn off all the pain."

Carlie smiled sadly.

"I mean, god, it's only six weeks since... well, since you lost Rowan," Rhiannon continued. "So you be as sad as you need to be, for as long as you need to be, and know that I am here for you now. For what it's worth, I really regret the way I treated you, and I promise I will be more considerate in the future."

Carlie reached over and hugged her friend, then looked down at their altar. Rhiannon got the hint. She picked up her wand to cast the sacred circle, then invoked the elements and directions.

Once she was done, Carlie called on the god and the goddess to join them, to aid them on this dark moon night as they went within on their own personal journeys of introspection and reflection. Rhiannon closed her eyes. Her mind whirled, and she saw an image of the woman in red from the other night. Was it Bridie, or Aideen?

"Does it matter beloved?" the being asked, voice deep and dark and ancient – and a little frightening. Rhiannon shivered. It must be Aideen. Surely Bridie would be kinder, gentler.

The red-clad woman's eyes glittered, cold and dark. "Do not be afraid Rhiannon. You have faced the storms, and tamed them. You have learned from the water, moved with it, and released what you no longer need. And now it is time to step into the fire."

"What does that mean?"

The woman laughed, her voice harsh. "That is for you to discover, to explore. It will not be handed to you on a platter. But just like the storms, fire is a part of you. It can destroy, yes, but it can create too. It can harm, but equally it can heal. It can burn away pain so you can truly open your heart – but you have to face it. You have to stare at it head on and acknowledge that it happened. Pretending it away will just leave you stuck."

Rhiannon glared at Aideen, unnerved and impatient. What was she talking about? She'd dealt with her grief. She'd apologised to Carlie. What more did she want from her?

"It is what *you* want beloved, what *you* need," she said. Suddenly flames licked at the bottom of the woman's long red dress, and Rhiannon felt the heat of them. As they climbed higher then reached out to her, panic overtook her. Was the woman in red *trying* to burn her alive?

There was an edge of cruelty in the sharp angles of Aideen's face, and her eyes flashed with danger, yet Rhiannon felt the flames lowering, then fading away. She inhaled sharply, trying to calm the racing of her heart.

"Let the power of fire fill you with courage," the woman instructed her, voice stern. "Stop hiding. Be brave enough to trust yourself, and risk everything. Let it burn away your pain, your blame, your shame, then spark your passion and intention."

Shame. Rhiannon shivered again, a faint thread pulling at her memory. But before she could lose herself, Carlie placed a hand on her arm, and her eyes snapped open. She was sitting in her friend's candle-lit bedroom, safe within their sacred circle. There was no fire, no flames, no woman in red accusing her of... *what?*

"Are you okay?" Carlie asked, and Rhiannon nodded, still feeling confused and not quite in her body. Her friend handed her a piece of pale green paper and a gold pen, and she tried to stop her hand from shaking so she could write what was in her heart.

Dear Bridie, goddess of healing and love and fire, of power and passion.
Tonight I call on you to help me release my guilt over how I treated Carlie, and to help her to forgive me. Please fill us both with patience and forgiveness and love.

Please help me listen to my own heart too. I thought I loved John, and yet I yearn for the kind of relationship Carlie had with Rowan, the passionate, all-consuming love that burns you like a fire. I know it nearly destroyed her, yet what is the point of anything else?

For a moment she chewed on the end of her pen, trying to figure out what Aideen had meant. *Shame.* Why had that word so unnerved her? A fragment of memory returned, of the psychic she saw when she was visiting her grandma. *"There's something painful you're trying to keep buried..."*

A flash of the woods at night.

Rough hands holding her down.

Determinedly, she shook the vision off.

Bridie, perhaps most importantly, help me be stronger so I can be there for my dad and for Brodie, and to help Carlie as she heals from this latest grief. And if I am supposed to work with your element of fire, please hold me safe. Make me brave.

So mote it be…

When she opened her eyes, Carlie was smiling at her. "Ready to burn it away?" she asked, as she passed her hands over the small cauldron on their altar, infusing the herbs within it with her intent, then igniting them. The scent of basil, bay and sandalwood gave Rhiannon strength, and she nodded.

She watched as Carlie fed her message to Bridie into the small flames, the paper blackening and burning away, curling upwards in sweetly scented smoke. For a moment it looked as though her friend was struggling with something – or someone – and Rhiannon reached out to her and gently touched her hand. "Are you okay?"

Carlie looked startled, but she nodded. "Yes, I'm good. Your turn," she whispered.

Nervous now, Rhiannon held her paper to her heart, then dangled it above the flames in the cauldron. It caught fire, and for an instant she thought she saw a figure in the flames – a red-clad woman admonishing her, or Bridie taking her message to the heavens? As the last of the smoke drifted skyward, both girls felt a shift in the room, and a great weight lifted from their shoulders, and their hearts.

Chapter 28

A Friendship Forged In Magic

Beth

Vivid memories slammed into Beth, threatening to swallow her whole, when she heard her daughter ask Carlie if their friend Jake could join their coven. Her own first magical workings all those years ago had been with Violet and Mike – their own Power of Three – so she wasn't surprised that Rhiannon would like the idea of Jake being part of their group.

Having Mike by her side in the circle had made Beth feel safe, and supported. Balanced. He had brought an earthiness to their spellworkings and ceremonies, a practical groundedness that allowed her and Violet to dance amongst the stars, knowing he would anchor them firmly to the present and guide them home. Mike had been fascinated by the rich history of the rituals they performed, while the girls loved the practise of magic itself. The tangible atmosphere as they cast circle and welcomed the deities. The physical sensation as ritual consciousness descended on them like a heavy cloak, a layer they could feel around their shoulders, weighing them down into their bodies and connecting them to the earth, and to the thread of enchantment they wove.

Despite that, Beth was glad the intensity of tonight's ritual with Carlie was reminding her daughter that she didn't need anyone else to work magic with, especially a boy she'd just met. There was an incredible intimacy that developed during ceremony and spellwork, a bond that left you emotionally naked and vulnerable. It was a beautiful thing to share that with someone you loved, and oh how she had loved Mike, but it would be too much for Rhiannon to tie herself to Jake right now, too messy. There were way too many things that could go wrong, way too many feelings that could unravel. Especially when she seemed so conflicted about her boyfriend right now.

The candles the girls had lit flickered in the breeze from a crack in the doors to the balcony, and Beth stared around in consternation. This was Violet's old bedroom, where she'd spent many happy times. Carlie must have moved into it at last, and for a moment Beth's heart ached for Rose, and how emotional that must have been for her. But then she was suddenly sucked backwards through time, through darkness, through memory, until she saw herself and Violet sitting where their daughters had been moments earlier.

"Come on Beth, Mum wanted to know if we'll call the quarters tonight, with her and Miri. You know you can do it, you don't have to be shy. You're filled with magic, and I for one am convinced you'll be absolutely fine. You have such an affinity with water, so that's the perfect element for you to call. You can wear my lapis necklace – it's blue for water, and it's associated with the throat chakra, and helping to open it up to aid speech and speaking. And it will look so pretty with your blue eyes."

Violet smiled at her, eyes daring her to agree, then reached out and touched her hand. Beth jumped in shock. How did memory have sensation? How did a ghost get to feel?

Violet sighed at her reaction, misunderstanding her confusion and hesitation. "Oh Beth, you have to stop doubting yourself, doubting your power, doubting your strength. Mike wouldn't have invited you to a ritual in the first place if he didn't like you. Mum wouldn't be welcoming you with open arms either. And I'm the best judge of character around, and I can see we'll be friends forever," she said, so certain of the truth of her predictions. Where had it all gone wrong? "And our hubbies will be friends, and we'll have daughters who will grow up and be friends too."

The lump in her throat kept Beth from speaking, so Violet continued, eyes dreamy, as she plotted out their lives. The houses they'd buy right near each other, the family holidays they'd go on, the magic they'd weave together.

Then she paused. "What's wrong Beth?"

"I so badly want all of that to be true Vee. But I thought you wanted to travel, to see the world, to meet new people..." And dump Mike for the older, more worldly shaman, but she couldn't say that.

Her friend laughed. "Sure, I might travel a little, but I know my home is here, in Summer Hill. I want to be a social worker, and help Mum in the shop too, doing reiki and herbalism, which will be a great combination. Think of all the people I'll be able to help."

Oh goddess, what on earth had happened to Violet to turn her into a high-flying lawyer on the other side of the world, who never spoke to her mother or visited the village again, and who turned her back on magic so completely?

Suddenly the scent of burning herbs overpowered Beth, and although she fought it, trying desperately to hang on to this precious time with Violet, she found herself dragged back to the present. Filled with sadness and nostalgia, she watched Carlie feed her list of wishes into the cauldron fire, followed by Rhiannon, and for a moment she imagined that she and Violet had got to live the lives they'd planned. A sob escaped her when she glanced across at Carlie, who looked so much like her mother. Would she be the one to live out Violet's dreams, working with Rose as a grief counsellor and healer, taking her mother's place in the ritual circle?

And how had the poor girl coped, suddenly being plunged into this strange world of magic, after growing up with a strait-laced mother who had rejected it all? Although truth be told, she seemed to be handling it better than Beth had. Recalling her own first stumbling steps into the Craft twenty years ago, and how shy and nervous she'd been, Beth envied Rhiannon and Carlie their confidence in casting circle and invoking the deities, in crafting rituals that were meaningful to them.

Had she helped her daughter with that at least? She'd been so excited when she took Rhiannon to her first public ritual a few years ago. So proud of the way she'd handled herself, and so happy that she could finally begin to share this deepest part of her heart and soul with her daughter. Admittedly most of it had gone over Rhiannon's head back then, but she'd been so wide-eyed and curious, so keen to absorb it all, and so grateful to be included.

Beth had longed to welcome Rhiannon into the circle proper, to initiate her as a full member of Rose's coven, rather than just coming to the occasional public rite. She'd thought seventeen would be the right age for her daughter's dedication – but she'd died before Rhiannon reached that birthday. The sense of injustice burned at her, but she was grateful that Carlie and Rose had helped Rhiannon continue her magical studies.

She wondered if the priestess still ran her Year and a Day magic course. When Rose had invited her to sign up all those years ago, she'd been hesitant, with no faith in her own abilities or potential, but somehow she managed to bury her fear and push herself out of her comfort zone, and it was the beginning of a spiritual transformation that changed her life.

Six weeks after Violet left home, as Samhain rang in the Celtic New Year, Beth and six other apprentices met with the priestess and committed to their path of learning. They gathered every week to study the sabbats, the moon phases, magical history, healing, divination and spellcasting. They celebrated each ritual together privately, on a deeper level, but also facilitated occasional public ones to share their magic with the community, who became more interested in their ceremonies every year.

All seven of the priestesses-in-training consecrated their own personal Book of Shadows when they began their studies, which continued to grow and evolve over the years. By the time Beth died, hers was a few thousand pages long. Some of the corners were jagged and the pages were slightly yellowed, but it was full of wisdom and learning, such an incredible charting of her magical journey, and she was so glad she had been able to pass it on to Rhiannon. The seven also contributed to the group book, which symbolised their learning, growing and becoming stronger together. They would take it in turns to record the sabbat and moon rituals, and would add spells and recipes and epiphanies whenever they had them. It was an astonishing document, which Rose had begun writing in when she first started doing magical workings twenty years before Beth joined her. She wouldn't be surprised if someone discovered it hundreds of years from now and put it in a national museum – the wisdom within that book was astounding,

After her initial hesitation, Beth adored the course. Over one enchanted year they celebrated the turning of the seasonal wheel, honoured the moon and the sun, cast spells for themselves and others, and invoked the gods and goddesses as they learned more about each one. Most importantly, the seven apprentices learned more about themselves, and grew and became stronger together. Rose had warned them that it would require a great deal of work, and a willingness to be fearless as they examined their life and their spiritual practice. And she was right, but it was rewarding beyond measure, and Beth blossomed as she found the magic within her and discovered an inner strength she'd had no idea existed.

It culminated in their initiation ceremony once they'd completed their training, and they became the founding members of Rose's circle, continuing to weave magic into their lives and the community.

She hoped Rhiannon and Carlie were doing something similar to her apprenticeship. It had been such a magical, life-changing year for her. The seven women had all been shy at first, but they grew together, forging deep bonds. Beth had been excited to learn that one of them, Laura, was also training to be a teacher, and the two of them became dear friends. When Beth's parents sold the house she'd been living in, she and Laura rented an apartment together, and for twenty years they shared their careers, their magic, their lives and their loves.

It made her so happy that her daughter seemed to have a friendship as deep and profound as she'd experienced. She'd been worried for a while, when she'd treated Carlie so badly, so unfairly. It had given her flashbacks of her own less-than stellar behaviour towards Carlie's mum, and she understood her daughter's jealousy better than she would have liked. But, just like Violet, Carlie seemed able to forgive and move forward. At least she hoped she could...

Chapter 29

The Back and Forth and In Between

Rhiannon

W hen Saturday dawned, Rhiannon smiled with relief. Their coven night had been illuminating, as she and Carlie used the energy of the dark moon to release their guilt and work a spell of forgiveness, and things had been wonderful between them all week. And now she was off to see John, and end things with him. She did like him, but Jake was right – if it wasn't all she wanted, all it could be, she was wasting her time, and his. This was better for both of them.

It also helped that she'd been gifted with the gorgeous candlestick holders by the woman in red – and more importantly, the beautiful note. She took it out now and unfurled it, although she knew it by heart. She still loved seeing the old-fashioned penmanship.

My dearest Rhiannon, here is some light to illuminate your own light, when you feel that you are drowning in darkness and cannot see what others see in you. Please trust yourself, and your worth.

Yes. She was worth more than "it was fun". Maybe other girls could do casual, and all power to them, but she didn't want to. She wanted the earth-shattering romance Carlie had experienced with Rowan, otherwise she'd rather be single. Yet when she stepped off the bus near John's house, her resolve evaporated. He was waiting for her, and pulled her into a hug then kissed her forehead.

"I've missed you," he said. "I hope you've had a good week?"

She nodded. "I missed you too," she said automatically. "And yes, it was fine." She couldn't bring herself to confess that she'd dissected their relationship with her friends and decided to dump him, not when he was being so nice, and normal. Had she talked herself out of wanting to be with him prematurely? Maybe she should wait for a sign either way.

"I have to buy a present for my brother, so would it be too annoying to do that first?" John asked. "It's his birthday tomorrow, and I could sure use your help."

"Um, sure. Okay." Hmm, that was pretty last-minute. Why hadn't he done it already? It's not like the date of his birthday was a surprise. As he led her from shop to shop and watched her consider gifts, making no effort himself, her annoyance grew. He was taking her for granted, and she hated it. Sign one pointing to breaking up with him.

After two hours of traipsing around the village, he finally chose something from her selection, agreed to the card she suggested, and nodded when he reminded him he needed wrapping paper. For a moment she considered going home, but he took her hand and led her to their cafe, and since she was now incredibly hungry, she reluctantly acquiesced.

"Thanks so much for your help Rhiannon, I couldn't have done it without you," he said.

Grudgingly she nodded, and her annoyance was defused when he ordered her usual – at least he remembered – then took her hand. Okay, she'd give him an hour and see how he treated her.

They chatted about their week, what was going on at school, and what their little brothers had been up to. "So, are you going to be on the summer ball committee?" he asked. "I'd love it if you are, because I've already volunteered. It will be great to get to see more of each other."

Grinning, she took a sip of coffee. Could this be the sign to stay with him? That he was planning activities so far ahead, assuming they'd still be together in four months because he thought their relationship was going well? "They haven't announced it at our school yet, but I'd definitely like to. It would be cool to see each other during the week again."

"And what theme will you recommend for this one?"

Yikes. This was her chance to reveal herself to him. "What about *A Midsummer Night's Dream*? It will be the summer solstice, which is about faeries and magic, so we could combine some of the pagan traditions with the literary ones, like at Yule," she suggested nervously.

"You mean like Shakespeare, all dressed as faeries and woodland creatures? You'd make a sexy Titania, the faery queen," John smirked. "Tiny dress, wings..."

Cheeks flaming, Rhiannon tried not to feel too deflated, but she was disappointed that he went for the sexier interpretation, not the magical one. Then she saw his smile slip.

"Are you okay?" she asked tentatively.

"Yeah, yeah. I'm fine." But he sighed, and Rhiannon noticed the furrow between his brows, and a tightness around his mouth. Had she been oblivious to his feelings, while being annoyed that he didn't care about hers? Or was that giving him too much of the benefit of the doubt?

"You can tell me..." she offered.

Their coffees arrived, and he took a long time stirring the sugar into his mug. "Mum and Dad told me last week that they're thinking about getting divorced. I'd noticed they were arguing a bit, but they've done that before, and got over it, so it was a bit of a shock."

Rhiannon sipped her coffee, trying to think of something comforting to say, but her mind was blank.

"Dad's been coming home late a lot, so I guess I figured it was his fault, that he must have cheated or something, so I've been really mad at him. Baiting him, blaming him. Hurling accusations and insults, and shouting him down when he's tried to explain himself. I said a lot of things I shouldn't have, that will be hard to get over."

"I'm sure he'll understand, and forgive you."

"Yeah, but I don't think I can forgive myself, because it turns out he *didn't* cheat, and he was telling me the truth. And it's Mum who wants to separate. And now they're both at me to take sides, and decide who I'll live with, but I can't really stand to be with either one of them right now. Then there are my brothers. They're too young to really understand, but they know something is up, and I'm not sure how to help them or ease their pain." He broke off, face flushed with emotion, and pain.

"I'm sure your brothers will be very grateful to have you, no matter how it turns out. And your parents will too." Rhiannon's voice was soft, not wanting to intrude, but wanting him to know she was there for him.

Finally John gave her a half-smile. "Sorry, I didn't mean to rant like that, and bring our afternoon down. I wasn't even going to tell you."

"What? Why not?" she asked, stung by his words.

"Nothing bad, it's just that I feel pretty selfish complaining to you about this when, whatever happens, I will still have two parents. And in the grand scheme of things I'll still have them both, even if one of them moves out."

"Pain is pain, and it's all valid. It's not a competition, and someone else's doesn't negate yours," Rhiannon said, remembering Rose's advice to her. "You're entitled to feel your emotions, and your pain, and it really will help to talk about it with someone, I promise."

Shrugging, he forced a smile, but he looked incredibly uncomfortable, and eager to end the conversation.

"Well, thank you so much for listening to me, I really appreciate it. I haven't wanted to talk to my friends about it, because to be honest I'm a bit embarrassed about it all. But telling you, even just saying it out loud, it's put things into perspective. If they do separate – and they may not – it won't be the end of the world." He paused. "Now, can I tempt you with some chocolate cake?"

Nodding, Rhiannon watched him walk to the counter and order, then take a deep breath and straighten his shoulders. When he got back to her, he was smiling, clearly wanting to change the subject, so she took his lead and turned the conversation to cheerier things.

When he had to leave a few hours later to pick up his brothers, she jumped on the bus back to Summer Hill, lost in thought. That morning, she'd been all fired up and ready to break up with him, but now she wasn't sure. Certainly she'd felt too guilty, once he confided in her about his parents, to end it then and there. But even before that had softened her feelings towards him, she'd felt conflicted. He was a nice guy. He'd held her hand and kissed her, without trying anything on, which she was relieved about.

She'd been obsessing over the whole "should she or shouldn't she" thing ever since they'd almost had sex, and maybe that was clouding her judgement. The fact that he hadn't tried to get her naked today made her feel a bit better about him – although he hadn't had the opportunity, so maybe that didn't really count.

Knock. Knock. Knock. The icy cold wind was making Rhiannon shiver, and she was relieved when Carlie opened the door. "Come in," her friend said, dragging her inside and giving her a hug. "Are you okay?"

Rhiannon shrugged. "I've been better, but I'm okay. I just had a really weird day with John." As she entered the kitchen, the warmth soothed some of her anxiety, and her tummy rumbled when she saw all the plates of cakes, biscuits and scones, and the baskets of savoury pies and tarts, spread out on the benches. "Wow, all this food looks amazing! What's the occasion?" she asked.

Rose told her to take a seat and brought her a plate, then put the kettle on to brew another pot of tea. "I'm afraid Luther passed away this morning," the priestess said softly. Rhiannon gasped with shock, then turned fearfully to her friend. No! This couldn't be happening. Surely she'd lost enough. Sadly she reflected on all of Carlie's losses – her parents, her friends, her childhood home, her school, her future in Sydney, her career as a lawyer, all topped off by the death of her first love, and now Luther, the first friend she'd made when she arrived in the village. Life sucked sometimes.

"Are you okay?" she whispered.

Carlie shrugged. "I've been better, but I'm okay," she said, voice quavering as she echoed the words Rhiannon had just uttered.

"What happened?"

"Gran said it was just old age, and there was nothing we could have done, so we're trying to focus on the fact that he had a great, and remarkably long, life. To be grateful for the time we did have with him. And he didn't suffer, so we're doing our best to convince ourselves not to be too sad, and that it's just part of the enchanted wheel of life – but it's really hard," she sighed.

"Do you think he knew he was going to die? Is that why he brought Luna to you?" Rhiannon asked, as she peered over at the kitten, curled up in Carlie's lap and seeming oblivious to their grief.

Rose spooned fresh tea leaves into the pot before she answered. "I think so. He was very old, although he never seemed that way. But I think he was worried about making Carlie face another loss, and of leaving her without a companion, so he found a replacement for himself," she said, pulling another mug out of the cupboard and pouring soy milk into a jug, then taking them over to the table.

The three were subdued as they drank tea, ate scones and chatted, then Rose excused herself, seeming to sense that Rhiannon had things to talk about. The moment her door closed, Carlie turned to her friend. "Are you okay? What happened today? How did it go?"

"We don't have to talk about it now. How are you doing? I can't believe Luther's gone. I'm so sorry," she said.

A shadow crossed Carlie's face. "I'm all right. We had a beautiful ceremony, and Gran reminded me that we should be celebrating and focusing on his life, not his death, and that he had an uncannily long one for a cat. But tell me what happened with John."

Rhiannon toyed with her mug of tea, then took a deep breath and managed to smile. "You know, death really puts things in perspective, doesn't it. I was stressing about John, wondering what to do to fix it, trying to figure out how much I liked him, or whether I just like having someone to be with. I'd worked myself up into a real frenzy, like it was the most important thing in the world, when really, what's the big deal? I date him or I don't date him, it's as simple as that. It's hardly an earth-shattering dilemma, so why was I tying myself in knots about it?" she asked, shrugging in an effort to seem nonchalant.

Carlie smiled. "You know, a wise person once told me that being a teenager is all about drama. That whole

'I'll die if he doesn't love me,' or: 'I love you, best friend, no wait, I hate you and I'll never speak to you again!' That we feel everything much more intensely than adults."

Rhiannon laughed, so hard that she ended up doubled over, tears of amusement running down her cheeks. It felt really good to release some of her pent-up emotions. "I can't believe you remember that!" she giggled. "That was at Brodie's party, the day after we met. My god, I really thought I knew everything, didn't I?"

"How could I forget? I was incredibly impressed by your maturity that day. Although it seems we forget all our great advice when something crops up in our own lives."

"Or it's: 'Do as I say, not as I do,'" Rhiannon added with a grin. "It's always so much simpler to see the answer to someone else's dilemma than your own. Yet I couldn't see it in myself. I don't know, I'd pretty much decided I should end things with John when we were talking about it with Jake the other day, but when we met up this morning I remembered all the reasons I liked him."

Smiling ruefully, Rhiannon rolled her eyes. "We had fun – I helped him buy a present for his brother, which was a bit annoying, then we drank coffee for hours. He asked if I was going to be on the summer ball committee, and said he'd love it if I was because he'd already volunteered. And then he confided in me some problems he's been having with his dad, and I felt honoured that he could tell me. So now I'm even more confused, because today I really like him, and want to be with him."

"That's great then, isn't it?" Carlie asked. "You really like him, he clearly likes you, and he feels close enough to you to share personal issues with. Isn't that what you want in a boyfriend?"

Sighing, Rhiannon nodded. "You'd think so, wouldn't you? But now that I'm away from him again, back here with you and Luna, and eating magical ritual food, I feel like I want more from my relationship. Which I know sounds insane!"

Carlie laughed. "It's not insane at all, it makes perfect sense. Especially as the reason you seemed to suddenly like Jake the other day was that he came to the ritual with us. I'm guessing you didn't bring up the witch thing today with John?"

Embarrassment made Rhiannon's cheeks flush red. "I'm not sure if I forgot or just chickened out. But it was going so well, I guess I didn't want to ruin things. Which in itself says something, I'm sure."

"Well, maybe you're over-thinking it now," Carlie said. "What if you try *not* to think about it for the rest of the weekend, and on Tuesday night at our coven meeting we can do an exercise to go within, and connect with our inner wisdom. Maybe you'll be able to figure it out then."

Rhiannon grinned. "You really are smarter than you look."

"Hey!" Carlie protested, and her friend laughed.

"Just joking. But I guess I'd better get home and let you get some sleep. And I'm really sorry about Luther," she added, leaning down to pat Luna on her tiny head.

"Thank you," Carlie said simply as she walked Rhiannon out to the front door and hugged her goodbye. "Now, no thinking, all right? We'll figure it out on Tuesday night."

Chapter 30

Letting Go

Rhiannon

It was hard to be patient with her brother or concentrate on school while Rhiannon waited for Tuesday night's coven ritual. She was tying herself in knots trying to figure out if she wanted to be with John or not. And backflipping every five minutes as she remembered dancing with him at the ball, and chatting about life over endless cups of coffee – then felt the intensity of her yearning for a boyfriend who shared her magical life.

Now it was almost time, and she wasn't sure she was ready for the answer. As if in response, a storm blew up while she was tidying her room, and she laughed when she opened the door and found Carlie wet and shivering on the verandah.

"How come you never bring an umbrella?" she asked.

Carlie shrugged. "It seemed like it was only the tiniest of sprinkles when I set out. And isn't it spring already? Why is it still storming?" she protested, voice petulant.

"It is, but it's still the very start of spring. And sometimes winter holds on longer than we'd like it to here," Rhiannon replied calmly, as she guided her out to the kitchen and put the kettle on. "Tea? And do you need some dry clothes to change into?"

Carlie stomped her feet to shake off some of the rain, then seemed to shake herself to rid herself of her bad mood.

"Sorry, I'm sure I'll survive. And tea would be great, thank you."

Mugs in hand, they climbed the stairs to Rhiannon's room, and she saw Carlie gaze curiously around her, clearly surprised there was no altar set up.

"I thought we could just use oracle cards tonight, and find the answers to our questions. Is that all right?" Rhiannon asked.

"Of course. You have a big decision to make."

Picking up the card deck from her desk, Rhiannon moved to the centre of the room, and waved Carlie over to one of the big purple cushions. Casting the sacred circle around them both, she sat down opposite her friend and asked if she wanted the first reading, but Carlie shook her head sternly.

"You're the one who desperately needs to figure out what to do, so ask your question as you shuffle the cards, then hand them over," she instructed, and although she sounded playful, there was a seriousness beneath her words.

Acquiescing, Rhiannon took the cards from the silk wrapping she kept them in and shuffled the deck, feeling panic rise with each flick of her wrist. *What should she do?*

"Hey, you know that you decide your destiny, right?" Carlie said, clearly noticing her nerves. "The cards are just to inspire and uncover your own heart, your own truth and choices, which you already know subconsciously. And if you don't like the answer, you don't have to take it on board – you can do the opposite, and they'll still have served a purpose by crystallising what you want to do. They're just a tool to help you see what you already know."

Rhiannon nodded. "I know, but I just have no idea what I want. When I'm with John I really like him and want to be with him, but as soon as I'm away from him I think we should break up."

"Yet deep down you know what to do, you're just not ready to face it. Maybe you'll get some clarity tonight though," Carlie said firmly. "Are you ready?"

Reluctantly Rhiannon nodded, still looking worried, and handed over the deck. Her friend grinned at her, then laid out three cards, face down, between them. As Carlie turned the first one over, Rhiannon was almost too scared to look, but she finally forced herself to do it, and to keep her expression blank. She didn't want to influence the reading with her fear.

"Okay, the first card represents the recent past, and it's Be Gentle With Yourself," Carlie began, smiling broadly. Then she turned over the next one. "The middle card is about the present, and it's Be True to Yourself. The third, which is about the near future and reveals symbols and wisdom to help you make a decision on this issue, is Learn to Let Go. Interesting..."

Rhiannon stared down at the three cards, entranced by their beauty, and relieved that she couldn't perceive a negative outcome from them and their position to each other. But they hadn't made it any clearer yet either – did Let Go refer to letting go of John, or letting go of her conviction that he had to come to rituals with her and share that part of her life?

Curiously she looked at Carlie, wondering what she was seeing in the patterns and positioning. For several long moments her friend seemed lost in thought, far away from this room and this sacred circle, and she tried to caution herself to be patient. Tried to temper her fear. God, what was wrong with her? Carlie was right, if she didn't like the answer, she could do the opposite. And she could decide to stay with him now, then break up with him a week from now, or a month. Whatever she chose tonight, it didn't have to be forever. She could change her mind at any time. Closing her eyes, she took deep, calming breaths, and felt the tension leave her body. Just as she started drifting off into dreams, Carlie's voice pierced the languid fog of her mind.

"Okay, for the first card, the one referring to the past, the message is clear – Be Gentle With Yourself. You've been beating yourself up over things you've done and choices you've made, but it's time to stop. The past can't be undone – you need to own your decisions and take responsibility for your actions, then let it all go so you can move forward. No one is perfect, so give yourself a break. And be as gentle and forgiving with yourself as you would be with anyone else."

Rhiannon nodded. That made sense, in regards to her relationship with Carlie most pertinently, but also with John. She had to give herself a break. She'd been good to him, good with him, as he had been with her. She'd been racked with guilt about running out on him the day he'd wanted to go further than her, then going hot-cold-hot the next day. But he hadn't seemed to mind, so she had to stop torturing herself over what she should or shouldn't have done.

"In relation to your question today, there is no blame to be cast, and you shouldn't have any regrets about the time you've spent together," Carlie continued. "Whether you stay with John or end it, you have both cared about each other, and enriched each other's lives, and nothing will change that. He's helped you learn more about yourself and what you want – and what you don't want – in a relationship. And he encouraged you to break through your shyness, to become more active with school committees, to communicate with people you normally wouldn't, and that's a valuable thing. He's helped you to grow and become stronger and more assured."

Rhiannon smiled. That was true.

"Don't regret your time together on his account either – you have helped him too, been a confidante when he needed one, and shown him a new way to look at the world. Whether your relationship endures or not, the things you have given each other will stay with you both, and you'll look back on your time together with fondness and gratitude."

Carlie looked up anxiously, eyebrows raised in question, then gulped down some tea. Rhiannon had forgotten that her friend was nervous about how well she'd be able to read the cards, so she grinned and nodded. She was impressed with her interpretation of the first card, and now she was curious about what she would get from the next one.

"This is where it gets interesting," Carlie grinned. "The present. Your card was Be True To Yourself, and at the heart of your question is insecurity about your own deepest self, and a fear that he won't like you if he really knows you. Yet it's also a wider feeling, about the whole world accepting you for who you are, and the fear you have of revealing yourself. We show a different side of ourselves to everyone we meet – we play up some aspects of ourselves with one person, play down or even hide others with someone else, and that's fine. It's not important that everyone knows everything about you. Fellow students, workmates, potential bosses, none of them need to know your religious, spiritual or philosophical beliefs if you don't want them to."

Sighing with relief, Rhiannon felt calm envelop her. So, she could stay with John. She kind of liked that idea. But Carlie hadn't finished.

"For real trust and real love to grow within a relationship, you can't pretend away the things that have the most meaning to you. You can't dim your light for acceptance, deny the beliefs that are central to your very being, or hide what's in your heart," she said. "Magic and ritual is vital to you, and any relationship where you feel you have to hide that will remain superficial in many ways. For a true heart connection, you have to be able to share that, not laugh it off or lock it away."

As much as Rhiannon hated to admit it, she knew that deep down this was the crux of her issue, which meant that she probably did need to end things with John. Then Carlie surprised her again with her insight and bravery.

"So don't deny him the chance to see you, all of you, and make up his own mind. Share your spirituality and what is important to you. Be brave enough to tell him you're a witch. If he has a problem with it, then it's not meant to be, and it would be better to find out now. But imagine how beautiful it will be if he does embrace it, and embrace you in all your complexities and depths. If he can share this precious thing with you, and come to rituals with you, it will make them even more magical."

Rhiannon was surprised to feel tears welling in her eyes, and she wiped at them impatiently. Carlie's words had touched her deeply, and she knew this was what she wanted, whether it was with John or with someone else. She almost didn't need to hear about the third card, because the reading felt complete to her. She had her answer.

"Nuh-uh," Carlie said, laughter in her voice. "There's still one left, and the future card is just as important as the others, if not more so. Yours is Learn to Let Go, and I think for you it refers to the fact that some people come into our lives for a long time, and that's wonderful. But others only come into our lives for a short time, and that's okay too. It doesn't mean the short-term people are less important, because sometimes you can learn more from, and grow more with, someone you only spent a few precious hours or days with, than someone you've known your whole life."

Rhiannon nodded, feeling the truth of the sentiment.

"So look for the good in your relationship, for the things you've learned and the things you've shared, and celebrate that, without feeling that you have to remain stuck there just because it was once good, or because it isn't bad," Carlie continued. "You deserve to be with someone who makes your soul sing, who loves all of you, not just the parts you choose to show, and who inspires you to be more yourself, rather than diminishing what's most important to you."

Then she broke off, and stared out the window, before muttering something under her breath.

"Are you okay?" Rhiannon asked. "Did you say something?"

Her friend shook her head, as if to shake off a memory or a vision. "Yeah, I'm fine. Just for a moment I thought I could feel... something. Sorry, what was I saying?" she asked.

Rhiannon was worried that her friend had been too distracted, and wouldn't know how to continue. "Someone who makes your soul sing, who inspires you to be more yourself," she reminded her.

And Carlie surprised her again. "Yes. Cherish the people who are in your life for the long haul, but also express your gratitude to those who only come into your life for a short time, then say goodbye with a clear heart. If John isn't the person who will share your magical life with you, that's okay. Don't be scared of letting him go so you can find someone who will embrace your spiritual side. It's better for John too, if that's the case, that you let him go and allow him to be with someone who shares the things that are most important to him."

Carlie paused, nervous again. "Thoughts?"

Rhiannon laughed. "When you put the cards down and I saw what they were, all I felt was relief. Relief that I should end it. And that last one made me really happy – I love that you said you can touch someone's life and heart, and be glad of that, but you don't necessarily need to stay with them. Because John is a lovely guy, and there's no real reason I can think of to break up with him. He hasn't been mean to me, he treats me well, it's just not… well, it's not what you and Rowan had," she admitted. "And I'd rather hold out for that than settle for something that's nice, but not amazing and magical and heart-opening. I want to love and adore someone, and feel inspired and passionate about them, about us, and I want to be loved and adored too. And I want that for John as well."

Carlie hugged her. "Oh Rhi, you'll find that for sure, I know it. And you deserve that. You both do."

"It feels strange though," Rhiannon said haltingly. "I mean, what do I tell him? Shouldn't I have a good, clear reason? And I'm not sure that 'you're not Rowan' will cut it."

"You don't need any other reason than that you want more for both of you. You care about him, but it can take more than friendship for a relationship to work, especially if you can't – or won't – share the thing that's most important to you with him."

"But what if he argues with me, and I can't explain why we should break up?" Rhiannon asked.

Carlie's brow furrowed. "You don't actually need a reason to break up, and you don't even really owe him an explanation, if it comes to that. If it doesn't feel right to you, then you should end it. You don't need to convince him or win him over with your reason, and you don't need an excuse. It's not a topic open to discussion. It's not a debate where the person who has the most convincing argument 'wins'. If you don't want to be in the relationship you shouldn't be, no matter what he says to convince you otherwise. I mean, would you want him to stay with you even if he wanted to break up?"

"Of course not!"

"Exactly," Carlie said. "And it doesn't mean he's a bad boyfriend, or you're a bad girlfriend. He'll be someone else's perfect boyfriend, he's just not yours, and that's okay. It totally depends on the chemistry of the two people involved. You and Rowan probably wouldn't have worked out either, but not because of any failing on either of your parts." She smiled sadly.

"Hell, I'm sure psycho shaman guy was a great partner to someone else, but for some reason he and Mum brought out the worst in each other, not the best. There's someone out there who will love and support you in ways that will make you want to be the best you that you can be, who will recognise the deepest parts of your heart, and see you as the embodiment of the goddess. And you'll bring out their best too, and support them in following their heart and manifesting their dreams into reality."

Rhiannon reached over and hugged her friend. "Thank you for your wisdom, and your truth telling. If I'm brutally honest with myself, I would say that John really likes me, and really likes spending time with me, but it's not as though he couldn't imagine his life without me. So that makes perfect sense. He'll be an awesome boyfriend to someone else, and no doubt someone else will be the perfect girlfriend for him, but we just aren't that for each other."

The more Rhiannon thought about it, the more sense the idea made. It wasn't a criticism of either of them, it was just a matter of chemistry, and what was important to each other them.

"Thank you so much for this Carlie," she said. "I know it can't be easy for you to talk about, but I really appreciate your analogy about me and Rowan, because he was perfect for you, but wouldn't have been for me, and vice versa. Besides, I have to remember that it's not the worst thing in the world to be single, especially as it means I'll get to spend more time with you. Now, do we need another tea before I do your reading?"

"I don't need a reading, I'm fine," Carlie insisted.

"We'll have a break for tea, but you're not going to get out of having your reading hon, it has to be an equal energy exchange," Rhiannon said, as they wandered downstairs to put the kettle on. Besides, she was hoping that she could get a little bit of a "Jake's so sweet, open your heart" message in there. Not in a pushing-her-to-date-him way, but her heart hurt when she thought of how much Carlie had lost, and she wanted her to at least allow Jake in as a friend. He obviously really cared about her, and it couldn't hurt to have another person like that in her life, when she'd been left with so few.

As Rhiannon was pouring their tea, her dad came home, and he sat down and had a cuppa with them, catching up on their lives and their magical adventures.

Then Carlie stood up abruptly. "Oh my, is that the time? I should get home. I need to finish that assignment for class tomorrow. It was lovely to see you Mike, and I'll catch up with you at school Rhi," she said, then picked up her bag and rushed down the hallway and out into the cold night air.

"Is everything okay?" Mike asked, and Rhiannon shrugged.

"Looks like she really didn't want to have a reading," she said, trying to sound light-hearted, but a little annoyed that her friend had run out like that, and uneasy that she hadn't been able to return the favour and the effort. "But I guess I should finish my assignment too. Night Dad. Love you."

"I love you too darling."

Chapter 31

Chai and Comfort

Beth

Black lace fluttered at her wrists, tickling her to awareness, and Beth stared around herself curiously. She was floating against the ceiling in Rhiannon's bedroom, and a wave of pride and longing washed over her as she observed her daughter setting out candles and mixing herbs and resins into incense. That would explain why she was clad in this long black velvet dress – it seemed she was crashing Rhiannon and Carlie's coven night. If this half-existence wasn't so tragic, she would probably laugh.

When there was a knock at the front door, Beth followed her daughter out, soaring above the banister while Rhiannon walked down the stairs, then watching her greet her friend. Carlie was wet and shivering from a sudden downpour, and Beth tried not to laugh.

She stayed with them while the girls made tea then hurried upstairs, and hovered all night, watching as Rhiannon cast the sacred protective circle, then shuffled the cards of an oracle deck. She was searching for answers about her relationship, and Beth was so frustrated that she couldn't be there to help, and to share the wonder and disappointment of first love with her daughter.

As Carlie flipped the cards over, Beth swooped down, gazing at the words and illustrations on each one as it was revealed, and sensing Rhiannon's fear as well as her hope when she looked at them and tried to guess the meaning. When Carlie began her reading, Beth was impressed with her divination skills, and the wisdom of her interpretation. Would she have been able to counsel her daughter as well as Carlie did, if she was still alive?

Although part of her wanted to drift off into memories of the past, of moments when she'd been able to hold her daughter, and talk to her – moments she'd taken for granted while she was in them – she forced herself to be present. All night she tried to communicate with Rhiannon, touching her face, throwing her transparent arms around her in an effort to hug her, even attempting to push herself into her body again and see through her eyes. But nothing worked.

Depressed, she curled up on the window seat and wondered what the point of these painful bouts of awareness was. She was just about to give up and allow herself to drift back into the void, into oblivion, when Carlie glanced up sharply and stared right at her. And froze. Beth froze too, excited and terrified all at once. For some reason she couldn't make herself known to her daughter, but would this girl, this granddaughter of wise priestess Rose and daughter of kind, sensitive Violet, be able to see her?

Frantically she tried to pull the molecules of herself together, to stand up straight and strong and firm. She focused on making herself visible, or at least substantial enough to disturb the air, or affect an object or something. She rushed towards the girl, arms open, calling her name, so desperate to be heard, or seen, or felt.

Carlie's brow was furrowed, as though she was trying hard to concentrate. Could she see her? Or maybe just feel her? Excited, Beth grabbed at her shoulders, waved her arms in her face, then shouted with all her might. Carlie smiled in her direction, and she felt hope for a moment – before it was cruelly crushed.

"Aideen?" the girl murmured softly, wonderingly, and Beth's heart plummeted. She wanted to sob. How frustrating, to not be able to cry and yell and rant. The living took so much for granted.

Rhiannon was staring at Carlie. "Are you okay? Did you say something?" Her friend turned to her, puzzled, and shook her head.

"Yeah, I'm fine. Just for a moment I thought I could feel... something. Sorry, what was I saying?" Carlie asked.

The girls got back to the reading, and Beth let a silent scream push up from within her. But even though she was discouraged, she hung around, not quite ready to give up on Carlie. When the girls went downstairs for more tea, she floated between them, listening to their chatter. And when Mike got home and joined them in the kitchen, Beth's heart ached, yet also filled with love. Maybe she would be okay, if she could remain this small part of their lives. Surely this strange half-existence with her family was better than nothing?

Suddenly she noticed that Carlie was looking at Mike with growing horror – then the girl stood up abruptly, made her excuses, and raced out the door. Intrigued, Beth slipped out behind her, gliding by her side through the beautiful dark. Maybe she could find a way to insert herself into Carlie's dreams, or even connect with Rose.

As she hovered beside Carlie down the High Street, Beth gazed around herself sadly. Despite hating this village as a child, when she'd felt so trapped by her cruel parents, she had eventually come to love it. It was a part of her, a part of her family, a part of her magic. The tor was sacred, filled with an incredible energy that made her vibrate and shimmer, but the whole village was special to her too, and in the chilly air of this wet early spring evening, she revelled in the enchantment of it reaching out to her.

And then she felt... something... trying to draw her into the churchyard, to pull her back up the road and out to the cemetery where she was buried. She shivered in fright. Was something... unsavoury... trying to lure her back, and imprison her in her grave again? Was following someone not in her family frowned upon and worthy of punishment? Or was she somehow bending the rules by being here at all, and something had been sent to return her? Was her time with her loved ones coming to an end?

Panicked, she drifted closer to Carlie, seeking protection, seeking warmth, seeking humanity. For some reason she couldn't explain, she felt a strange kinship with this girl, this stranger who was so much like her friend Violet had been. There was something so beautiful, so poetic, in their daughters becoming friends. That there was this link between the two loves of Mike's life.

Now this thought of Mike having loved another before her just made Beth sad, rather than jealous, and she was pleased that she was no longer so torn up about Violet. Did ghosts evolve? Had she been sent here as penance for something she'd done, as a punishment of some kind? Would she only be able to stay until she learned something, or achieved something? Did she have a mission that she was unaware of? And if so, what was this girl's part in it? Why was she so drawn to her? So connected to her?

Her musings halted when Carlie opened the door of Kylie's Cafe and walked inside. Beth felt her shiver of delight when the warmth hit her skin, and she smiled. Such simple pleasures. Earth and fire, air and water. The elements she'd honoured and acknowledged for so long. Taking a deep breath, she focused all of her will on appearing visible, or at least being sensed – then was shocked to feel resistance when she tried to pass through the door into the cafe.

Stunned, she reached for the door handle, and was astounded to feel the smooth chill of the brass under her fingertips. Hardly daring to breathe, and unable to believe she'd *really* managed to manifest physically, she pushed against the door, exhilaration filling her when she heard the bell tinkle above her as it opened.

The scent of coffee, the heat of the crackling fire and the warm glow of the candles enchanted Beth, and for a moment she lost herself in the sensation. But she couldn't afford to waste time. Carlie was sitting in a cosy armchair next to the fire, and had pulled out her Book of Shadows and started to write. Beth was about to approach her when the woman behind the counter looked at her and smiled.

"It sure is chilly out there isn't it? What can I get you?" she asked. Beth turned and stared behind her, certain she must be talking to someone else, but the woman laughed.

"It's just you," she grinned. "What will it be?"

Beth gasped. She was visible. "A hot chocolate would be lovely, thank you," she stammered. Her voice was croaky, but apparently audible.

"No problem, I'll get it for you now. Take a seat." The waitress smiled, then turned away to pull down a jar of cocoa from above the coffee machine.

Elation shimmered through Beth, along with relief and joy, frustration and shock. Someone had seen her. Her heart skipped with excitement – then sadness and confusion flooded her. Why couldn't Rhiannon see her? Or her husband, who she'd been spending so much time with? Or Rose for that matter, the priestess and wise crone of the community, teacher of magic and divination, communicator with gods and goddesses. It didn't make sense.

But as she gazed down at her solid form and saw her long velvet skirt made physical, she knew she had to pull herself together. She had no idea how she'd achieved her current state, or how long it would last. Whether she was getting stronger, or this was just a one-off thing, and she would be sucked back into the void at any moment. Yet none of that mattered right now. This was her chance, possibly her only one, and she couldn't blow it. She had to find out why Carlie had looked at Mike so strangely before saying a hasty goodbye and running out of the house. And she'd also like to know why the girl who was so new to magic was the only one who'd come close to sensing her.

Before she lost her nerve, Beth strode over to Carlie's table – and was overwhelmed by the pulsating wave of wild emotions emanating from her. The girl was worried about Mike and Rhiannon – Beth could physically feel her pain – and she felt guilty. *Why?*

She cleared her throat. "Excuse me?"

Dropping her pen in surprise, Carlie looked up in confusion at the stranger who'd approached her. "I'm sorry," she said automatically, picking up her pen then turning her eyes back to Beth. There was confusion, and a flash of fear, in them, and Beth almost backed away and left her alone. Then she realised that Carlie's reaction wasn't because she looked like a ghost – she was just worried that she'd been introduced to her before but had forgotten her name.

"Didn't your friend tell you to stop apologising?" Beth asked, then winced at her foolishness in revealing that she'd overheard her conversations. Talk about creepy. "Do you mind if I sit with you?"

Hesitantly Carlie nodded. "Of course," she said politely, closing her book and stuffing it into her bag while Beth sank elegantly into the armchair next to her. When the waitress placed her drink on the table between them, Beth leaned in, closed her eyes and inhaled the sweet scent of the chocolate, then let out a deep, contented sigh. For a moment she allowed memories of being here with her family soothe her. She missed being able to touch things, feel things, smell things, affect things.

Then she became aware that Carlie was staring at her, waiting for her to go on. "Sorry," she muttered. She had to focus on her mission, and she had to speak before Carlie freaked out and ran away.

"They really do make the best hot chocolate here," she said, then sighed. *That was the best she could come up with?*

"I'll have to try it one day," Carlie replied, pouring a cup of chai tea from her pot, then staring intently at Beth again.

Bless her, she was still racking her brain to try to figure out who the crazy woman was. "We haven't met before Carlie, so you can stop struggling, and thinking you're rude to have forgotten me."

Bad move. Now Carlie's confusion had transformed to worry, and Beth swore under her breath. Inexplicably she could sense the girl's thoughts, but she had to hide that. She didn't want to scare her off before she'd managed to talk to her.

"You could say that I'm a friend of Rhiannon's," she said hastily. "I can sense that you're worried about her. And I'm so glad that you've both reconnected. That you've been able to forgive her, and are such a good friend to her. She's true to you too, and she'd never knowingly hurt you."

Carlie nodded cautiously. "I know," she whispered.

Did she? Did she know Rhiannon had been as jealous of Carlie as Beth had been of Violet? Did she know Rhiannon had been devastated to discover that her father had loved someone else before Beth – and that it was Carlie's mum, who she'd never heard mentioned before? It was understandable that it had made her daughter suspicious. And it was entirely Beth's fault, because she had forced Mike to create and maintain the strange altered history of their early life, erasing Violet as a friend, and as his beloved. Erasing her entire existence. No wonder Rhiannon was defensive when she first met Carlie, the daughter of the woman she'd just discovered had been so loved by her dad.

Beth sighed. She felt like she was drowning. What did she say to this girl she'd never actually met? This girl who looked so much like her old friend? As Carlie picked up her cup and took a sip of her tea, Beth stared at her, trying to figure it out. Why was this girl so worried about Mike? And why was she feeling guilty, as though it was all up to her to fix?

When the answer came, Beth almost broke apart and surrendered herself back to the void. She heard the word curse, loud, like the girl had shouted it. And now she was confused. Somehow Carlie knew about the curse, but how? Beth only knew about it because of Mike's crazy ramblings just before she died, when he'd reluctantly confessed that he'd gone to see the shaman who lured Violet away from him all those years ago and begged him to let her go. Of course Andre had refused, threatening Mike instead. He said that if he came between him and Violet, he would curse him so that everyone he loved died at age forty.

Beth didn't believe in curses, yet it turned out she'd died on the morning of her fortieth birthday, as promised. Would Mike have said something to Carlie about that? Asked her about Violet's death perhaps? But Violet was a couple of years younger than Beth, so she should have been safe. And didn't she die with her husband in a random car accident, on the other side of the world? How could that be part of the shaman's curse? And how could Carlie think she was responsible for it?

But the girl was staring at her expectantly again. These long silences were making her anxious. *Get it together Beth.*

"I can sense how much you're worrying about Mike too," she blurted out. "You have a beautiful heart Carlie. Your grandmother must be so proud of you."

The girl blushed, and tilted her head in acknowledgement of the compliment, without actually agreeing with it. Then she took another sip of her tea, and a deep breath. She was looking a little scared now, Beth could sense it, and hoping this was all just a dream, or some other rational explanation.

"Maybe it is some kind of dream," Beth said urgently, no longer as worried about scaring her. Somehow she had to get Carlie to help Mike, put his mind at ease. Maybe that's why she'd become physical tonight. "But you're awake now. And the thing is, you really need to wake up. Not from sleep, but from the fog in your brain, from the fog of your memories. You already know why the curse isn't real, why Rhiannon is safe, but you're too scared to linger on how you know."

"That's not true! I'd do anything to put Mike and Rhiannon's minds at ease," the girl protested, but she'd paled when Beth mentioned the word curse.

"I know," Beth replied. "You're kind like your mother."

Carlie gasped. "You knew her?" she asked, pain in her voice.

"I did. Everyone here loved her, and felt her loss when she left the village. I know Mike never stopped loving her."

Brow crinkling, Carlie stared hard at the woman. "Who are you? How do you know this stuff?" she begged. "And how could you know about Mike loving my mum? Because that's not true. He was married to an amazing woman who he adored, who he adores still, and whose children miss her terribly."

Tears pricked Beth's eyes, and she smiled sadly. "I'm sure she misses them more than anything too," she managed to choke out. Wow. She'd mentioned Violet being kind because she wanted to give Carlie a gift, a link to her mother's past, but it turned out that it was the girl giving the present to her, with her fierce denial that Mike had loved anyone other than his wife. She really was like Violet.

For a heartbeat Beth allowed herself to be distracted by the glow of her husband's love, and the warmth and heavenly sweetness of the cafe, gathering her thoughts while she watched the swirls of steam curling and uncurling as they danced towards the ceiling. Tentatively she reached for her hot chocolate, and almost dissolved back into the nothingness in shock. She could feel the warmth of the drink, and the solidity of the mug!

All at once her senses became real. Alive. What was making her able to touch the mug tonight rather than have her transparent hand slide right through it? How was she able to appear to Carlie and the waitress tonight, when nothing had worked before? When her fingers had passed right through her beloved husband, and her hand trying to stroke Rhiannon's head had sunk into it. When her darling son had seemed a phantom as she'd attempted to hug him.

Was it Carlie doing it, this stranger who'd only become aware of magic a few months ago? That seemed unlikely – but then again, she was the daughter of Violet, and the granddaughter of Rose. Had she had any chance to avoid her witchyness?

Shaking with a mixture of fear and hope, Beth lifted the mug to her mouth and inhaled deeply. Pleasure swept through her, until she almost swooned from the memories it evoked. But fear stopped her from actually taking a sip. She couldn't risk it. What would it look like to Carlie if she faded at the wrong moment? A floating mug suddenly tipping over in mid-air, spilling the hot, sweet liquid onto her chair? Reluctantly she placed it back down on the table. Besides, she had to focus. She didn't know how long this would last.

"Rhiannon is going to need you, need your support," she said. "And Mike needs to know it's not his fault that his wife died. That he's not cursed." As Carlie gasped at her words, Beth saw a flash of gold out of the corner of her eye, and panicked. Was something really going to take her away right now?

"This is too long a story for tonight, but all you need to know for now is that you already have the answer to Mike's fear of a curse, you just have to dive within and rediscover it. I have faith in you Carlie," she said, then stood up abruptly and walked out of the cafe.

The door banged shut behind her, making the candles on the tables flicker, and she watched Carlie shiver in the cold draught that rushed in. Beth gazed down and saw that she'd become transparent again, and the disappointment tore her apart and shot her back out into the atmosphere in a million jagged pieces.

Chapter 32

Stained Glass Heart

Rhiannon

Heart thumping, Rhiannon stepped slowly off the bus and dragged her feet up the road to John's place. She hadn't slept all night, too busy tossing and turning, trying to figure out what she felt, what she wanted. It was easy to say it was over when she was drinking tea with Carlie in Rose's kitchen, filled with magic and camaraderie, and all fired up with the promise of a boyfriend who would embrace every part of her. But now in the cold light of their impending meeting, she was feeling tongue-tied and fuzzy on the details, and grumpy from exhaustion.

It didn't help that her night-time panic had kept her up until the early hours, which made her oversleep and miss the bus she'd planned to get. So she was stressed out and running late, and now that she was almost there, reluctant to knock on his door.

But eventually she could put it off no longer, so she steeled herself for the confrontation – and was relieved when John's mum answered the door. *God, she was such a coward.*

"Rhiannon, come in, it's so lovely to see you."

"Hi Mrs McGowan," she said, before remembering that his mum's marriage was in trouble. Would she be offended to be addressed as Mrs? Or was she just trying to obsess over some issue she had no control over, to avoid the more pressing one?

"Um, how are you? How are the boys?" Rhiannon asked politely, as she followed her down the hallway.

His mum turned around and smiled. "They're great. And thank you for helping John with the present last week, it was a big hit."

"Oh, I'm so glad!"

"Would you like a coffee before you head off with John? I think he's just finishing an assignment or something upstairs, but he shouldn't be long."

Rhiannon halted in surprise. He was always ready to leave the minute she arrived, as though he'd been waiting for her. And today she was later than she'd expected, so it was even more unusual that he wasn't prepared to go. Which might mean he wanted to end things too. And that could be a good thing. No guilt.

"Are you okay?" his mum asked, when she realised Rhiannon had stopped walking.

Forcing the frown from her face, she nodded and stepped into the kitchen. "Coffee would be great, thank you."

His mum bustled around the room, handing Rhiannon a steaming mug of caffeine-y goodness, then pulling a tray of shortbread biscuits out of the oven and offering it to her.

The sweet scent of sugar made her stomach rumble, and she blushed. "I'd love one, thank you. I was rushing too much to have breakfast this morning, so I'm a little hungry."

Mrs McGowan beamed at her. "Here, have as many as you like," she said, placing a plate of the biscuits in front of her. "Would you like anything else? Toast, eggs, a sandwich?"

"No, I'll be fine, we'll be having lunch soon. But these are delicious, thanks!"

Rainbows started dancing around the kitchen as sun filtered through the window and hit the crystal hanging from its frame, and Rhiannon felt herself relaxing. She hadn't spent a lot of time with John's mum before now, but as they chatted about school and springtime and the books they were reading, she realised how much she liked her. She would actually miss her. *Was that weird?*

"Thanks for being so lovely to John," his mum said.

Rhiannon gaped at her in surprise.

"I know he was able to confide in you, and I'm grateful for that. And you don't need to worry. His father has been really stressed at work for the last few months and, well, I won't bore you with it all, but things are slowly improving."

Rhiannon's smile was genuine, and relief rocketed through her. She had felt a twinge of guilt at breaking up with John while he was upset over this. "I'm so glad. I know how much time and energy work can take up – Dad really buried himself in it after Mum died, and it took a while for him to emerge, and come back to us."

When she saw the sympathy on Mrs McGowan's face, she regretted being so honest. Had she known that Rhiannon had lost a parent? Had John mentioned it to her?

"I'm so sorry about your mother. I can only imagine how hard that must be. My parents – all John's grandparents in fact – are still alive, a blessing I'd taken for granted, I must admit. If I can ever do anything, or you want to talk... Well, just let me know, okay?"

Tears welled at her kindness, and Rhiannon tried to keep herself together. She couldn't start crying in this warm kitchen in front of John's mum, especially when she might never see her again.

"Thank you," she whispered, taking a huge gulp of coffee and biting into another shortbread to try to distract herself.

Before Mrs McGowan could comment further, John bounded into the kitchen with a half-hearted apology, and asked if she was ready to go. She'd been ready for ages, but she bit her tongue. It had been nice to talk to his mum, and surprising herself as well as the others, she hugged her as she said goodbye.

"What was all that about?" John asked as they headed to the cafe.

"What was what?"

"You hugging Mum."

She sighed. "I don't know. We had a good chat while I waiting for you," she said, emphasis on the *waiting*.

"I'm sorry," he replied, voice contrite. "I just had to get a maths assignment finished before I completely lost the thread of it. But enough about that, how are you?" he asked, and leaned in to kiss her cheek. Which was odd, that he kissed her so innocently, without his usual ardour. She was perplexed, but tried to shake it off.

As they sat down in their usual booth, Rhiannon's nerves returned. Although she still felt good about her decision to end things, she was worried that she'd back out again if he was nice to her, like she had last time. Had she always been this frightened of confrontation? So racked with guilt at the thought that she might hurt someone's feelings? Either way, that wasn't a good enough reason to stay with someone she didn't want to be with.

"So, how has your week been?" John asked when he returned from ordering.

"It was okay. Lots of homework, hanging out with Brodie after school, seeing Carlie a bit."

John raised his eyebrows, and she rolled her eyes. He'd never got over his first, unfair impression of her best friend, which was awkward. And it reminded her just how amazing Carlie's boyfriend had been to her, how much he'd included her, even when he would have preferred to be alone with Carlie. Which was one more comparison where John unfortunately came out looking... not the better of the two.

"How about you?" she asked, determined to change the subject.

"Much the same. I've had extra soccer training, so I'm tired, but it's been great to hang out with the guys."

Rhiannon tuned out for a while, trying to work up the courage to ask him about his spiritual beliefs, or how he felt about hers anyway. She was scared though. How would she cope if he was really disparaging? But Carlie was right, it was better to know now if that was the case. How had her friend worded it? Something about the beauty of revealing her true self, and being brave enough to risk her heart and risk his judgement for a hopefully wonderful outcome.

"Earth to Rhiannon," she heard, at the edge of her awareness. Blinking rapidly, she focused on John. He was looking at her closely, waiting for her to say something, but the moment stretched out, an awkward, uncomfortable silence. They'd never had those before.

"Um, what do you think about witchcraft and the goddess, and rituals to honour the cycle of the seasons and nature?" she blurted.

To her shock, John laughed.

"What?" she asked defensively.

"Oh, sorry, I thought you were joking," he replied, still smirking.

She shook her head. "No, I was just wondering... Um, like the Yule Ball, that was steeped in pagan traditions."

"Oh god, you're serious," he said, and she knew she wasn't just imagining the mocking tone of his voice.

Mortified, Rhiannon nodded.

"Okay, well, if you want to know the truth, I think it's all superstitious nonsense that ancient peasants believed in because they didn't understand what made the sun rise and the earth turn. It was a symptom of their times, because they didn't know better. But since then we've learned so much about the world, and the universe. We've been to the moon. We know that the sun will rise every morning, without the need for sacrificed virgins."

She gasped, too stunned to respond. Not that he was waiting for anything from her.

"I can't believe there are still people who really believe in all that. They'd have to be seriously lacking in intelligence."

Rhiannon's mind spun, and she wondered how she could have been unaware of his feelings all this time. Had he been hiding his true self just as much as she had? And how could he not know that she *did* believe in all of that? It wasn't a secret. From the first day they'd met they'd been talking about Yule and the Wheel of the Year and the symbols of the goddess.

"So, I guess you don't want to come to the Beltane rite with me and leap over the bonfire together?" she said before she could stop herself. Oh well. In for a penny, in for a pound.

John stared at her like she'd grown an extra head, and she wondered what had possessed her to say that. It seemed her inner self wanted to burn this relationship to the ground. When he laughed, she stared at him in astonishment. He found this funny? Demeaning and belittling her beliefs was a joke?

"Oh Rhi, I do like your sense of humour. What are you talking about?" he asked, before collapsing against the back of the booth, amusement obvious.

Anger mixed with mortification, and Rhiannon opened her mouth to tell him – loudly – where to go, but before she could, the waiter came over with their drinks and their cake. John followed him back to the counter to get her some honey, which was surprisingly thoughtful, so she took a deep breath and tried to figure out how she felt about his response, and what he really meant by it.

Maybe she had to explain it to him a little better than she had. Possibly all he knew about witches were the stereotypes, and perhaps he'd just been caught off guard, and hadn't meant to be so rude. Maybe he didn't understand what she was asking, so she supposed she could offer him the benefit of the doubt.

"So, um, is that really how you feel about pagan spirituality?"

John gave her a strange look, but he considered his words more carefully this time. "Okay, what exactly do you mean by the term? Because there are a couple of girls at school who have started dressing all gothic, wearing pentagrams and wandering around holding crystals and muttering under their breath about casting spells and putting curses on people. And seriously, anyone who believes that curses have any power needs to have their head read."

Playing for time, and for calm, Rhiannon stirred the honey into her coffee as she tried to gather her thoughts. "No, I don't believe in curses, or casting spells on people without their knowledge, or even that black clothing makes a witch – Carlie and I have loads of beautiful, colourful dresses for our rituals. To me it's about being in tune with nature and the earth, observing the cycles of the seasons and of the sun and the moon, protecting the environment, doing rituals of healing and connection, becoming more aware of your own inner self, and being conscious about creating the life you want."

She smiled as she warmed to her theme. "It's hard to describe just how amazing, and how powerful, it is to work magic with Rose, the high priestess in our town. There's an electricity in the room when she welcomes the elements, and the god and the goddess, an energy and a tangible sense of connection that is so empowering. It's truly beautiful to be in her presence, and I know it helped me work through my grief over Mum."

The look on John's face silenced her. He was disappointed in her, disgusted and horrified, so she knew there was no point mentioning her coven work with Carlie, or the comfort and enchantment the Otherworldly beings of mist had brought to their lives.

John took a big mouthful of cake, then sighed. "I must admit that I'm shocked you could believe this Rhiannon, I thought you were smarter than that. But I suppose we can get around your ill-informed views – we don't have to agree on everything, and I can overlook this, as long as you don't try to drag me to some stupid hippie circle to commune with the *earth mother*," he laughed.

It was his sarcasm that did it. Anger pumped through her veins, and she no longer cared about being careful of his feelings. "Maybe there's no point in us being together then, if you're so dismissive of something that's so important to me," she said furiously. "Is that it?"

John shrugged. "Fine, if that's what you want."

"But –" She broke off. She was actually speechless. With no idea how to come back from where their argument had led, she stood up and grabbed her bag. "Fine. Well, it's been lovely spending time with you. Please give your mum my love. Goodbye."

And she ran out of the cafe and down the road to the bus stop.

*T*ears streamed down her face, although she didn't really know why. She'd been fine for it to be over – she'd planned to end it herself – so why was she so upset now that it was? She supposed it would have been nice if he'd cared. She wanted him to be sad at the prospect of them breaking up, not completely indifferent. Which she knew was irrational, but no one ever said love was fair...

Thankfully the bus came before she could rethink her actions or be tempted to go back and apologise, and she sighed as she dropped into the seat, then stared blankly out the window all the way home. As soon as she jumped off the bus she hurried over to Carlie's, eyes dry but her mind a jumble.

"How did it go? Are you okay? Want a cup of tea?" Carlie asked as soon as she opened the door.

Rhiannon smiled. "It was fine, I'm okay, and I'd *kill* for a cup of tea," she replied, following her friend out to the kitchen.

As Carlie put on the kettle and grabbed tea leaves and the teapot, Rhiannon leaned against the bench, still feeling shaken and confused.

"So, we broke up," she announced.

"I'm sorry," Carlie said, and Rhiannon raised her eyebrows in surprise. "Well, even when it's for the best, I'm sure it's still difficult, and I know that you really did like him," she clarified.

"You're right, thank you," Rhiannon admitted. "And the whole way back I've been feeling really strange, wondering if I did the right thing, to-ing and fro-ing with my decision…"

Carlie handed her a mug of tea and led her to the table to sit down, then put some homemade gingersnap biscuits on a plate and brought them over. Rhiannon laughed as she took one. All she'd eaten today was cake and biscuits. No wonder she felt so scattered and all over the place. So totally ungrounded.

Taking a deep breath to try to centre her thoughts, she told Carlie about her day, from coffee with his mother and how much she'd miss her – understandable, Carlie suggested, since she'd lost her own mum, which made Rhiannon shudder – to the cafe and her weird conversation with John, and his eventual declaration that he could oh-so-generously overlook her idiocy. She had to admit that it was reassuring when her friend looked just as shocked by his cruel comments about magic and rituals as she'd been, because she'd spent a few minutes on the bus wondering if she'd over-reacted.

"Then I suggested that maybe there was no point in us being together if he was so dismissive of something that was so important to me, and he just shrugged and said fine, if that was what I wanted."

Carlie was staring at her in horror. "What did you do?"

"I said 'fine' too, and ran out of the cafe," Rhiannon sighed. She still felt a little hurt by it all. Bruised.

"Are you sure this is what you want?" Carlie pressed. "Does it really matter if he won't come to a ritual?"

Rhiannon smiled. "I am sure, which was a good realisation. I mean yes, we could have differences of opinion, no sweat. And if he'd not wanted to come to a sabbat festival or moon ritual with me but respected that I was going, that would have been okay. But for him to be so scathing and judgemental, and to say that anyone who enjoyed such a ceremony was stupid... well, why would I want to be with someone like that?" she asked.

"Rose is the cleverest person I know, as well as the kindest and most compassionate, and he was insulting her as well as me," Rhiannon continued. "Plus it showed how closed-minded he is. I mean, we got together at the Yule Ball! We were part of the planning committee that made it solstice-themed. Surely he knew what I believed and how I felt about these things from the day we met, so he was either being deliberately cruel, or wilfully ignorant and uncaring, and none of those are desirable traits in a boyfriend."

Carlie smiled sadly. "I guess not."

"But the best thing?" Rhiannon ventured. "I'm actually relieved. I did think for a minute: 'Oh god, did I act too hastily? Should I have given him a chance to explain?' But I'm not filled with regret, and I'm not wishing I hadn't said anything."

She gazed into her empty cup, and Carlie jumped up to put the kettle on and make more tea, motioning for her to keep talking.

"I'd rather be single than be ridiculed for what I hold dear, just to say that I have a boyfriend. I figured John wasn't pagan, but I was shocked that he would be so disparaging of those who are. And I guess we could have continued on for a while, but how could I be with someone like that for the long term? And how could he? And since I see no future with him, isn't it better to cut my losses now and free us both?" she asked.

"I guess the answer to that is how do you feel now?" Carlie replied. "Are you really relieved that it's over, or do you think you'll be regretting your decision in the morning? And be honest. Be brave enough to look within and discover what you're really feeling. It's no point of pride to say that you're over it if you're not, and not all relationships are the same."

Rhiannon stared at her friend. "When did you grow up and get all mature and kick-arse-advice-y?" she asked.

Carlie shrugged. "I guess I've just had more time to ponder the alternative. And someone has to play devil's advocate," she grinned. "I just remember how much you liked him at the Yule Ball, how happy you were when he kissed you, how ecstatic when he came to your place and decided you were dating. But I'm not trying to convince you to take him back, I promise."

Rhiannon's brow furrowed for a moment, then she smiled. "He is sweet, and we got on well – but I need to be with someone who I can express all of myself with. And surely if he was so totally unfazed by the prospect of it ending, he couldn't have been that into me anyway. But most importantly, if I really cared about him, if I *really* wanted to be with him, I wouldn't be feeling so relieved right now."

"That's your answer then," Carlie said, and reached over to give her friend a hug. "And you'll meet someone lovely, I'm sure of it."

When Rose came in soon afterwards, the girls were sitting out the back, laughing as Rhiannon tried to pinpoint which traits would define her ideal boyfriend. She'd realised she needed to be more specific than when they'd cast their love spells the year before. She wanted magical to be on the list. And smart.

She grinned. "Independent. Creative. Mature. Tattooed. Slightly wild," she giggled. "And a witch. *That* would be awesome."

Chapter 33

Unweave Your Fears

Rhiannon

The smell of coffee woke her, and Rhiannon stretched luxuriously, revelling in the freedom of a week off from school. Rolling over, she saw the other bed was empty. Usually when she and Brodie had to share a room on holiday with their grandparents, he woke her up stupidly early and demanded she get up and play with him. He really was growing up.

When she headed to the kitchen, she was surprised to find her father on his own, standing over the stove, drinking coffee and humming along with the radio.

"Morning Dad."

Mike spun around with a huge grin. "I wondered if the smell of coffee would wake you. Would you like a cup?"

"God yes," she replied, then grimaced. "Sorry, but yes, that would be great. Thanks."

He laughed and poured her a mug, then got the milk from the fridge. "I'm frying eggs and tomatoes too, if you want some? Just pop some bread in the toaster."

"Thank you." She sat at the table, smiling at the bright tablecloth and the sunny daffodils in the window box. "So where is everyone?"

"Your nan and pop took Brodie down to the lake – he's determined to spot a fish, or at least a tadpole or two."

Rhiannon giggled as she pictured Brodie holding a fish, then sighed with pleasure as she took her first sip of coffee. While her dad cooked, they sang along to the radio together, laughing when they got the words wrong. But when he brought the platter of eggs and tomatoes to the table and sat down with her, his tone turned serious.

"So how are things with you darling?" he asked carefully, and Rhiannon froze. She'd managed to avoid any deep and meaningfuls with her dad, but now she wondered if he'd sent Brodie and his folks out to give them time together. Still, she supposed he meant well.

"I'm okay," she said, trying to keep her tone casual.

"I don't want to pry, I just want you to know that you can talk to me. I realise I'm not the preferred parent in terms of love and relationships and all that stuff, but I promise I'll do the best I can."

He broke off, and Rhiannon saw how worried he was about her, and how desperate for her to know she could confide in him, no matter how awkward he found it.

"Well, I broke up with John on Saturday..."

Mike reached over and squeezed her hand. "Are you okay? I know how much you liked him, and he seemed like a lovely guy."

"Yeah, it's all good. I actually decided to end it. Not that he did anything wrong, or treated me badly!" she added quickly, when he frowned. "He is a nice guy, we're just more different than I realised. And he was very disparaging of Rose, and her magic and beliefs. And of Carlie too, come to think of it. And I just... well, I'd like to have a boyfriend who will come to rituals with me. Or at the very least, be happy for me to go. Who'll like all of me, you know?"

"Oh darling, I totally understand. And you should definitely hold out for that. It's important to you, and it should be respected by whoever you spend time with. I know how glad your mum was that I came to rituals with her – well, that I introduced her to them in fact," he said proudly.

Rhiannon smiled at him. Sometimes she forgot that her parents had lived a whole life together that she was completely unaware of – unaware because her mother had sworn her dad to secrecy over it, for some strange reason. They'd been friends with

Rose and part of her magical circle for years. Maybe her dad had been like Rowan, the perfect boyfriend for her wild, magical mother.

As she poured another coffee, her dad started to say something, then broke off. He bit his lip, and focused on cutting his toast, and was having trouble looking her in the eye.

Finally Rhiannon took pity on him. "It's okay Dad, we didn't... you know. We kissed a bit and stuff, but we didn't have sex."

She wasn't sure which one of them was the most uncomfortable with where the conversation was heading, and for a moment she wished her grandparents would return and interrupt them. Her father seemed to be thinking the same thing, but then he took a deep breath and plunged in.

"I must admit that's a relief to hear, since I'm absolutely clueless with all this, but I am here for you if you want to talk, or need advice, or whatever. I was young once, and I remember how scary it all seemed, and how dramatic. And I know how... persistent... guys can be. So I hope you never feel pressured into anything, and you never feel ashamed either, if you do find someone you love, who you want to... be with, so to speak."

"Thanks Dad," she said quickly, mortified and more than keen to change the subject. "It was really cool to see how much Jake enjoyed the Imbolc ceremony, and I know Rowan always encouraged the magic in Carlie, and I'd like something like that." Was she babbling? Anything to avoid the sex talk with her father.

He grinned. "Okay, point taken, you don't want to discuss this right now. But if you ever do, I'm here for you. And if that's too weird, you can talk to Rose."

When she scrunched up her nose at that suggestion and shook her head, her dad smiled. "All right, maybe Rose is a bit too priestessy, or a bit too grandmotherly, to confide in about these things, but you could chat to Laura. She was your mum's best friend, and she's a wise woman. And a *wise woman*," he said. "Pun intended."

Rhiannon rolled her eyes, but had to laugh.

"First love can be tough..." her dad said tentatively.

"It wasn't love," she said quickly, sharply. "I did really like him, and it was nice to have someone to share the school dance with, and spend time with, but when I realised he was so anti-magic, and so anti-Rose, I couldn't stay with him. It wouldn't be fair to either of us."

Mike raised his eyebrows. "And Jake?"

Rhiannon blushed. "That was just an example – I'd like someone *like* him, but not him. He's awesome, and I really like hanging out with him, but I think he's in love with Carlie."

She sighed. "I don't know why all the good ones fall for her. Maybe it *is* magic. Wasn't her mum like that too, everyone falling for her? Is it a Tyler family spell?" She was only joking, but it suddenly seemed strangely plausible. Could something like that work? Kind of the opposite to a curse that lingered down the generations...

When her dad abruptly stood up and went to get more coffee, she panicked that she'd upset him. "Sorry Dad," Rhiannon said quickly. "I didn't mean to –"

"No, it's okay darling, I know you have questions, and it wasn't fair that we kept it all from you, especially since Rose was like a grandmother to you. But your mum felt really guilty about Violet, I still don't understand why, and I just wanted to protect her. And Violet had disappeared, so it didn't seem like such a huge omission. Who could know that her daughter would turn up all these years later? I can't even begin to imagine how your mum would feel, knowing you're best friends with Violet's daughter."

Rhiannon swore under her breath.

"No, it's not a bad thing! I actually think she'd love it," he said. "Before Violet left home, she and your mum were really close. Your mother would be delighted that you have such a close friend, who's strong and good and brave and kind, just like you. And I know she would want you to be loved by someone who sees all of you, loves all of you. You'll find someone soon, someone worthy of you."

"Rhi-Rhi, you're up!" Brodie squealed, as he came flying into the kitchen and threw his arms around her. "I caught a fish!"

Laughing, Rhiannon looked at her grandparents, who nodded and showed her the bucket, which had a shiny silver fish in the bottom, still flapping its tail, and opening and closing its mouth in panic.

"He did. We thought we'd fry it up for an early lunch," her grandfather said, to much excitement from Brodie.

"I've just had breakfast, so I'll leave you to it," Rhiannon said, wrinkling up her nose at the fishy smell. "But do you want to go down to the park this afternoon?" she asked her brother, so he wouldn't feel bad that she was racing out of the house now.

Brodie nodded enthusiastically, and she picked up her coffee mug and headed down to the lake.

Thoughts swirled around her head, and she breathed in the fresh country air as she tried to get a handle on them. She was relieved that her conversation with her dad had been interrupted, because she knew why her mum had felt guilty about Violet – she'd cast a spell on Mike to make him love her instead of her friend. Violet had already moved on from Mike and was in love with someone else, but it had still played on her mum's mind all her life.

But the spell had worked.

Gazing out at the mist-wreathed water, and the pattern of tree branches dancing on its surface, she smiled. Should she cast a love spell on Jake? Carlie swore she didn't like him like that, that she would never want to date him.

"Beloved, did you learn nothing from your mother's spell?" a low and stern voice hissed in her ear. Smothering a scream, Rhiannon whirled around, wondering how anyone could have gotten so close to her without her noticing.

The shadowy figure looked like it had emerged from the earth itself, from the twisted tree trunks and green mounds that littered the lake shore. As she peered more closely, the woman in a long green gown became more solid, less mist-formed. Her eyes were gentle yet strong, and more soothing than her words had conveyed.

A ripple of fright passed through Rhiannon, then faded as she felt herself drowning in the being's gaze.

"Just breathe," the figure seemed to whisper, directly to Rhiannon's soul. "There is no need to worry."

Nodding, Rhiannon took a step closer. Was this the woman – being? – who had gifted Carlie with the athame when Rhiannon had received the chalice at their coven dedication? The one who had later presented them with the pentacle and the elder wand?

The woman inclined her head gracefully. "That was I. Some call me Brianna, but I have no need of a name. I am the heart of the nature and landscape of this country, and you can call on me when you need to ground yourself and connect back to the earth, or to feel my nurturing and protection. When you are considering doing something you know is wrong."

Great, she was a mind reader like the rest of them.

"I wasn't really going to cast that spell," Rhiannon insisted, although was that actually true? She had been tempted.

"Beloved, please know there is someone for you. You do not need to twist anyone's will in order to be cherished, and you know that doing it that way would only make you doubt yourself and them anyway. Learn from your mother's story. Be patient. Release the beliefs you are clinging to, the fears you are swamped by, the memories that are crushing you."

Rhiannon laughed. "I'm not being swamped or crushed, I'm fine."

"You must be honest with yourself, even if you cannot be so with me," the green-clad woman said, her voice stern again.

"This is crazy! I really am fine!"

The figure started to waver, and Rhiannon sighed. "Okay, I'm sorry. You're not crazy," she called out, voice conciliatory. "But I really don't know what you mean."

"So wise and yet so stubborn. We have tried to tell you. One of us came to you at Samhain with messages to guide you."

Rhiannon thought back to that strange night when she'd journeyed into the water temple. What had the blue-robed woman sung to her?

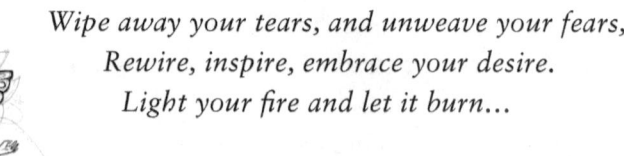

Wipe away your tears, and unweave your fears,
Rewire, inspire, embrace your desire.
Light your fire and let it burn...

But what the hell did that mean? Light what fire? And Brianna had just said messages, plural. Desperately Rhiannon racked her brain, until she finally recalled the cryptic comment: *Look for the raven.*

"Yes, Brauna told me about fear and fire, and mentioned a bird," she conceded grumpily. "But I don't know what she meant. How is that supposed to help me?"

The woman ignored her distress. "Rose also instructed you to work with the element of fire to banish your fears, and offered to help you use the passion and heat of the element to reignite your self-belief, and your self-love."

A ripple of anger and fear raced up Rhiannon's spine. Did they listen in on all her conversations? Had they been watching her and John when they... kissed and stuff? Or argued? *How creepy.*

Brianna's voice became gentle, soothing, almost apologetic, and a sensation of calm settled around Rhiannon.

"Aideen counselled you also, to let the power of fire fill you with courage, to let it burn away your pain, your blame, your shame..."

Shame. Rhiannon shivered. "I don't know what that means!" she screamed. Her voice echoed back to her, then the air around her wavered, and dizziness washed over her. She swayed where she stood, and knew she was about to hit the ground face first.

But strong arms caught her before she fell, and there was a soothing hand on her face. Energy pumped into her, and light, and the fogginess began to clear. Slowly she regained her balance and composure – just as she heard her name being called. Opening her eyes, she discovered that she was standing alone, tears pouring down her face, and her father was walking towards her along the lake shore.

"Hey, are you okay sweetheart?" he asked, drawing her into the safety and warmth of his embrace.

Sighing, she scrubbed at her eyes. "Yeah. I just miss her, you know?" she whispered.

"I know darling. Me too. It's not fair."

She felt the pain in his words, and his loneliness, and suddenly she saw him in a new light. He was alone, he was single, and she knew how loyal he was. He would stay single forever if it was left up to him. But it had been almost eighteen months since his wife died. Was he holding back because he was worried about how his kids would react? Would she have to tell him he was allowed to love again, allowed to open his heart? Was she ready to do that?

She might have to work up to it. "Um, Dad, how did you and Mum end up dating? Now that I've finally learned you were with Carlie's mother before you were with Mum, and they were both friends, I want to know how that worked. Was it awkward? Did it take time? Who made the first move?"

In the back of her mind she realised that part of her wanted to know on the off chance that Jake might transfer his affections from Carlie to her, but mostly she just wanted to talk about her mum, and hear her dad speak about her too. Often they avoided conversations about Beth because they made them so sad, yet what more perfect topic to discuss while they stood together beside a Scottish lake, out in nature, as the wind picked up and the sun fought through the clouds. She was desperate to know more about her mum when she was younger, and her dad looked despondent, but also excited at the opportunity to wax lyrical about his beloved.

Chapter 34

Sparkle and Fade

Beth

Sparkling lights disorientated Beth as she struggled to solidify back into some semblance of form. Her eyes were shut tight against the dancing sunbeams, but the warmth was comforting. As she finally peeked at her surroundings, her confusion increased. Where was she? She was hovering over a vast body of water, which glittered below her and made her blink rapidly before she could finally focus. Sensing the nearest land, she made her way towards it, and smiled as the trees and small rocky lake shore revealed itself through the mists.

It was Scotland, if she wasn't mistaken, near the lakeside cottage Mike's parents rented every year for a family holiday. Oh, she missed the rugged beauty of these hills and lochs so much. The earthy scent and soft colours of the heather fields. The air of enchantment in the woodlands. The wide open skies. And there was an ancient, weathered stone circle nearby, where she and Mike had drawn down the moon and embodied the god and the goddess a few times over the years. One morning they'd even woken up there, naked and shivering, after an intensely moving vow renewal ceremony and a sweetly seductive bottle of golden mead.

The memory tore at her heart, its exquisite beauty matched only by the pain of her loss. But if she was here, that must mean her family was too, so she finally coalesced into her transparent body and focused on the here and now, letting the wisps of memory warm her and give her strength before she regretfully released them.

It was enough for her to home in on her loved ones. Mike and Rhiannon were sitting on a fallen log beside the lake, gazing out over the water. Her daughter looked upset, and as Beth swooped down and perched between them, she felt their sadness and yearning for her like a stab in the heart. But then Rhiannon smiled bravely up at her dad, and asked him to tell her about how he and her mum had moved from friendship to romance, and whether it had been awkward because she'd been so close to Violet.

For a moment Beth burned with shame, feeling terrible that she'd made Mike cover up the early part of their life, the part that involved Violet, because of her insecurities. Made him lie to his daughter, at least by omission, to make his neurotic wife feel better. Then she forced herself to let go of all that as she dove into the memory.

While it had taken Beth no time at all to fall for Mike, he'd remained oblivious to her romantic feelings for a year. She had tried to be patient. At first he needed time to get over Violet dumping him, and then to come to terms with her sudden disappearance. Then there was the friendship thing. How did you move out of that zone once it got comfortable? And it was wonderful, their friendship. It had even made her pause, the risk that she could lose that if she pushed for something more.

While it had been frustrating to keep her feelings secret so she didn't scare him away, in the end she was glad that it had taken them so long to turn from friends to lovers, and eventually to spouses. Not at the time, admittedly, but she had been insecure enough about living in Violet's shadow, so to have had to wonder if she was just a rebound fling would have crippled her.

And it was such a beautiful moment when Mike finally, to his great surprise, had the epiphany that he wanted to be with her, that she wouldn't have swapped it for a single extra day. When she'd asked him about it later, he couldn't pinpoint exactly when his feelings for her had changed – it had been a slow realisation, a creeping build-up of emotion as friendship turned to romance.

Now she smiled as she recalled when everything had changed. It was after one of Rose's rituals. Beth and Laura were members of the priestess's small, tightly knit circle of magic by then, often calling the quarters, and usually staying back to help her pack up afterwards. But on this night, the priestess had asked that Laura help her on her own, as she had something to discuss with her.

Shrugging, Beth had picked up her bag and headed for the stairs, thinking nothing of it. When Mike asked if he could walk with her, she almost said no, but something in the way he looked at her made her curious, so she followed him down the stairs and out into the moonlit night, and tried to stay calm when he took her hand...

Beth shivered and pulled her coat tighter as they wandered up the High Street. She had no idea where they were going, or what he intended, and she was too scared to ask.

Trust.

The word echoed around her, and within her, and she tried to obey. When the moon emerged from a cloud and shone down on them, illuminating a golden pathway forward, she decided to surrender herself to whatever was ahead. The warmth from Mike's hand holding hers felt comforting, safe, and when she glanced up at him, the stars were sparkling in his eyes, tiny pinpricks of light swirling around, an entire constellation contained within his gaze.

What magic was this? Was she dreaming? Or had her deepest wish been made manifest? Anxiety rushed through her. She didn't know what had changed, but it was clear that something had, and she was worried that she'd stuff it up, ruining her chance at whatever this was. Should she ask, or wait for him to speak? And where was he leading her anyway?

"So, um, I was wondering if you'd have dinner with me tonight?" Mike said, almost in answer to her silent plea.

Disappointment washed over her, and she shrugged. "Sure." They often grabbed a bite to eat together, so she didn't know why he was looking so nervous, or holding her hand.

When they got to their usual cafe she turned towards the door, but he shook his head and pulled on her hand. "No," he whispered.

"Not there, not tonight." And he led her to the only expensive restaurant in their town. She'd never actually been there before, and she nervously lifted a hand to the flowers woven through her hair, then gazed down at her floaty green dress. Could she even wear her witchy clothes here?

Mike smiled at her as he pushed open the door. "You look perfect. Absolutely beautiful."

Blushing, she allowed him to lead her inside, and followed in a daze as the formally attired waiter ushered them to a table in the corner. There was a vase of sweetly scented red roses in the centre, and two candles, their golden flames dancing. If she imagined a perfect date night, this would be it. But... she and Mike were just friends, weren't they?

The waiter fussed around them, placing linen napkins on their laps, handing them elaborate menus, and pouring glasses of blood red wine. While Beth had been to a fancy restaurant or two with her parents, she felt totally out of her depth here, worried she would knock something over or embarrass Mike in some way. This strange upending of their established friendship rules meant she wasn't sure what she was supposed to say or how she was supposed to act.

But finally their orders were taken and they were left alone, and Mike tightened his grip on her hand, turning it over and stroking her palm in a soothing, calming way.

"Sorry to spring this on you Beth, I hope it's okay," he finally said, and she noticed again how apprehensive he seemed.

"Of course, it's lovely." She took a big gulp of wine. His nerves were rubbing off. "I've never been here before, but it looks wonderful."

Mike continued smiling, continued holding her hand.

"So, um, are we celebrating a special occasion tonight?" she asked hesitantly.

"Sorry! Oh god, look at me all tongue-tied. It's just, well... I've been thinking, and –"

He broke off. Blushed. Bit his lip... Then stood up, leaned over the table, and kissed her.

Head spinning, Beth felt herself coming undone as she lost herself in the tingle of her lips when he pressed his to hers, tasted the berry flavours of the wine on his tongue as he gently explored her mouth, sensed the acceleration of her heart rate as blood and joy, and merlot and confusion, raced through her veins.

What the hell was going on?

As shocked as she was, she didn't want the moment to ever end. When Mike finally broke the kiss, she felt grief and loss, and a chill and sense of yearning that settled deep within her.

Too flustered to speak, she just stared at him, and a small, hopeful smile crossed her face as she thought – *hoped?* – that she saw something new in his eyes.

"Sorry," he whispered. "I couldn't help it."

"That's okay." *But what did it mean?*

At that moment the waiter brought their meals, and they did the awkward dance with him as he settled their dishes on the table, refilled their wine glasses and their water ones, then hovered, checking if there was anything else they might want. Beth wanted to scream, to push him away, but Mike remained his usual polite self, patiently responding until the guy finally headed back to the kitchen and left them to it.

"Beth, I'm so sorry to have put you on the spot like this. I had a speech all planned out, about how I've started seeing you in a new way, and wanting to be more than just your friend, if you'll have me. I wanted to ask you first, not just spring it on you like that, by kissing you in a room full of people, but gazing at you in the candlelight, I was overcome. And now I'm babbling, because I'm terrified that you're angry I kissed you, and are about to tell me you have no interest in me romantically. And if that is the case, I can only apologise again, and hope you can forgive me, and are able to assure me that I haven't totally destroyed our friendship."

Smiling at him, she took his hand, then reached out with her other to caress his cheek, just the way she'd always wanted to. "You haven't destroyed our friendship, I promise," she began, but he interrupted her before she could say any more.

"But you don't like me like that," he stated softly, sadly, shrinking down into himself.

"No. I mean yes! Yes I do, of course I do. I always have."

His jaw dropped, and he stared at her in astonishment. "Really?"

Reluctantly she nodded. Maybe she shouldn't have admitted that. Would he be put off that she'd liked him even when he was with Violet, and change his mind about her?

"Why didn't you say something?" he asked.

She shrugged helplessly, suddenly wishing the waiter would return. "So, um, what does this mean?" she asked instead.

Mike's cheeks flushed with heat, from the wine or embarrassment, she couldn't tell. "I want to be your boyfriend. Although that sounds so silly and juvenile. What do people even say about this? I want to be in a relationship with you? I've only ever been with Violet, so I've never had to describe it before..."

Beth pulled her hand back and placed it in her lap, his ex's name a slap in the face. How could she compete with her? Violet had been the perfect girlfriend, the high school sweetheart, the dream woman, loved by everyone in the village.

"Hey." Mike had come around to crouch beside her, and he took both her hands in his. "I want to be with you Beth, no one else. I want to take you on dates, and share your dreams, and cook for you, and read you stories, and spend time with you. I want to plan a future with you, if that's not too forward."

She gazed at him, hope and fear in her eyes. "Really?"

"Oh Beth, of course. This isn't something I just thought about today, and wondered if it would be fun, I'm very serious. And it's not a rebound fling. I've been single for more than a year, and I'm grateful for the time alone, and grateful for the friendship we've developed, but I want more. I want you."

"But –"

"I love you Beth. I've always loved you, as a friend, but now I've realised that I'm falling in love with you too." He sounded almost pained at the confession.

"Is that a bad thing?" she whispered.

"No, not at all. Well, not if you reciprocate my feelings," he offered, looking anxious again.

Beth grinned. "Of course I do." She gazed at him curiously. "When did this occur to you? What changed your mind?"

Mike took a big gulp of his wine. "Well, it wasn't just one big thing, one moment, I guess it was a few smaller things, a few realisations. Watching your friendship with Rose. Being ridiculously proud of you when you received that award for your teaching course, more than just a friend would. Then seeing you at the party that night, radiating joy, and accomplishment, and purpose." He blushed, which made him look even more adorable.

"Then when you went away with Laura last month, I missed you with an ache that brought me to my knees. Maybe that was it, the absence that made me finally understand just how precious you are to me. Which makes me feel terrible, that I've taken your presence in my life so for granted. I'm just glad nobody else swept you off your feet in the meantime."

She was silent. Last month she had been out on a few dates, with a guy from college, but she'd ended it when she realised that he just wasn't Mike.

He mistook her silence, and groaned. "Unless someone else already has?"

Quickly she shook her head. "No, it's just been you that I've loved, ever since I came back here last year."

"Thank god!" he said. He stood up, kissed her on the forehead and poured her more wine, then resumed his seat and took a bite of his now-cold dinner.

A cheeky grin lit up his face. "So, you've loved me for a year?"

Blushing, she ducked her head, embarrassed, then laughed. "I wouldn't go that far," she lied. "But I haven't fallen for anyone else."

Satisfied, he raised his glass in a toast, then they both looked relieved when they were interrupted by the serving of dessert, and Mike steered the conversation to lighter topics.

Later, he took her hand again and walked her home, and when they got to the entrance of the flat she shared with Laura, he drew her into his arms and kissed her. Passion spread through her body like fire, sparking her to life, to love. His lips were gentle, tentative, yet there was a possessiveness she liked.

"Coffee?" she asked, when they finally paused for breath. He quirked one eyebrow, and she laughed. Mike often came in for coffee, but would it be different now? Did "coffee" suddenly mean something else? Nerves stole over her, but she put her key in the lock, opened the door and determinedly led him inside.

Laura was sitting on the couch reading a book, but she looked up and grinned as soon as she saw their clasped hands and dazed smiles. "It's about time you two!"

Beth sighed. Had it been obvious to everyone but Mike?

"Coffee?" she asked again, then hurried into the kitchen to put the kettle on, without waiting for an answer. Her flatmate followed her out and stood in the doorway, a smirk on her face.

"So, what happened?" she asked.

Remembering how the strange night had begun, Beth swiftly changed the subject. "Is Rose okay? Are you? What happened? How come she only wanted you to stay back?"

Laura laughed. "Really, that's what you want to talk about?"

Beth blushed, but nodded.

"No idea, to be honest. I just figured she was letting you have a break, because it was the same as always – I just had to pack away twice as much stuff as usual. Then again, perhaps our wily priestess knew what was going on and was helping your relationship along. Tell me what happened! How did you get to the hand-holding stage in one evening? And is that all you did?" she demanded, eyebrows raised suggestively.

"Shhh!" Beth whispered. "I'm not sure I know enough to explain it. But we were walking downstairs after the ritual, and Mike asked if I wanted to have dinner. I said sure, since we often grab something together at the cafe. But he took me to the Orchard!"

Laura gasped, suitably impressed.

"When the waiter finally finished pouring the wine, and taking our order, and hovering for what felt like forever, Mike said he had to tell me something, but kept stumbling over his words – then all of a sudden he just leaned over, right there in front of everyone, and kissed me!"

Jumping up and down, Laura squealed with excitement.

"It took a while, but he finally confessed that he'd started looking at me in a different way recently, and figured out that he wanted to be more than just friends. If I wanted to. Which, duh, of course!"

Her friend hugged her. "So what changed for him?"

"He couldn't really explain it, but he was confused by how much he missed me when you and I went to Spain, and started wondering then. He also said he felt bad that he'd taken me for granted for so long, and not realised his feelings were changing and deepening. But I must admit, although it's been so frustrating waiting, I'm glad it took him this long. If it was any sooner I would have worried it was a rebound thing on his part, and that would have been awful."

Beth broke off, remembering the spell she'd cast on him in the woods that full moon night a year ago. But it couldn't be that. She was saved from the panic clutching at her heart when the kettle boiled, and she centred her self and her thoughts while she made coffee for the three of them, then took it out to the lounge room.

Mike was sitting in his usual spot on the beanbag, flicking through a magazine, and Beth had to stifle her disappointment that he'd left the couch for her and Laura. She wondered if things like that would change now, all of their usual patterns disrupted, which made her smile. She handed Mike his coffee, and the three of them chatted idly for a while, the way they always had, until Laura faked a few yawns and headed to bed, with a wink in Beth's direction.

Oh goddess, bed! Beth went cold all over. Would Mike assume he'd be staying the night now? Did she want him to? How did you transform a friendship into a romance without any awkwardness?

As if sensing her thoughts, Mike stood up, put his mug on the coffee table, then sat next to her and took her hand. She shivered, with nerves, with uncertainty, with fear. What if it did ruin their friendship?

"Sweet Beth, don't stress about this."

"I'm not," she blurted out, but her voice gave her away.

Mike laughed. "I think I know you pretty well, and that is definitely your anxious face."

"Oh..."

Grinning, he kissed her forehead, then cupped her chin in his hand and forced her to look at him. "There's no rush for us to do anything... well, anything that we're not ready for. I know it's a little strange that we already know each other so well, and yes, there could be a few odd moments while we negotiate the path from friendship to romance, but we can figure it out together. Just tell me how slow you want to take it, and what you need from me. I can be patient, I promise. Although to be honest, I can't think of anything more natural than two best friends falling in love."

A shy smile lit up Beth's face, and she put down her mug and reached for him. Tentatively touching her lips to his, she pulled him closer, until they were pressed up against each other, no more space dividing them. A fire ignited between them, and their kiss deepened, growing more intense, and more demanding.

It wasn't long before she'd unbuttoned his shirt and slid it off, her fingers stroking his chest, her hands clutching at his shoulders. Mike's passion rose to meet hers, and soon he'd dragged her dress over her head and thrown it on the floor. Staring at her with smouldering desire, he bent his head to kiss every inch of her.

Patience smatience. Beth had wanted to feel his naked body on hers for an eternity, and she couldn't wait to be burned in his fire.

Chapter 35

Burning Up, Breaking Down

Rhiannon

Rhiannon woke up in a sweat, heart racing and body shaking. It was the same dream she'd had before, of the tall, dark-haired guy leering down at her, dragging her from the path and pulling her roughly into his arms, smashing her head up against his hard, broad, suddenly naked chest. Her breath coming in ragged gasps as she struggled against him. Lust blazing in his eyes as he looked her up and down, gaze lascivious, breath hot on her face. Then he was crouching next to her, ripping her shirt open and forcing her down onto her back in the long grass, pulling off his own shirt and lying on top of her, his weight pressing down on her, his body hot and heavy against hers.

Last time, John had been in her dream too, and had saved her from the stranger who wanted to hurt her. But there was no John now. And there was something disturbingly familiar about the guy. Shivering as she huddled under her blankets, she tried to think about other things, force the too-real scene away. But the images in her mind were changing from the sunny grass of her dream to the cold woods on a dark night, and there was a haunting sense of deja vu. As she hugged her knees to her chest, her heart beat faster, her limbs trembled, and sweat trickled down her back.

Noooooo!

She must have screamed, because all of a sudden the light was on in her room, and her dad was holding her tight, fear in his voice.

"Rhiannon, what's wrong? Are you okay?"

It took long moments before the terror subsided enough that she could speak, although she couldn't stop the tears pouring down her face, dripping on her dad's shoulder.

"Nightmare," she finally managed to gasp.

"Darling, it's okay," he murmured, relieved. "I'm here. It's all right. Let's go have a warm drink. Shake it off. Nothing can hurt you."

Numbly she dragged herself out of bed and followed her father downstairs. Having the light on helped, and while he heated two cups of milk then sat with her and talked, she managed to keep her mind empty of the chilling images.

But once back in the dark of her room, she felt herself break apart as memories drowned her. Heart pounding, she shook from the weight of the pain shuddering through her body. Her head spun, her brain struggled for clarity, and then in a single light-bulb moment she realised what was destroying her. What she'd hidden, even from herself, for the past eighteen months.

This was what the woman in blue had alluded to. What the woman in green had been more direct about. What the woman in red was forcing her to see. The shame and blame she'd concealed.

How could she have forgotten *the thing that happened*? Although apparently she hadn't totally forgotten, since it was here right now, replaying in technicolour detail. She'd just... ignored it. Buried it. Suppressed it. Her mother had died the next day, and so she had pushed down her pain, repressed her tears, submerged her shame. Blocked it out as she dissolved into the far more pressing, immediate, devastating and understandable grief over the parent she'd lost.

The thing that happened hardly seemed important compared to the horror of her mum's death. And there was no way her dad could cope with what she'd been through, not after losing his wife. So she'd diminished her pain for his sake, and for hers. Concealed it completely. She couldn't face it then, and she didn't want to face it now.

Shuddering, she pulled the blankets tighter around her, barely able to breathe as the images slammed into her mind, tormenting her, taunting her. Again she felt the harsh fingers on her shoulders, trying to pull her closer, trying to compel her. Cold wraiths intent on ruin.

She'd been trying to find a healing spell, an enchantment that would fix her mum and make her world right again. When her friend Debbie's older brother told her he performed healing rituals and would be happy to help, she was so filled with gratitude that she focused only on that. But he hadn't wanted to help her – he'd just wanted to have sex with her, whether she liked it or not.

Trembling, she tried again to force the images of him pushing her down onto the cold ground away, to not feel his hands all over her, his body on top of her, sweaty and heavy and hard and horrible...

She took a deep breath. She could bury it again. She'd done it before, and besides, it hadn't affected her, right? She was fine. She went out with John for a few months, she kissed him, and fooled around a little, and she was okay with it. She hadn't fallen apart when he touched her.

Except that she had. Her blood ran cold as she recalled her desperate flight from his house when he'd tried to get her naked.

And then she got a sinking feeling in her stomach, and fiery regret rushed through her body, a physical sensation that made her skin crawl. *This* was why she'd over-reacted when Carlie told her about Rowan trying to turn their kisses all hot and heavy for a minute when he was half asleep. She'd wondered why she was *so* angry at him about that, why she'd refused to listen to Carlie's explanation, and been mean to her about it. Why she'd tried to break them up.

This was the reason. It was *her* anger. *Her* sense of injustice. She'd assumed a pagan healer and teacher would harm Carlie, because a pagan healer and teacher had harmed *her*, had betrayed *her* within the sacred circle. She'd conflated Rowan's actions with her own long-buried experience.

It was all too much.

Finally, too emotionally drained and exhausted to torture herself any longer, she passed out into a troubled sleep.

She had no idea how, but the next morning when her brother woke her early, Rhiannon got up and got dressed without complaint, then followed him downstairs to make breakfast and watch cartoons together. A simple white lie about hay fever explained away her red eyes, and by the time Mrs Pearson came by to take Brodie to soccer with his friend Ben, Rhiannon had managed to put on a brave face.

But being home alone was making her crazy, so finally she grabbed her keys and headed outside. Maybe a wander through the village in the bright sunshine would keep her nightmares at bay for a little while, and illuminate the darkness she was drowning in.

"Rhiannon."

Fear slithered up her spine at the voice, and she wanted to run as far as she could, as fast as she could. But he'd already overtaken her and swung back around so he was blocking her path. Had she dreamed him into being last night? She hadn't seen him since that night in the woods eighteen months ago, yet here he was on the High Street, like he'd slunk out of her nightmares right into her waking life.

The one who did... *the thing that happened.*

Her throat was dry, and she couldn't speak, even if she'd wanted to. Even if she'd known what to say. When he reached out a hand towards her, she opened her mouth to scream, and he quickly pulled back without touching her, regret on his face. She was grateful for that small mercy, and she wondered if it was the anger in her own expression that had warned him off, or something else.

"Can we talk, just for a minute?" he asked, and there was pleading and nerves and anxiety in his tone.

She gaped at him blankly. It wasn't like her body was capable of getting her away from him anyway – she was frozen, rooted to the spot in terror, as an avalanche of memories swamped her and a dizziness buzzed in her head.

The next thing she knew he was holding her up, and leading her to the bench in front of the church. Had she fainted? Dear god, that was all she needed, to fall helplessly unconscious at the feet of her attacker.

As soon as he'd helped her sit down, he scooted away from her, right to the other end of the bench, as though touching her skin burned him. She kind of hoped it did.

"I just…" He blushed, and looked away, then seemed to draw his own strength in, up from the earth. He was a witch too, she reminded herself, though how any follower of the goddess could do what he'd done to her, she had no idea.

She raised an eyebrow. What did he want with her? If he was looking for sympathy, he'd come to the wrong place.

"I'm so sorry," he finally managed to get out, holding her gaze. "From your reaction, I know that what happened between us was very much unwanted, and I apologise."

What happened between us? He made it sound like it was something she'd agreed to, something she'd asked for. She stared at him in horror, stunned by his casual mention of *the thing that had happened*. She tried to reply, tried to say something, but she couldn't. She was totally flabbergasted.

With a great effort, she steadied her breathing, but she still didn't know what he wanted from her, or how she should be reacting.

She sighed, but stayed silent. What did he expect her to say?

"It's okay?" She couldn't say that. She wouldn't.

"Don't worry, you haven't made me terrified of all men and screwed up my relationships forever?" At that thought, a hammer smash of pain slammed into her, making her double over, and robbing her of oxygen. Was this why she'd broken up with John? Had this guy and what he'd done to her made her incapable of a normal relationship? Her breath hitched, and she gasped desperately for air.

"Rhiannon," he said, voice calm, and a hand on her back as he tried to comfort her, to reassure her, to lead her back from the edge of the panic attack surging within her. Numbly she shrugged him off her, and stared at him with furious eyes.

"How could you?" she cried.

She saw regret envelop him, and there was anguish in his expression, although how genuine it was she had no idea. "I don't know, but I'm sorry. I don't expect you to forgive me, and I'm not asking you to try, I promise. But I do hope that if there's *any* way for me to make amends, you will tell me."

She shrugged. What on earth could he do to help, besides leave her the hell alone?

"You are beautiful Rhiannon, and magical. And I say that not as an excuse, but so you will know it. If I made you feel shame in any way, made you feel bad about yourself or your magic, please let that go. Let me carry that burden."

Shame. The message the women of the mists had been trying to give her. Trying to make her face. Tears began to well, but she fought to hold them in. She would not cry in front of him. She would not give him the satisfaction of knowing he had any power over her.

Not again.

"Is there anything I can do?" he asked, voice small, and gentle.

Helplessly she shook her head. How could he do anything to change what had happened, unless he could travel back in time? The pain and fear of that night began to swamp her again, and the fury and frustration of the morning after, at school.

"Wait. Yes, there is something you can do. You can tell your friend Rory that what you did is not okay. Tell all your mates that it's not okay. That it's not cool. Tell him that I didn't want it then, from you, or from anyone else. Tell him no woman owes him anything. That consent is not something to take from a person by force."

He regarded her blankly. "What do you mean?"

"The next day at school, when I felt lower than I ever had, Rory called me a slut in front of everyone, then told me I should have sex with him. He seemed to think it was a great thing, what you did to me. He wanted me to meet him in the woods that night, to do... things I didn't want to do..." Somehow her voice remained calm. Her anger was lending her strength. It was a life raft in the ocean of pain and flashbacks she was drowning in.

"But I –"

"But nothing. Whatever you told him about me – which must have been before we even met that night, which, frankly, shows premeditation – it made him think he had the right to harass me, to shame me, and to demand sex from me. Your actions have consequences – believe me, I'm just beginning to discover that – but your words do too. Your casual insinuations made him, and who knows how many others, feel they had rights to me. To my body. If my mum hadn't died the next day, so I missed a few weeks of school, my life would have been ruined, my reputation destroyed, and god knows how many people would have thought they had the right to be sleazy to me, to call me names, to expect me to do stuff."

His face was pale, and he stared at the ground, too embarrassed to look at her.

"Well?" she demanded.

"I'm so sorry Rhiannon, really I am. I have no excuse, and I won't insult you by trying to justify my behaviour. You're right, I was big-noting myself with Rory and his mates..." He had the good grace to look embarrassed. "I was more concerned about looking cool to them than how any of it would affect you. In fact I wasn't thinking of you at all, I was only thinking of me, of what I wanted. But I've changed, I promise."

Fat lot of good that did her, yet there was no benefit in labouring the point. "What brought this on?" she asked instead. "After all this time, what made you want to apologise?"

Blushing, he finally met her gaze. "I started dating a girl at college a few months later, and we've been together ever since. A few weeks ago, we stayed up talking, and she revealed to me that she'd been..." He paused, and looked like he wanted to be sick, then he took a deep breath and continued.

"Um, well, she told me that she'd been raped the year before. A man had followed her when she left the library one night, then forced her into his car with a knife and attacked her. It broke my heart to hear it. I wanted to find the guy and beat him to a pulp. I wanted to tattoo the word rapist on his forehead. I wanted to hurt him, the way he'd hurt her. But that wasn't what she needed from me."

Rhiannon felt the anger vibrating through him, through his words.

"As she sobbed her heart out, and slowly revealed what had happened, and how it had made her feel about herself, feel about men in general, and about relationships, it made me think of you, and wonder if I'd damaged you in any way."

His voice trembled, but he kept going, wanting to get everything out now, before he lost his nerve.

"I pretended it away at first – I'd had no knife, I wasn't a stranger abducting you, it wasn't the same thing, surely – but as she opened up more, and I started reading about sexual assault, I finally had to acknowledge that I'd forced you. Admit to myself that, no matter how much I tried to convince myself otherwise, I knew you didn't want to, yet I did it anyway. And I'm mortified about that."

"Sorry." It came out automatically, her standard response, and it made her furious.

"No! You have nothing to be sorry about Rhiannon. This is all on me, and I want to do anything I can to help you. To make sure you know it was not your fault. It took me a while to realise this, but in some ways it must have been even worse for you because you knew me. You trusted me, and I betrayed you."

She remembered his face that night. His hands. His silken words. The flashbacks threatened to sink her, and her body shook. She didn't know how much more of this she could listen to, or deal with.

"It's no consolation, but I got a part-time job just so I could give money to a sexual assault service at college," he continued. "And I'm training with them now so I can volunteer my time to help. I need you to know that I regret what I did. That I'm remorseful, and trying to make amends. And I swear I will never do it again."

She shrugged. She couldn't deal with his feelings. She couldn't even deal with hers. And she really wasn't going to be the one who let him off the hook. "Is she okay?"

He stared at her, blank again.

"Your girlfriend?"

"Oh. Yes. She went to counselling, and it helped her a lot. A friend of hers was also... assaulted... but by someone she knew. And for her, confronting him was really important in dealing with it and starting to move forward. That's why I want to give you that opportunity, in case it could help you."

Vaguely she nodded. It felt so surreal. And it was too much. She didn't know what to do with everything he was saying. Until last night she'd repressed the whole thing, denied it ever happened, hidden from it for eighteen months, and now all of a sudden it was spilling out of her, and spilling out of him. Consuming her. Burning her up.

"I'm also concerned for you, because after my girlfriend finally told me what had happened, she revealed how ashamed she felt. It was completely absurd to me, that she could blame herself for what happened, but she did. And she'd been too scared to tell me, because she didn't know if I could still love her, knowing it had happened."

Dizziness swamped Rhiannon again, and she swayed, before quickly managing to brace herself. She didn't want him to touch her again, even if it was to stop her fainting at his feet. Her skin was burning, yet she felt cold inside, dead, and she wondered if she was going to pass out. Forcing herself to get a grip, she turned towards him and gazed at him, eyes swimming with tears.

"What did you say?" It was a whisper, a prayer, and by the look on his face, a knife right through his heart.

"I said of course!" There was horror in his voice, and his expression. "What do you mean?"

Sweat trickled down her back, and a clammy sensation rippled over her skin. "That's what I wonder too. How could someone love me, knowing this? Knowing I'm so... damaged..." Her voice trailed off, and she gulped air in huge, desperate breaths. She didn't know if it had subconsciously affected her relationship with John – but now that it had emerged so fully into her conscious awareness, what would it do to her going forward? The thought of any guy touching her made her feel sick, and there was no way she would ever be able to tell anyone. Would she have to rebury it? Could she?

"Rhiannon," he said, gently but firmly. "This does not reflect on you, it reflects on me. The shame is mine alone."

She blinked rapidly. Shrugged. She didn't believe him.

"If anything, I love my girlfriend even more now, because she trusted me enough to tell me."

She raised her eyebrows in surprise. "So if I start seeing someone, you think I should tell them what happened? What you did?" she asked, voice small. "You don't think they'd break up with me if I did?"

"I promise you, he will not break up with you because of this. If he's the right guy, he will be honoured that you confided in him."

Tears finally spilled from her lashes, and she desperately wanted to get away from him. *Needed* to get away from him. He seemed to sense it.

"Is there anything I can do?" he begged her.

"Don't ever speak to me again."

"But..."

"No. I don't care how awkward that makes it for you with your sister. Is that what you were going to say?"

Reluctantly he nodded.

"You wanted to know what you can do. Well, do that. Think about the way you speak about women – to them, to your friends, to the world. And don't talk to me."

"But if I could help you –"

"*That* is how you can help me."

And she stood up, turned on her heel, and ran.

Chapter 36

Slaying the Ghost

Rhiannon

Blinded by tears, Rhiannon wandered aimlessly up and down country lanes for hours, before finally finding the courage to go home. Relieved to discover that her dad and Brodie were still out, she made a cup of tea, but she felt too sick to eat. Hearing voices in the lounge room, she walked in to turn the television off – then froze where she stood. A woman whose face had been cast in shadows then pixelated was talking on the screen, softly, hesitantly, voice dripping with pain.

"It was hard, the aftermath of the assault. I tried to forget about it, to pretend it hadn't happened, to just move on with my life and act like it hadn't affected me. But a few years later something triggered the memory and I had a breakdown, which finally made me realise that it had damaged me enormously. I was more reserved after it happened, more afraid. I cut myself off from people, and life… I dated, but I never let anyone get close enough for a real relationship – I always chose people who were unavailable for some reason – then freaked out and ran away when that changed."

Another girl, another shadow, another shaky voice. "I was terrified of guys afterwards, I didn't trust any of them. Finally I agreed to go on a date with a friend I already knew, and I took it slow – but when he tried to, you know, I flipped out and ran out of the room, out of his house. I was too embarrassed to face him again, so I lost him as a friend as well."

A third shadowed face, a third modulated voice. "It destroyed me. Destroyed my self-worth. I thought that was all I was good for. That guys would only like me for sex, so I would go home with any sleazy guy who came onto me, because I didn't think I deserved to choose, deserved to say no. If I did meet someone I liked, I would make the first move, initiate it to get it over with. Which made me feel terrible about myself, caused me to choose terrible partners, and got me a terrible reputation..."

Rhiannon sank down onto the carpet, unaware of her actions, or of her self, as she clutched the remote control she'd picked up and stared at the screen in horror. She'd freaked out when John tried to have sex with her, and run out of his house in a blind panic. Then she'd swung the other way and initiated it herself, in an attempt to prove that she didn't have a problem with it, that she was a normal girl. Undamaged. Functioning.

A sob wrenched free and she tried to swallow it down, then as statistics on sexual assault flashed up, she fell apart, shocked by how prevalent it was. She definitely wasn't alone, which was appalling, yet it also gave her a tiny bit of comfort. If others could survive, could thrive even, *could be normal,* maybe there was hope for her.

Another face flashed up, this time in high definition. The voice was clear and calm, unmodulated, the woman's credentials spelled out across the screen: Dr Edith Halliwell, psychologist and rape counsellor. "Those who have been assaulted can react in different ways. Some remain in complete denial, and manage to repress it altogether. Some become scared of all men and shut themselves off, refusing to date, to be intimate with anyone, to fall in love. Others become *more* sexual, trying to assert some control over their life, to prove to themselves that they aren't weak, to choose the sexual situations they're involved in and take their power back. Some use a variety of coping mechanisms at different times. They are *all* normal reactions..."

Rhiannon stared at the screen, frozen and numb.

Normal.

She wanted to swallow that word and make it part of her.

"For those who can't deal with it at the time, who tuck it away and pretend it never happened, some time later – months, even years – a trigger may bring it back to the surface, and they will fall apart then. It could be a song, a movie, an article, a news report, a meditation retreat, an intimate moment with someone they love, running into the perpetrator, or it could be a completely unrelated situation," Dr Halliwell explained, voice filled with compassion.

"Whatever it is that brings the trauma to the surface, acknowledging what happened and being able to talk about it can be a very important step in the healing process, helping a person move from victim to survivor. And it's important that they are gentle with themselves while they deal with it, and get some support, be it a counsellor, a friend, a partner, a crisis line, whatever they feel comfortable with."

The program had finished and a football match had begun before Rhiannon realised tears were pouring down her face. Dazed, she turned the television off and collapsed onto the couch, staring listlessly out the window as darkness descended. She wanted to fall into that darkness and never return.

Maybe she could rebury *the thing that happened*. Hide it away once more. Go back to pretending it had never occurred. Because she didn't know how she would ever find the light again.

The sound of a key in the front door made her leap up and scrub at her eyes in panic, trying to erase the treacherous tears. Treacherous memories. Treacherous disconnect from her very self.

It was chilling how quickly she switched to autopilot, cooking dinner for her family, making small talk with her dad, reading Brodie a story and tucking him in. But once that was done, she crawled into bed and the tears returned. She felt herself breaking down, coming undone, all the shattered pieces of her soul flung so far apart. And she had no idea how she was supposed to put herself back together.

She couldn't think straight. Her mind was too blurred. Now the tears soaking her pillow were a purely material reaction, a release of the emotional pain she'd been carrying physically in her body, the trauma woven into her cells and stored in her skin, in her bones.

As she felt herself drowning, she clung to that word. *Normal.*

When she woke late the next morning, Rhiannon's eyes were red-rimmed and scratchy, and she was aching all over, battered by the emotional storm she'd endured. Knowing that Brodie and her dad were out for the day, she breathed a sigh of relief that at least she had the house to herself. Her brain was scattered, unable to focus on a single thought. She tried to go back to sleep, but was plagued by flashes of memory. When hunger forced her out of bed, she dragged herself downstairs for a piece of toast, but almost choked on it. After that she attempted some homework, but eventually had to give up in defeat. And she stopped trying to read when she realised she'd been staring at the same page for half an hour.

Finally she ran a hot bath and sprinkled dried lavender, chamomile and lemon balm into it, resorting to magic in her search for calm. Climbing in, she drew the healing steam of the herbs into her lungs in huge, ragged breaths. Then she slid down under the surface, totally submerged. Opening her eyes, she gazed up at the ceiling, her vision muted by the water. Everything looked fuzzy, and gentle. Peaceful.

As she watched her long hair swirling in the water above her, she flashed back to the water temple on that chilly Samhain night, where the woman in blue had pushed her into the black water and forced her under, and she'd thought she was trying to drown her. But it had been a baptism, not an attempted murder, and now the words that echoed around the cavern that night returned to her.

Divine... dive in... die within...
Submerge yourself to emerge from self...
Lose yourself to find your self...

What would she find now though, when her whole world had been torn apart? For a split second she considered remaining in the soothing cocoon of the underwater world, free from the pain and turmoil of her life. Letting it end. Letting go. It would be a relief, surely, to no longer feel this distress, this fear. This unworthiness and loss of self.

But when she closed her eyes, she saw an image of her mother in a long white dress, dancing amongst a vast star-strewn blackness on the back of her lids, and she was holding out a hand to her, reaching down to drag her back to life. Reluctantly Rhiannon thought of her dad and her brother, and the trauma she would cause them if she gave in to her misery, and so she reached up and took the hand being offered to her, and felt herself being hauled up above the surface.

Coughing and spluttering, she gasped in as much air as she could, in huge, heaving lungfuls, until her breathing returned to normal. And despite her dark thoughts, and her panicked search for a mother she knew couldn't really be there with her, she felt cleansed as the flower-scented water streamed over her. Calming her. Soothing her.

Then she heard the blue-clad woman's voice again.

Wipe away your tears, and unweave your fears,
Rewire, inspire, embrace your desire.
Light your fire and let it burn...

She almost laughed. Enough already with the fire signs.

As she stepped out of the tub, she noticed lavender and chamomile petals in her wet hair, but she left them there, loving the fragrance as she towelled herself dry and sunk into the soft warmth of her dressing gown. The flowers made her feel like she was part of nature still, part of the earth. They gave her strength and hope. Would it be enough to last though? To get her through the hell she was enduring right now?

Once she was back in her room, Rhiannon gazed around with new eyes. Frantic eyes. In a whirl of activity, she started cleaning and sorting, ripping down posters, dragging the sheets from her bed, tearing clothes from their hangers and throwing them in a pile to get rid of. Some part of her hoped that if she could get her room clean and under control, she would feel that way herself. She needed to feel safe, stripped bare of the past, to create a space both mentally and physically where she could deny entrance to any doubt or pain or regret. Any awful memories.

She was normal. Her reactions were normal. She was not alone. And she would be a survivor like all the women in that TV show.

As she clumsily pulled her Book of Shadows from the shelf, the book next to it moved forward too, and started to fall. Catching it just before it hit the floor, she reached up to return it to its place – and noticed a piece of paper poking out of the top. Curious, she sank to the floor, note in hand, then felt tears threaten again as she realised what it was.

My darling girl,
It broke my heart to see you so vulnerable tonight, so full of fear and shame. I wish I had been able to get there faster, to have spared you any pain, any tearing apart of your faith in humanity.

Right now you are grieving – my impending loss, the loss of your innocence, the loss of your trust – but I want you to know that not all men are like that. Some are, yes, I won't lie to you. Before I met your father I was involved with a man who hurt me, and manipulated me, and used me terribly. He made me into someone I wasn't proud of, someone who was not her best self, who did things she regrets. But now, years later, I realise he wasn't worth the energy I spent on hating him. That giving him even a moment of my time, my anger, my energy, was a waste. Was doing myself a disservice.

Don't hold on to your rage darling, and don't allow this guy to make you bitter. I almost messed up my chance with your father because I was so consumed with hatred and vengeance. But hating that guy won't punish him, it won't teach him anything, it will only affect you.

It's easier said than done, believe me I know, but I say this for your sake, not his. Let it go. Let him go. Let your anger go. I am confident he will get his in time, but whether or not he does, don't punish yourself. Because then he wins. Then he really does have power over you. The only way for you to win is to find a way to move forward.

You can talk to me and your dad.
You can go to Rose for a healing.
You can see a counsellor.

Or you can heal yourself, if you'll trust yourself...

We can talk more about this tomorrow after school, and make a plan, but until then I just want to let you know how much I love you, and trust you, and how proud I am of you and your strength.

All my love,

Mum xx

Her strength. Rhiannon shuddered. Did she have any? She felt so weak, so distraught, so broken. But she wanted to believe her mother. And finding the letter now, after all this time, had to be a sign, right? It made her feel as though her mum was still with her. How else could it have appeared right now, just when she needed it most?

That thought gave her a glimmer of courage, and of hope. She wanted to be strong, to be healed. To not be controlled or defined by what he'd done to her.

Which meant she had to go back to the woods and slay another ghost – not a person this time, but a memory. Walk into the shadows, into her past, and face what had happened. Face herself. Find herself. Throw herself into the fire.

Chapter 37

Beth

It was her daughter's anguish that brought Beth back this time. Her scream of terror reached her even in the darkness of her starless void, forcing her molecules together and her awareness to painfully reawaken. When she emerged from wherever she disappeared to when she wasn't with her family, she was hovering in Rhiannon's room, and Mike was sitting on the edge of their daughter's bed, trying to comfort her, but feeling as helpless as Beth did in the face of her obvious distress.

He made them warm milk in the brightly lit kitchen, and for a while he kept Rhiannon's demons at bay, at least until she returned to bed, where she spent the rest of the night huddled under her blankets, shaking, with tears pouring down her cheeks even when she finally fell into an exhausted sleep.

Beth stayed with her all night, trying to hug her, to comfort her, but growing more and more frustrated as her ghostly hand kept sliding from Rhiannon's shoulder and fading away into nothing. What had so spooked her daughter? Was it just a garden-variety nightmare, or something more? And why could she sense Carlie's thoughts, but not her own daughter's?

Just after the sun rose, Brodie crashed into his sister's bedroom and woke her up, and Beth cringed, hoping she wouldn't lash out at him in her pain. But she'd clearly misjudged her children. While Rhiannon's eyes were raw and red from all the tears she'd cried, she greeted her brother with a smile, and followed him downstairs to make him breakfast. Relief coursed through Beth, and she relaxed her grip on her awareness, allowing herself to drift aimlessly amongst the sunbeams filtering through the kitchen window, the aroma of coffee making her sigh with something close to contentment.

She didn't realise she'd dissolved back into the nothingness until a jolt of terror slammed into her, and she was suddenly blinking in the bright light of midday. Wildly she stared to left and right, trying to figure out where she was, and why. Her heart lurched when she saw Rhiannon sitting on a bench in front of the church, trembling and pale while a guy pleaded with her. It was the man from Beth's premonition, the one she'd had the night before she died, of her daughter out in the woods and at his mercy. She thought she'd made it there in time to save her from the worst of it, but the pain and fear crippling Rhiannon right now made Beth realise how wrong she was. Sorrow and regret pulled at her centre, trying to tear her apart, but she couldn't let it. She had to be strong now, for her daughter.

Steeling herself, she floated across the road and settled on the bench between them, trying to provide a barrier, to protect Rhiannon from the torment he was causing her. Yet it was Beth who was coming undone. She was mortified that she'd let her daughter down, first by not being able to rescue her in time, and then by dying when she'd needed her most, in the aftermath of such a traumatic event. For the first time in her life, or her death, Beth cursed the goddess she had believed in so fervently, paid her respects to so diligently, and made magic with so often.

But that wasn't going to help her make amends. She had to find a way to protect her daughter, and heal her. Listening to her recount the ways that night had affected her was heart-wrenching. Hearing the guy tell her how many women he knew who'd also been assaulted filled her with despair. But when Rhiannon told him firmly to never speak to her again, then stood up, turned, and walked quickly away from him, Beth wanted to cheer for her brave warrior child. She was growing into an amazing young woman.

Hovering beside Rhiannon as she wandered aimlessly along narrow country lanes and around the gentle slopes at the base of the tor, Beth tried to wipe away her daughter's tears, but her lack of physicality was driving her to distraction. It was devastating her that she couldn't comfort her.

Yet a tear had fallen from her eye onto the page when she read the note her husband wrote her. Another tear had dripped onto the floor when she thought about Rose having to perform her funeral service. And somehow she'd managed to become visible and speak words that Carlie heard. Surely she could figure out a way to connect with Rhiannon and help her through this. Maybe *this* was the reason she'd been reborn into this strange existence – so she could be there for her daughter in a way she hadn't been able to at the time. A second chance to make things right. Or as right as they could be.

After a while she sensed Rhiannon's mind begin to calm, and her stride lengthen and quicken as she turned and headed towards home. But the more purposeful her daughter became, the frailer Beth felt. Her grip on awareness faltered, and no matter how hard she tried to stay present, her translucent self split apart, and she scattered back out into the sweetly scented air and was lost.

It was an echo of a thought that made Beth solidify back to awareness. The echo of a voice. *Wipe away your tears, and unweave your fears...* In the cold empty darkness of the void, she heard the sentiment crooned, and knew she had to get back to Rhiannon. Gathering the starlight to her to give herself form, translucent and etheric though it was, she focused all her attention on her daughter – and abruptly found herself back in her bedroom, watching the early spring sunlight streaming in the window.

Rhiannon was curled up in the window seat, staring vacantly outside. She was still in her pyjamas, and her eyes were red and bleary from crying. Beth's heart ached as the pain rolled off her daughter in waves and headed towards her, trying to shatter her fragile presence. She floated closer, and reached out a hand to gently stroke her hair. When Rhiannon leaned into it, Beth wondered if she was finally being felt, but then her daughter stood up and walked right through her, and down the hall to the bathroom.

Sadly she followed her, watching as she ran a bath. The fragrance of chamomile and lavender lulled Beth into a false sense of security, and she smiled as she gazed at her daughter. She looked so peaceful lying there under the water, her eyes closed and her hair swirling gently around her, with none of the pain and trauma of the last twenty-four hours marring her expression.

Beth almost drifted off, and away, until a new wave of pain rushed into her. Concentrating all of her effort, she tried to communicate with her daughter, to feel her heart, or read her mind – and what she discovered terrified her. Her baby girl was being seduced by the peace of the underwater world, of oblivion, but Beth knew there was no peace in oblivion.

"No my darling!" she screamed. Desperately she tried to send thoughts to Rhiannon, to bombard her with memories of her father and her brother, of the love they shared, and of their need for her. She didn't want to play the guilt card, but desperate times called for desperate measures, and there was no way she was going to allow her daughter to be swept from the world, from the land of the living and all the love she had here, if only she would remember it.

A wall of resistance rose up against her, but for an instant it softened slightly, and Beth seized the moment and quickly thrust her arm down into the water – and was shocked when she felt her daughter grasp it, and allow herself to be hauled up above the surface. But it had taken every bit of power and will that she had, and while Rhiannon gasped and coughed up water as she struggled into a sitting position, Beth felt herself falling apart from the effort.

When she came together again, she was weaker. Nebulous. Swimming in an ocean of confusion, unable to form words or thought, the world blurred around the edges, and her mind vague and foggy. Peering at her surroundings, it took Beth a while to decipher that she was in Rhiannon's room, and that little time had passed since she'd come undone. Her daughter's hair was still wet from the bath, and there were flower petals strewn through it, but they were no longer inducing calm. Instead she was in a frenzy, ripping down posters from the walls, rifling through drawers and throwing things onto the floor. Fury unabated, she started pulling clothes from her closet, adding them to the pile of discarded items.

Beth floated over to her, trying to soothe her daughter, but she was even more translucent than usual, even less effective. She became frantic too, drawn into the wildness of Rhiannon's emotions. Eyes darting over her surroundings, Beth saw the beautiful red dress she and Rose had sewn, just before she died, for Rhiannon to wear to the Yule ritual. It was hanging, unworn and neglected, at the back of the closet. Summoning all her will, she forced her form into it, and was pleased to see a slight ripple of movement in the fabric.

Somehow Rhiannon saw it too, and slid it curiously from the coat hanger and over her head. Hands smoothing the soft velvet over her hips, she seemed to draw strength from it, and calm, and she turned towards the shelf next to her bed.

As she reached out a hand for her Book of Shadows, Beth noticed the slim tome next to it. It was a beautiful collection of flower spells, which she'd slipped a letter for her daughter inside on the night before she'd died. Fighting harder than she ever had, Beth concentrated all her strength and all her spirit, and dove towards the book, shoving against it and pushing it forward with all her might as her daughter's hand lifted the one beside it.

As her awareness dimmed and everything became hazy, Beth smiled one last smile when she saw Rhiannon catch the book and curiously slip the letter from its pages. There was a sensation of pain as she was ripped apart, but Beth had no regrets. If helping her daughter to heal was the reason she'd been granted this second chance at existence, and her time was now up, it had all been worth it. And she beamed as she shattered into pieces and disappeared back into the starless void.

Chapter 38

Fire and Fury

Rhiannon

Standing on tiptoes, Rhiannon pulled out the boxes on the top shelf of her wardrobe and reached behind them, to the darkest corner of her room, and of her mind. The black velvet cloak she'd worn on that awful night felt soft under her fingers, but as she dragged it out, she heard whispers of the past, of the pain, of that moment. Heard her frantic breaths, her racing heart, her desperation as she clawed at him, as she tried to escape his hands on her body, his touch on her skin, the weight of him crushing her into the earth, pounding against her, beneath her, within her.

It was a symbol of her rage and helplessness, but no more. Defiantly she draped it over her shoulders, over her long red dress, picked up her ritual bag and left the house, determined to reclaim the cloak's magic and power.

The thing that happened had not only stolen her innocence and trust. It had also stolen her love of magic. Her connection to magic. Disillusioned by what he'd done to her within the supposed safety of the sacred circle, Rhiannon didn't go to any of Rose's rituals. The priestess had implored her to take her mother's place in their group, to learn to use magic for spiritual development and personal growth, and to do healings for herself and others. But she'd refused. And now she realised that was one more thing he'd taken from her.

For almost a year after *the thing that happened*, Rhiannon cut herself off from magic. And she would have stayed cut off if Carlie hadn't arrived from Australia and begged her to come to a ritual with her. So *he* would have been the reason she turned her back on the goddess, and her mother's legacy, and never returned. Never felt its healing power, or its strength. Never developed the profound coven relationship she and Carlie had carved out together. Never found the strength to hopefully survive this now.

She was only just beginning to understand how much he had taken from her, and the realisation made her furious. But no more.

The sun was low in the sky when she slipped out the back gate into the laneway and hurried off into the gathering fog. By the time she reached the edge of the forest the mists had thickened, and a shiver ran up her spine as she faced the gloomy woods. The path could barely be discerned, but despite the hammering of her heart in her chest as real fear hovered around her, she pushed on. She had to do this. She had to face her fears. She had to put him, and *the thing that happened,* behind her.

Although she hadn't been back since that night, she remembered the way, perhaps because it had been the landscape of her nightmares. Nightmares she'd managed to bury beneath dreams of John, and she was grateful to him for that, for holding her safe at night, even though he had no idea he was doing it. Had her knowingness of what happened resurfaced because he was no longer part of her life? No longer keeping her demons at bay?

Breathing deeply, she tried to centre herself, to ground herself into the earth, into nature, into her self. Treading purposefully along the narrow path, she stopped abruptly when a black feather drifted downwards directly in front of her. She caught it before it hit the ground, then smiled up at the black raven perched on the branch above her, who was gazing at her with intense beady eyes.

"Thank you," she whispered.

As she watched it fly away, a pit of yearning opened up in her stomach, and she remembered the woman in blue telling her to look for the raven and she would find her love. As the memory hit, she staggered and almost fell. It pained her physically to contemplate how close *he* had come to stealing her magic. To consigning her to a life without her Otherworldly mentors, without the courage and confidence Rose and her rituals gave her, without the shimmer of possibility she felt in the circle with Carlie. She was shaking with rage – but that made her more determined. Today she was changing that. She was taking a stand, and reclaiming her power, her strength and her magic.

W hen she reached the clearing in the middle of the woods, she started trembling, memories darting around her, and the fear crashing into her so suddenly that she thought she would vomit. But no. She pulled back her shoulders, straightened her spine and stood tall. This was the new Rhiannon. The strong Rhiannon. She would own her emotions and her actions. She would acknowledge that it was her issues that had made her over-react to Rowan, and be more conscious in the future. Maybe it was her buried trauma that had destroyed her relationship with John too. Maybe not. Either way, she was aware now. Conscious.

Slowly she sank to the ground in the small grassy glade, the deep red fabric of her dress billowing around her. She'd found it in the back of her wardrobe, unworn, which was odd, but it was perfect for today. It made her feel strong, and defiant. Fiery. Empowered. In control, and in charge of her destiny and her choices.

With great reverence, Rhiannon set up her altar on the small, flat slab of stone in the middle of the glade, grateful for all the magical tools she'd been gifted. Her altar was the focal point of her ritual, the physical manifestation of her spellworking, and a piece of her soul.

In the centre was her small black cauldron, for she had surrendered to the promptings – of priestess Rose, and the mist-wreathed women – and was ready to work with the element of fire to burn away her pain. In the north she placed a chunk of rose quartz, to provide the grounding of earth and the essence of self-forgiveness and self-love. In the east, the midnight-dark raven feather, to represent air and her connection with the natural world. In the west, the beautiful chalice she'd been gifted by blue-robed Brauna at her coven dedication, to symbolise water and bring its nurturing properties to her working. And in the south, perhaps most importantly today, a deep red pillar candle in a pretty glass holder for the heat and power of fire.

After filling the chalice with spring water, lighting the candle and pouring her herbal blend – hawthorn flowers for a more resilient heart and to release fear and grief, yarrow for courage, rosemary to sweeten bitter memories and help her forgive, and a pinch of ground angelica root and dragon's blood for protection – into the cauldron, she stood up, athame in hand, and gazed skyward. The late afternoon was fading into the beauty of dusk, and the shadows were lengthening. Soon the sun would set and the full moon would rise – as it had on that long-ago night that had brought her here today – but for now she treasured the light that comes before the dark.

Raising her ritual knife high, she stepped out the boundary of her sacred circle, long blonde hair floating out behind her, long red dress billowing around her like flames. She felt powerful, invincible, and at one with nature and the earth. And with her self.

By my will a circle formed,
Between the worlds a boundary drawn.
To guard without and hold within,
The powers and the magic raised herein.
This sacred circle is cast...
So mote it be.

Settling back down on the grassy earth, Rhiannon solemnly invoked the directions and the elements, and the god and the goddess, then gazed into the flame of the red candle, losing herself in the golden glow as she felt the magic gathering around her. She breathed in, smiling at the soothing sweetness of the chamomile flowers in her hair, then exhaled the last remnants of fear that had gathered in her throat to choke her. It was time. Time to lay this ghost to rest.

Suddenly she saw a flash of movement and looked up – and cried out in fright. There was a woman sitting opposite her, wrapped in a long red cloak, her dark eyes glittering with power and strength. Aideen. The woman in red. The woman of fire. As Rhiannon watched in awe, she reached out a pale, elegant hand, and with a flick of her wrist, ignited the herbs in the cauldron between them.

The heat hit Rhiannon first, making her eyes water and her cheeks burn. Then the flames grew, scorching her body, singeing her hair, blistering her skin. Peeling away the layers within.

Eyes wide with terror, she staggered backwards, opening her mouth in a silent scream as fire surrounded her, then seemed to move within her, burning her up inside. Was she going to combust? Explode into a thousand shattered pieces and rain down glowing embers to destroy the woods?

"Do not be afraid little one. I am here to help you," the woman said, and with another wave of her hand, all the pain in Rhiannon's body left her. Fearfully she peered down, but her flesh was not blackened or charred. It had just been an illusion, albeit one that felt so sickeningly real. Anger flashed through her, but she didn't know why. She wasn't angry with this woman. *Was she?*

"Do not fight your emotions. Let yourself feel them. Acknowledge them. Dance with them even," Aideen crooned. "You cannot release it until you have spoken it. Named it. Felt it."

Rhiannon shrugged. Fine. She was angry at him. That was a no-brainer. But she'd faced him. She'd told him how she felt about *the thing that happened*, how it had affected her and how to help her, and banished him from her life.

"Faced who?" the woman asked.

"Him," she muttered.

"Name him."

Her body shook as much as her voice. "Evan," she whispered.

"And what did he do?"

The trembling got worse. *"The thing that happened."*

"What happened?"

She couldn't do this. She couldn't say it. She wouldn't. She wanted to leap into the fire to escape the woman, wanted to burn away to nothing and disappear from the world.

Aideen's voice softened. "Okay beloved, that can wait. Let us go back to your anger. Reach out for the spark that ignited your pain, and ignited this wild fire you are being consumed by."

Rhiannon closed her eyes. Breathed in, then out. Saw Carlie's face crumpling with pain as she ranted at her about Rowan.

Her fury built and swirled, grew and whirled.

Anger not just at what had happened, but at what it had created.

How it had shaped her and changed her, without her even knowing. Influencing her actions, making her react so harshly based on her own messed up issue, not her friend's.

What else had this secret, unacknowledged anger and bitterness made her do? She thought of her dad, and the times she'd lashed out at him with no real reason. Saw the hurt and confusion in his eyes as she'd unleashed her wrath on him.

Regret washed over her. Denial of what had happened may have protected her in some ways, yet it had crippled her too, made her cruel. Her heart caught fire, flames rising within her, blazing with ire. She felt herself sway. Did she have to confront him again? But what good would that serve?

"You are not only angry with him," the red-clad figure sang. "Look deeper. Look closer to home. Look within."

Shaking her head, Rhiannon tried to block the woman out, tried to look away from her coal-black eyes, but she was entranced. Trapped. Soon, without any effort on her part, waves of emotion started washing over her, shocks of rage cramped her muscles, and there was a bitter taste in her mouth that made her gag.

"I don't know!" she insisted. "Who am I angry at? You?" But she wasn't being honest, was she? She felt tears gather as realisation hit her. She was angry at herself.

"How could I have been so stupid? How could I let it happen?" she wailed. "Anyone else would have been suspicious of a guy who wanted to get them alone in the woods at night. Who insisted on secrecy. Who claimed they both had to be naked to make the spell work. Had to come together as the god and the goddess did in order to heal Mum." Bile rose in her throat. The woman gazed back at her calmly, unblinking. Her face was still, her eyes serene. And then in an instant she was beside Rhiannon, her arms around her, and warm, calming energy was pouring into her. Comforting her.

"Beloved, stop. You are not stupid, and it was not your fault. You *know* that – he told you as much yesterday."

Suspicious, Rhiannon stared at the woman. How did she know what had happened yesterday? But that concern fell away under Aideen's harsh gaze. *Right, that wasn't what she had to focus on.* Somehow she had to find the courage to admit that she was furious with herself – because there was a part of her that thought she'd made it happen, that she deserved it because she'd been so foolish.

"I'm so ashamed," she finally conceded. "Of my actions, my naivety, my gullibility. Carlie wouldn't have fallen for it. No sane person would! It *was* my fault, for being so stupid."

The woman sighed. "There are many covens who work in secrecy, and many witches who believe working skyclad amplifies the energy. That does not mean they should not be trusted. Forcing you to be naked when you did not want to be is a warning sign, but you cannot blame yourself. You were so focused on the promised result of making your mother well that you would have done anything."

Aideen's hand on her back was so soothing, and her voice so hypnotic, that Rhiannon felt herself starting to believe her.

"There have always been a few who use magic to take advantage of people, to prey on others, but most do not. Did your mother not tell you the same thing, in the letter she wrote you that night? You must not let one person's bad act destroy your trust, in yourself or others. You can learn from this – learn to trust your intuition and your instincts, trust your inner knowing. Do not allow it to change your world view. To destroy your goodness. *This was not your fault.*"

Numbly Rhiannon nodded, and in that instant the stress and strain left her body. As soon as she realised it had shifted, the mysterious woman was suddenly back on the other side of the altar from her, staring into her very soul.

"Say it Rhiannon. Tell me this was not your fault. Tell *yourself.*"

She opened her mouth, but her voice wouldn't come out. The comforting feeling blanketing her intensified, and she smiled in gratitude as it loosened the tightness in her throat.

"It's not my fault." It was barely a whisper, barely audible, but it was her voice. She was finding her voice, after being silent so long.

"It's not my fault."

She was a little louder this time, and the woman smiled at her approvingly. For a moment she felt content. Then she heard words murmured on the wind, and a chill ran up her spine.

Your cup runneth over with power and passion.
Your heart will be calmer when you develop compassion.

"Compassion for him? How can I feel that?" Rhiannon cried, feeling betrayed all over again.

In a flash, Aideen was at her side, drawing her close. "No beloved, compassion for yourself. Can you do that? Can you feel that?"

Rhiannon shrugged. "I'll try." That would have to do for now.

The woman bowed her head in acknowledgement, then thrust a hand into the fire that still burned in the centre of the altar. Rhiannon shrieked, feeling a corresponding pain in her own hand, but there was no scent of scorched flesh, and the figure beside her calmly withdrew her arm. A gold chain was wrapped around her fingers, with a large pendant hanging from it.

As the woman held it out to her, Rhiannon regretted that she was already wearing a necklace, yet when she raised her hand to it, she realised it was no longer there. It must have fallen off along the path into the woods. *Strange.*

She allowed Aideen to lift her hair and do up the clasp, then gasped as she looked down at the deep ruby red of the crystal, which glinted in the firelight and gave off an eerie glow, mesmerising her as she focused on the deep shadows within its surface.

Running a finger over the beautiful crystal, she felt a calm, soothing warmth seep into her body. It was a garnet, which was fittingly referred to as living fire. A stone of physical love and psychic protection, it represented love, devotion, understanding, trust, sincerity and honesty, which she supposed would come in handy.

"Beloved, do not despair. Love is coming for you, real love, and you will be ready for it when it gets here. Trust that you are enough, just as you are. You are not broken, and you have nothing to be ashamed of. Let the power of fire cleanse you of those false beliefs."

"How?"

"Facing it, acknowledging what happened, that is the first stage to healing, and you have done that now. It is understandable that you buried it beneath your grief at your mother's death, but now that you are conscious of it again, you can start to work through it, and be free of it. It will not happen overnight, and there will be setbacks along the way, but you have taken the hardest step."

She paused, watching Rhiannon with eyes that glittered with compassion now, rather than the enigmatic, impenetrable judgement she'd regarded her with earlier.

"And now you know that you are not the only one," Aideen continued. "Shame has silenced and isolated so many, so there is strength in knowing you are not alone. Knowing it is not your fault. Allow that knowledge to remove the shame you feel, remove the blame you feel. Then use the passion and heat of fire to reignite your self-belief, and your self-love, and begin to heal. And remember that those cracks you feel – that is how the light gets in. You will be stronger in the places you thought you were broken."

Rhiannon smiled. She liked that. She reflected on the words this strange being had whispered to her during her dark moon ritual. "Let the power of fire fill you with courage. Stop hiding. Be brave enough to trust yourself, and risk everything. Let it burn away your pain, your blame, your shame, then spark your passion and intention."

Yes. She could do that. She would do that.

She stared at Aideen, nodded, then slipped the cloak from her shoulders. When she'd worn it that night, she had felt herself dissolving into the ground, into the earth, into the nothing, at the violence that was done to her.

But now it was time to become solid again. To condense back into form. To find her courage and reappear, free from shame...

Handing the black velvet fabric across the altar, she released it into the keeping of the woman of fire and flame.

Then, head held high, she slowly walked back home.

Back to herself.

From the Ashes

Fire above, fire within, fire without.
She had been ordered to step into the fire, and so she did.
Through the gateway. Across the threshold. Into the flames.
Into the spiral of shame, the silence of blame,
The dead and buried weight of pain.
To another land, another realm, another piece of herself.
Into the ether and the ever-light, and ever-flame and
ever-more, that's ever-clear, from here.

For too long she had buried her trauma,
and denied its power.
Let the grief at her mother's death suppress it,
oppress it, repress it.
Wall her up, wall her in.
Lash out at everyone to avoid what was within.
But now it had bubbled to the surface.
Boil, bubble, toil and trouble. Fire burn, and cauldron bubble.
It was a poison forcing its way out through the tiniest
of cracks, billowing into the air she breathed.

In the quiet, in the silence, she came undone, and broke apart.
Numb, she split into a million tiny pieces, with no idea how
to tape together her shattered heart.
But in this rawness of being alone, she allowed a little fire in,
through the cracks in her soul, and it forced light into
the darkness of her deepest, most shadowy corners.
It provided warmth to the chill,
A spiritual balm, to all the harm.

It was the old trick. Walking on coals.
Revealing her soul.
She must accept what she'd wrought,
realise how hard she'd fought.
And become stronger in the places she was broken.
Right now her anger was keeping her warm,
lending her strength, yet she knew this righteous fire
would smoulder out to ashes, cold and dark and empty,
and she would be left bereft, burned up, spat out.
She had to ignite the fire of passion and forgiveness,
stoke the flames of kindness and compassion,
and focus on love not hate, truth not fate.

So she would burn away this pain, and this blame.
Play with the fire, and dance in the flame.
Trade blows with the devil who created her shame.
He taunted her, that she would burn on the pyre,
be destroyed by the fire.
But she roared back: "No! I am the fire."

She would rise from the ashes she had become,
and allow her crushed and shattered heart to fly.
A phoenix emerging, reaching for the sky.
Her spirit revealing a new truth from the lie.
And now she knew she wouldn't get burned,
because she was the heat of the fire,
the strength from the pyre,
the spark to inspire.
She had been forged in the flames, and she was transformed.

Rhiannon and Beth's stories continue in *Into the Air...*

"And just as the phoenix rose from the ashes, she too will rise.
Returning from the flames, clothed in nothing but her strength,
More beautiful than ever before."
Shannen Heartzs

Thank You!

Thank you so much for reading this book, and
sharing the magic of Rhiannon and Beth's stories.
As an indie author, I rely on word of mouth and reader reviews
to get the word out. If you enjoyed *Into the Fire*, I would be
so grateful if you could take a moment to leave a review on
any book site. Reviews help improve sales and ranking,
and are of immense help to all indie writers.

If you'd like to stay in touch and receive free exclusive content,
be the first to hear about book news, events info and giveaways,
win prizes and more, you can sign up for my newsletter at

www.sereneconneeley.com/subscribe.

(And don't worry, you can unsubscribe at any time...)

With love and gratitude,
Serene xx

"Ignis reddit – Fire restores."
Kjerkius Gennius, Roman philosopher

With Thanks

I am so grateful, as always, to my sweet hubby, for his love, support and belief in me. For talking me down from my doubt-filled moments, being patient when I'm on deadline, making me tea while I write, and asking for Rhiannon's story (not sure we knew what we were getting in for there!). Thank you my precious beloved, for our enchanted life together, and our magical adventures at home and away.

I am more grateful than I can express to amazingly talented artist Selina Fenech, for allowing me to use her beautiful paintings for my covers – and for serendipitously creating the perfect one at the perfect time, every single time. You are the sweetest person I know, my absolute favourite artist, and a wonderful writer too...

With love and gratitude to my dear friends Selina Fenech and K. A. Last. I value your honesty, your encouragement, your suggestions, your beta-reading skills and your wisdom sharing. Thank you for the laughter, the long conversations, the occasional venting – and the support, the focus and the action. I'm so excited for what's ahead...

I'm so grateful to the readers who have such faith and trust in me, especially those who pre-ordered *Fire* (I'm so sorry for the delay – thank you for your patience!). You have no idea how much it means to me to know you want to read Rhiannon's story. Writing is such a solitary thing, and I'm always a little scared when I send a new book out into the world. Your messages and support help ease the fear...

Love and blessings to my writer friends, Felicity Pulman, for belief and gentle nudging, and Lucy Cavendish, Kylie Matthews and Cheralyn Darcey. To my NaNoWriMo and Camp NaNo buddies, to L. L. Hunter and the Story Queens, and to all the indie authors who share this crazy journey. To my gorgeous hubby, and my faery friend Daniella, for the illustrations. To sweet Voula for coffee and chats. To Janine and my fit group friends for strength and sanity. To my wonderful family who have supported me always.

And love and honour to Tori Amos and Bif Naked, for their music, their wisdom, their activism, and for sharing their stories with me all those years ago, and to all those who speak up and speak out... Time's Up.

With much love, Serene xx

"You must be ready to burn yourself in your own flame.
How could you rise anew if you have not first become ashes?"
Friedrich Nietzsche, German philosopher and poet

About the Author

Serene Conneeley is an Australian writer with a fascination for history, travel, ritual and the myth and magic of ancient places and cultures. She's written for magazines about news, travel, health, spirituality, entertainment and social and environmental issues, been editor of several preschool magazines, and contributed to international books on history, witchcraft, psychic development and personal transformation.

She's the author of the Into the Mists Trilogy – *Into the Mists, Into the Dark* and *Into the Light* – the Into the Storm Trilogy – *Into the Storm, Into the Fire* and *Into the Air* – and the non-fiction books *Faery Magic, Mermaid Magic, Witchy Magic, Seven Sacred Sites and A Magical Journey,* and creator of the meditation CD *Sacred Journey.*

Serene is a reconnective healing practitioner, and has studied magical and medicinal herbalism, bereavement counselling, reiki and many other healing modalities, plus politics and journalism. She loves reading, drinking tea with her friends, working out and celebrating the energy of the moon and the magic of the earth. Her pagan heart blossomed as she climbed mountains, sat in stone circles, climbed into ancient burial mounds and stood in the shadow of the pyramids on her travels, and she's also learned the magic of finding true happiness and peace at home.

www.SereneConneeley.com

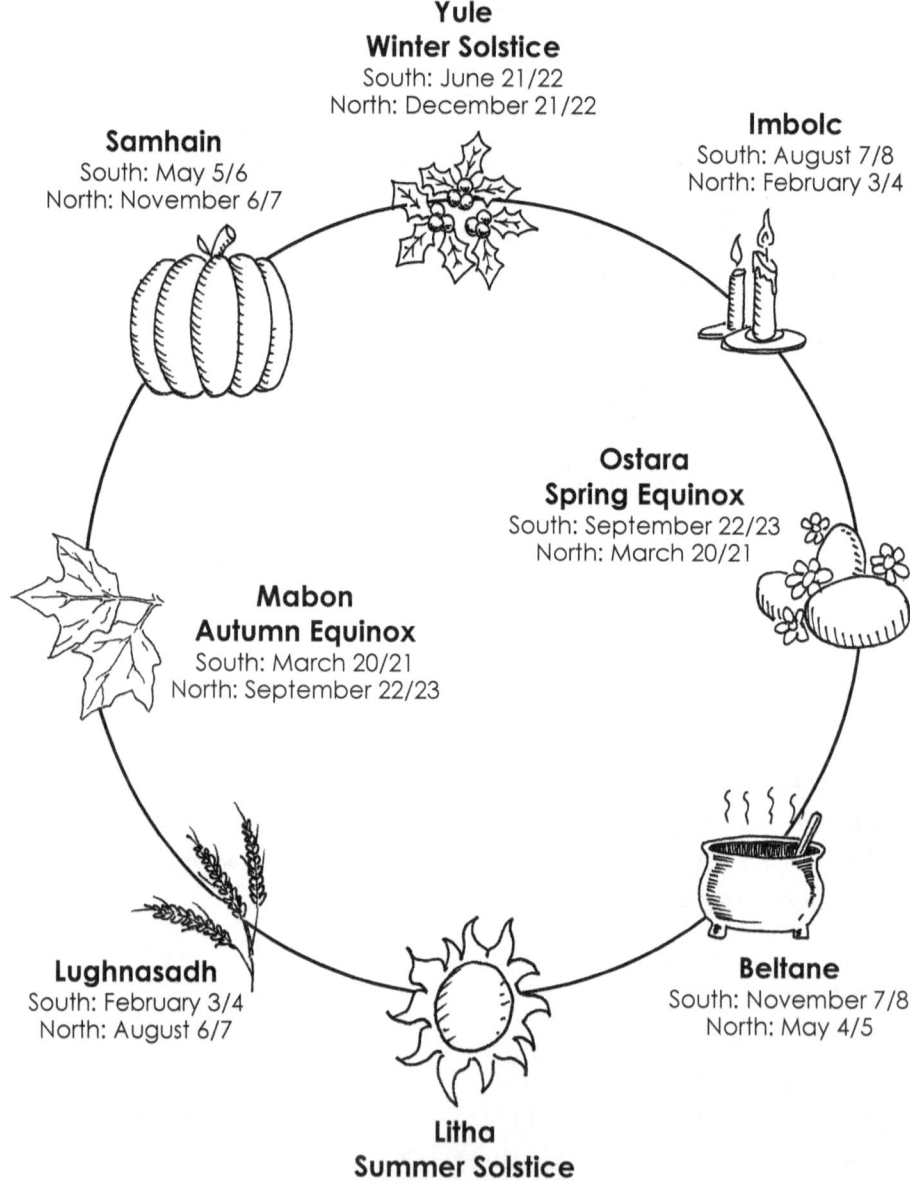

Yule
Winter Solstice
South: June 21/22
North: December 21/22

Samhain
South: May 5/6
North: November 6/7

Imbolc
South: August 7/8
North: February 3/4

Ostara
Spring Equinox
South: September 22/23
North: March 20/21

Mabon
Autumn Equinox
South: March 20/21
North: September 22/23

Beltane
South: November 7/8
North: May 4/5

Lughnasadh
South: February 3/4
North: August 6/7

Litha
Summer Solstice
South: December 21/22
North: June 20/21

The Wheel of the Year

Rose and her witchy circle, including Beth and Violet in the past, and Rhiannon and Carlie today, celebrate the eight sacred sabbats, or festivals, of the Wheel of the Year, as ancient druids, priestesses and magical practitioners once did, and modern pagans around the world still do. In *Into the Fire*, the story begins at Samhain, the final harvest festival, when those we have lost are honoured and celebrated, and ghosts are said to walk.

"The festivals of the Wheel of the Year are defined by the cycle
of nature, by the dance of the weather gods and spirits of place.
They require us to look not to the heavens but to the earth.
They are set within our soul, watching the leaves on the trees,
feeling the shifting temperature and the changing light,
within and around."
Emma Restall Orr, British druid priestess, ritualist and author

A powerful way to become more aware of your inner world is to harness the natural magic of the cycles of the seasons. The shifting energies of the earth's turning have been celebrated and utilised for thousands of years, and even today, when most of us are so far removed from nature, you can still tangibly feel the introspection of winter, the crisp change of autumn, the potent energy of summer and the vibrant power of spring, and see the changing moods reflected in the colours of nature and the behaviour of plants and animals.

Attuning yourself to the vibrations of the eight sacred festivals that make up the enchanted Wheel of the Year will fill you with strength, magic and a sense of grand possibility and potential. You will become more in sync with your inner self and your intuition, and start to connect with your own emotional tides as you connect with the earth's.

These special days, determined by the position of the earth in relation to the sun, mark the beginning, midpoint and end of each season, and are measured today by astronomers and scientists. In the past they were calculated by druids, the philosophers and scientists of their age, and recorded in stone circles and cairns, or by shamans who created calendars in pyramidal structures. These events have been honoured for thousands of years in cultures throughout the world, so the imprint of their energy can be tapped in to and absorbed.

Long ago, when life revolved around agriculture, and the sun and the moon were considered deities to be worshipped, the Celtic peoples of Europe, and many others around the globe, were in tune with nature. They had to know when each season began and how long it would last so they could plant and harvest crops, hunt migratory prey and prepare for the harshness of the winters. They divided their year by seasons, not months, and honoured each change, celebrating eight festivals that marked the cycles of these seasons and the cycles of the earth.

There are four astronomical and four agricultural festivals. The astronomical celebrations are determined by the position of the sun, and include the spring and autumn equinoxes (Latin for "equal night"), which occur when the sun is directly above the equator and the length of day and night is equal, and the summer and winter solstices (Latin for "sun stand still"), which occur when the sun is at its northern or southernmost extreme, the furthest it ever gets from the equator. These four events are the midpoint of each season – thus the summer solstice being referred to as Midsummer's Day and the winter solstice as Midwinter. The agricultural celebrations are known as cross-quarter days, because they fall midway between the astronomical festivals. Traditionally they were tied to agricultural events such as the sowing and harvesting of crops, and they mark the beginning of each season.

Even today, when most of us no longer live in harmony with the earth's rhythms or agricultural cycles, magical practitioners celebrate the Wheel of the Year as an honouring of nature and an acknowledgement of the continuing cycle of life, death and rebirth, both literally and symbolically.

Literally this refers to the changing seasons – the planting and rebirth of spring, the fertility and vibrant life force of summer, the harvest energy of autumn, and the introspection and endings (death) of winter. Mythologically it was tied to the story of the god and the goddess. At the spring equinox they meet and court, before consummating their love during the rites of Beltane. At the summer solstice the goddess blooms into the mother, pregnant with new life, and the sun god reaches his energetic peak. He weakens through the harvest time of Lughnasadh and the autumn equinox, before journeying to the underworld at Samhain to learn new wisdom. Then he is reborn at the winter solstice, when the goddess gives birth to the infant sun god, and the Wheel turns again, playing out the cycle on and on through time.

Once this creation story was regarded as fact. Today some people still think of it as a literal retelling of a historical truth, while others feel it is simply a parable that humanises and anthropomorphises nature. Either way, it's now the symbolic meaning that's most relevant to our lives – planting the seeds of our dreams in the metaphorical spring, watching them grow and manifest in the world, then giving thanks for our literal harvest, and allowing the things that no longer serve us to die off or be released, before starting all over again with new dreams as we celebrate our own rebirth.

Becoming aware of the seasonal shifts and the patterns of nature wherever you live, and celebrating these ancient but still relevant festivals, is a simple way to tap in to the magic of the earth and start to connect with nature and your inner self. Channelling this energy and creating meaningful rituals in your life doesn't conflict with any religion or require a belief system, as it's a celebration of the science of nature and the cycles of the planet. Many pagans, like Rose and her friends, do call on gods and goddesses, and have a personal concept of the divine as a universal creative force, but others don't believe in any form of deity, simply revering nature as sacred and as the source of life, and believing that divinity is an inner not an outer power, an energy within themselves and every other person alive.

Samhain : First Day of Winter : Death

Samhain, which is celebrated in early November in the northern hemisphere and early May in the southern, is a cross-quarter day marking the end of autumn and the beginning of the cold and dark of winter.

Symbolically it is about rest and renewal, of preparing for what's ahead and withdrawing a little to conserve your energy, and releasing the things you've been holding on to, in order to ready yourself for new challenges and experiences. It's also the night when the veil between the worlds is said to be at its thinnest, when people honour their ancestors and try to commune with the dead. Some set a place at the dinner table for any loved ones passed over, as Rhiannon and her dad Mike did at their Samhain ritual, while others cast spells to bring their spirit back, or use divination to converse. This magical time and its purpose has been conserved in the modern festival of Halloween, which celebrates ghosts, witches and restless spirits.

The beginning of winter is a period of reflection, so spend time in contemplation. If you've lost someone close to you, light a candle and remember them. Look at photos or letters and feel their presence with you. This shouldn't be morbid – you're celebrating their life and all they mean to you. Also honour those who are here now. Call your mum and dad, visit your grandparents, or write to someone who meant a lot to you when you were growing up and thank them.

Long ago, Samhain was the end of one year and the start of the next, so it's a powerful time to let go of the energy and old memories of the previous year so you can move forward with lightness and strength, and new resolutions. Light another candle, and by its flickering illumination, write out all the worries, frustrations, regrets and seeming failures you've held on to. Then burn the list in the flame as you visualise the element of fire burning them all away, helping you release your attachment to those emotions and their power over you. Breathe in this positive new energy and feel refreshed.

This is the time to prepare yourself for the rebirth you'll experience at Yule, but for that to happen there must be death – the death of fears and doubts, and anything holding you back.

Yule : Winter Solstice : Rebirth

The winter solstice, known to pagans as Yule and Midwinter, falls around December 21/22 in the northern hemisphere and June 21/22 in the southern, and marks the middle of winter. It's the shortest day and the longest night of the year, and marks the transition between dark and light, both emotionally and physically. It's the lowest point of the Wheel in terms of daylight and energy, with the sun rising later and night falling earlier. The land is barren and cold, there is less light, and energetically people feel tired and unmotivated.

Winter is a time to rest and reflect, to acknowledge sadness and loss – of dreams, of friendships, of parts of your self – and conserve your energy. But the solstice is the turning point in this time of darkness, introspection and dreaming. Considered the dark night of the soul, it also marks the period when the dark half of the year relinquishes its hold to the light half. From this time forward, the days will start to lengthen, the sun will become stronger, and the energy within and without will start to increase and build.

In pagan times an evergreen tree was brought inside as a symbol of the hope of spring's return, and Yule was a time of feasting, celebration and gift-giving in honour of the birth of the sun god – traditions that live on today in the Christmas tree we decorate, the presents we put under it, the huge meal we cook for family and friends, and the celebration of the birth of the son of God.

To attune yourself to this festival of rebirth, light a candle on solstice eve to symbolise the sun and its activating energy, and list your dreams for the coming year. Traditionally people stayed up all night to await the return of the light, but if you can't do that, get up for the sunrise to toast the dawn and give thanks for this energetic reawakening. Open yourself to the promise of new growth and achievement, and the rebirth of your own self and your creativity, as the sun is also reborn. Symbolically and energetically it's a time to honour your inner wisdom, consider the lessons you learned during winter's introspection, and integrate them into your life so you can start to initiate change and prepare for the rush of growth of the coming springtime.

Imbolc : First Day of Spring : Purification

Imbolc, which is celebrated in the first week of February in the northern hemisphere and the first week of August in the southern, is a cross-quarter day marking the end of winter and the start of spring. It celebrates the return of light to the land, and to our own hearts, and is a time of hope, renewal and fresh starts after winter's sluggishness. Energetically it's a time of awakening, rebirth and re-emergence. Nature fills with life force and quivers with the energy to grow again, and we start to emerge from the chill of winter, shaking off our lack of motivation and re-engaging with the world, making it a great day to sow the seeds of what you want to achieve in the coming year.

Imbolc is dedicated to Bridie, the goddess of inspiration, creativity and fire, who was later supplanted by Saint Bridget, whose festival is also celebrated at this time. Talk to Bridie – or Bridget, or the higher-self aspect of yourself – or write her a letter, and tell her what you want to create in the next twelve months. Meditate on your goals and what you hope to achieve. Don't worry about how to do it, as that will be revealed later in flashes of inspiration, guidance or outside help.

Physically it's a time of purification and cleansing after the long dark of winter, so clean your house and clear your space, sweeping out old energy and thoughts so the new will thrive. It's a good time to write about your beliefs and examine how you feel about your spiritual path too, exploring the reasons you think the way you do, and perhaps questioning if there are other viewpoints you might also embrace.

Imbolc is all about new beginnings, and in some magical traditions it is the day chosen for initiations and rededications, so if you want to make a pledge to a new path or a new goal, or a personal vow of any kind, you will be supported by the energy of the season. You may also like to ignite a candle to represent the coming back of the light, and do some candle magic. Stare into the flame as you concentrate on what you want, then blow it out, sending your desire out to the universe. Making a wish as you blow out the candles on your birthday cake is a magic that has survived from pagan times, and is a potent way to begin manifesting your wishes into reality, whatever day it is.

Ostara : Spring Equinox : Blossoming

The spring or vernal equinox, known to pagans as Ostara, is celebrated around March 20/21 in the northern hemisphere and September 22/23 in the southern. It's one of only two times in the year when the length of day and night is equal, as the sun sits directly above the equator on its journey north or south, creating equal light and dark in both hemispheres.

This equinox is about growth and passion, and the unfurling and release of the immense potential within you. On a universal and a personal level, it's a period of balance and harmony, of union between the physical and the spiritual, and the integration of your heart and your soul. This can be harnessed to anchor your dreams in reality and enhance your own inner harmony as the balance of universal outer energies is reflected within. Relationships are also harmonious now, making it perfect for weddings and for healing rifts.

It's a time of growth and fertility, when new crops are sown, new shoots break through the earth, buds on the trees open, birds build nests and lay eggs, and new life is celebrated. Thanks was traditionally given to the fertility goddess Ostara, whose symbols were an egg and a hare, and who is still honoured around the world today, albeit unknowingly, in the form of chocolate eggs and the Easter bunny.

Energetically it's also a very fertile time, as the seeds you sowed of your goals at Imbolc begin to sprout and gain momentum. Paint some hard-boiled eggs with symbols that represent your desires, or buy or make the chocolate version, meditating on your own metaphorical fertility and your ability to manifest dreams into reality. Choose an affirmation related to your desired outcome, then write it down and pin it up where you'll be able to see it often.

Go outside during the day and breathe in the fresh spring air, filling your heart with new energy and inspiration as you fill your lungs with oxygen. In many ancient cultures, including the Roman one whose calendar we have based ours on, the spring equinox was the first day of the year, and the sense of new hope and optimism reflected in this time remains today. It's a celebration of new life, hope, passion, growth and energy.

Beltane : First Day of Summer : Growth

Beltane, celebrated in early May in the northern hemisphere  and early November in the southern, is a cross-quarter day marking the end of spring and the start of the heat and energy of summer. Evidence of new life is everywhere, in abundant blossoms, the hatching of birds, and bees pollinating flowers, showing that time is moving forward and life is progressing. Women bathed their faces in the dew gathered from their garden on Beltane morning to harness the energy of youth, and flowers were brought inside to symbolise fresh beginnings and the power of nature.

Beltane was the major fertility festival. Handfasting rituals were conducted, and lovers leaped over bonfires then came together in sacred union in the fields to bless the crops with fertility. Maypole dancing, representing the union of the god (the pole) and the goddess (the ribbons), was performed to join the forces of masculine and feminine, and May Day remains a popular day to wed in the northern hemisphere.

It's a time of lovers and spells to attract love, and celebrating the fertility of life, not just physically, but also of your dreams and ambitions. Symbolically this day marks the igniting of the fires of creativity and passion, of the fertility of your dreams being made manifest, and is the time to take steps to achieve what you want. Check in on the projects you started at Ostara, and write about their progress and the ways in which they've sprouted into reality. If you need to fine tune anything, learn a new skill, or let go of one aspect so it can germinate further on its own, the energy of this day will support you. Make a commitment to yourself – start a new project, apply for a new job or take up a new hobby, knowing the universe is bursting with raw energy and power that you can tap in to.

It's also a powerful time to repledge your love to your partner. You don't have to build a bonfire and leap over it, although you can! Simply lighting a red or gold candle as you stare into each other's eyes and speak your love and commitment will invoke the power and passion of the element of fire. If you're single, make a commitment of some kind to yourself, nurture a friendship, or if you seek love, sing your intention and wanting of a romantic partner to the universe.

Litha : Summer Solstice : Fruition

The summer solstice, known to pagans as Litha, is celebrated around June 20/21 in the northern hemisphere and December 21/22 in the southern. It's the longest day and the shortest night of the year, and marks the peak of energy and solar power for the year. On this day the sun reaches its northern or southernmost latitude before it turns and heads back towards the equator, so near the poles daylight lasts for twenty-four hours – the sun just doesn't set for weeks at a time. In nature, everything is ripe and abundant, and life is blooming.

It's a time of high, hot and active energy. Creativity and expression is at a peak, so stand in your power and express your needs, saying what you want rather than assuming that people know. Whereas the winter solstice is slow and introspective, its opposite is fast and effective. Make use of the active energy – this is a time to do, to get out there and harness the energising earth power and make things happen.

Follow your passion, take a chance, say yes to new opportunities, and express your creativity and your inner self. This is not the time to be withdrawn or shy, it's for getting out amongst it and making your dreams come true. It's also a time when relationships – and you – will mature, and you'll apply new wisdom and forethought to your passion. So give thanks for the lessons you've learned, and allow the person you are maturing into to unfold.

It's a time of celebration too, of acknowledging how far you've come and what you've achieved. Enjoy the happiness and abundance of this season and soak up the sunshine and festive atmosphere. Traditionally people stayed up all night on solstice eve, partying around bonfires or within sacred circles of stone, then watched the sun rise the next morning, feeling it bathe them in warmth and light.

At dawn, stand with your arms outstretched and breathe in the sun's life-giving power. Let it wash over you with its healing energy and burn away anything you no longer need. Take note of how your dreams and goals are manifesting into the world, and meditate on anything that could be blocking your progress. Be open to letting go of whatever isn't working so you can move forward in a new direction.

Lughnasadh
First Day of Autumn : Gratitude

Lughnasadh, named for the Celtic god Lugh and also known as Lammas, is celebrated in the first week of August in the northern hemisphere and the first week of February in the southern hemisphere, and marks the end of summer and the beginning of autumn. It's the first harvest festival, traditionally a time of feasting and of thanksgiving for the life-giving properties of the grain and nature's bounty, as well as a recognition of the cycle of sowing and reaping of the crops.

It is also the time to honour the things you have grown and created in your life, a day to harvest the fruits of your labours, and acknowledge your successes and what you've achieved in the past year. Celebrate the goals you've reached and have your own festival of gratitude, in whatever form that takes. Toast your success, throw a party or do something special to mark the occasion – maybe reward yourself for your hard work with a gift you've long wanted, or some precious time off to rest and chill out. Make a list of all the things you've gained over the past year – the gifts you've been given, the new talents you've developed, the friends you've made, the experiences you've had, the healings you've received – and give thanks for it all.

Then, out of gratitude and in the spirit of the ancestors who shared the bounty of their harvest with those less well off, pay your good fortune forward. Donate to a local charity or collect food for the homeless, as Rose and her friends do, lend to a business in the developing world (Kiva.org does great work), or give your time to help someone, ensuring the energy of abundance continues and is strengthened. Give joyfully, with no expectation of receiving anything in return. And work out small ways in which you can make a difference to the people around you all year long as well.

As the energy begins to subtly slow, this is also a time to be patient and to trust that everything is as it should be, because there are still harvests to come. Not everything has to be achieved right now – some things take longer to manifest. The lesson of the Wheel of the Year is that everything continues, everything happens when it should, and everything is eternal.

Mabon : Autumn Equinox : Harvest

The autumn equinox, known as Mabon and celebrated on September 22/23 in the northern hemisphere and March 20/21 in the southern, is characterised by the length of day and night being equal as the sun travels back across the equator to the other hemisphere. From this point on, the days will become shorter and cooler, but this is a moment of balance in nature and within – a point of harmony and calm.

Vibrationally Mabon is a season of withdrawal, of being alone to meditate, recharge, reassess and ponder where you're at in life. The energy of the earth retreats and goes within, as does your personal power, but from this period of introspection you will emerge with strength and wisdom. It's a time to honour your achievements, experiences and growth, and to ensure balance by integrating all parts of yourself. Acknowledge and celebrate what you've reaped in your own life. Feel fulfilment from each goal reached, releasing what no longer serves you in order to move forward. In the wild, old growth is cleared. In your life, cut out anything that's preventing new life and love from flourishing, whether it's work, people, a belief system, regret or the past.

On this day, when all is balanced, witches traditionally renewed their magical commitments, and you can renew any vows you've made or pledge a new one, be it to do with magic, love, friendship, career or anything else. As the shadows lengthen, it's also a good time to scry for insight into your future. If you can, light a fire and stare into the flames, allowing your mind to go blank and your vision to blur a little, or go outside and watch the clouds scuttling across the sky, analysing the shapes and symbols you see within flame and cloud. Without over-thinking it, write down what they mean to you.

Pyromancy (fire reading) and nephomancy (cloud reading) are forms of divination that have been used for millennia. You should develop your own dictionary of symbols, as you know better than anyone what any shape or image means to you, but you can begin with standard readings, such as a heart indicating romance, a cat referring to a need to trust your intuition, a tree meaning you will make new friends and a plane foreshadowing travel.

The Magic of the Moon

Rose works with the phases of the moon in her spellcasting and her healings, and performs rituals at the new moon, dark moon and the full. Carlie and Rhiannon planned their coven dedication for a full moon, and did a ritual to banish negativity on the dark moon, and witches, druids and shamans have long harnessed lunar power too.

The moon is a thing of mystery, enchantment and wonder, linked to intuition, inner power and imagination. To the Celts, its phases reflected the phases of a human life – birth, adolescence, adulthood, death and rebirth – and were associated with the Triple Goddess who included the aspects of maiden, mother and crone, represented by Rhiannon, maiden goddess of inspiration and the waxing moon, Arianrhod, mother goddess of fertility and the full moon, and Ceridwen, crone goddess of death, rebirth and the waning moon. In countless other cultures the moon was also seen as a goddess, who not only marked the passing of time, but increased fertility, deepened psychic powers and improved wellbeing.

Harnessing the energy of the phases of the moon can help bring a goal to fruition. These phases are determined by the moon's position in relation to the earth and the sun, as it orbits our planet every 29.53 days. The moon has no light of its own – it's illuminated by the light of the sun reflecting off its surface, and its phases are created by the amount of the illuminated side we can see from earth.

You can picture these phases by imagining a clock. The earth sits in the centre of the clock face, with the sun above twelve o'clock. The moon is at the end of the minute hand, circling around the clock face, and the earth, in an anticlockwise direction. It begins its cycle at twelve, directly between the sun and the earth, which makes the moon invisible to us because the side that's reflecting the light of the sun is facing away from the earth, towards the sun. This is the dark moon.

A day later, as the moon moves towards eleven o'clock, a tiny sliver of the illuminated side can be seen, which appears as a thin crescent. This is the new moon. In the southern hemisphere it looks like a C, while in the northern hemisphere it's reversed, appearing as a backward C, and at the equator it's horizontal rather than vertical.

The crescent continues to grow as the moon moves from between the earth and the sun, and the angle between them allows us to see more of the moon's reflected light. By the time it gets to nine o'clock, which takes about a week, it's at right angles to the earth in relation to the sun, and we see a half circle. This is the first quarter moon.

When the moon gets to six o'clock, it's on the other side of the earth from the sun, with the earth in between. The whole of the side that is visible to us is reflecting back sunlight, so we see a round moon in all its shining, golden full moon glory. The size of the moon hasn't changed, it's just that we're seeing the fully illuminated side.

After that it appears to decrease again as it progresses back to the dark moon. When it gets to three o'clock we see a half moon again, but this time it's facing in the other direction. This is the third or last quarter moon. From there it continues back to twelve, with the crescent getting smaller each night, until it returns to the beginning, where it's invisible again, and the cycle starts over.

Lunar phases are printed in newspapers, moon diaries and websites like www.sunrisesunset.com, and you can also determine the phase of the moon by its shape, as well as by the time it rises, which occurs about fifty minutes later each day. It can be remembered by the old adage: "The new moon rises at sunrise, and the first quarter at noon. The full moon rises at sunset, and the last quarter at midnight."

As the moon progresses from dark to full it's the waxing or growing period, a time of new beginnings and increasing energy. As it goes from full back to dark it's the waning period, a time of lowering energy and introspection. Magical practitioners use the cycles of the moon to increase the power of spellworking, harnessing the energies inherent in each phase. So do fishermen, who understand the incredible pull the moon has on the tides of the ocean and its creatures.

Gardening also operates to the rhythms of the moon, as the lunar phase can enhance or hinder plant growth. To boost it, sow crops that produce above the ground between new moon and full, as the light and energy increases, and crops that produce below ground, such as root vegetables and bulbs, between full moon and dark.

Surfers understand its power too. The full moon magnifies weather patterns, so a winter full moon will bring stormier swells and bigger waves. Tides are more extreme at both the full moon and the dark moon – high tides are higher, and low tides lower. These two phases have an intense influence on the ocean, heightening conditions and drawing huge swells – or, if the ocean is flat, making it even flatter. Surfers going to Indonesia for a wave-riding safari book around a full moon, so they'll have optimum conditions and even bigger waves.

Hair growth is also influenced by the moon. If you want your hair to grow faster, trim the ends between the new moon and the first quarter. If you want it to grow thicker and fuller, trim it during the full moon phase. And if you really like the style and want to maintain it, have it cut around the third quarter, so it grows out more slowly.

The moon affects tides, plants, animals and the behaviour of people. Some can't sleep during the full moon, others feel more emotional or have strange dreams. It's common to feel more energetic during the waxing phase, and more tired when it's waning. There are also many tales of accidents and psychic breakdown increasing at the full moon. Today the moon's journey across the sky is often obscured by buildings, and even women's cycles, which used to be connected to it, can be controlled by chemicals. But the moon still impacts on our energy and emotions, and can be used to influence the outcome and power of rituals, and empower any project you want to complete.

Phases of the Moon

One lunar cycle runs for 29.53 days, beginning with the tiny crescent of the new moon, building in energy through the waxing phase to the full moon, then decreasing and withdrawing through the waning period to the dark moon, before starting a new cycle. Here are some ways to take advantage of the phases of the moon to set your goal or intention, then watch it grow to beautiful, abundant completion.

New Moon – Day 1

The new moon rises just after dawn and is up all day, so it is often unnoticed in contrast to the sun and the bright sky, and sets just after sunset. From the moment the tiny new crescent moon is first sighted, and for a day or two afterwards, there is heightened energy, so it's a good time to start new projects, make resolutions and vows you want to stick to, go in a new direction, invite something new into your life, or look for a different job. Chinese New Year always falls on a new moon, as it brings energy and vitality to the coming year.

This is the time to plant seeds, both literally and metaphorically, be it in the garden or in your life, sowing the seeds of new ideas, dreams and hopes. Magical workings are most powerful during the day, when the moon is visible – during this phase there is no moon at night.

A simple yet powerful new moon ritual is to sit outside as dawn breaks, watching the sun rise and feeling the energy of the new moon as it peeks above the horizon, and write down your wish for the coming month. Work out an affirmation to support it, and keep it somewhere you'll see it often. You can also invoke maiden lunar goddesses such as Rhiannon, Bridie and Persephone to add sweet, innocent yet powerful energy to your intent.

Waxing Moon – Days 1 to 14

During the two weeks from new moon to full, the energy is strong and positive, so concentrate on attracting and drawing things to you. It's the optimal time for magical workings to manifest love, abundance and new career opportunities, and for learning new things, expanding your outlook, increasing spirituality and boosting fertility. In this waxing period the lunar energy continues to build, so whatever seeds you planted at the new moon will sprout rapidly. It's an energy of gathering, growing, strengthening and increase, so if you need to release something while the moon is waxing, reverse the intent of the spell so it fits with the energies. Rather than giving up smoking by releasing your addiction, create a ceremony to attract willpower.

If you're doing healings, draw good health to you as the moon is waxing, and release illness when it's waning. Maiden goddesses can be invoked, such as Bridie, Artemis, Athena, Aphrodite and Aine.

Waxing crescent moon: Days 1 to 6

In the week following the new moon, it rises a little later each day, through the morning, and sets after sunset. This is the sprouting phase, when you nurture the seeds you planted at the new moon. It's the time to set things in motion, and brings energy and new growth to projects, helping you manifest them into reality and flooding you with strength and the energy of growth. The sliver of light represents your growing consciousness and the dawning of your potential.

Waxing half moon – the first quarter: Days 7 to 8

At the end of the first week is the first quarter moon, which rises at noon and sets at midnight (this is why you can see it in the evening but not in the morning, as it's appearing to the other side of the world then). It's halfway between new and full, and looks like a half moon. This is the growth phase, where you build upon what you've already begun, although the energy can be challenging at times, pushing you towards achieving your goals and urging you to work hard to get the projects you've planned completed. Issues can come to a head, which can be uncomfortable, but it's all part of the process of growth.

Waxing gibbous moon: Days 9 to 14

In the second week of the lunar cycle, as the moon moves towards full, it rises in the afternoon and sets in the early hours of the morning. This phase is conducive to expressing yourself, getting in touch with your feelings and taking action. It requires some patience, as things are almost, but not quite, at the peak of their potential and energy.

Full Moon – Days 14 to 16

The full moon rises as the sun sets, which is why it's so obvious and clearly seen, because it sails across the sky all night, contrasting with the velvety blackness, before setting around dawn, just as the sun is rising. The three days of the full moon – the day before, day of and day after – can be used to boost any intention or project. It represents achievement, culmination and abundance. The world is filled with energy and potential, so it's a great time for healing and manifestation.

Midnight is the most powerful time for magical work, as the moon is directly overhead. Stand beneath the golden orb and give thanks for what you've achieved so far, and breathe in the energy and power so you can harness it for self-expression and strength.

Perform a Drawing Down the Moon ritual, bringing the energy of the moon, and the moon goddess, into your heart and soul. This is also a great time to charge crystals and amulets with the moon's energy, and cleanse your own physical and etheric bodies. Psychic abilities are thought to be at their strongest now, so practise any divination methods you are drawn to, looking within to find answers to your questions and clues to your future.

The full moon is the high tide of power in a lunar cycle, so cast spells for completion, things you want to achieve, and anything requiring a boost of intensity, such as healing work, job hunting or love. You can also invoke mother goddesses Arianrhod, Isis, Selene, Diana, Lakshmi, Quan Yin, Demeter, Ishtar and Mama Quilla, who embody the full moon, motherhood, fertility, the earth and creation.

Waning Moon – Days 16 to 29

During the two weeks from full moon to dark, the energy is slowing, so it's a time for banishing and release work. Do a ritual to let go of anything that no longer serves you, such as a past relationship, a bad habit, a trait like procrastination, or any material objects or issues weighing you down and blocking your progress. If you need to attract something while the moon is waning, reverse the intent. Rather than doing a spell to draw love to you, which works against the energy of this phase, cast one to banish loneliness. This is a time of retreat and withdrawal, when you can invoke darker crone energy goddesses such as Ceridwen, the Morrigan and Grandmother Spiderwoman, who hold the wisdom and power of transformation, endings and rebirth.

Waning gibbous moon: Days 16 to 21

In the first week following the full moon, it rises a little later each night, between dusk and midnight, and sets in the morning. This is a phase of introspection and self-assessment. In the garden this energy promotes root development; in life it's a time to stand strong and find your inner power, bravely delving within for the answers imparted by the full moon. Magical workings are most effective from midnight to dawn, particularly releasement rituals to banish things, people or situations from your life.

Waning half moon – third quarter: Days 22 to 23

At the end of the third week is the third quarter moon, which rises around midnight and sets at midday, so if you see a half moon in the morning it's this waning one, but if you see it in the afternoon it's the waxing first quarter moon. This third quarter moon brings a reflective energy, and is a great time to assimilate what you've learned and achieved, and determine what you still need to do. If an issue requires resolution, work your magic and put your intent out to the universe. The energy is waning, and you can work on banishing illness, addictions, negativity and bad habits, and releasing anything that will slow the fruition of your earlier spellworking.

Waning crescent moon: Days 24 to 29

In the fourth week, as the moon moves towards dark, it rises in the early hours of the morning and sets in the afternoon. This is the letting go phase, a time to release and banish anything you don't need so you can prepare again for the fresh beginnings of the new moon. It's the closing of this lunar cycle, the time to reap what you sowed at the start of the month and integrate the lessons you've learned along the way. You've done the inner work, and now you must release the outcome to the universe.

Dark Moon – Day 29

The dark moon rises at dawn, with the sun, and sets at sunset. It is between the earth and the sun the whole time, making it invisible to us. While some practitioners take this day off from magic, others use it to go within, using the introspective energies to examine their feelings and thoughts and delve deep within their psyche.

While the moon is hidden it's also a powerful time to scry and perform any kind of divination that will uncover your hidden truths, and for getting in touch with your inner wisdom and approaching the Mysteries. This energy helps you explore the darkest recesses of your mind and your heart, and acknowledge your passions, your fears and your anger so you can release them to the approaching light.

You can rest and renew your strength, and also evaluate your life, your purpose, and your progress. The powerful, deep and transforming energy of the dark moon is an internalised vibration, so be aware of your thoughts. Avoid focusing on negativity or self-loathing in case you manifest the fears you want to banish. The dark moon celebrates the crone, so you can invoke Ceridwen, Kali, the Cailleach, Hekate, Baba Yaga or Nephthys to help you descend to your metaphorical underworld and examine the layers of your subconscious.

Eclipses of the Moon and Sun

Lunar and solar eclipses, while fairly rare, also affect the energies of the universe, and our emotions. An eclipse occurs when one celestial body obscures another, either partially or fully. Because of the angle of their orbits, the sun, moon and earth rarely align precisely, which is the condition required for an eclipse. But when the moon is directly between the other two, which can only happen at the dark moon, it blocks the sun's light from reaching the earth, creating a solar eclipse that makes the sun appear either totally or partially invisible. And when the earth is directly between the sun and the moon, which can only happen at the full moon, the earth blocks the sun's light from reaching the moon, producing a lunar eclipse that dims or even totally obscures the moon for a brief time.

Energetically, eclipses create opportunities for change. They can sometimes push you a bit further than you wanted to go, forcing you to move forward and continue along your path. To some they are a wake-up call, nudging you on and making sure you don't lose sight of your dream. A solar eclipse, when the moon blocks the sun, is considered a peak of feminine power, and gets you in touch with your intuition. It is the perfect time to take stock of where you're at and examine your inner self. The energy of a lunar eclipse, when the earth blocks the sun and plunges the moon into darkness, gives you the strength to be honest, to yourself and others, about who you are, and to move forward without fear of judgement.

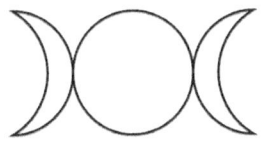

Books By the Author...

The Into the Mists Trilogy

Into the Mists

Into the Dark

Into the Light

Into the Mists: A Journal

The Into the Mists Trilogy Omnibus

The Into the Storm Trilogy

Into the Storm

Into the Fire

Into the Air

The Magic Series (with Lucy Cavendish)

The Book of Faery Magic

Mermaid Magic: Connecting With the Energy of the Ocean
and the Healing Power of Water

Witchy Magic

The Sacred Series

Seven Sacred Sites: Magical Journeys That Will Change Your Life

A Magical Journey: Your Diary of Inspiration,
Adventure and Transformation

Sacred Journey: A Meditation To Connect You
To the Magic of the Earth

Sacred Sites: Egypt

Sacred Sites: Glastonbury

Sacred Sites: Hawaii

Sacred Sites: Peru

Sacred Sites: Stonehenge

Sacred Sites: The Camino

Sacred Sites: Uluru

Before she leaped Into the Fire, Rhiannon journeyed Into the Storm...

A spell to weave. A life to save.
A heart to break. A storm to brave.

When Rhiannon's mother dies, her whole world falls apart, and she withdraws from her family, her friends and her life. As grief and anger rage within her, she connects with the wildness of the winter storms – until she's consumed by the powers they unleash. A priestess tries to help her, a woman from the mists seeks to comfort her, and her little brother attempts to reach her, but she doesn't know how to find her way back.

Entwined throughout is the story of her mother, which reveals a haunting mystery. Why did her parents keep such a dark secret? How will a spell she casts in the woods one full moon night unravel her? Who is the woman in red she encounters atop the sacred hill? And what chaos will be wrought by a girl from the other side of the world with a strange link to her father?

As the darkness of her shadow self is revealed, Rhiannon must find the courage to go into the storm and face her greatest fears. But if she does, will she be transformed by its terrible power, or broken and lost in the wreckage?

"*Into the Storm* takes you on such an emotional journey, and makes you believe in real magic. I loved it."

Selina Fenech, author of The Memory's Wake Trilogy

In the Works

Into the Air: Into the Storm Trilogy Book Three, plus new Into the Mists Chronicles, featuring other characters, including *Into the Earth* and *Out of the Shadows*.

Rhiannon's story was first told in the Into the Mists Trilogy, which centres on Carlie and her mum Violet. But there are two sides to every story, so Rhiannon got her own series too...

Into the Mists

Enter the swirling mists of an enchanted land, and open your heart to the mystery...

Seventeen-year-old Carlie has the perfect life. A wonderful family and a best friend she adores. A house by the beach so she can go surfing after school. A clever, rational mind and big dreams of becoming a lawyer. A future she's excited about and can't wait to begin.

But in a split second her perfect life shatters, and she is sent across the world to live with a stranger. In this mystical, mist-drenched new land, she is faced with a mystery that will make her question everything she's ever known about her parents, her life and her very self. A dark secret that made her mother run away from home as a teenager. An old family friend who is not what he seems. A woman in blue who she's not convinced is real. A shadowy black cat that she'd swear is reading her mind. A deserted old cottage she can't always find. And a circle of wild-haired witches who want her to join their ranks.

Will she have the courage to journey into the mists, and into her own heart, to discover the truth? And can she somehow weave together a life that she'll want to live – or will she give up and allow despair to sweep her away from the world forever?

"I can't put this book down. It's so compelling and beautifully realised – there's so much magic. Absolutely recommended!"
Lucy Cavendish, author of Spellbound and White Magic

"This is Amazing with a capital A. It's healing, empowering, inspiring and, like all the author's work, truly magical. It's one of my favourite novels ever. It opened my heart and inspired the magic within me."
Sarah Byrne, reviewer

Into the Dark

A best friend. A forever love. A promise. A betrayal. An ultimatum. A choice...

Carlie coped with moving from her home in Sydney, Australia to a small village in England to live with a stranger. She battled her way through the mists she thought would drown her, and emerged transformed. She was even starting to think she would survive the death of her parents. But now an old diary, which promises to reveal the mystery of her mother, threatens to tear her world apart. How will the words she reads affect her? Will she wish the truth had died with her mum? And what is the connection to her own life hidden within the pages?

In the second book of the gripping Into the Mists Trilogy, a new relationship with her grandmother is opening Carlie's soul to the energy of the earth. A new friend is opening her mind to the magic and potential within her. And a new love is opening her heart to the sweetest enchantment of all. Yet betrayal hovers, and she will face an ultimatum, a sacrifice and a cruel choice that may break her.

Will Carlie find the courage to go into the darkness of her own heart to seek the wisdom and strength she needs to survive, or will the tragedies and the pain of her life break her into a million little pieces?

"A compelling novel that haunted my dreams while I was reading it, and lingered in my mind long after I'd finished. It's very powerful writing, and very real – and very haunting, the mark of a good novel."
Felicity Pulman, author of I, Morgana and The Janna Chronicles

"Serene Conneeley's magical and very intoxicating new novel *Into the Dark* has me totally under its spell – I relish every shiver Carlie's descent into darkness is giving me. *Into the Mists* was wonderful, but this is another level, a huge leap. I LOVED this book so much – it just ended way too soon!"
Lucy Cavendish, author of Spellbound and White Magic

Into the Light

**A friendship torn apart. A love lost forever...
A curse to break. A mystery to solve.
A heart to heal...**

When her parents died in a tragic accident and her life fell apart, Carlie was sent across the world to live with a stranger. After a harrowing journey through the enchanted mists of an English village, she finally found peace with her grandmother, magic with her new friend, and first love with her druidic soul mate. But then she was plunged back into darkness. Now, haunted by loss and betrayal, and worried her shattered heart is beyond repair, she must decide if she has it in her to find her way back into the light.

In the stunning conclusion to the trilogy, the wheel of the year turns from the bleakness of midwinter to the new hope of spring. Can Carlie break a decades-long curse and save the person she's closest to? Will she unlock the mystery of the sad woman she meets late one night? Which of the Otherworldly beings can she trust? And how far is she willing to go to forgive and be forgiven? For a chance at happiness, she must challenge the wise priestess and embrace her darkest fears. But is she already fated to echo the lonely life of her grandmother, or can she find the courage to open her heart again?

"I'm absolutely blown away by this book and this series. It is beautiful from start to finish – magical, realistic, gentle, harsh, sad, joyful... I've been on a total rollercoaster ride, and am now feeling so bereft at the thought that these wonderful people will no longer be part of my life. What the author has created with these books is just beautiful."

Kylie Matthews, reviewer

Audiobooks

Into the Mists, Into the Dark and *Into the Light* are also available as audiobooks, narrated by British voice actor Gabrielle Baker, from Audible, iTunes and Amazon.

Into the Mists: A Journal

Awaken your inner voice and unlock the power and strength within you...

Keeping a journal is a powerful way to make sense of the world, and of your inner universe, whether you're recording the events of your life or journeying within to discover your truths. It's a valuable tool of self-discovery and self-knowledge, a sacred place to reveal your inner being, and a mirror to show who you truly are, and the beauty of all you are becoming.

Including words of wisdom from priestess Rose, the Otherworldly women and more beloved characters, *Into the Mists: A Journal* will inspire you to look within and express the feelings at the core of your being, encouraging you to let go of past pain, forgive yourself and others, and move forward with joy and confidence so you can achieve all that you dream of. Whether you use it as a daily diary, a gratitude book, a travel record or a place to write your novel, this will help awaken your inner voice, unlock the power and strength within you, and allow you to start seeing the magic in every moment.

"This is *divine!* The lovely quotes throughout are inspiring, and the feel of the journal is heart-warming. It sits on my bedside table for writing in during quiet times of reflection. It is just beautiful."

Cheralyn Darcey, eco artist and author of Flowerpaedia

Into the Mists Trilogy

The three books of the Into the Mists Trilogy are also available in a beautiful hardcover omnibus.

"A mystical, magical tale of forgiveness and love. I couldn't stop reading once I started – I had to know what happened next! I recommend this to anyone."

L. L. Hunter, author of The Aqua Saga

Also by Serene Conneeley

Seven Sacred Sites: Magical Journeys That Will Change Your Life is part spiritual adventure story, part history, part travel guide. Discover what makes these places sacred, when to go and how to get there, the fascinating histories, the rituals performed there, the cultural and magical significance of each sacred site, both now and in the past, and the many ways in which they still inspire, touch and initiate growth and learning in all who visit.

"By far the best travel book this year. Her style evokes the great travel writers like James A Michener, who weave cultural anthropology into an entertaining traveller's tale – a recipe for pure reading pleasure."
Joanne Lock, Spheres magazine

A Magical Journey: Your Diary of Inspiration, Adventure and Transformation combines a diary where you write the story of your life with a guidebook that includes the physical, mental and spiritual health benefits of journalling, and tools to release emotional blockages and unleash your authentic self. Make a wish come true using the cycles of the moon, celebrate worldwide festivals, and create magic in your life by harnessing the sacred energy of the seasonal turning points of the year.

"This helped me connect to self, and venture forth with boldness and compassion. I am so much more aware, and I thank the author from the depths of my heart and soul for the opportunity to grow."
Marissa Clarkson, bereavement counsellor

Sacred Journey: A Meditation To Connect You To the Magic of the Earth is a CD of seven guided meditations set over beautiful music. Each runs for around seven minutes, and can be done on its own, or all together as a fifty-minute journey. Attune yourself with the sacred elements and energies of the earth to soothe your soul, uplift your spirit and heal your heart.

"A gem to treasure. Serene is a gentle, loving, wise teacher of wisdoms we can all benefit from. This takes us on a sacred journey into the earthly and heavenly elements and realms, and into history, spirituality and self-love."
Lucy Cavendish, creator of As Above, So Below CD

Sacred Sites: The Pocket Guides To Your Magical Journey are seven mini books that are perfect for travelling or collecting. They include each of the places in *Seven Sacred Sites*, with extra practical information and websites added, plus pages for your notes, the better to plan your magical adventure.

Witchy Magic (with Lucy Cavendish) is an enchanting adventure into the Craft of the Wise, with clear guidance on how you can access this ancient knowledge to create the life you dream of. It is an earth-honouring spiritual path and an empowering, beautiful way to be at one with the universe, taking responsibility for your life and transforming every word and action into an alchemical tool of change. Step into the world between the worlds and the wisdom of your inner witch to create an inspiring, magical life.

"This is a definitive reference for the would-be witch, and entertaining and enlightening for the witch-curious... For the history buff, nature lover and ritualist, to the magician, pagan and spiritualist, and well beyond."
Kylie Matthews, book reviewer

Mermaid Magic: Connecting With the Energy of the Ocean and the Healing Power of Water (with Lucy Cavendish) is brimming with sea magic, inner journeys, marine conservation and rich research, and will help you develop a deep connection with the element of water. Work with the ocean and its creatures, learn about tides and lunar phases, divine your future with sea oracles, absorb the healing energies of sacred wells and springs, become an eco warrior, and discover the beauty of mermaid lore and love.

"This is a wonderfully inspiring read. It really made me want to shed my twenty-first century shackles and dive into the ocean to embrace its wonderful healing powers. Thank you magical ladies for the journey!"
Sabina Collins, freelance writer

The Book of Faery Magic (with Lucy Cavendish) is rich in tradition, history, research and lore, and filled with whimsical interactions with the fae, grounded guidance on how to work with them, and beautiful ideas for reconnection with nature and the magical realms. Whether you believe that faeries are truth or fantasy, *Faery Magic* is your portal to a state of being where fun and healing energy will help you fulfil your dreams, transform your life, and improve your relationship with the earth, your self and others.

"The ultimate guide to all things faery – entertaining, informative and enthralling. Whether you believe in faeries or are just curious, there is much to learn in this book, from their history and legends, their magical gifts and nature sites, to the unique beings from around the world."
Larissa Chapman, Good Reads

www.BlessedBeeBooks.com

www.ingramcontent.com/pod-product-compliance
Lightning Source LLC
Chambersburg PA
CBHW020656110726
47901CB00001B/214